VORAGO RETURNS

THE MERMAID CHRONICLES

BOOK SEVEN

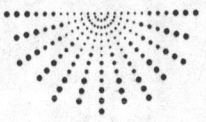

MARISA NOELLE

THE MERMAID CHRONICLES SERIES

REVIEWS FOR VORAGO RETURNS

"If I could give this 10 stars, I would!" — Goodreads Reader

"Romeo & Juliet for today." — Amazon reader

"Romance, mermaids vs sharks - what more do you need? This is a thrilling read with great characters that you won't want to put down!" — **SJ Willis, best-selling author of** ***Bite Risk***

"Packed with twists, could not stop reading!" — **Louie Stowell, best-selling author of** *Loki: A Bad God's Guide to Doing Good*

"A refreshing take on an emerging genre. I found this book so hard to put down. Lots of drama mixed with a dollop of romance and just a touch of the supernatural." — **Melissa Welliver, author of** *My Love Life and the Apocalypse*

"The perfect balance of action, heart, and sacrifice. Gal's journey will stay with me long after the final page." — ARC review

"The stakes have never been higher, the power never more

dangerous—this is fantasy romance at its peak!" — GoodReads reviewer

"Fans of **Throne of Glass** will love this explosive, heart-wrenching end to Gal's story." — Amazon review

"Deliciously romantic!" — Goodreads reader

"This series is so good, it got me out of my slump!" — ARC reader

"Gripping, emotional, and utterly enchanting!" — ARC reader

CONTENT WARNINGS

This book contains themes and references that some readers may find distressing, including, but not limited to:

- Explicit Sexual Content
- Seduction and Non-Consensual Magic Influence
- Strong Language
- Violence and Battle Sequences
- Death and Loss
- Mental Health Themes
- Emotional Abuse and Conflict
- Trauma and PTSD Elements
- Mentions of Drug Use
- Magical and Supernatural Themes
- Religious or Spiritual Themes
- Implied Nudity and Sexual Humor

VORAGO RETURNS PLAYLIST

On Top of the World - Imagine Dragons
Drag Me Down - One Direction
Antihero - Taylor Swift
Daylight - David Kushner
Hurricane – 30 Seconds to Mars
Slow It Down - Benson Boone
High Hopes – Panic at the Disco
Crazy - Gnarls Barkley
Another Love – Tom Odell
I Miss You, I'm Sorry - Gracie Abrams
Everybody Hurts - R.E.M
The End of the World - Skeeter Davis
Outnumbered - Dermot Kennedy
Solo - Myles Smith
Hold Me While You Wait – Lewis Capaldi
Waves – Dean Lewis
Unsteady – X Ambassadors
Whatever It Takes - Imagine Dragons
Your Song - Elton John
Happiness - McFly

For the ones who swam all the way to the end.

*Thank you for diving in with open hearts, braving every wave,
every storm, every whispered prophecy.
You held your breath through the darkest depths and surfaced
with me in the light.
This final tide is for you.* 🩶

RECAP OF BOOK 1 – SECRETS OF THE DEEP

On the approach of Cordelia Blue's eighteenth birthday, she decided it was time to break free from the shadows of her tragic past. The loss of her mother and twin brother in a devastating shark attack had haunted her for five long years, forcing her to abandon her once-promising swimming career. She even shied away from taking a simple bath.

With unwavering support from her best friends, Maya and Trent, Cordelia embarked on a journey to conquer her deepest fears head-on. Little did she know, this leap of faith would reveal a world of enchanting secrets lurking beneath the surface. As she dipped her toes into water for the first time since the attack, Cordelia unearthed her astonishing destiny—she was a mermaid, and her long-lost twin, Dylan, was alive too. Trapped in an aquatic realm, he was unable to shift into human form. Dylan entrusted Cordelia with a mystical pearl, a key to locating the elusive High Council—the sole authority capable of granting mermaids their precious legs once more. However, the mermaids weren't the only ones hunting for this gem. The selachii, shark shapeshifters cursed to the depths, yearned to regain their legs too. And they would stop at nothing to find it.

Old flame, Wade Waters, swam back into Cordelia's life. Sparks flew, but lurking in the shadows were Wade's shady cousins, and Cordelia couldn't shake the feeling that he was harboring a deep, dark secret. And keeping her own secret concerning her mermaid lineage under wraps took a toll on their relationship.

When the pearl mysteriously vanished from Cordelia's grasp, she discovered Wade's secret—he was one of the selachii and had betrayed her. Worse yet, Trent, her loyal friend, fell victim to a brutal shark attack and was transformed into one of them.

With trust shattered and alliances uncertain, Cordelia turned to Maya and the ancient tome, *The Mermaid Chronicles*, which held the key to unraveling their intertwined destinies. Maya insisted that merfolk and selachii must unite to reclaim their lost glory. Cordelia delved into the book's secrets, uncovering a forgotten era of harmony between merfolk and selachii on the fabled island of Atlantis.

As Cordelia unmasked Zale, the leader of the selachii, as the thief behind the pearl's theft, she and Wade joined forces to retrieve the precious jewel, but it almost cost Wade his life. When Cordelia and Wade reunited, the pearl's secrets unraveled, whisking them away to another dimension to confront the enigmatic High Council.

The High Council, comprised of representatives from merfolk, selachii, dragon kings, and eelusionists, agreed to grant them legs once more. Yet, it came at a price—Cordelia and Wade were tasked with the monumental quest to unearth their lost homeland, the mythical Atlantis. The epic adventure had only just begun, and the fate of two worlds hung in the balance.

RECAP OF BOOK 2 – QUEST FOR ATLANTIS

When mermaids began mysteriously disappearing, stolen away by humans for display or sinister experiments, the hidden realm of mermaids and selachii was unveiled. Cordelia, Wade, and their friends fought valiantly, rescuing one of their own from a science lab. Yet, the global onslaught continued, casting an ever-growing shadow over their existence.

Their mission was clear: unveil the enigma of the lost island of Atlantis—an aquatic sanctuary where all ocean shifters could find refuge. To unlock its secrets, the team embarked on a quest for the fabled, scattered jewels that held the key to Atlantis' portal. But their journey was fraught with peril.

Beneath the icy depths of Mount Rainier and the treacherous Puget Sound, Cordelia and Wade faced near-death encounters with ice demons. Gal, a formidable dragon king and council member, defied convention to save them. The Power of the Sea surged through them, healing their wounds and bestowing incredible gifts—Herculean strength for Wade and the untamed power of fire for Cordelia.

Tensions flared as Wade's ex, Stephanie, intruded on the mission, determined to win him back, fueled by his mother's approval. Cordelia grappled with doubt, their bond tested by misunderstandings and painful infidelities, fracturing their once-unbreakable unity.

Maya's life hung by a thread after a harrowing accident, compelling Dylan to transform her into a mermaid. But the toll of their perilous journey didn't end there—Cordelia's father faced certain death in the unfathomable Mariana Trench, only to be transformed into a selachii through a desperate ritual led by Wade.

Amid near-tragedies and heartaches, Cordelia and Wade rekindled their love, poised to confront those who sought to tear them apart. Armed with the keys to Atlantis, they crossed dimensions into a magical realm. But a harrowing sight awaited them—an island in ruins, guarded by legions of dragon kings. A savage battle ensued, with Cordelia mastering her fiery abilities to vanquish the malevolent force at the cost of her dear mentor, Gal.

As the Power of the Sea was plunged into the Fountain of Youth, the island blossomed anew. Amidst the rejuvenation, Cordelia made an astonishing discovery—a long-lost captive, her mother, believed dead for over five years, was alive and well.

In a joyous reunion, Cordelia found her family and a newfound sanctuary where all could walk on land, hidden from prying human eyes. Amidst the serenity, Wade proposed to Cordelia, promising a blissful future...until the pages of *The Mermaid Chronicles* started turning once again.

RECAP OF BOOK 3 – FIGHT FOR FREEDOM

A year after the discovery of the long-lost Atlantis and their showdown with the fierce dragon kings, Cordelia and Wade tied the knot, ascending to their rightful thrones as the rulers of the mystical island. Hidden away from the prying eyes and judgmental gazes of ordinary humans, Atlantis basked in tranquility, shielded by an enchanting veil that isolated it from the rest of the world.

As the brave folks of Atlantis cautiously reconnected with their mainland families, a shockwave of devastating news rocked their world. A cataclysmic nuclear war had erupted, and fingers were pointed squarely at none other than the merfolk and selachii.

This apocalyptic nightmare was set in motion when a wealthy baron's wife met a watery demise. With no ocean shifters around to perform the life-saving resuscitation ritual, the baron pointed the finger of blame at the mysterious Atlantis, threatening to unleash nuclear annihilation unless the world revealed the whereabouts of the elusive merfolk. But nobody had a clue where the merfolk had vanished to, and humanity paid the price with widespread devastation.

Venturing back to the mainland, Cordelia, Wade, and their loyal friends stumbled upon two distinct groups of surviving humans. There were those desperate for survival after the nuclear apocalypse and a faction hell-bent on extracting vengeance from the ocean shifters.

Wade and Trent fell into the clutches of a former mercenary turned captor, the enigmatic Sean Wilson. Meanwhile, Cordelia found herself face-to-face with her high-school rival, the determined Babette, who pledged to aid her in freeing Atlanteans from the clutches of hostile humans, and gave them hope surrounding the latest prophecy in *The Mermaid Chronicles*. While distracted, Wade's ex-girlfriend, the ever-jealous Stephanie, resurfaced as a formidable sea witch, swearing vengeance on Wade and Atlantis.

While Cordelia and her fearless squad embarked on a daring rescue mission to free Wade from the clutches of mercenaries, they crossed paths with Blaze, the last surviving dragon king and Gal's only son, Cordelia's late mentor. With Blaze's remarkable abilities and Cordelia's fiery powers, they launched a mission to free the ocean shifters from captivity. Their journey back to Atlantis, however, took a treacherous turn when Stephanie and Aquaria unleashed the dreaded Hound of the Ocean, a venomous sea monster with lethal breath.

Simultaneously, Sean Wilson invaded Atlantis, leaving a trail of death and destruction in his wake, including the loss of crucial High Council members. As the situation spiraled out of control and their people faced annihilation. Cordelia's powers went haywire, forcing an uneasy alliance with Babette, her father, and their human army, thus fulfilling the prophecy.

Just when all hope seemed lost, Cordelia's wedding ring revealed astonishing powers, creating an impenetrable forcefield around the ocean shifters and saving them from the deadly breath of the Hound. But humans were still dying. After vanquishing Aquaria, Cordelia confronted the monstrous sea beast with her fire abilities. Entrusting the ring to Babette, it extended its protection to the humans too, truly uniting all three species. With Wade by her side and a glimmer of the Power of the Sea from Edward, a High Council member, they finally achieved victory, though Stephanie managed to slip away.

Back on Atlantis, Cordelia and Wade threw open their island's gates to the surviving humans, offering refuge from the radiation and nuclear chaos ravaging the mainland. Babette was entrusted with the guardianship of the Power of the Sea by the last surviving High Council member as he breathed his last, ensuring that humans would forever feel a part of Atlantis.

In a poignant ceremony honoring those lost in the attack and the venerable High Council, Stephanie unleashed her venomous snakes, poisoning Atlanteans. Jordan, Wade's devoted cousin, who had once been enamored with Stephanie, delivered the fatal blow, stabbing her through the heart and ending her reign of terror.

Only then did tranquility return to the island, with Cordelia dropping the bombshell that she was pregnant. But the pages of *The Mermaid Chronicles* never remain still for long.

RECAP OF BOOK 4 – GHOST PIRATES

In the seven years since Cordelia and Wade's son, Gal, came into the world, Atlantis enjoyed a period of relative tranquility under their rule. However, Cordelia's inner turmoil festered as she battled the shadows of her past, haunted by the ever-present fear that something might befall her beloved son. As the Fountain of Youth didn't work for Gal, Cordelia rarely let him out of her sight, believing she was the only one who could protect him from harm. Despite concerns from friends and family about her mental well-being, Cordelia remained fixated on Gal's safety, pushing him to train in martial arts for self-defense.

When the pages of *The Mermaid Chronicles* began to turn, indicating a new prophecy was on the way, Cordelia's anxiety heightened, and she suspected one of her oldest enemies would return. The arrival of a reclusive shifting clan, the orcana, brought an unusual winter to the ordinarily temperate island, and the kids discovered a new sense of joy along with a fresh blanket of snow. Until one of them went missing. Searching for the young girl in the tunnels beneath the island led to devastating land collapses. Cordelia and Gal were trapped in a cave-in and accidentally discovered a powerful elemental orb, which enhanced Cordelia's affinity with fire. While Gal recovered from a concussion in the hospital, more children went missing, leading the Atlanteans to believe there were nefarious motives behind their disappearances.

All became clear when the leader of the orcana admitted to placing a cursed stone in the Fountain of Youth, ultimately blinding Maya, the oracle of Atlantis, and stunting the prophecies within *The Mermaid Chronicles*. Ghost pirates were behind the children's disappearances, and they returned each night to steal more, lashing with their poisonous whips and scattering their venomous spiders on the island. Cordelia discovered they were not merely undead, but immortal. Only by combining all six elemental orbs could they be turned to flesh and therefore become mortal. With two orbs in their possession, a hunt for the remaining orbs ensued. When Gal was taken, Cordelia risked everything, including her own life, in her desperate search for the elemental orbs, shunning those close to her and turning the residents against her with her rash actions.

Then Caol, an evil selachii from her past, appeared on the island. His arrival confirmed Cordelia's suspicions that her oldest enemy, Zale, was after her. Caol claimed he had the last remaining orb in his possession and she killed him without remorse. The island was thrown into a deep depression as they realized the last orb was lost to them, and therefore all the children.

Cordelia vowed to make it up to her people, and with the help of her friends and family, discovered the last orb and turned the pirates to flesh once more. The Atlanteans accepted her apology, and it took uniting all the ocean shifters as well as the humans to defeat the ghost pirates in a deadly battle. Reunited with her son once more, Cordelia's joy was short-lived as Zale finally launched his attack. Protecting her son, she threw herself at Zale's mercy, only to discover he had none. With her powers depleted and unable to defeat him in his new megalodon form, Zale got the better of Cordelia and put an end to her life, leaving her son and husband distraught.

The entire island mourned the loss of their queen, but the story was far from over...

RECAP OF BOOK 5 – VENDETTA

For twelve long years, Gal burned with the desire for revenge. His target was Zale, the murderous selachii who had stolen his mother's life. Furious at being chained to prophecies that had done nothing to save his mother, Gal destroyed *The Mermaid Chronicles*. Yet, as the pages burned, fragments of a new prophecy caught his eye:

> *Celestial Abyss...*
> *Vorago's Trident...*
> *Parting the sea...*

The cryptic words sent a chill through him, but he shoved his fears aside as well as the information that he could now read the encoded book, and focused on his plan of revenge. On the anniversary of his mother's death, Gal set sail on his perilous quest, only to discover two stowaways aboard his boat: Ember, his cousin and the last remaining dragon king, and Una, the ever-optimistic daughter of his mother's best friend. Though furious about now being responsible for their safety, Gal reluctantly allowed them to join, unwilling to lose time returning them to Atlantis.

Their search for Zale led them to the unforgiving Antarctic, where they sought guidance from the orcana. Directed to the Lady of the Lake in England, they set course north. But before they could travel far, a brutal storm capsized their boat, plunging them into the depths. As Gal battled to keep them alive, guilt churned within him—he cursed himself for allowing Ember and Una to follow him into danger.

Salvation came in the form of Gal's reclusive grandfather, who plucked them from the storm-tossed ocean. As they sailed north, his grandfather recounted tales of Gal's parents' legendary love. To Gal's surprise, his grandfather had never disapproved of his mother but admired her courage instead. Slowly, Gal's icy demeanor thawed, and he begrudgingly admitted that his friends had made the journey less lonely. But when he caught Una casting lingering glances in his direction, he vowed never to fall in love. He couldn't risk doing to someone what his mother had done to his father—leaving them heart-broken and alone.

Reaching England, the trio entered a post-apocalyptic Lake District filled with ominous danger. Mutant dogs, known as muttwalkers, stalked their every step as they hurried toward the lake. On its shores, they presented offerings symbolizing the six elements and recited a poem to summon the Lady of the Lake. She emerged from the waters, revealing that the only weapon capable of defeating Zale was Vorago's trident, hidden deep in the Galapagos and fiercely guarded by seawolves. To charm the seawolves into submission, Gal would need to carve and play an ice flute made from the whispering ice of an Icelandic glacier.

A near-miss with the muttwalkers forced the trio to seek shelter in an abandoned house. With Ember on watch and only one bed available, Gal and Una shared the first shift of sleep.

Despite his growing feelings, Gal remained too stubborn to admit the truth.

Their journey to Iceland began with Babette, Gal's uncle's on-again, off-again girlfriend and the guardian of the Power of the Sea. Babette brought them to a local couple for shelter and guided them in their search for the magical ice. Overwhelmed by guilt over the dangers his friends faced, Gal set out alone to find the ice—only to end up stranded, requiring rescue. His recklessness resulted in a polar bear attack that left Una gravely injured and missing an eye. Gal, overcome with grief and guilt, finally admitted to himself that he was in love with her.

As Una recovered, Gal resolved to accept help from his companions. He successfully found the magical ice and attempted to carve the flute, drawing closer to Una as they both acknowledged their feelings. Though still terrified of loss, Gal could no longer deny his love for her.

Frustration mounted as his first two attempts at carving the flute failed. A volcanic eruption forced an evacuation of the island, cutting short any further attempts. Before they could leave, Babette was mortally wounded in a violent storm, leaving Gal, Una, and Ember to continue the trio's mission alone.

From Greenland, the trio journeyed across Canada, finally reaching the west coast, where they commandeered a boat. Along the way, Gal successfully carved and played the ice flute, while also learning to rely on his friends and let them in.

When they arrived at the Galapagos, they dove into the depths with the flute in hand. The seawolves attacked, wounding them all before Gal's melody subdued the creatures. Guided into a hidden cave, they discovered the ancient trident. The moment Gal picked it up, it glowed with radiant power, and all the nearby creatures bowed in respect.

But their victory was short-lived. Zale awaited them outside the cave, determined to claim the trident's power for himself. In a vicious battle, Gal defeated Zale. Though victorious, the fight brought him no solace. His heart still ached with grief, yet his newfound closeness with Una gave him a glimmer of hope.

Returning to Atlantis, Gal placed the trident in the Fountain of Youth, allowing its curative waters to heal humans as well. To his shock, *The Mermaid Chronicles* was reborn, hinting at a new prophecy on the horizon...

RECAP OF BOOK 6 – DENIZENS OF DARKNESS

When the trident suddenly granted Gal new powerful abilities, he realized he needed to isolate himself so as not to harm the inhabitants while he mastered them. Moving to the secluded north of the island with Una, Ford, Ember and Ember's half siblings, Cyra and Ash, Gal pushed the limits of the ancient weapon, all too aware of the looming prophecy.

The Denizens of Darkness crave Vorago's trident.

While he trained, Ash battled his inability to breathe fire, while Cyra uncovered a jaw-dropping gift—she could inhale fire and spit it back out. As Gal's bond with the trident deepened, Una and Ford suspected it was preparing him for the war to come.

It arrived in the form of Nautalun. Once a stranger in his uncle's bar, she returned with devastating seduction. Gal, bewitched, believed he was making love to Una—until he realized Nautalun had possessed her. Wracked with guilt, Gal confessed, and though Una's devastation was quiet, it cut deep.

There was no time to heal as Dagonar, the Weaver of Shadows, attacked, plunging Atlantis into eternal night. When he seized Una, Gal teleported midair to save her, severing the shadows and driving Dagonar back, but leaving a bloom of venomous jellyfish in his wake.

When the group returned to the palace, Nautalun struck again, causing Gal to waver under her spell. Although Gal came to his senses and ultimately rejected Nautalun, Una witnessed the infidelity, and walked away.

When Nautalun went after Una, Gal and Ember struck back, killing Nautalun and breaking her spell. Una saw the truth and forgave him. But the next wave hit harder.

Tidal waves and fireballs rained from the heavens. Ember and Cyra, stronger together, inhaled the fire and redirected it skyward, while Gal lured Maelstrom away from Atlantis. The battle dragged him to the lava lake that had once been Lake Echomere. Ember followed, saving Gal from a deadly fall but losing his wing in the process. Gal fought with everything he had. It wasn't enough. Gal was battered, losing ground. He needed help.

With his newfound teleportation ability, Gal brought Cyra to the battle. She and Ember sucked up the lava and expelled it over Maelstrom, encasing the Denizen in obsidian rock where he could no longer survive.

Returning to the palace, Gal and Ember were treated for their wounds. Ember seethed. His anger at losing his wing caused him to lash out at Gal and accuse him of reckless decisions and selfish pride. For the first time, Gal wondered if Ember was right. Had he put his friends in danger? Had his thirst for control blinded him to the risks? But their anger didn't last. They had fought too many battles side by side to let resentment linger. Their bond, though strained, endured. Both had been cured by the Power of the Sea and were informed that as a result, they would develop a new ability.

Gal developed the power of cryo-aquaism, where he could freeze water and moisture into any shape. Ember developed the ability to produce pyro shields, which could shrivel Dagonar's shadows where Gal's powers had been useless, ultimately defeating the Denizen and ending the eternal night.

But the final threat was rising. A monster beyond comprehension, Karkenloth rose from the depths as a giant squid. Gal formed frozen steps with his cryo-aquaism, climbing to gain an advantage while his father tore through the writhing tentacles with sheer force. Una and their allies wielded explosive swords, carving a path through the beast's limbs. From above, Blaze and Ash attacked, while Ember and others fought below. But victory came at a cost. Gal feared the trident's grip on him was growing too strong.

Gal removed the jellyfish from the water channels, allowing the ocean shifters to rejoice in the water once more. With all four Denizens defeated, Gal returned to Una. The wedge Nautalun had driven between them began to close as they confronted their feelings, reaffirming the love that had endured even during the darkest of storms. But before one night could pass, he found a new prophecy in *The Mermaid Chronicles*—one that left Una in despair.

The man becomes the god.

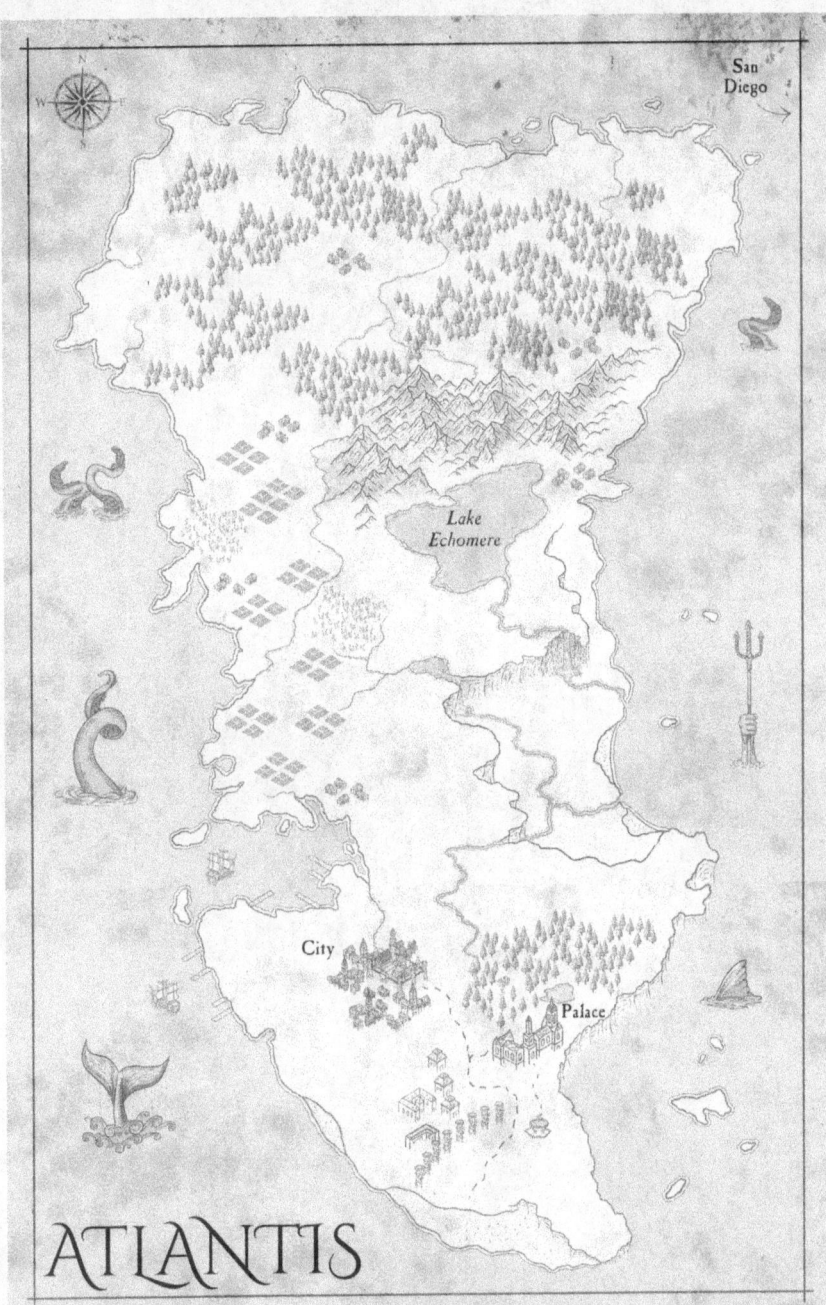

San Diego

Lake Echomere

City

Palace

ATLANTIS

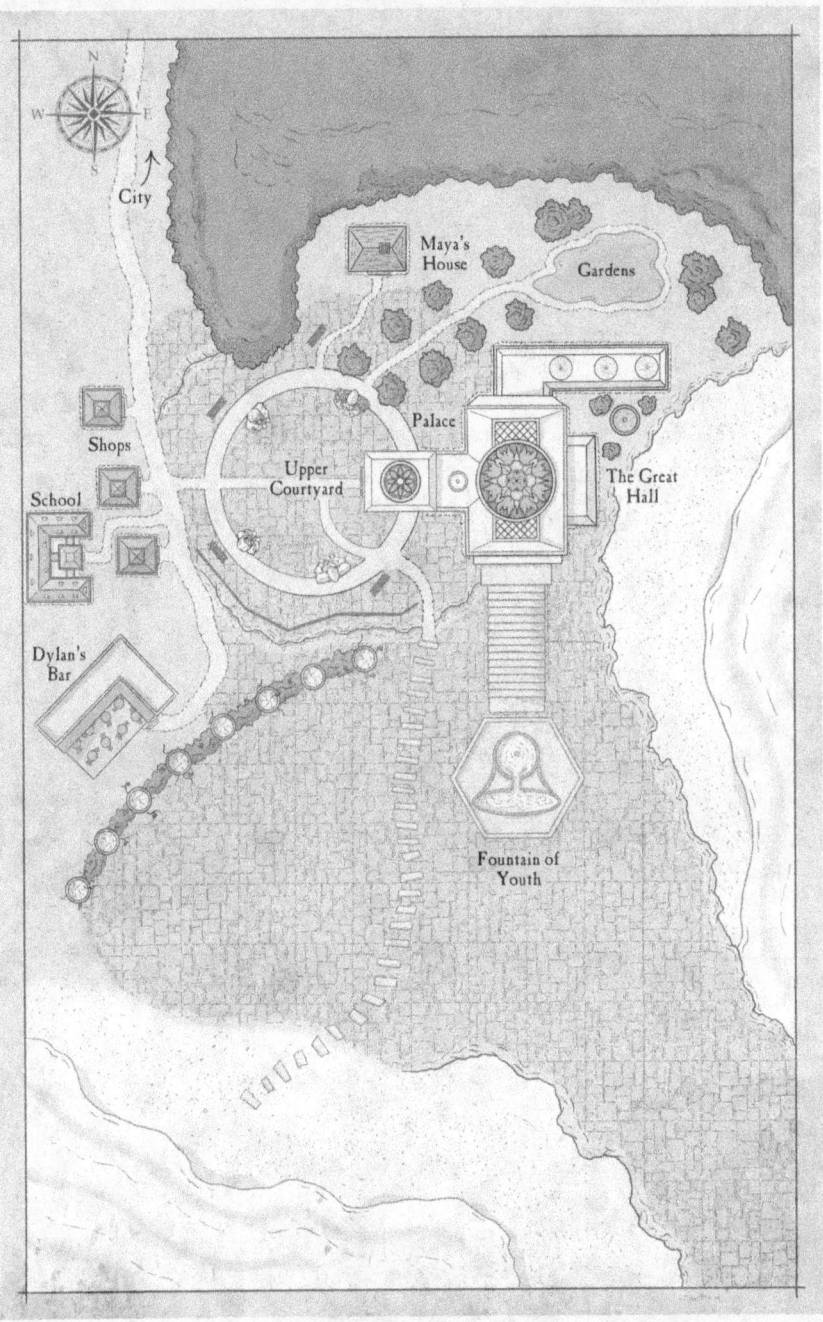

CHAPTER ONE

*P*erfection.

Una was perfection personified.

She walked toward me, her blonde hair catching the sunlight like it was spun from gold, her single blue eye fixed on me with an intensity that stole the air from my lungs. Her dress, made of a delicate seafoam fabric, clung to her figure before flaring out like the crest of a wave. Around her neck hung a string of pearls, each one said to be blessed by the gods.

She was radiant. Fierce. *Mine.*

"Relax, cousin." Ember's voice drifted from my left, low and laced with amusement. "You look like you're about to face a firing squad, not marry the love of your life."

I shot him a look, but the smirk on his face only widened. His dark eyes sparkled with mischief.

"I'm fine," I said, leaning toward the dappled shade of a fig tree near the altar. Red heads and sun did not mix so well, and I was already sweating. "This is the day I've been waiting all my life for."

Ember chuckled. "Tell that to five-year-old you when you thought Una was about as attractive as an ashray."

I laughed at a memory. Una had spent her formative years following me around. With a two-year age gap between us, that was quite a distance when we were young. But it didn't stop her. And If I remembered correctly, I had reveled a little in her adoration, teaching her to jump kick the head off a snowman, and other such displays of my developing strength.

She never gave up when she wanted something. And today, I was counting all my blessings that I was the thing she wanted.

It was a perfect day. Sunlight spilled like liquid gold across the surface of the ocean. Geckos darted through the low shrubs and up the palace walls. It was a day for beginnings. For promises. For hope. At least, that's what I told myself.

The sound of music swelled and the crowd fell into a hush. I caught my father's eye and he gave me a reassuring nod. Several years ago, he had stood in this exact spot and married my mother. Now Aunt Raina flanked his side, her arm tucked in his. And I was happy for them.

Movement caught my eye at the end of the aisle. My heart thudded against my ribs as I spotted Una rounding the corner of the gathered crowd, her feet gliding over a carpet of moss and petals arranged especially for this day. I held my breath. Tried to smile. Was overcome by her utter perfection. By the thought that she wanted me. Forever.

She drifted along the aisle, her arm tucked into her father's, her face nothing but a beaming smile. *Perfect*.

I expelled the air that had been trapped in my chest, then inhaled deeply to steady my nerves. The sweetest scent of jasmine filled my nose, and only strengthened the closer Una got. Her scent. One I would never tire of.

"You got this, buddy." Ember squeezed my shoulder.

I stood at the center of the sprawling gardens, surrounded by the murmurs of the crowd—selachii, merfolk, and humans mingling in a show of unity. Everyone had gathered to witness the most important event of my life: my wedding.

I straightened, forcing myself to breathe as Una approached, Trent accompanying her. She walked with a grace that could charm kingdoms, the eyepatch covering the scar she'd earned in Iceland only adding to her regal ferocity.

When she reached me, Trent gave her a kiss on the cheek before stepping back. Una's gaze never left mine as she placed her hand in mine, her touch grounding me in a way nothing else could.

"You ready for this, prince?" she asked, a teasing smile tugging at her lips.

"Always," I said, no trace of doubt in my tone.

Una leaned in and gave my hand a gentle squeeze. "I love you," she whispered.

"I love you too," I whispered into her ear as the minister began the ceremony.

I didn't hear a word. I couldn't peel my eyes off my soon-to-be-wife. The way her dress swished around her ankles. Delicate ankles I wanted to press my lips to and trail my tongue along. The way her pale skin shimmered under the sunlight, like she had been dusted in stardust. The way her hair fell over her shoulders, begging me to tangle my fingers into it. When she spoke, her lips curved into an infectious smile. My gaze skimmed over the sparkle in her eye, the swell of her cheek, and the elegant column of her throat. I knew Una's body like the back of my hand, but today I was taking her in anew.

Perfect.

The ceremony passed in a blur of words and vows, but it wasn't until I slipped the ring onto Una's finger—my mother's ring, a pearl surrounded by tiny diamonds—that the enormity of the occasion hit me.

"I love you so fucking much," I said, gasping under the weight of emotion that had chosen that moment to land on me.

Una placed a hand on my chest. "Not nearly as much as I love you."

Lies. But I didn't have time to protest. When Una looked at me with that familiar spark in her blue eye, the rest of the world faded into nothingness. The soft rustle of the ocean breeze, the distant applause of our guests, the strength of the sun on my face, the geckos circling our feet, the hum of insects in the air—it all dissolved until there was only her. My wife. My Una.

I cupped her face, my fingers grazing the hem of her eyepatch, and tilted her head toward me. Her lips parted, her breath warm against my skin, and that was all the invitation I needed. I didn't care that everyone was watching. I didn't even know if the minister had given me permission to kiss my bride. But nothing was going to stop me.

I kissed her with a fervor I couldn't hold back, pouring every ounce of love I felt into the connection. Her hands slid up my chest, her fingers curling into the fabric of my shirt as if anchoring herself to me. I angled my head, deepening the kiss, and her soft moan ignited a fire low in my stomach. She tasted of salt and the ocean, a tantalizing mix of sweetness and strength that made me crave her even more. Her body pressed against mine, fitting perfectly, as if she'd been carved from the same essence as me.

Someone let out a wolf whistle. Probably Ember. Or Ash. I didn't care.

My hands slipped to Una's waist, fingers curling around her hips as I held her against me. Her skin was warm under my touch, and when her nails grazed my scalp, I groaned into her mouth. Every nerve in my body came alive, every touch and taste sending a current of electricity through me. She nipped at my bottom lip, a teasing spark that set me on edge, and when I opened my eyes, the fire in hers mirrored my own.

I broke away to catch my breath, my forehead resting against hers. Her eye searched mine, full of the same longing I felt, her lips swollen and glistening.

"You're mine now," I whispered, my voice rough with emotion.

"Always and forever, my prince," she whispered back.

Flashes of golden light spilled out of the windows of the great hall, as if the trident was blessing our union. The crowd erupted into cheers, the sound echoing across the gardens and into the open sea beyond. And because I couldn't resist, because the day was perfect and I wanted to show the world I was more than ready to take on whatever fate threw at me, I raised my arm and called the trident to my hand. The weapon slammed into me with a loving force, its whispers immediately caressing my mind, easing any lingering tension. I raised the weapon and spun it in a dazzling arc. The crowd gasped as the trident's glow intensified, sending streams of light into the air that twisted and danced like ribbons.

Una elbowed my ribs and threw a mocking look at the trident. "Already cheating on me?"

"I've only got eyes for you." I kissed her cheek. "But I do have my people to lead."

"You mean to *entertain*," Ember said from my side as he clapped my back. "You've become quite the showman."

Ember was referring to my tours of the great hall where the magical artifacts of Atlantis were kept. Since the tours resumed after the Denizens' attack, people regularly requested my presence. My people wanted an accessible ruler, someone they could identify with, talk to, even touch. And I had enjoyed getting to know more inhabitants. Sometimes I would pluck one or two unsuspecting guests off their feet and teleport them to the north of the island. And back again. I wouldn't leave them stranded.

I cocked a shoulder as I looked into the dark eyes of my best friend. "It's what they expect. We all know Atlanteans don't like it when their rulers go rogue." It was a vague reference to the time my mother's powers had turned chaotic when I'd been kidnapped as a young boy. Both Una and Ember knew me well enough to guess what I was referring to.

Una put a hand on my arm, the one holding the trident. "No one will expect you to entertain today. It's about both of us today."

But I couldn't resist. The trident was whispering sweet nothings, its words almost a physical caress. Over the years, I had learned that the trident was part of me. And I was part of it. That it was an almost sentient being. A long time ago, I'd tried to hang it on the wall and ignore it. But the trident didn't work like that. And so we had found our way together. It wanted to be used. It longed to be held. And I loved wielding it.

I wrapped one arm around Una and arced the trident with the other, making us float into the sky above the crowds' heads. People looked up and gasped as I spun Una in a circle to the rhythm of our island's waves. "I can do both," I told her as I dipped her in my arms.

The last prophecy came back to me. *The man becomes the god.* It had appeared five years ago. And I was still very much mortal. The Fountain of Youth still refused to heal me. There were no timeframes on the prophecies, but I was growing impatient. If I became a god, I could protect the people I loved. I could protect Una.

Ember whistled low. Then he flicked his hand and a series of small, fiery disks flew from his palm and into the sky, circling us as we floated in the air, lighting up the gardens, the display a thousand times better than fireworks. Even in daytime.

Una rolled her eye. "You two are as bad as each other."

I grinned and placed us back on the ground as the crowd broke into wild applause.

"Well, that's one way to get back down the aisle without everyone staring," Una said as she smoothed her dress.

"Oh, I think everyone was staring alright."

"And hopefully not at my underwear."

I raised an eyebrow. "Now I want to see your underwear."

She swatted my hand away as I moved to touch her. Before I could engage in my second attempt, a waiter placed full champagne flutes into our hands. After sending the trident back to its resting place, Una and I crossed arms, stared into each other's eyes, and toasted.

"My prince," Una said.

"My queen," I said. "Forever."

We drank, and as I tipped my head back, my gaze flicked to a figure watching by one of the stone columns. Bay. Una's brother. He stood with his arms folded and a disapproving look set on his face, his short swords crossed over his back like he was on duty. *Sanctimonious bastard.* He was all about the blacks and the whites and none of the fun. He was taking his apprenticeship under Ford far too seriously. If he was going to be the head bodyguard of the royal family, he was going to have to learn to like me. At least a little bit.

The band struck up and I gave Bay no more thought. I placed our empty flutes on a nearby table and guided Una to the temporary dance floor that had been assembled on one of the lawns. The golden hues of the late afternoon sun stretched across the gardens, casting a warm, honeyed glow over the crowd. The soft murmurs of conversation faded as the first notes of music floated through the air. I rested my palms on Una's waist and prepared myself for our first dance as husband and wife.

She looked up at me, her beautiful blue eye shining with something that made my chest tighten. Love. Admiration. A spark of playful mischief. Her eyepatch matched her dress and only added to her fierce beauty. It had become so much part of her I couldn't imagine her without it. The wind caught the loose strands of her golden hair, and I had to remind myself to breathe.

The music wove through the gardens and we began to dance. I curled my fingers a little tighter around hers as I guided her. Her dress shimmered in the sunlight, each step catching the light as if the ocean itself had blessed the fabric. I spun her, and the material flared like waves cresting the shore.

"You're better at this than I thought you'd be," she teased.

I smirked, pulling her closer. "The trident makes an excellent practice partner."

The song shifted into a quieter melody, the violin carrying an ache that made the moment feel even more intimate. I leaned down, my lips brushing her ear as I murmured, "You know I'd do anything for you, right?"

Her hand tightened on my shoulder. "I know. That's one of the few things in this world I really do know."

"Nautalun—"

"Too soon." She placed a finger over my lips. "And not on our wedding day."

"Agreed." Nautalun was one of the Denizens I had killed five years ago. She was known for her spells of seduction, and I had fallen prey to it. Thank Vorago Una had forgiven me.

After placing a soft kiss on her lips, I twirled her once more, her laugh echoing between us. When she returned to me, I slid my hand up her back, holding her as close as I could, her head resting against my shoulder. The music slowed, the final notes lingering in the air, and I pressed a kiss to the top of her head, breathing in her familiar scent of salt and jasmine.

"Forever, Una," I whispered, just for her. "I'm yours forever."

We ate. We drank. Everyone came to offer their congratulations. My father shook my hand and wrapped me in one of his bear hugs. Una's parents wore beaming smiles. Coral, her youngest sibling, trailed along behind Ash and Cyra, her big blue eyes never leaving Ash's handsome face. Until it was her turn to wish us well. She was Una's spitting image. All wild blonde hair and compact muscle. She had none of Una's confidence, but she made up for it with smiles and warmth. She was the nicest damn person I knew.

"I'm so happy for you two," Coral squealed and threw her arms around both of us, refusing to let go as the line of people behind her grew alarmingly long. Ripple, her pet sea otter, danced across her shoulders and cooed at us. I took that as a sign of his approval. "If only Vorago could see you now!"

"Vorago does not need to concern himself with one marriage," I said.

"But you are the best couple in Atlantis!"

Una laughed and squeezed her sister's arm. "You're just saying that because I'm your sister."

Coral shook her head vehemently, causing Ripple to flee her shoulders and slink down her dress. She tucked loose strands of blonde hair behind her elfin ears as she looked up at us with wide blue eyes. "Nope. I speak the truth. I'm an oracle in training and I know things."

I laughed and kissed her cheek. "Oh yeah? What kind of things?"

She tapped her temple with mock seriousness. "Deep, prophetic, mysterious things. Like...that Una is totally going to be the bossy one in your marriage." She grinned up at me, eyes twinkling with mischief.

Una scoffed. "Like that was ever in question."

Coral giggled, then sobered slightly, a thoughtful expression crossing her face. "And I know something else."

I arched a brow. "What's that?"

She hesitated for a second, the shift so small I might not have noticed if I hadn't known her so well. "That you two will do great things together. You'll change Atlantis for the better." Her voice softened. "I know it."

Something in the way she said it made my chest spasm. Maybe it was the conviction in her tone, the utter belief she had in us. Or maybe it was just Coral—full of light, full of unwavering optimism, seeing the best in the world even when it didn't deserve it.

"Thank you," Una said, pulling her into another hug. "That means more than you know."

Coral beamed. "Just don't forget me when you're ruling the world, okay? I expect a nice little island of my own. With unlimited sunshine and fruit trees."

"You're not going anywhere," I teased. "You'll be too busy keeping us humble."

She grinned. "Damn straight."

The line of well-wishers behind her started to complain.

Moby, Una and Coral's other brother, plucked her from the courtyard in front of us and planted her at a table a few feet away. Ripple scampered after her, snatching dropped prawns from the ground on his way. Moby threw a wave of apology behind him, but was quickly swallowed by a group of fans. He was Atlantis' biggest movie star. The production company had been established a few years ago and he'd played roles in every single film produced. And he was only nineteen. Coral settled at the table next to Ash, already talking his ear off and batting her eyes at him. She was all motion, and energy, and life. I couldn't imagine Atlantis without her in it.

Uncle Dylan came by with Aunt Marina and they offered

their congratulations. Followed by my dad's cousins and my grandparents until I felt like I'd been standing there for an hour hugging and kissing and shaking hands and I was bored out of my mind. But one person hadn't come by, and his absence was glaringly obvious.

When the crowd thinned for a second, I glanced at my wife. *My wife.* "Your brother really does have a problem with me."

Una shook her head. "He's just...serious."

"*I'm* serious," I said. "He takes it to a whole new level."

She took my hand. "We all have our scars to bear."

"What scars? He wasn't anywhere near the fight with the Denizens."

"He comes from a family whose parents are on the High Council and senate. A sister who is an oracle. A brother who is a movie star. That's a lot of pressure. For all my siblings." Ever the empath. There was a reason Una was the guardian of the orb of Spirit and Soul.

I raked a hand through my hair as a sigh escaped my lips. "You're right. I'm sorry. I'm not used to people...holding me at arm's length."

She patted my chest. "It'll keep you grounded."

"Why do I need to be grounded?

The man becomes the god.

"So that trident of yours doesn't fly you off to space never to return." She laughed, but there was an edge to it.

I circled my arms around her waist. Throwing my head back, I glanced at the stars winking above. Then frowned. The constellation that depicted the trident was...different. The three stars that constituted its left prong had shifted, like it had been bent somehow. The constellation had first appeared when I'd returned home from defeating Zale. I'd come to rely on it, to take it as a sign that all was well. But now...

Something is wrong.

11

The internal thought filled me with dread.

"Look at that." I pointed to the constellation. "Does it look different to you?"

Una stroked my cheek. "Everything looks different to me now."

"I'm serious."

"So am I." I lifted her chin so she was staring at the sky with me.

"Maybe it's a blessing from the heavens," she said. "Either that, or we've both drunk too much."

I chuckled, but the unease that had slithered into my stomach remained. I gave the constellation one last glance. Still bent. Still out of place. Maybe I *had* drunk too much.

Ignoring the spike of concern burrowing into me, I returned my attention to my wife. "Enough about family and tridents. Today is about us. It's time to shower you with affection."

"I think I like that idea." Una trailed a finger down my arm, a seductive smile flickering over her lips. I responded immediately.

Suddenly, I was tired of the wedding, the people, the music...and I wanted Una all to myself. I'd had her countless times, but I never grew tired of her naked body. Of the way her skin felt under my fingertips. Of the way her hips rolled when she straddled me. Of the taste of her exquisite center. Always the ocean, salt, and jasmine.

I wanted her now. *Now.*

I took her hand and tugged her toward the palace steps.

"Gal..."

I threw her a wink.

"We can't." She tried to yank her hand out of my grasp. "People will know."

"So? It's our wedding. We can do whatever we want."

A fire lit in her lone blue eye. "What about the cake?"

"They'll wait for us."

I started moving again, and this time she followed, her pace increasing as she lifted her dress so as not to trip on it. We made it to the top step at the same time.

"The great hall," we said in unison, then let out a breathy laugh.

As we approached the guards stationed outside the vast room and opened the doors, I said, "Don't let anyone in."

The one on the left smiled. "Of course not."

The one on the right winked. "Congratulations."

"Thank you for protecting the artifacts during the wedding." I gave them a curt nod before I shut the door.

Una headed for the little alcove around the corner, but I tugged her back into the center of the room near where the Power of the Sea hovered atop its plinth. The six smaller orbs surrounded the Power of the Sea and pulsed with their individual lights. Couches and chairs were positioned nearby in front of a cold hearth. The trident lay in its brackets above the mantle and *The Mermaid Chronicles* sat in a glass case in front of it. The heart of the room.

"Not here," Una said, her face half amused and half horrified.

"I'm the Prince of Atlantis. The Trident Wielder. The guardian of the orb of Snow and Ice. I have the power of cryo-aquaism. You are an oracle and the guardian of the orb of Spirit and Soul. If we want to consummate our marriage in the middle of the great hall, then that's exactly what we're going to do."

Una giggled. The most adorable sound, and it warmed every corner of my heart.

I placed a hand on the small of her back. "I take it you're in agreement."

She nodded, a hand over her mouth to stifle her laughter. "You are brazen, Gal Waters, but I kind of like it."

The mischievous glint in Una's eye set my blood on fire. Her laughter melted into a soft, breathy anticipation and her cheeks flushed with a rosy hue that made her utterly irresistible. I wasted no time closing the space between us, my hands finding her waist and tugging her against me. Her body molded perfectly to mine, soft where I was hard, welcoming where I was blazing with need.

Her lips parted as I kissed her, her taste still as intoxicating as the first time. My tongue teased hers, and her quiet moan sent a thrill racing down my spine. The room's glow—soft blues, greens, and reds from the orbs—cast her features in ethereal light, but there was nothing otherworldly about the heat growing between us. It was raw. Consuming. Somehow different now that we were married. Good different.

Una arched into me, her fingers weaving through my hair, pulling just hard enough to cause heat to flash over my skin and a tightness to coil in the pit of my stomach. She tugged on the tips of my ears, a playful torment that got to me every single time. It made me abandon all thought and give into my most base needs. The coil in my stomach threatened to unravel.

I trailed kisses down her neck, sucking on the tender spot below her ear. Her head tipped back, her breath hitching as I slid my hands along her sides, over the curve of her hips, and to the small of her back.

"Gal..." Her voice was low, breathless, and it spurred me on.

I spun her around, pressing her against me so her back met my chest. My hands roamed over her, her warmth searing through the fabric of her dress. I brushed my lips against her ear. "Let me take care of you, Una."

She gasped as I slipped my hands beneath the hem of her dress, my fingertips grazing her thighs. The fabric slid up, pooling around her waist as I bent her forward. Her palms braced against the edge of the plinth that supported the Power of the Sea, and for a fleeting moment, the juxtaposition of our intimacy against the room's sacred artifacts sent a thrill of defiance through me.

Una shivered as my lips skimmed the nape of her neck and then the length of her spine. I coasted my hands over her hips, dipping my fingers past the waistband of her sheer panties, and cupped her. I teased her with light touches that made her whimper, my thumb circling her clit in the way she loved, my fingers poised at her entrance. She shifted, her body pressing back against mine in silent invitation.

"You're perfect," I murmured, my voice thick with need as I ripped her panties away. I undid the zip on my trousers and let my boxers drop to the floor. A low growl escaped my throat as I freed my erection, so hard, aching with need.

I guided myself to her, my hands firm on her hip, holding her steady.

"Gal..." she breathed and shuddered when I positioned myself at her opening. The heat of her enveloped me, her sharp inhale matched by my own guttural groan.

I pushed into her welcoming warmth, savoring every tiny contraction of Una's that spasmed around me. When I was fully inside her, I released a long sigh of relief. How I craved this feeling far more than I should. Needed it. How could one person love another so completely? If anything happened to Una, I would simply cease to exist.

As I began to thrust inside her, each stroke gaining speed, Una's back arched with each movement. Her hands gripped the plinth, knuckles whitening as soft moans spilled from her lips. The way her body responded to me unraveled every last thread of control I possessed.

"Gal," she gasped, her voice trembling with both need and pleasure.

I tightened my grip on her hips, my movements quickening,

more purposeful. Each thrust drew a cry from her lips, her body meeting mine with equal fervor. The world around us blurred, the soft glow of the orbs turning into streaks of light in my periphery. The only thing that existed was her—the feel of her, the sound of her, the way she called my name as if it was the only word she ever needed.

Her body tensed, a shudder rolling through her as she cried out, her release triggering my own. I buried myself deep, holding her against me as wave after wave of pleasure crashed over us. Our breaths tangled, fast and uneven, as silence settled over us like a shared secret.

As I pulled her upright, I wrapped my arms around her, holding her close. Her hair was damp against her neck, her body still trembling in my embrace. She leaned her head back against my shoulder, a satisfied smile tipping her lips.

"You really are brazen," she murmured.

I kissed her temple, my chest still heaving. "And you love it."

"I do," she whispered, tilting her head to meet my gaze. Her eye shone with both mischief and tenderness. "But next time, maybe somewhere a little less...public?"

I grinned, brushing my lips against hers. "We'll see."

It was then I caught the new spark of light in the room. Amid the soft glow of the magical orbs, it could have been missed. But my stomach clenched when my gaze landed on the glowing pages of *The Mermaid Chronicles*. A new prophecy was coming.

CHAPTER TWO

"*Vorago Returns*." Una traced the ominous two lines with a shaking finger, her voice equally tremulous.

"Why?" I paced the room, not taking in any of the orbs or magical artifacts, lost in my own staccato thoughts. "Why now? What does he want?"

"I wasn't even sure he was real," Una muttered, almost to herself.

I pivoted on the ball of my foot and came to a stop facing her. "Me neither."

We stared at each other. Una, so beautiful in her seafoam dress the palest shade of blue, seashells fastened in her hair, my mother's ring winking on her finger...but the tension in her face was the last thing I wanted to see on our wedding day.

I glanced at the Power of the Sea, willing it to impart its secrets, but the orb remained in its usual amorphous form, swirling with every hue of blue imaginable. "I guess our world had to come from somewhere."

For its entire history, Atlantis had existed behind a veil that barred human entry. Until my parents had dropped that veil and allowed survivors of the nuclear war to find sanctuary in

MARISA NOELLE

our sacred land. Now we existed in the human world. But we had to have come from somewhere. The magic had to have come from somewhere.

Una's fingers hovered over the glowing page of *The Mermaid Chronicles*, hesitant, as if touching it might burn her. "I've always believed in this book. It's mapped out our lives. Our parents' lives. So I guess Vorago must be real."

"Do you think the constellation is a message? That it's trying to tell us something?"

Una placed both palms on the book. "I don't know. That's what we have the book for. We don't need constellations that can't speak to portray messages of...ambiguity."

I glanced out the window at the wedding guests dancing in the gardens, their faces full of smiles, their glasses full, their buoyant chatter floating through the windows. At the trident constellation that still displayed a bent prong. What did it mean?

A whispering breeze floated around me, bringing with it a foreign voice that entered my head like the echo of a forgotten dream.

Your time is coming.

I spun at the sound of the words, but it was only Una and me in the room.

"Are you okay?" Una asked.

I scanned the room once more. The breeze rustled the heavy drapes. No one else was here. So where had that voice come from?

I glanced at the trident, dull without my touch. It often whispered to me. But its whispers caressed the back of my mind, they never offered ominous warnings.

Unless something had changed?

"Gal?"

I returned my attention to my wife. "I'm okay. Why would Vorago return now?"

Atlantis had been lost for centuries. If there was a time to wreak punishment on his people, it would have been then. But the island had been recovered twenty-five years ago. I was the second child born on fresh soil, so to speak, so why did its creator want to return now? To show thanks?

I had my doubts. There wasn't a single prophecy in *The Mermaid Chronicles* that could be considered benign. Except for one. *The man becomes the god.* That one had appeared five years ago just after the defeat of the Denizens. I had taken it to mean me, that I would, somehow, become a god. Did Vorago's return relate to that?

Una looked up at me with her big blue eye. It was filled with an unshed tear.

"What is it?" I asked as my stomach twisted into knots. Una was an oracle. Although the book had granted me the ability to read it, it was Una and her family who received special insights into the meaning of the prophecies. "Do you know something?"

She shook her head, wiped her eye, crossed the room and planted her face in my chest. Automatically, I wound my arms around her. She was shaking.

"It's just a prophecy," I said as I kissed the top of her head. "We've dealt with them before."

"It's different this time."

I stepped away from her, gripped her by the forearms. "You *do* know something. Tell me, what is it, Una?"

Her gaze dropped to the pearl ring on her finger, then back up to my face. "Nothing specific. But I have this terrible sinking feeling."

Her words sent a flash of fear through me. I thought I'd put fear behind me a long time ago. With the Denizens. And now that I had mastered all the trident's powers...there wasn't anything in our world to be fearful of...except the look on my wife's face. That scared the hell out of me.

Before we could continue our conversation, Ash flew through a window and landed beside us, his wings almost knocking one of the orbs off its plinth. He wore nothing but a loose linen shirt and shorts and a cigarette dangled from his lips. Probably rolled by Ember.

"It's time to cut the cake." Ash blew a smoke ring skyward. "Everyone is wondering where you are." He surveyed the room, his gaze resting on the magical artifacts on display. I followed his eyeline to *The Mermaid Chronicles*, but the pages had dimmed, as if not yet willing to share its secrets with all. Ash wasn't a High Council member anyway. He threw us a wink. "Good choice for a quickie. Always around to be a third if required."

Una flushed. I punched his shoulder. Ash cracked up, then headed for the window. "I'd offer to fly you back but that comes with a charge, even on your wedding day, and I only just oiled my wings. Need to let it set." He flexed his wings, and I noticed they shone with some kind of ridiculous shimmer powder that darkened the green and added golden sparkles. And was that where the scent of musk and clove was coming from? His vanity never ceased to amaze me.

Taking another drag of his cigarette, Ash stretched his wings and climbed onto the sill. "Oh, and I want the biggest slice of cake. I left a pretty stacked plate to come and find you. Not to mention the wine." He left with a backward gust of air and the scent of marijuana trailing after him.

"I have no words," I said.

Una laughed, then cut herself off when she glanced at *The Mermaid Chronicles* once more. The book was glowing again.

"I guess we should gather the High Council," Una said, slipping her hand into mine.

I shook my head. "Not tonight. Tonight is our wedding

night. Tonight, we are going to enjoy being married. We are going to love each other. We are going to make love...all night long." I couldn't keep the emotion from my voice. Nothing would stand in the way between me and my wife. Nothing. "I mean it, Una. Tonight is ours. We deserve it."

"You're right," she said, tugging at the loose collar of my shirt. "The last prophecy appeared five years ago and nothing has happened yet. We have time."

I closed the cover on the book, wishing that small action could stop it glowing or delete the prophecy. No such luck.

Una gave the book one last lingering glance as we left the great hall. We descended the steps together, our hands clasped, not talking, but sharing the last few moments of calm.

Coral met as at the bottom, Ripple dancing figure-of-eights between her legs. "Come on, everyone is waiting!" She squeezed between us and took both of our arms, dragging us toward the crowd and a giant, towering cake that was a surprise for both of us.

"No need to gape." Ember stood beside me. He placed a hand under my jaw and shut my mouth.

I couldn't take my eyes off the cake. It was a masterpiece, a towering work of art that captured not only the essence of Atlantis, but the very heart of Una and me.

Each tier told a part of our story. The base was a rich aquamarine, swirling with deeper blues that mirrored the ocean's shifting currents, edged with silver pearls no bigger than water droplets, and cascading waves of sugar frozen mid-motion. The second tier shimmered with an iridescent sheen, delicate coral and seaweed patterns winding up its surface like nature's lace, tiny edible sea creatures peeking out—so very Una in its beauty and grace. The third tier was mine—bold and commanding, cloaked in deep navy with jagged silver and white streaks, cracks of ice symbolizing my cryo-aquaism and guardianship of the orb

21

of Snow and Ice. At its peak, a sugar wave curled over, poised to crash, yet nestled in its hollow was a single glowing pearl. And at the very top, a hand-blown glass sculpture of two ocean shifters intertwined, their tails forming a heart as they held a trident between them. It wasn't just us—it was our bond, our unity, the idea that together we were stronger than the sum of our parts.

Speechless, I stood there staring, a lump hardening in my throat. This wasn't just a cake, this was...*everything*. It was the ocean, the land, the storms we'd weathered and the calm that followed. It was the future we were stepping into, no matter how uncertain or daunting it felt. No matter what that damn book said.

"It better taste like jasmine," I said the first thing that popped into my head.

"It's so beautiful," Una said, a hand over her mouth.

My Aunt Raina approached. It was a gift from her. "I hope you like it."

Una laced her fingers through mine. She beamed at my aunt. "It's perfect."

I nodded, swallowing the knot in my throat. "It is."

For a fleeting moment, I was able to hang on to an image of a perfect future. Una and I together. Always. Swimming beneath the surface in our ocean forms. No kids. Of course not. Una was all I needed. All I wanted. All I would risk. I turned to my aunt. "Thank you."

She gave me a hug and kissed my cheek. "I love you so much."

"And I love you." And I really did. For a multitude of reasons. Not just because she was my mother's sister. But because she had brought a new happiness to my father with their unexpected relationship. Together for five years now. Not married. They never would. And it was a different love from what my father had with my mother. But it was love all the same. Quiet, soft, but fierce.

Dad joined us and handed us the knife to cut the cake.

"I can't cut it," Una said. "It's too pretty."

I laughed and slid my arm around her. Pushing thoughts of the prophecy and the whispering into a lockbox for intrusive thoughts, I pressed the knife into Una's hand, wrapping mine around hers. A crowd gathered around us. Uncle Dylan caught my eye and raised his glass in a silent toast. Trent offered me a wide smile and a nod of encouragement. Moby grinned at me from across the cake, surrounded by a swarm of females vying for his attention.

Just as Una and I touched the blade to the edge of the bottom tier, I felt eyes on me. Not the eyes of the crowd, or a god, but the eyes of something equally terrifying. Maya, Una's mother, stood on the other side of the table, her face sapped of joy, her brow furrowed. She was the first oracle of the new Atlantis, the one who received the most insight, the one who had discovered *The Mermaid Chronicles* on a dusty shelf in a second-hand bookshop on the mainland so long ago.

Una and I slid the knife through the cake, but I couldn't tear my eyes from Maya. She knew.

As the band played in the background and stars reigned over the courtyard, servers descended to slice the cake and hand out plates to the wedding party. Una and I were given the first slice, Coral the second. Una took a bite and offered it to me. I nibbled on the sponge. It did indeed taste of jasmine, but the cake turned to ash in my mouth. I looked across the table for Maya once more, but she had moved.

"Your mother knows," I said to Una, a chill running through me despite the warmth of the evening. No matter how many times I tried to ignore fate or push morbid thoughts into a deep recess in my mind...it never worked. The prophecies ruled me like I was in chains.

A breeze toyed with my hair. But there was something different about this breeze. It was heavy, unnatural, out of place. I braced myself, and the voice followed seconds later.

You think you can fight what's coming?

I pretended I didn't hear the voice. I had a feeling it was after a reaction.

Una's smile didn't drop. She was good at maintaining face in public, but tension crossed her brow.

She placed the half-eaten cake on an empty table. "I've lost my appetite."

"This isn't how I wanted our wedding day to go."

She cupped my cheek, held my gaze. "I know. But this is Atlantis. We are bound by prophecies and magic."

"And curses." I kissed the pad of her thumb. "I destroyed that book once. I kind of feel like doing it again."

A wisp of a smile flickered across her lips. "You can't blame the book. It's there to protect us."

I squeezed my eyes closed, biting the inside of my cheek as my frustration boiled over. Maybe Una and I should sail away to a remote island where magic didn't exist and I was no longer a prince. But then who would be here to protect the people I loved in face of another threat? No. I had rid myself of those childish dreams years ago. I knew my place was here. But it wasn't always easy.

"So what do we do?" I asked.

"We gather the senate and High Council," Una replied. "We discuss the possible motivations of Vorago. And we prepare."

"Spears and swords and guardians?"

"And the trident, cryo-aquaism and pyro shields."

"Did someone say pyro shield?" Ember joined us, wolfing

down what looked like his second piece of cake. His one wing was nowhere in sight. It had been five years, but I still couldn't get used to Ember with only one wing. And since its loss, I'd never seen him in his dragon king form. "Best damn cake I've ever eaten."

"I can tell," Una said. "You've got icing all over your beard."

"That's for the girls to lick off later," Ember replied, not missing a beat.

I snorted, the cake lodged in my throat almost spurting out my nose.

"What?" Ember splayed a hand in mock innocence. "Weddings bring out the love in people."

"Oh I do hope so," Coral said, joining us. She clamped her hands together as if in prayer, her eyes cutting to a particularly handsome dragon king holding court with Moby.

Una laughed and tugged on her sister's hair. "I don't know what you see in him."

Coral flushed bright red. Obvious even under the moonlight. I felt for the girl. Ash had a certain reputation with the ladies. Coral was his opposite. But the heart wants what the heart wants.

Coral turned to Ember, but before she could utter a single word, Ember threw a hand in the air. "Oh no. Don't get me involved in this. You're on your own with my brother."

She battered her blue eyes at him and widened her smile. Ember backed away, still munching cake, holding his free hand high to ward her off.

"Maybe don't try so hard." Una slipped an arm around Coral's shoulder. "Love will find you when it's ready."

Coral faced her sister, raised an imperious brow. "Oh, like how you waited for Gal to notice you?" She prodded her finger into her chin in an exaggerated thinking pose. "If I remember correctly, you started chasing after him when you were five years old."

"Yeah, well..." Una stuttered a laugh. "Do what I say, not what I do."

"Actions speak louder than words," Coral retorted as she dashed off into the crowd in the general direction of her brother and Ash, Ripple on her heels.

"She is going to get her heart broken," Una said.

I wrapped my arms around her waist. "So let her. She's an adult."

"Barely."

"You were barely an adult when you had your wicked way with me."

"That was different."

"Because it was you?" I chuckled and kissed the tip of her ear. "It's her choice to make."

"But she's my little sister."

"I know." I didn't have siblings, but Coral was the closest thing to it. She was a mini version of Una, but wore her emotions so plainly on her face I couldn't help but love her, in the most brotherly kind of way, of course. As for Una's brothers. Moby and I got along okay, and he knew how to have a hell of a good time, although he preferred to stick to the sidelines when it came to government and prophecies. And Bay? Well, let's just say we knew how to be civil to each other. Being Una's closest sibling in age, he'd been aware of my infidelity with the Denizen Nautalun. Aware of how much I'd hurt Una. And he'd never forgotten. I guess I couldn't blame him. "If it's meant to be, it will be. And there's nothing we can do about it."

Una stroked my cheek. "When did you get so wise?"

"You tend to have that effect on me."

"Gal. Una."

We turned at the voice, softer than the night breeze, but

laced with warning. Maya stood in a flowing aqua dress, her hair tied up in a tiara and fastened with seashells to compliment Una's outfit. Every bit the mother of the bride.

Maya laced her hands together. "We need to talk."

I gritted my teeth. "Not tonight we don't."

Sympathy softened her features. "There was a prophecy on the night of your parents' wedding too."

"You've seen the book?" Una asked, squeezing my hand.

Maya shook her head. "You know I don't need the book."

That was some badass level oracle shit right there.

Una lifted her hand, fiddled with her eye patch. "You know what it says?"

"I do." Maya touched her daughter's arm. "And I know you've both read it. I came to tell you not to worry—"

"Not to worry?" My voice came out louder than intended and a few people nearby glanced my way. I took a breath, lowered my voice. "Our creator plans to pay us a visit and you don't think we should worry?"

Una dropped her hand from her patch, toyed with the shells in her hair. "It could be good news. I mean, as you say, he's our creator, maybe he wants to see how we're getting along. Maybe he wants to check on Atlantis now that it's flourishing again. Hell, maybe he wants to move in..." she trailed off when my eyebrows hit my hair line.

"I'm looking for the positives," Una said, a defensive under-current in her tone.

"And that's one of the many things I love about you." I took her hand and kissed her palm. "But we need to be realistic."

"Gal is right," Maya said. She paused to let a group of laughing teenagers stroll by, then stepped closer and lowered her voice. "Prophecies don't appear in the book because they are good news. They are warnings."

I frowned. A different prophecy echoed in my mind. I'd

never discussed the idea of me becoming a god with Maya, but Una had. "I don't know if I believe that."

Maya nodded. Gave me a fragile smile. "I can understand why. Whether you become a god or not is undecided. As is your pathway to it. The prophecies may not be set in stone, but the one thing I do know, is that they *are* warnings."

I dropped Una's hand, a cold flush erupting over my skin. "Me becoming a god is good thing." I pushed through gritted teeth. "Think of all the possible threats Atlantis could face. The myriad of monsters listed in *The Mermaid Chronicles*. If I'm a god, I have more power. I can protect everyone I love. Hell, I can protect the entire island."

Una laid a hand on my shoulder, a silent message to calm down. People were staring again. My voice had risen. It was our wedding night and this was supposed to be a joyous occasion.

"With great power comes great responsibility," Maya said.

I rolled my eyes. I'd heard that phrase, or something close to it, my entire life.

"What is it I've done to disappoint you?" I asked my mother-in-law.

Maya let out a soft sigh. "Absolutely nothing. I'm incredibly proud of you, Gal. I love you like one of my own. You know that. Your mother..." Her gaze dropped to the ground and she took a few seconds to collect herself. Took a deep breath before she leveled her gaze at me once more. "You are so very special to me. I promised your mother I would always look out for you." She closed the gap between us and took my hands in hers, squeezed them with more force than I thought her capable of. "Nothing runs smooth forever. Whether we're in Atlantis or back on the mainland. Life is a rollercoaster. But Atlantis does come with its unique challenges. And I'm doing my best to guide you through them. Your parents...they faced tremendous threats too..." She released one of my hands and put hers across my chest. "I just want you to stay true to yourself."

"With all due respect, Maya, I'm twenty-five. I don't need a mother anymore. Haven't had one for quite some time."

Disappointment flashed across her face as she dropped her hand. "That may be true, Gal. But there is a High Council. And you are a prince. Your actions have consequences for the entire island. The High Council have one job, and that is to protect Atlantis."

CHAPTER THREE

$\mathscr{I}$ carried Una over the threshold of our home and kicked the door shut behind me. Finally, we were alone. I'd thought my wedding day was going to be the happiest day of my life, and in several ways it was, but the new prophecy had cast a shadow over it. Maybe if Una and I had never ventured to the great hall...or if I'd avoided Maya for the night...but there was also the deformed constellation and the whispering voice.

I shook my head. I would no longer bury my head in the sand...except for tonight. Tonight, Una and I would spend together, no one else. No magic. No trident. No prophecies.

Una stroked my cheek, a warm smile softening her features, and I placed her gently on the floor.

"You're still thinking, Gal Waters. I know that face." She touched the flower pinned to my shirt, a tiny bundle of wilting jasmine.

"I'm doing my best." I rubbed my hand over my forehead.

Una placed her hands on my shoulders and eased me down to a chair. She undid a button on my shirt, then the next, until they were all undone and my shirt hung open, and something stirred in the pit of my stomach.

"Mom said we didn't have anything to worry about tonight."

I winced. "Can we not talk about your mother when we're about to have sex?"

Una laughed. "I only said it to make you relax."

"Yeah...no."

"We have tonight, Gal." Una wound her arms around my neck and planted a kiss on my lips. "Tomorrow we can worry about the future."

Deciding she was right, I gripped her around the waist, digging my fingers into the solid surety of her, and buried my face between her breasts.

"That's more like it," she sighed as I kissed one of her breasts through the fabric of her dress.

I slid my hands down her waist and kissed a line to her stomach. With a soft sigh escaping her lips, Una leaned into me and ran her fingers through my hair. A delicious sensation rolled over my scalp in the wake of her touch and heat spread from the pit of my stomach to my groin. *Fuck the book.* Tonight was all about Una. I planned to devour her inch by inch and savor every one of her exquisite flavors.

Una slipped her hands inside my shirt and eased the material off my shoulders. She helped me to release my arms until I was sitting in front of her bare-chested with my erection straining in my pants.

"We need to take care of that." Una pressed her leg into my crotch, causing a tiny lick of friction that pulled a growl from my throat.

I wanted her. Naked. Now. *Right fucking now.*

Lurching to my feet, I plucked her into my arms and carried her into our bedroom. A few vases of jasmine dotted the surfaces and petals covered the bedspread. "What the hell happened in here?" I asked. "It looks like a florist vomited all over the room."

"Coral," Una replied with a soft chuckle. "She's such a romantic."

As was I, but I couldn't give two shits about flowers right now.

"I'll make sure to thank her when I see her."

I lowered Una to her feet. She turned and lifted her hair, allowing me access to the zip on her dress. Taking my time, I slid the small metal clasp the length of her spine, her exposed flesh prickling with goosebumps. She looked at me over her shoulder, gave me the sexiest smile.

"You don't know what you do to me," I groaned.

Una smiled. "I think I have a pretty good idea."

I slid the thin straps of the dress off her shoulders and the material slipped to the ground and puddled at her feet. Now she was completely naked, the panties she had been wearing earlier still rolled in my pocket.

Jesus Christ.

Una turned to face me, moonlight from the open window dancing across her pale skin. She lifted her hands to her breasts and teased her nipples between each thumb and forefinger. "Is this what you want?"

"*Fuck*, yes." I didn't think I could get any harder.

Una draped herself across the bed, her breath hitching in little delicious moans that I couldn't wait to swallow with my lips. As she shifted, the petals strewn across the bed released delicate notes of jasmine, making me salivate for Una's taste. She bent her knee and slid her hand down her taut stomach, nearing the juncture of her legs.

"Don't you dare touch yourself."

My command was met with a grin.

I strolled toward the bed, undid the fastening on my pants,

and slid them off in one smooth motion. Giggling, Una cupped her hands over her mouth as I joined her on the bed. I leaned over her and planted a rough kiss on her lips, giving her the promise of many more to come. She kissed me back, wrapping her hands around my neck, pulling me close. Rising to meet me, she pressed her naked flesh against mine and drew me down to the bed.

After another breathless kiss, I propped myself up on an elbow beside her, and entwined my leg with hers. I brushed my fingers over her face, rubbing my thumb over the old scar under her eye. Then I pushed her patch over her head, exposing her healed wound, and laid a soft kiss on the scar tissue. She was so. Damn. Beautiful.

"Gal..." She ran her hand up and down my arm.

I trickled my fingers up her thigh. Una closed her eye, arched her back. I smiled at the look of pure lust on her face.

"I love you so fucking much," I said.

"I know," Una replied, making me laugh.

I moved my hand over the curve of her hip, around the soft swell of her stomach, until I reached her breasts. Rubbing a thumb over her nipple, it immediately hardened.

Una opened her eye and stared at me, a lazy smile on her lips. "You are the best thing in my life."

I swallowed her words with my mouth. I flicked my tongue between her lips, deepening the kiss until I forgot where I was. Una's hands roamed over my back, tracing the definition of my muscles, then she dug her fingers into my rear. The hard length of me pressed against her side as I molded her breast into the palm of my hand. I bent my head to take a nipple into my mouth and reveled in the taste of the ocean, salt, and jasmine.

"Gal..." she sighed.

"We've been living together for five years," I said between kisses. "But tonight, I really feel you belong to me."

"Always," she said, shifting to look at me. The ring was the only item she wore. My mother's ring. And not only was our love as fierce as my parents' had been, but the pearl in the center of the ring would always protect her. I'd heard stories about the battle with the Hound of the Ocean when the ring was used to produce a force field of protection from its noxious breath. I never wanted Una to be unprepared. The ring not only symbolized our love and the history of Atlantis, but it also meant Una would be safe from other sea monsters that dared to emerge from the depths.

I kissed the ring, then the pad of each finger, then trailed my lips up her arms until I found the soft, lush skin between her neck and shoulder. I brushed my lips along the column of her throat, all the time listening to her breathy moans.

She arched into me, pressing herself against me. I shifted so I was positioned above her, my weight on my elbows, my aching length poised at her entrance. I smiled at my wife. *My wife.* Nothing could mar this moment. Not the prophecies or the trident or Vorago.

Una placed her hands on my ribs, a gentle pressure guiding me toward her. I pushed into her, reveling in her delicious warmth.

"I wonder if it will feel like this when we make our children," she said on an exhale.

The smile plunged from my lips. I flinched as though I'd been slapped, jerking away from her, tearing myself out of her.

Startled, she sat up. "Gal? What is it?"

I shook my head. Backed off the bed until I was standing. Suddenly, the flowers smelled too sweet. The room was too claustrophobic. The night breeze too cold. I stood there, wilting, my desire waning as my anger grew. The temperature in the room dropped, ice crystals forming on the windows, a slick sheen of ice coating the bed frame. My breath misted in front of my face as I tried to control my breathing, tried to get a hold of my powers.

Una pulled the covers over her chest. "Gal?"

I frowned, gnawed the inside of my cheek. "Please tell me you haven't stopped taking the prevention herbs?"

Una's mouth fell open. The ice on the windows thickened, then cracked.

"Una! Please!"

A tear rolled out of her eye. She shook her head. "No, of course not. And you've been taking them too, so it's not like it would matter if I stopped—"

I stormed forward and grabbed her arm, ignoring the goosebumps dotting her skin. "That is so not the point!"

"Gal! You're hurting me!"

Mortified, I released her arm, turned my back.

I sensed her shifting behind me. Then I felt her hand on my shoulder, a tentative touch.

"I told you I never wanted children."

Una's hand dropped from my shoulder. Tension filled the air between us. Tension and ice.

"That was five years ago..."

I whirled around to face her. "Nothing has changed."

Pity whirled in Una's lone blue eye. Pity that had no business being there.

"I thought, in time—"

"You thought wrong."

Una winced. I looked away. I knew I wasn't being fair, but this was the one subject I wouldn't negotiate on. And she knew it.

Una wrapped the covers tight around her and kneeled back on her heels. "I don't want to fight."

"If I'd known that's what you wanted..." I shook my head, unable to articulate my thoughts.

"What? You wouldn't have married me?"

I stared at my wife. *My wife.* Her lips blue, her breath pluming, her face the picture of confusion and hurt. Of course she would want children. That's who she was. She came from a big family and she had so much love to give. But I thought we'd put the topic to bed. Loving her was difficult enough for me. After losing my mother, I couldn't risk more loss. My mother's death had crippled me for years. There was still a painful ball lodged inside my chest. I'd learned to live around it, but I wouldn't do that to a child of mine. I was the Prince of Atlantis. Most of the prophecies in *The Mermaid Chronicles* would involve me. And if Maya was right, the prophecies were all warnings. Danger would always be a part of my life. I could accept that for myself. I could even accept that for Una. She had shown me we were stronger together. But I would not abandon a child.

"I will never not love you," I said. Delicate ice structures hung in the corners of the room.

"I know."

"But I can't have children."

"Can't, or won't?"

"Both. Either. What does it matter?"

"You're still living in fear." Her voice was gentle, but her words cut to the bone.

"What would you know about losing a parent?"

Una rose to her knees. "That's not fair."

I grabbed my pants from the floor and slipped back into them, not bothering to do the button and letting them hang low on my hips. Then I raked my hands through my hair as I attempted to collect my thoughts and salvage our wedding night.

"I'm not perfect, Una," I said, my gaze resting on her beautiful face. "And I do have scars. Some have healed. Some will always be there. Every day I try to live around the fear in my heart. I've gotten good at it too. But this is something you can't ask of me. I thought I'd made that clear."

Una stepped off the bed, letting the covers drop, and stood before me completely naked. Exposed. Her love for me evident in not just her one blue eye, but in the way she held herself, and how she let me see her so totally vulnerable.

"I never asked for perfection. I knew what I was walking into the day I decided to love you. I knew you had scars. And I know some of them will never heal. But I want to be there to help you try."

Heat built behind my eyes, and before I knew it, a tear rolled down my cheek. The ice in the room thawed and the temperature rose.

"I love you," Una said. "I always will. If one day we have children, that will be wonderful. If we don't, that's okay too. So come back to bed and let me love you."

I did exactly as I was told. I took my wife in my arms and got back into bed with her. We made love. It wasn't the fiery, heated joining we had started with, but a soft and slow exploration of each other. Not merely our bodies, but our minds and souls. I had never loved anyone more and I was so damn lucky to have someone who loved me back. Who understood me better than I understood myself. And that was enough. Hell, that was everything.

CHAPTER FOUR

*T*he decay was expected. But the silence was soul-destroying. No gulls cawed overhead. No distant hum of engines. Just the sound of our boat slicing through the water, the lap of waves rhythmic against the hull. Although laced with the familiar scent of salt, the air was heavy, like it carried the weight of everything that had been lost.

It had been over five years since I'd set foot on the mainland, and even though I told myself I was prepared, my stomach knotted. The last time I'd been here, I'd killed Zale and lost Babette to the fury of a storm. Memories of England's muttwalkers—those hideous, mindless zombie dogs—still clawed at the corners of my mind. Part of me wondered what new nightmares this side of the world might hold.

It is coming.

The voice arrived on the wind once more, but somehow penetrated the deepest recesses of my soul. Sweat slickened my palms.

What *is* coming? I asked the wind, but there was no response.

So it was like that. Intruding in my mind during vulnerable

moments, hiding at the edges, never fully revealing itself. Was I going insane? Or was something else at play?

"Gal? Are you okay?"

I looked at my wife. *My wife.* So achingly beautiful. Concern etched into her brow. "You didn't hear it? The voice?"

"What voice?" Her frown deepened.

"The one that comes with the wind. It talks to me, it..."

"It what?"

"Do you think the book is whispering to me? That the prophecies are being entered right into my brain?"

"I guess it's a possibility," Una replied. "But Mom always said she got a feeling, then saw images. Nothing about a voice or whispering. But it could be different for you, I suppose."

For a reason I couldn't identify, I didn't think the book was responsible. "Maybe I'm going crazy."

She smiled and took my hands. "You went crazy a long time ago."

A laugh spilled out of me. "Thanks so much."

"You're not going crazy," Una said, rubbing her thumb over the back of my hand. "But you have been under a lot of stress. It's not a surprise your mind is playing tricks on you."

I gnawed on my lower lip. "You think that's what it is? You don't think it's somehow part of the prophecy?"

Una squeezed both of my hands. "What is it saying to you?"

"It's...threatening me. I think."

"It could be stress."

Stress. Great.

Una stood and came behind me, wrapped her arms around me in a fierce hug. "I love you, Gal Waters."

I leaned into her embrace. "I love you too."

"Now how about we put the wind and mysterious voices behind us, and go see about your Mom's old house."

My gaze drifted back to the shore. "I wasn't ready before. To come back here. To face this."

This isn't where you're supposed to be.

The voice curled over me with a breeze that snuck down my shirt. The hairs on the back of my neck bristled as a cold warning trickled down my spine. I clenched my teeth, attempting to ignore the voice, but I had a feeling it would only get louder.

"I get it," Una said. "You needed time. I'm glad I'm with you."

I nodded, but unease coiled in my ribs. I'd either be able to put the past behind me...or this trip would be my undoing. "Two days tops, then we'll sail to the north of Atlantis where you can have your wicked way with me every night."

"And day," Una said, her blue eye twinkling. "In fact, I may never let you leave our bed."

"Perfect." I kissed her cheek.

I inhaled a deep breath of sea air and took in my surroundings. San Diego's marina wasn't as desolate as I'd imagined. The docks were weathered, warped by years of saltwater and neglect, but some of them still stood, like skeletons of a world that refused to die. A few boats remained moored, their sails tattered, their hulls covered in barnacles and rust, the strong summer sun highlighting every depressing detail. Some had sunk halfway, their bows pointing skyward as though pleading for rescue. Others were little more than charred husks, evidence of desperate fires that had burned long ago.

"It's hard to believe the High Council agreed to this trip," Una said, as we tied up the boat and stepped onto the creaking dock. "I thought they'd put up more of a fight."

I shrugged, tugging at the rope to secure the boat. "I think they recognized we shouldn't put our lives on hold for something that might not happen for months, or even years."

Una planted a hand on her hip, her gaze drifting toward the skyline. "Do you think they're right? That Atlantis can cope without us for a little while?"

"They'll manage," I said. "The High Council isn't merely a group of figureheads. They've dealt with crises before, and they're more than capable of handling things while we're gone. Besides, they've got Ember and my father and Ford. That's plenty of manpower."

You sure about that? The voice whispered in the wind.

Yes, I spat back. Una hadn't heard it. It was only me. Intended only for my ears. *Just stress.*

"Don't forget Cyra." Una pumped an arm. "Representing for the women."

"Of course."

Una searched my face. "And what about you? Are you okay with leaving Atlantis behind, even for a few days?"

I pointed to the trident resting on the seats. "We can be back in seconds if we need to."

She nodded. "In a way I'm relieved. Vorago won't think to look for us on the mainland."

"I don't care what he does," I said as I took Una's hand and steered her along the floating dock. "As long as I've got you by my side, that's all I need. Hell, if he wants to take over ruling Atlantis, he can have at it. We can escape to the north and never have to face a senate meeting again."

Una poked my ribs. "You say that now, but I reckon you'd miss it."

After a few minutes, we reached solid ground. I took a deep breath as I looked out over the town, Ocean Beach. The town my mother grew up in. "This place is like a graveyard," I said. "A graveyard of broken dreams."

Una squeezed my hand. "We have Atlantis now."

I noted the rusted hulls of several cars, a vehicle we didn't

41

MARISA NOELLE

have in Atlantis. I had driven one during my last visit to the mainland with Una and Ember, and I wondered if I still remembered how.

The two-block walk to my mother's house felt like crossing into another world. The shopfronts were shattered or boarded, their signs faded and illegible. Trash skipped along the pavement and broken glass was strewn across the tarmac, winking in the sun. Somewhere in the ruins was my mother's home, and with it, the remnants of her life. Although I had put her death behind me years ago, I had never visited her childhood home and I felt there was a piece of me that needed to.

We passed a surf shop with a tangle of broken boards piled against its doorway, their once-bright decals barely visible under layers of grime. Would Trent be able to salvage them? He still surfed. The entire Summers family did.

A breeze crept down the collar of my shirt as we walked along the ruined road. I braced myself for the voice's appearance, but it remained silent.

"It's so quiet," Una said, breaking the stillness. "I can't believe this used to be...alive."

"Mom used to say it was the happiest place she'd ever been. It was where she learned to swim...found my dad." My voice faltered. "Doesn't look like much now, does it?"

Nature had crept in to fill the void. Weeds sprouted through cracks in the pavement, their roots sprawling like veins across the ground. Ivy climbed what remained of the streetlights, and palm trees leaned at awkward angles, their trunks scarred by wind and decay.

"This is still her place," Una said, giving me a sidelong glance. I knew she was waiting for me to break down. "Her memories live here, even if the people don't."

I wanted to believe her, but it was hard to reconcile her words with the surrounding desolation. My mother's stories

42

were painted in bright, warm colors—this place was nothing but muted grays and browns. It felt wrong, like walking through someone else's dream.

The house appeared as we turned the corner. A jolt of tension locked my muscles. It stood in the middle of the block, a weathered two-story structure with white siding and pale blue trim. Or at least, it had once been white and blue. Now the paint was peeling in long strips, revealing patches of bare, rotted wood beneath. The front yard was a jungle of wild grass and ivy, spilling over the cracked walkway that led to the door. A shattered bay window overlooked the street and ocean beyond. Her bedroom.

"This is it?" Una asked, threading her arm through mine.

I nodded. "Yeah. This is it."

It wasn't much to look at, but it felt like a piece of her was still here, waiting for me. I imagined her sitting on the porch with a book in her hand, the ocean breeze ruffling her hair. I imagined her calling to the neighbors, waving at passing surfers. I imagined her alive.

"Maybe I should wait for Dad," I said.

"He told you to go without him," Una reminded me. "He was only coming to support you, remember? But you've got me for that."

The knot in my chest loosened. "Did I ever tell you I loved you?"

Una smiled. "Once or twice."

We stopped at the gate, its latch rusted shut. I gave it a hard shove, and the wood creaked in protest before it swung open, the sound echoing across the empty street. The house loomed ahead.

"You ready?" Una asked.

I wasn't. Not really. But I nodded anyway. "Let's go."

I pushed open the front door and stood in a dusty hallway,

muted sunlight streaming in through the grimy windows. No one had been here in years. Dust coated everything.

I progressed down the small hall, Una trailing behind, and emerged into an open-plan kitchen and living area. Ahead were a couple of couches centered around a large flat screen TV. To my left was the kitchen, the breakfast bar sporting dirty dishes growing something brown and sludgy that made me wrinkle my nose. Dead plants lined the kitchen windowsill, nothing more than pots full of dirt. A large clock lay on the counter, its batteries missing. When I opened the fridge, against my better judgement, amongst moldy cheese was a six-pack of the beer Uncle Dylan used to talk about. I wondered if it had a sell-by date. I could bring it back for him. Although in recent years he'd quit drinking as much. Aunt Marina seemed to have a positive effect on him. And she'd never said a word. Never laid an ultimatum on him. Just gave him time to heal.

I left the kitchen and followed the hall toward the bedrooms, remembering Dad's instructions. The wall was dotted with family pictures and I paused to examine the photos of my mother and Uncle Dylan as young teens. Several of my grandparents. Another of my mom and dad. I raised my hand to take one off the wall, intending to gather them and bring them back to Atlantis so Dylan and my grandparents could see. But then I figured if they wanted them, they could have come back for them. They belonged here, in another life.

I found my mother's bedroom. The door was ajar and I nudged it open with my foot. There was the shattered bay window overlooking the ocean. The window seat looked like a few birds had spent the night on more than one occasion, and a bundle of twigs and leaves implied the suggestion of a permanent relocation. Clothes spilled out of the wardrobe, but the bed was still neatly made in sheets that looked to be light blue, albeit covered in inches of dust. I pulled open a few drawers to find socks and underwear and jewelry and a few pieces of mainland technology I hadn't come across before. A photo stood on the bedside table. The photo Uncle Dylan had spoken about from their thirteenth birthday only days before their world imploded. I placed it face down. No one needed a reminder of that. The temperature of the room dropped as my cryo-aquaism power kicked in, mimicking my mixed emotions.

"You've got this," Una said.

I nodded, took a couple of deep breaths, and the temperature thawed.

Una turned in a slow circle. "Somehow it still smells like her."

I inhaled deeply, and beneath the dust and damp and mold, I caught a lingering trace of my mother. A smell I had almost forgotten. My chest clenched tight and my eyes heated.

"Is there anything you want to take home?"

I looked over the various knickknacks, the vase full of seashells, the jewelry, the clothes, the bottles of perfume, and shook my head. "This all belongs here. I just wanted to see it for myself."

"Are you okay?"

"I am." And I meant it. This visit had the desired effect. It closed a door on my grief. Not that I would ever forget my mother, or want to, but that last lingering curiosity about her life before was now satisfied.

This wasn't a place I had ever known. It wasn't a place I needed to linger. My mother's heart was in Atlantis.

We headed back to Atlantis a couple hours later, the sun sinking into the horizon. Una and I sat snuggled together at the helm, nestling into each other as the wind picked up. I listened for the voice, but it remained alarmingly silent. It had only spoken a handful of times, and yet I sensed it was going to become a permanent fixture in my life. How quickly things changed.

The trident lay at my feet and a couple of the decaying surfboards were propped against the seats. Una thought her dad could use the wood, and she had her eye on an old board with bright tropical decals.

When I turned the tiller to head to the north of the island, Una put a hand on my arm.

"Let's check the book before we go. Then I won't worry while we're gone."

I gave her a kiss, then adjusted the sail to bring us on course with Atlantis' southern marina. A little less than half an hour later, the island appeared. As we approached, I noted a gathering in the courtyard and trailing along the beach. More than a gathering. A crowd. I'd only seen crowds like these during annual festivals.

Una frowned. "What's going on?"

My stomach sank. "We've only been gone for a day."

Una pinched my arm. "Maybe they're celebrating our departure."

I tried to laugh, but it got stuck in my throat. Maybe Una's sixth sense was rubbing off on me, because I instinctively knew one or more of the prophecies had arrived. And I was pretty sure I hadn't mysteriously turned into a god during our short voyage. Which meant...Vorago.

Vorago returns.

The prophecy screamed inside my head. Not the voice this time, but my own internal thought.

As we entered the marina under a blanket of watchful stars, a suffocating tension turned my lungs to soup and my muscles to painful knots. People stared as we secured the boat. They lined the clifftop, the beach, the pathways, and every square inch of space in between. Smiles, laughter, and excited chatter competed with the ominous thud of my heart.

I leaped from the boat, the trident firmly in my grasp. Its familiar weight grounded me as I helped Una climb out. She placed a reassuring hand on my back as she scanned the unfamiliar faces lingering near the dock. The crowd parted as we approached the path leading to the main courtyard.

My father stood at the forefront, his face carved in stone, his jaw set with a tension I hadn't seen in years. He didn't wave or greet me. That wasn't like him. Next to him stood Maya and Trent, Una's parents, their expressions equally guarded. The senate was present too, flanking the High Council like ceremonial guards. Ford was there, his piercing gaze locked on me, analyzing every move I made. And in the center of them all, three figures I instinctively knew weren't mortal.

The gods.

CHAPTER FIVE

stared at the tallest of the three gods. It wasn't his height that drew my eye, it was the power radiating off him like a surging storm that insisted on being acknowledged. It brushed against me with the force of a riptide.

His features were chiseled to the point of unnatural perfection. His aquamarine eyes glimmered with the intensity of the deepest ocean, and his hair, completely silver, flowed like water down his back. He wore deep blue armor that looked carved from coral and was decorated with bioluminescent patterns, complementing his seafoam skin. A golden crown rested on his head.

"Vorago." I kneeled in the cooling sand at his feet. No wonder a crowd had gathered. Our creator had returned. The prophecy had come true.

I moved my gaze to the second god. Tempest, his frame lean and taut, exuded barely-contained chaos. His dark skin contrasted with his aqua armor, and long black braids trailed to his waist. There was something about his demeanor that reminded me of a ticking bomb.

Cascadia stood on Vorago's other side. Her serene beauty

was no less intimidating, her skin color was a tone between her two siblings and glowed as if moonlight coursed through her veins. Her gaze was more penetrating than I was comfortable with, as though she could see every doubt buried within me.

I adjusted my grip on the trident, its glow uncertain, like it too was holding its breath.

Una kneeled at my side, her hand grazing my wrist before she bowed her head, her diplomatic mask slipping into place.

Vorago's voice was the first to fill the beach, smooth and deliberate. "Gal Waters, I presume. Wielder of the trident." He stepped forward with a practiced smile. Behind him, many people clapped and cheered. "You hold in your hands a legacy that predates Atlantis itself."

I swallowed, feeling every set of eyes on the beach fixed on me. "The trident—it's yours. Rightfully."

Vorago's smile widened, but it still didn't reach his eyes. "You are as respectful as I hoped. Yes, it is mine, forged in the depths of the abyss, imbued with primordial power. And yet..." He glanced at the trident. "During my absence, it chose you."

Tempest snorted, folding his arms across his chest. "A mortal wielding a god's weapon. I'll never understand how it came to this."

Okay. So Tempest was a dick. At least he wasn't the one who created us. Or Atlantis.

"Tempest," Cascadia murmured, her voice holding a reprimand. "Do not belittle the boy. He has proven himself worthy."

Boy? Irritated, I stood, bringing Una with me. We'd been on our knees far too long already. I caught the hint of dissatisfaction flash over Vorago's face. He was a god. He was probably used to people on their knees for hours at a time, sucking his dick like it dispensed miracles, metaphorically speaking, of course. But he hadn't been around people for centuries.

Swallowing my pride, I offered the trident to Vorago. Its

glow intensified, as though responding to my intentions. "It belongs to you. If you want it back, it's yours."

Wind lifted my hair. **Don't let him have it.**

It belongs to him! I snapped back.

It *did* belong to Vorago. He had crafted it a millennium ago, and yet as I stood there with the weapon in my hands, offering it to him, it took everything inside me not to close my fingers around the trident's hilt and renege on the offer. To do what the voice wanted.

Vorago stepped closer, his hand outstretched. The courtyard turned deathly silent. Even the sea breeze held its breath. All the while, I was aware of the broken trident constellation above my head.

When Vorago's fingers brushed the trident's shaft, a crackling sound filled the air. His face twisted, and he recoiled with a sharp cry. A faint wisp of steam rose from his hand, the skin reddened as though burned, and the brief acrid stench of charred flesh was carried away on the breeze.

The crowd gasped, murmurs rippling through the assembly. Tempest stepped forward, his eyes alight with anger. "What did you do to it?"

I was about to answer when Cascadia held him back with a firm hand on his arm.

Through our joined hands, I felt Una's fingers trembling.

Vorago's eyes darkened as he stared at me, his fury almost burning through his restraint. "It...It seems the trident has truly chosen you," he said through gritted teeth. The burn on his hand was already healing, the redness fading as if it had never been there.

A breeze curled around my neck, looping tighter, almost a tangible thing.

You will pay for this.

There is nothing I can do about it.

I felt the weight of his anger, and his terrifying gaze alone seemed capable of flaying me alive, but he masked it quickly, forcing his expression back into one of calculated calm. He clasped his hands behind his back, nodding as if he was merely conceding a point in a chess match. "The trident's loyalty is...unexpected. But no matter. Perhaps it needs time to remember its true master."

The crowd rippled with noise, the whispers growing, speculation catching like wildfire. But all I heard were the waves crashing at my back, the harsh power of them signaling my uncertain future.

Beside me, my father tensed, and I caught Ford's faint nod of approval. Una squeezed my hand again. I reminded myself she was the guardian of the orb of Spirit and Soul. Her mere presence should be enough to diffuse a difficult situation.

"Perhaps it's not a matter of remembering," I said quietly, though my voice carried as people strained to hear. "You've been gone so long. Maybe the trident thought you had forsaken it."

Tempest's nostrils flared and his gaze pinned me to the sand. He opened his mouth to yell something, but Vorago waved a hand.

"It's quite alright, brother. The boy may be impudent, but he is correct." Vorago's forced smile returned. "It is a small, temporary matter. The trident will remember who it truly belongs to."

It doesn't belong to anyone. It is a partnership.

Vorago turned to address the gathered council, his tone smooth and commanding. "I am pleased to see the future of Atlantis is in...capable hands." He waved at the crowds beyond and was met with resounding cheers that shook the rocks for a full five minutes.

Tempest's sneer was subtly concealed as he muttered, "For now," before turning on his heel.

Cascadia lingered, her gaze meeting mine. Her expression was softer than her siblings', almost pitying. Then she, too, turned and followed her brothers along the path and toward the palace.

I watched them go, the crowd trailing after them along the lantern-lit paths, hanging on their every word and swamping them with questions and offerings. It was only when they reached the palace steps that I remembered to breathe again.

The trident was still in my grasp, its glow steady in my embrace. I tightened my grip as the reality of the gods' presence finally sank in.

"Gal," Una whispered. "What just happened?"

I didn't answer immediately, my eyes fixed on the gods' retreating figures. "I don't know

"How long have they been here?" Una asked our family and friends.

Dad rubbed his forehead. "They arrived an hour before you docked. But the entire island already knows."

"We knew who they were instantly," Maya said.

"Vorago said he'd only talk with the Trident Wielder," Ford said. "But he did grant an audience with the public."

"Ego," Uncle Dylan said. "He has an ego bigger than..."

"A god?" Dad finished for him. "Not surprising."

"So he only came back for the trident?" I asked.

No one volunteered an answer. I stood under the night sky, sweat dripping down my spine in spite of the cool evening breeze, my palms slick, my teeth gritted, my stomach twisting with nerves.

"We don't really know why he's here," Maya eventually said. "We can only guess at his motivations."

Ford rested his hand on the hilt of one of his short swords.

"Vorago's already making waves. He's only been here an hour, but he's wasted no time making his presence felt. Atlanteans have been gathering outside the palace grounds in droves, hoping to catch a glimpse of him. When he stepped outside to greet them, it was like they'd seen a living legend."

"A legend who demands an audience," I muttered.

"The amount of flowers and shells and other gifts already piling up..." Dad trailed off.

"He's not stupid," Ford said. "He played it well. He gave a short speech thanking the people for their loyalty to Atlantis, mentioned his connection to our history, and then performed a few... demonstrations."

"What kind of demonstrations?" I asked warily.

"He created a shrine. Right there, in front of everyone." Ford pointed to a towering sculpture of water and coral that glowed with bioluminescence a few yards away. People formed circles around it. Whispered compliments concerning its beauty swept between them, some comparing it to the Fountain of Youth. Offerings were laid at its base. The rings of people were at least ten deep.

I stared at it, nestled between the figures of the old High Council and the Fountain of Youth. "Why a shrine? Why not a..." But I couldn't think of anything Atlantis was lacking.

"It was about display," Ford said. "Power. Symbolism. He's making sure they remember who he is—and that they revere him."

"And look at it," Maya said, sweeping her hand toward the shrine and gathered people. "He's already achieved what he set out to do. People are praying."

"Praying?" I couldn't remember the last time someone had prayed to Vorago in a way that didn't take his name in vain.

Uncle Dylan scoffed. "That's what gods do, isn't it? They show up, put on a spectacle, and boom—instant worship."

Dad sighed. Although he only wore his crown on ceremonious occasions, his height and stature never failed to indicate his level of royalty, even when he felt deflated. "It doesn't take much to reignite faith. Atlantis has been searching for something greater to believe in for years. Vorago gave them a reason. He's stepping into a role that's been empty for generations."

Ford dipped his chin in agreement. "Exactly. The temples that were abandoned are reopening. The first vigil is scheduled for tonight. I think Coral organized it."

"Bless her," Una murmured. "She loves anything to do with the gods."

I squeezed my wife's hand.

Maya crossed her arms. "As much as I love my daughter and admire her good will, we don't know what Vorago's intentions are. Once faith like that sets in, people stop asking questions. Vorago could do almost anything now, and they'd follow him without hesitation. Including my youngest."

"We'll keep her safe, Mom," Una said, giving her a quick hug.

A cold knot twisted in my stomach. "He's doing this in plain sight. No subtlety, no pretense."

Ford rubbed a hand over his shaved head. "And the people love him for it. He's gaining their trust faster than any of us expected. Faster than you, Gal."

You will lose the love of your people.

I blanched at the warning, but covered it with a cough. Why did I have to live on an island where wind was a constant? I had a feeling this voice, whatever it was, would never leave me alone.

I turned my thoughts back to the problem at hand. Vorago could take over Atlantis without a single show of force. He didn't need to fight; he merely needed to keep dazzling them with his enigmatic presence.

54

"You're still their prince, Gal," Dad said. "And I'm still their king. They'll follow us, but we must give them something real to believe in. Atlantis has managed just fine without the gods for centuries, and if it comes to it, we'll do it again."

The pressure mounted inside me like a rising tide. I had fought, sacrificed, and bled for Atlantis. But now, that wasn't enough. If I didn't find a way to counter Vorago's influence, we could lose everything.

CHAPTER SIX

*T*he great hall pulsed with tension, every sound echoing louder than it should, every flicker of light casting shadows that seemed to stretch farther than before. I stood near the plinth where the Power of the Sea had rested for centuries, the trident humming in my grip. The faces of those gathered around me reflected a mix of concern, confusion, and unease.

Una sat to my right, her hand brushing mine in silent reassurance. Across from me was the High Council—Ford, Maya, and Blaze—each wearing expressions as sharp as blades. Beside them sat the senate, their ranks filled by Dad's cousin Jordan, the ever-practical Trent, my grandmother and my Aunt Marina. My father sat at the head of the circle, his brows furrowed as he leaned forward, fingers steepled.

Ember, Bay, Ash, Cyra, and Coral were scattered around the room, their postures ranging from guarded to openly wary. Apart from Coral, who couldn't stop staring at Ash.

Ember nudged me. "We got crazy shit going on right now, buddy."

"Tell me about it."

"We got crazy shit going—"

Smirking, I elbowed his ribs, hard. "Not literally."

"We need to figure out why they've come back," Dad began, his voice slicing through the murmur of speculation. "The gods don't do anything without a purpose."

"We don't know anything about the gods," I said. "Not really."

"I always thought if Vorago came back it would be a good thing." Dad rubbed a weary hand over the back of his neck, absentmindedly putting his toned physique on display. "After all the years the selachii were persecuted by the ashrays..." he shook his head. "I thought they would be...*proud*. Was I wrong to think that? To hope for it?"

"Of course they're proud," Coral spoke as she stroked Ripple, who was curled up in her lap. "But they are gods, and they deserve our respect."

"Do they?" I questioned Una's youngest sibling. "That depends on the cost."

She rolled her eyes. "Respect doesn't cost us anything."

"I know you want to believe in them." Maya sighed, then smiled at her daughter. "We all want to believe the best in our creators, but the very fact that his return was documented in *The Mermaid Chronicles* is sign enough he brings...trouble."

Coral frowned. "No, it doesn't. I've studied the book almost as much as you, Mom. Not all the prophecies were bad. *Cascadia's tears, when offered to the Ocean's Heart, can grant the most profound wishes of the faithful*," she quoted an early prophecy. The insistence in her voice caused Ripple to wink an eye open. "And how can Gal becoming a god, one of *them*, be bad?"

"Oh, I could name a few," Ash said, throwing me a wink to let me know he was joking.

"But what kind of trouble?" Jordan, recently back from an expedition to Atlantis' single mountain, paced a line behind the chairs. "I can understand if he wants the damn trident. He made it after all. So why couldn't he take it?"

"Because Vorago abandoned it and the trident chose Gal." Blaze stood by his guardian orb, Fire and Heat.

"The trident values loyalty," Ford confirmed.

"But if the trident doesn't want Vorago back," Cyra said, emerging from the corner of the room. "They should leave, right?"

It wasn't like her to be so naïve. Although rare that she offered her opinion in council meetings, Cyra usually saw straight through people to their real intentions. I guessed no one wanted to believe that Vorago, our creator, the very god who had gifted us Atlantis, would turn out to be a dick.

"Where did they go, by the way?" Uncle Dylan asked. "I saw them walking toward the palace, but where did they go?"

"They've taken rooms in one of the royal cottages in the gardens," Maya replied.

Una raised her brows. "And we're all okay with that?"

"We don't have much of a choice," her father answered. "Even without the trident, the three of them have an undocumented amount of power."

"So if Vorago can't hold the trident...what will he do?" I asked.

A thick silence fell over the gathering.

Maya stood and walked to *The Mermaid Chronicles* where it rested in a glass box on top of a marble plinth. "The book has not imparted any further information, nor revealed Vorago's true intentions. So perhaps it can't, for fear of altering our fates for the worse. And I am not receiving any more mystical information either. We can only speculate."

"If he created ocean shifters and gave us an island to live on away from persecution, he can't be all bad, can he?" Aunt Marina asked, looking at Uncle Dylan like he would have answers. Uncle Dylan preferred to bury his head in the sand. The fact that Aunt Marina had forgotten that was a testament to the amount of stress in the room.

Coral threw her hands skyward, causing a *harrumph* of protest from Ripple. "Vorago is not *bad!* Why can't you all give him a chance?"

"We *can* give him a chance." Steam poured from Blaze's nostrils as he spoke. "But we need to be prepared at the same time. And let's hope he proves us wrong."

"I'd be more worried about Tempest," Ash said, rubbing his knuckles across his thigh. "That one is a total loose cannon."

"Agreed." Ember nodded at his brother.

Restless, I pushed off from where I was leaning against Una's chair. "Vorago created Atlantis so long ago it's hard to know what his original intentions were. Did he create us merely for his amusement? As an experiment? We don't know. And after centuries in slumber, who knows what side of the bed he's woken up on."

Blaze nodded, his wings catching the glow of the room's magical light. "They're playing a long game. Vorago's reaction to the trident tells us something. He wanted to reclaim it, yes, but it also exposed something else—if he needs it, he can't be *all-powerful.*"

Maya pursed her lips. "I've always suspected Vorago gifted some of his power to give life to the trident. But he is still a god and we cannot underestimate him, nor Tempest, nor Cascadia."

"Power," Bay said from where he stood propped against a wall like he was no more than furniture. I never understood why he was privy to council meetings. Just because he was a Summers didn't mean he would inherit oracle powers. Moby certainly never bothered showing up. Why was Bay so invested? Probably so he wouldn't lose an opportunity to show me up or criticize whatever decision I'd made. "It's always about power."

I glanced at him, his calm demeanor making my unease spike. He didn't look nervous or uncertain—he looked the same as always, stoic and expressionless. He stood near a window, sunlight highlighting the strength of his features, the natural muscles in his arms. Not a single brown hair was out of place. He crossed one ankle loosely over the other, and his two short swords were sheathed at his waist. A mimicry of Ford.

Grams stood, laced her fingers in front of her, and cleared her throat to get everyone's attention. "I think we're getting ahead of ourselves. While I understand that many of you are worried, and that the gods have been absent from our world for some time, we cannot assume they mean us ill will." Coral beamed like she'd won a prize. "They could be here to help us, to aid the advancement of the island, or even to live among us as they did in ancient times. I urge you all not to jump to conclusions until we know more."

"Wise words," Aunt Marina said.

Sat on the chair beside me, Una shook her head and reached for my hand. Although I respected my grandmother's wisdom and experience, I trusted Una's gut more.

"Or maybe there's another oceanic battle in another corner of the world or universe and they need the trident." Jordan rolled his shoulders and tossed his head from side to side. "Or Gal."

"Maybe," I admitted, gnawing on the inside of my cheek. "But they don't see me as an equal. Vorago didn't respect me, he tolerated me because I wield the trident."

"That could change." Ford stood with his arms crossed, his expression composed. "The gods respect power, and you've already proven you can wield it, and wield it well."

"Or they see me as a means to an end," I countered. "What if they're just waiting for the right moment to take it from me?"

It doesn't belong to you.

60

The breeze and voice had trickled in through an open window. I was tempted to growl at it, but that would only raise questions.

"Then we'll be ready," Dad said firmly. "Atlantis isn't defenseless."

"The prophecy has only been in the book for forty-eight hours," Maya said, placing a hand on its decorative cover. "We've never had to prepare for something like this."

Before I could respond, the Power of the Sea—hovering on its plinth in the center of the room—glowed brighter. Its blue light pulsed, permeating the room, and drew every gaze in the hall. The smell of the ocean filled the hall and the sound of waves reached my ears. The temptation to be in the water in my ocean form was almost too strong to resist.

"What's happening?" Ember whispered, his voice breaking the spell. "I knew this day was going too smoothly."

"Vorago returning is smooth?" I shot back at him.

He shrugged. "Better than a Denizen."

He had a point.

"The last time the Power of the Sea was this animated," Una said, her eye tracking the orb as it pulsed, "it chose Babette as its guardian."

I squeezed Una's shoulder, and she returned my touch by resting her hand on mine. The Power of the Sea rose from its plinth, floating toward our circle. I rocked on my heels, the trident glowing in response, expecting it to stop in front of me and bathe me in its blue approving light.

Wind whispered through the room once more.

You think you need more power?

Maybe I really was going insane. There wasn't another explanation for that damn voice intruding on my thoughts.

"Stay calm," I said, mostly for myself.

The large blue orb ignored me, moving with deliberate

purpose until it stopped in front of Bay. It hovered there, its light reflecting in his wide blue eyes, until he stumbled back a couple of steps and almost got lost in the velvet drapes.

"Bay," Ford said sharply. "Do not be afraid."

"Is it about to smite me, or something?" Bay's hands were clenched at his side, one of them hovering over his sword as if he could kill the Power of the Sea. His eyes tracked the blue sphere as it dipped lower, almost like it was bowing to him. Then, slowly, it rose again, stopping at chin level.

Coral leaped to her feet, causing Ripple to dart from her lap and hide between her ankles. She clapped. "Bay! This is so exciting!"

"*By the depths*," Blaze muttered. "It's chosen him."

"Chosen him for what?" I demanded in an unintentional shout. My pulse raced. My muscles locked. My jaw ached. In front of me, Una paled and tightened her grip on my hand.

Ford's gaze didn't waver. "The guardian of the Power of the Sea."

"What's wrong with everyone?" Coral plucked Ripple from the floor and nestled him in her arms. "This is *amazing*. The Power of the Sea has been without a guardian for years."

"That's not possible," I said. "It's been years since Babette died...Why now? Why him?"

Bay looked as shocked as I felt, his back pressed against the wall as if trying to escape its blue light. "I...I don't know," he stammered.

"It makes sense," Aunt Marina said. "If the Power of the Sea has chosen a new guardian, it must mean something is coming. Something big."

"Like the return of Vorago?" I asked.

"Or the ascension of a god," Maya replied.

Dad gave me a sympathetic look. "They're probably linked."

Ember eyed me cautiously. "And so the Power of the Sea needs a new guardian to help it look after the island."

"The Power of the Sea doesn't need a guardian when Atlantis has me," I said.

Jordan scoffed and slapped the back of my head. "Someone needs to knock you down an inch or two."

I arced the trident through the room and golden light filled the large space. "I'm only speaking the truth."

Una stood and came to my side, linked her arm through mine. "Do not forget my husband has saved our island on more than one occasion. The island chose him as its protector. He is the Trident Wielder. He has the power of cryo-aquaism. These are all big, enormous things. Scary things. Wonderful things. Let's not belittle the power Gal does have. But..." She turned to face me. "You are not a god. Not yet anyway. And if it comes to it, we will need everyone in this room with all their unique abilities to deal with Vorago or any other threat that comes our way."

Maya and Trent beamed at their daughter.

"Exactly," Coral said, pumping a fist, the seashells in her hair clattering with her exuberance. "Atlantis is stronger with Bay and Gal working together."

I folded an arm around Una's waist and brushed my lips against her ear. "And that is why you are the guardian of Spirit and Soul." Her orb glowed a little brighter, as if in response to my words.

"What do I do with it?" Bay asked, the Power of the Sea still hovering by his face.

I turned to Bay, who was staring at the orb like it might explode. "You didn't ask for this," I said, trying to keep my voice steady. "But if you're the guardian, it means you'll be granted...powers."

"Powers?" Bay repeated, his usual even tone cracking with traces of fear.

"Guardianship of the Power of the Sea comes with abilities," Blaze explained as he approached Una's brother. "Control over currents, defensive shields, maybe even more. It's a role meant to protect Atlantis."

"Okay..." Bay drawled, his features tightening. "And here I thought I was going to be a bodyguard."

"You *will* be a bodyguard," Maya said to her son. "But it will be to the entire island, not just the royal family."

Bay gulped.

I stepped closer to him. "Do you even want this?"

Bay met my gaze, his pupils blown wide. "Does it matter? It's not like I have a choice."

"That's not an answer," I said.

"Gal," Una said, with a light touch on my arm. "It's not his fault."

I pulled away, something tightening in my throat, tension threatening to choke me. "Fault or not, this changes everything. He's not ready for this. He's only twenty-one. Babette was much older when..." I trailed off, realizing that none of my protests would matter.

"I don't think the Power of the Sea cares whether we're ready," Maya said. "It's chosen Bay, and that's that. We need to focus on what this means moving forward."

She would say that. She was his mother.

"This isn't about who deserves what," Dad said, with all the authority of a king. "The gods have returned, and now we have a new guardian. We need to figure out how this changes things."

The room fell silent again.

I glanced at Bay, the orb still hovering near him, its light unwavering. My instincts screamed that this wasn't right, that it should have been me.

When the breeze irritated the back of my neck, I knew the voice was coming.

It should have been you.

Finally, the voice and I agreed on something.

But the Power of the Sea had chosen differently, and there was no undoing its decision. Was that how Vorago felt when he'd tried to take the trident? No. I couldn't compare myself to a god. The two situations were entirely different.

Doubt crawled over me, digging its claws in.

The man becomes the god.

Was the prophecy even about me?

CHAPTER SEVEN

I marched toward my home in the palace gardens, Una on my heels yelling at me to slow down. I did *not* slow down. The scent of jasmine floated around us, but I took no pleasure in it and swore at the bugs who dared to get in front of my face. I cut along the path with the trident swinging in my hand, the violent flashes of light it emitted mirroring my mood.

"Gal, stop!" Una called.

I turned to face her, almost tripping over a pile of offerings to the gods stacked near a fountain. "It's not right."

She frowned, her one blue eye scanning my face, pity creeping into her expression.

"Don't look at me like that."

"Like what?"

"Like I'm a little kid throwing a tantrum."

"Aren't you?"

"No."

Una straightened her eye patch and gave me a hard look.

"The Power of the Sea is our most special, most powerful,

most revered source of magic," I said, unsure how to express what I was feeling.

"I'm aware."

"Bay is twenty-one."

"I'm aware of that too. You were nineteen when you became the Trident Wielder—"

"And he hates me."

Una's brow wrinkled once more. "I don't know why you think that."

"Really? It oozes out of him every time we're in the same room."

"He's just a very serious—"

"Don't give me that bullshit."

Una closed the gap between us and planted her hand on my chest. "You are the Trident Wielder. You possess cryo-aquaism. You are the guardian of the orb of Snow and Ice. What more do you want?"

"I figured if I was going to become a god, I'd need more power than I already have. And believe me, I'm conflicted about the idea. I do not need more power or responsibility, but if they were granted to me, I would never worry about your safety again—"

"Gal, that's not—"

"Let me finish." I drew in a breath, scanned the gardens to make sure we were still alone. "The fact that the most powerful artifact in our world chose your brother...it makes me wonder if the prophecy is about me at all."

I lowered my head and looked at her through my lashes, too afraid of her reaction to face her.

Una sucked in her cheeks. "You think Bay will become a god?"

I raked a hand through my hair. "Is the idea really so preposterous?"

Una dropped her hand from my chest and laced her fingers through mine. "I suppose, considering recent events, I can see why you'd think that. But I don't feel it. In my gut. And I've learned to trust my gut."

I nodded. Una was usually right about these things, but something in *my* gut told me this time, she was wrong.

"I don't understand how someone who doesn't support the royal family, the history of Atlantis, can possibly become a guardian?"

"He's training with Ford to become the head bodyguard!" Anger flared in her voice. "How can you say he doesn't support the royal family? My entire family are entwined with yours."

I sighed, tried to draw in a steadying breath of jasmine, but the sweet fragrance did nothing to calm me. "I feel like he has a hidden agenda."

"Hidden agenda?"

"To keep an eye on me. To make sure I don't..." I hated bringing up my infidelity, but there was no avoiding it now. I reminded myself to stay calm as ice crystals snaked across the lawn and the fly that had been annoying me dropped out of the air, frozen. "He might try to drive a wedge between us. He's never forgiven me for Nautalun."

Understanding pooled in Una's eye. "It's not his job to forgive you. *I* forgave you. And that should be all that matters." She stared at me, waiting for me to agree.

"It is," I began, "for us. But I can feel the depth of the grave he imagines me in whenever he's in the room."

"You need to get over that."

I laughed. "That's your solution?"

"Yeah. You're the older, more mature male. Get over it."

"Maybe we should rethink your role as the guardian of Spirit and Soul."

Una chuckled, her cheeks crinkling in genuine amusement.

"I didn't mean that as a joke."

"That's why it was funny."

"Una—"

"Empathy is important. But sometimes people need a kick up the backside. And I will never lie to you, Gal Waters. Bay is a serious guy. He takes his duties seriously. His family seriously. And infidelity seriously. Yeah, maybe he's hung up on the Nautalun thing, but that doesn't mean he'll serve you any less."

"I'm not so sure—"

Before I could say more, a voice boomed from the darkness. "Trident Wielder!"

I turned to see Tempest striding toward us, still wearing his imposing aqua armor, his dreads swaying with virility. "You're requested to dine with Vorago." He waited, as if expecting me to drop everything there and then.

I frowned at the obnoxious god. "I'm in the middle of a conversation."

"Finish it later," Tempest ordered.

I looked at Una.

"You'd better go," she said.

"I will not bow—"

"Yes, you will," she said. "For now."

"Bring your woman," Tempest called.

I raised an eyebrow. Una's face took on an expression of pure fury. "Did he just call me, *woman?*"

"I believe so." I smirked. "But there's nothing to complain about. You *are* my woman."

Una's lone blue eye was so full of indignation it was like she had the power of two. "How very dare you—"

I kissed her button nose before she could continue. "Come on, let's go see what he wants." I kissed her again, this time on the lips, making it linger to annoy Tempest, then grabbed her hand and followed the god into the woods.

It didn't surprise me that the gods had chosen the grandest of the palace's cottages, a sprawling estate surrounded by lush greenery and nestled close enough to the sea that the eternal motion of the waves hummed a low melody through the windows. And it was easy to find because offerings lined the path the entire way. There were flowers and seashells, coral figurines and smooth driftwood carved into sacred symbols. Bowls of saltwater sat beside delicate starfish, their arms curling gently, while polished stones, some etched with prayers, formed a winding trail toward the front door. It was...a lot. I had no idea our people, *my people*, were so desperate for their deities to return.

The wind picked up. I sighed.

You are not the ruler they desire.

"Fuck off," I muttered.

"You okay?" Una asked.

"You really can't hear it?"

"The voice in the wind? No. I hear leaves and trees and bushes and—"

"I get it."

She put a hand on my arm. "Breathe, my prince, just breathe."

The air thickened with the overly sweet reek of too many flowers in one place as Una and I entered the cottage and were led through to the dining room. A large round table of polished coral dominated the room, its surface etched with swirling oceanic patterns that glimmered in the soft glow of candles. Platters of food had been placed across the surface and the aromas they gave off made my stomach rumble. I couldn't remember the last time I'd eaten. On the boat? Vorago sat at the head, his hands steepled under his chin, his silver beard reaching the table's surface. Cascadia sat to his left, her presence more serene. I got the distinct impression she was the most reasonable of the three.

Vorago rose as we approached, his coral crown catching the light, his gaze landing on the trident I carried. "Ah, Trident Wielder, Princess Una," he said, his voice a deep rumble. "You honor us with your presence."

Una schooled her features, all signs of her earlier indignation gone. "The honor is all ours."

I tilted my head. I was pretty sure Vorago was all about gracing *us* with *his* presence, not the other way around. What game was he playing at? "I thought it would be my father's presence you would seek."

Tempest led us deeper into the room, his smirk resembling a gathering storm cloud, promising chaos. I did not trust him one little bit.

"He may be the king, but it is you I am interested in, Prince Gal," Vorago replied.

"I see," I replied, my tone light, but my grip tightening on Una's hand.

Vorago gestured for us to sit. "Let's not waste time on pleasantries. Sit, eat, and let us speak openly."

Una and I exchanged a glance before taking the seats opposite him. There was an extravagant spread of grilled fish, jeweled seaweed salads, and crystalline pitchers of water and wine. Unwilling to release the trident, I held it at my side and lifted a fork with my other hand.

"Atlantis has changed much since I last swam its channels," Vorago said, raising a goblet of wine in a toast. I dropped my fork and repeated the gesture. Una followed suit and the five of us sipped. It was the best damn wine I'd ever tasted. A vintage that certainly did not come from Uncle Dylan's bar. Did the gods have their own source? "Humans living among ocean shifters. Commerce. A senate. Is this what you call progress?"

Una stiffened beside me, but I spoke before she could. "At its finest."

"Finest?" Vorago echoed, his displeasure clear. "You've spent your whole life thinking this place belonged to you. But you have no idea what Atlantis was meant to be."

I frowned, clutching the napkin in my fist. "I know it was built as a refuge for ocean shapeshifters—"

"Yes. And now look at it." He turned, eyes burning, sweeping a hand toward the window. "You call this paradise?" His lip curled, disgust dripping from every syllable. "A kingdom filled with mixed-bloods and humans?" He spat the last word like poison. "This was never meant for them. They are the very thing we built this place to escape. And yet, when I woke from my slumber, I found them everywhere—thriving, ruling, corrupting."

I stiffened. "We live in peace—"

"Peace?" Vorago let out a cold laugh. "Atlantis has forgotten its purpose. Forgotten its gods. Do you know what it was like to wake after centuries of nothingness, expecting to return to my people, only to find myself a *stranger* in my own world? Everything I bled for...everything we built...gone." His voice cracked like a whip.

"But the people worship you. Humans and ocean shifters alike." Una leaned forward. "You've seen them, their offerings, their gifts. They couldn't be more delighted to have you return."

"Delighted?" Vorago said the word as though he'd never heard it before. "Tell me, what right do they have to stand in my domain?"

I forced myself to hold his gaze. "They belong here just as much as we do."

Vorago's expression darkened. "No. I created Atlantis. I ruled it. And when I left it to the ocean shifters, they should have protected it. But instead, they let it slip through their fingers. *They forgot us.* They let our home be shaped by human hands, let it be defiled by their presence, their weaknesses, their mortality."

His anger pulsed like a living thing. He pointed at me, ripples of water rolling across his arms.

"They're not our enemies anymore." Anger flashed through me. I gritted my teeth to contain it. Una placed her hand on my thigh and squeezed. "They're our allies. Our people."

Tempest snorted, swirling his wine. "Allies? Or parasites?" He white-knuckled the stem of his glass. "Your rediscovery of Atlantis was, in part, due to human persecution. Only twenty-six years ago."

I took another sip of wine and prayed I wouldn't lose my shit. But I didn't know who to send the prayer to. "I wasn't even alive then."

"Enough," Cascadia said gently, her soft voice startling after Vorago and Tempest's sharp tones. "The past cannot be undone, brothers. The world is not as it was when we last ruled. The people have been nothing but respectful. And this boy has not had long enough to shape its destiny."

Boy?

That is what you are, is it not? The tickling irritation of moving air swept around my shoulders, swarmed my face, jabbed at my nose.

"He is merely a mortal," Tempest added, derision dripping from his words.

"A mortal who wields my trident," Vorago said.

Was that a question?

"He also possesses the power of cryo-aquaism, and is the guardian of the orb of Snow and Ice," Una said, her hand tensing on my thigh. "And he is the Prince of Atlantis."

I covered her hand with mine and squeezed gratefully.

"But still a mortal." Tempest pointed his fork at me. "The

Fountain of Youth doesn't even deem you valuable enough to cure. You'll be gone from this island's history in the blink of an eye."

Furious, I lurched to my feet. "Why exactly have you all come back?"

"Sit down," Vorago said.

"I'd rather stand."

He pinned me with his bright blue eyes. "I said, *sit*."

I sat.

"You, Gal Waters, are the Trident Wielder," Vorago said. "Tell me, do you even comprehend the depths of the power you hold?"

I bristled at the condescension, but forced myself to remain calm. "I've mastered its abilities. It's why I'm still here. Why this island is. *Your* island."

A shadow of a smile crossed Vorago's face. "Mastered? How quaint. Tell me, did you know the trident can bend time? That it can shape the fabric of reality?"

My breath caught, and I glanced at Una. Her expression was carefully neutral, but I felt the tension radiating from her. "Time manipulation?"

"Time manipulation," Vorago confirmed.

Tempest shook his head. "He doesn't deserve such power."

Vorago whirled on his brother. "Quiet!"

Tempest's jaw tightened, but he did as he was told, gulping the rest of the wine and refilling it from a carafe.

"I didn't know such power was possible," I said. I could give Una back her eye. Could I bring my mother back from the dead?

Vorago leaned forward, his gaze piercing. "Why would it not be? The trident is more than a weapon. It is the key to Atlantis' past, present, and future. And yet, you wield it as a mere tool. It must be frustrating, knowing there's so much you cannot yet unlock."

My grip on the trident's staff tightened. Frustrating wasn't the word I'd use, but the idea of untapped power gnawed at me. During the five years the trident and I had been together, not once had it hinted at hidden powers. Was this how I would become a god? By bending time? The possibilities were endless, and yet each one boggled my mind.

"Gal," Una said, her voice pulling me back to the present. "It took you a long time to block the trident's whisperings...its temptations..." Is that the voice I was hearing now? Was it the trident? But the trident had never been mocking before. And she was right. Overcoming the trident's power over me had taken a concerted effort, but that was in the past. We had come to understand each other, and no longer did I fear the weapon would turn me into something I didn't want to be. But if it really could control time...perhaps I needed to risk addiction once again. I was willing to snatch any carrots it saw fit to dangle in front of me. I would do anything to keep Una safe. *Anything*. "You don't want to go back to that place. You don't want to...push it too far."

"Too far?" How could *too far* be defined? It wasn't like it was a number, or a risk assessment. And if I could learn to control time, then future enemies and prophecies would become redundant. Una would be safe. Forever.

Tempest smothered a smile as his eyes darted between Una and me. Cascadia's expression portrayed concern, but she didn't voice any warnings.

"It is a weapon of gods, Gal," Vorago said. "You cannot, as a mortal, expect to understand all its powers or to understand how it influences you."

"That's my point exactly," Una said, fiddling with her eyepatch.

Vorago's gaze shifted to her, and for a moment, I thought I saw amusement flicker in his eyes. "Princess Una, your caution is admirable. But greatness requires risk. Surely you see the potential your husband has. The destiny he could fulfill."

"Destiny is earned, not given," Una replied evenly. "And power without control destroys everything."

Tempest chuckled darkly. "Control is overrated. Isn't that right, Gal? You didn't win your battles by holding back."

"I didn't win them by being reckless either," I snapped, my patience fraying.

"I could teach you," Vorago said, laying his glass down carefully. "I could show you the powers the trident has kept hidden from you."

The trident hummed in my hand, golden light streaking down its hilt.

"It seems to approve," Cascadia said.

"Why would you do that?" I asked. "When you clearly only awoke to reclaim it for yourself." Although I didn't feel as though I could trust Vorago, I did want to learn the secrets the trident had kept from me. My instincts told me I'd need the knowledge, and soon.

Vorago arched a brow. "Do you not desire to learn how to bend time?"

"It's not that. It's your motivation that concerns me."

"You dare to question the motives of your most revered god?" Untapped fury laced each word. "The one who created you? The one who gave you this land, safe from human persecution. The one who made it possible for you to touch that trident you're wielding? The one who has now returned to bless his people."

Una and I shared a glance. I was well aware I was walking a tightrope. Gods certainly had power. And egos to match. It wouldn't do to get on their bad sides.

"Of course not," I said, and Vorago's shoulders visibly relaxed. "I just wondered why now, after all this time."

The three gods exchanged meaningful looks. "Because we have awoken and decided it was time to return," Vorago answered, as if his response actually explained his intentions. He cut into a piece of grilled fish, chewed methodically, all the time keeping his eyes glued to mine. "Well? Do you wish to learn?"

"I do." It would mean spending more time with Vorago, which I wasn't entirely happy about, but instinct told me I should amass as many abilities as possible. I injected a pleasant and grateful tone into my words. "I would like that very much."

"Gal—"

I turned to my wife. "This is what must be done."

Her blue eye pleaded with me. I knew she was concerned. And she was right to be. But for now, we had to follow this path. Vorago, Tempest, and Cascadia were the most powerful beings on this island. They possessed ten times the abilities of the Denizens. It would be foolish to anger them. And there was so much I could learn.

You shouldn't play with powers you don't understand.

I will come to understand them.

It probably wasn't a good idea to talk back to the voice, but I was running out of options.

"Then it is decided," Vorago said.

"And the guardian of the Power of the Sea?" Cascadia asked.

I startled. "How did you know about that?"

She gave me a wry smile. "It is the ocean's most powerful artifact, a concentrated amount of energy gathered from the universe's primordial forces, do you think we wouldn't know when it chose a guardian?"

"Bay," Una blurted. "It chose Bay. My brother."

"Earlier today," I said.

Vorago's attention shifted between Una and me. "Interesting."

"Your family is becoming very powerful," Cascadia remarked.

"Bay isn't interested in power—"

Una was cut off when Vorago slammed his palm on the table. "Everyone is interested in power."

Una shook her head. "That's not true. I only aspire to be an oracle so I can help the inhabitants of Atlantis."

"You may wrap it up in altruistic motivations," Vorago said. "But it is still power."

Beside me, Una tensed, but didn't argue further.

"Perhaps we should strip the island and its inhabitants of all its power," Tempest said, flicking his dreadlocks over his shoulder. "Start again."

Cascadia dropped her fork. "Don't be foolish, brother. What has been set in motion cannot be undone. Even with the trident. Nor should it be."

Una nudged me. Did they just slip up? Did they admit to a weakness? That they weren't all-powerful?

Vorago focused on Una. "The Power of the Sea does not make mistakes, but its choices are often...strategic. If it chose this Bay, it is because he will serve a purpose. But be wary, Trident Wielder. Those who gain power often seek more. We must protect the trident."

"Bay's loyalty is to Atlantis," Una said. "Not to himself."

"We shall see," Vorago murmured.

The rest of the dinner passed in a tense dance of veiled comments and forced civility. Vorago continued to prod, dropping hints about the trident's hidden powers and its potential to reshape Atlantis. Tempest relished every moment of my discomfort, while Cascadia remained a quiet observer, her gaze shifting between us as if cataloging every word and expression.

As the meal concluded, Vorago stood. "We shall meet tomorrow to discuss the trident's true potential, should you be able to claim it."

I nodded, my mind a whirlwind. Una gripped my hand as we rose to leave, her silence speaking volumes.

As we stepped into the cool night air, I finally exhaled. We walked along the forest path, heading toward our home. "What do you think?"

She didn't answer immediately, her gaze fixed on the moonlit path ahead. "I think there is far more to Vorago than meets the eye. I think he is dangerous. And I think you're tempted by what he's offering."

I stopped walking, turning to face her. "Is that so bad?"

She toyed with her ring, rubbing her finger over the central pearl. "I'm undecided. But knowing you, who will do anything to keep the people you love safe, you'll be all in...but there is a danger of going too far."

I shook my head. "I'm not as reckless as I once was."

"I know." A soft smile warmed her features. "But I think power is seductive. And Vorago knows exactly how to exploit that."

Her words struck deeper than I wanted to admit. As we continued toward our cottage, I couldn't shake the feeling that I'd been granted an opportunity. To give Una back her eye. To talk to my mother again. To fill the holes of grief that plagued so many. I couldn't turn my back on that.

CHAPTER EIGHT

$\mathcal{T}$he cavern was alive.

I felt it the moment I stepped inside. The water flowing down the waterfall was heavier, thrumming with something ancient, something old enough to remember the first stones laid in Atlantis. Bioluminescent moss crept along the walls, their blue-green glow pulsing in slow waves, as if the cave itself was breathing. The floor was smooth beneath my bare feet, worn down by the tides of millennia. I hadn't been down here in the caverns and tunnels since the collapse, when the rocks had caved in and trapped me with my mother right before the ghost pirates' attack. And now, I was surprised it didn't bring back an onslaught of negative memories. It was just a place.

Is that what you think? That memory and emotion no longer have a hold on you?

I didn't bother responding to the voice. I knew what my weaknesses were. I didn't need the voice to remind me.

As I moved deeper inside, the roar of the ocean at my back abated. Vorago stood motionless at the heart of it all, his silver hair catching the cavern's dim glow.

"The greatest power of the trident is not its ability to call the tides or smite enemies," Vorago said, his voice smooth as flowing water.

"If I can control time, then I can change things." I kept my voice even, but the thought pulsed through me like a heartbeat. "I can give Una back her eye. My mother..." I couldn't finish the thought, the lump in my throat strangled further words.

Vorago tilted his head, studying me. "You misunderstand." His words carried no anger, just an unnerving certainty. "Time is not a river you can force to flow backward. It is a tide—relentless, moving only forward. You can slow it, speed it, stretch it, even step between its currents—but you cannot turn it back."

A sharp chill prickled along my spine. I lifted the trident, feeling its power simmer beneath my skin, restless, waiting. Nothing but disappointment filled me. I had been hoping...I shook my head, angry at my naivety. Of course it would never be that simple. "What's the point of bending time if I can't change the past?"

Vorago chuckled. "It is a skill far more useful than you realize."

Irritation flared. "But if I could go back, just a few years, I could change things. I could give Una her eye—" I stopped myself, jaw clenching. I didn't need to say it. We both knew how it had happened. That it was my fault.

Vorago's eyes gleamed with something I couldn't place. Something close to pity, but not quite. "Try," he said simply.

I blinked. "What?"

"Try to go back," Vorago repeated. He stepped aside, giving me space. "Focus on the moment. Feel the weight of it. Use the trident to take you there."

I hesitated, but then I closed my eyes and tightened my grip on the trident. The memory surfaced—Una, before everything. Before the Denizens, before Zale, before I told her I loved her. I pictured her standing on Mýrdalsjökull, her hair whipped by the wind, her sharp blue gaze meeting mine, filled with challenge. If I could go back, if I could stop the polar bear before it ever touched Una, I could fix everything.

The trident vibrated, a low thrumming sound filling the cavern. The air around me rippled, distorting like a heat mirage. A pull yanked at my core, a strange, stretching sensation as if I was being unmoored from the present.

For a second, I thought it was working.

But then, as quickly as the power surged, it slipped from my grasp. The tension snapped back like an elastic cord, slamming me into the present. I stumbled forward, gasping as my surroundings blurred back into clarity.

Nothing had changed.

I was still here. Still now.

Of course you are.

How the hell did wind get into a cave?

I am not the wind.

The statement sent alarm ricocheting through me, but I had little time to react before Vorago spoke.

"You see? The past is a fixed point." Vorago's expression remained impassive. "No matter how much force you exert, you will never reach it."

Frustration burned through me. "Then what the hell is the point of this?" I gestured sharply with the trident.

"The point," Vorago said, stepping closer, "is not to dwell on what you have lost. It is to ensure you never lose again." His voice was low, but it carried the weight of something deeper. Something I wasn't sure I wanted to name. Regret?

I swallowed, trying to work moisture back into my dry throat.

"You cannot bring back the dead, Gal Waters. You cannot undo what has already happened. But you can bend time's flow in battle. You can make a second stretch into an eternity, long enough to shift the tide. You can slow your enemy's blade, see their strike before it lands." He pushed a blade against my throat, so fast I never saw it coming. "In a fight, this would mean death for you. But with time manipulation, you would be invincible."

Vorago stepped away and lowered the blade. I touched my throat to find a small drop of blood had escaped. *Not so invincible right now.*

I waited for the voice to chime in, but it remained silent.

I rubbed my temples, my thoughts a storm of frustration and reluctant understanding. "So, that's it? I can't change fate, but I can manipulate the way time moves around me?"

Vorago's smile was sharp. "You still do not understand." His voice lowered, became something dark and coaxing. "Altering time is not small. It is the difference between life and death. Power and powerlessness. It is the difference between being a man—" he paused, "—and becoming a god."

A shiver ran down my spine. *The man becomes the god.*

I met his gaze. Una's warnings echoed in the back of my mind, but I pushed them down, locked them away. Vorago was showing me the trident's greatest power. He was showing me how to defeat him. Why would he do that if he meant us harm?

"Then teach me."

Vorago's smile widened as he planted his feet. "Good. We have much to do."

The cavern walls pulsed around us. And despite the small voice in my head telling me this was dangerous, despite the way Una's voice whispered for me to stop—I knew I couldn't ignore this opportunity.

"How does it work?"

Vorago laughed, a surprisingly light sound that contrasted with the gruffness of his voice. "It is beyond human comprehension."

I didn't anger at the slight. He was right. I couldn't wrap my mind around the idea that I could slow time. "Then how do I learn it?"

"By imagining all the threads of time in front of you. By picturing everything that led to your current moment."

"It's that easy?"

Vorago raised a disapproving eyebrow. "It is *never* easy."

"But you can do it."

His face turned to thunder. "Not without the trident. Which is currently in your possession."

Okay then.

Skirting over the dip in Vorago's volatile mood, I made my voice as gentle as possible. "So I just picture the threads of time..." I shut my eyes and blocked out the cavern, the dripping water, the smell of damp, even Vorago's presence. When I blinked them open again, everything remained the same.

"How can you see time if you shut your eyes?"

Embarrassment warmed my cheeks. "Time isn't visible."

"Isn't it?"

I sighed.

"Try again."

The distant sound of water dripping echoed, each drop a slow, rhythmic reminder of time slipping away. I stood in the center of the cavern, gripping the trident until my knuckles turned white. My breath came in ragged pulls, my body aching from each failed attempt.

"Again," Vorago commanded for a fifth time.

You will never wield the power of time.

Yes, I will.

I ground my teeth and adjusted my stance, feeling the cold press of the stone beneath my feet. The trident hummed, its power restless in my grip, waiting for me to do something— anything—other than fail.

I focused.

The world around me blurred at the edges as I reached for time, trying to mold it, bend it, force it into submission. The cavern's echoes stretched, the dim glow from the walls flickering erratically. For a moment, I felt it—like I was skimming the surface of a wave, catching the pull of something deeper beneath.

Then it slipped.

Time snapped back into place, rushing past me like a tidal current. Vorago's figure sharpened, unimpressed, as if he had expected my failure.

Frustration flared hot under my skin. "Damn it."

"Again."

I scowled but obeyed, bracing myself. I cleared my mind, pushing aside the frustration and doubt. I focused on the cavern, on the way time pulsed like a second heartbeat beneath everything. I reached—

And it shattered.

Nothing changed.

Nothing bent.

Nothing obeyed.

I let out a sharp breath, struggling to quash the urge to slam the trident into the ground. "It's not working," I snapped. "It's like trying to hold onto water with my bare hands."

Vorago wore a stony expression. "You forced it," he said. "Power is not commanded, Gal. It is understood. It is surrendered to."

I frowned. "I thought the whole point was learning to control it."

"The illusion of control," he corrected. "True power does not bend to will alone. It comes when one surrenders to destiny." He gestured at the trident. "Do you think this artifact bends because you demand it? Or because it has chosen to reveal itself to you?"

I swallowed, the implications of his words stirring an acid pool in my stomach.

Vorago studied me for a long time, then asked, "Why do you think the trident chose you, Gal?"

The question landed like a punch to the gut.

I opened my mouth, then hesitated, my mind scrambling for an answer I didn't have.

Why *had* it chosen me?

Yes, why did it choose you?

It was clear to me that the voice was not coming from *The Mermaid Chronicles.* So either I needed to address the status of my mental health...or there was an explanation I hadn't yet considered or discovered. I didn't know which option I preferred.

Choosing to ignore the worrying situation, I focused on Vorago's question.

Why had the trident chosen me? Was it because of my leadership? The sacrifices I had made? Or was I simply in the right place at the right time? Or was it my birthright?

Doubt crawled up my spine. What if it had been a mistake? What if I wasn't meant for this?

"I don't know," I admitted finally. "I want to believe it's because I earned it. Because I fought for Atlantis, because I protected my people. But sometimes...sometimes I wonder if it was just chance. If anyone could have wielded it, had they been standing where I was."

Vorago's expression clouded. "Chance?" He towered over me. "You are more special than Atlantis even realizes, Gal. The prophecy confirms it."

I forced myself to hold his gaze. "The prophecy could mean anything."

"*The man becomes the god,*" he murmured, his eyes gleaming. "It does not speak of chance. It speaks of inevitability."

Ice crawled down my spine, though I wasn't sure if it was from his words or the way he said them—like they were undeniable.

I had spent years trying to outrun prophecies, trying to carve my own fate instead of being bound by one. But Vorago spoke as if destiny wasn't something to fight. As if it was something I should embrace.

I looked at the trident in my hand. What if he was right?

What if I was meant for something greater than even I understood?

The voice didn't utter a single word, it merely laughed. Before I could retort, the sound of slow, deliberate footsteps interrupted.

I turned as Tempest emerged from the cavern's shadows, his expression one of barely restrained disdain. The glow of the bioluminescent moss reflected in his electric eyes, making him look even more detached, more otherworldly.

"This is pathetic," he remarked, voice laced with contempt. "I expected more."

I stiffened, biting back the immediate retort that burned on my tongue. Between the voice and Tempest, I couldn't decide which was worse.

Vorago didn't react, his focus still on me. "He is learning."

Tempest scoffed. "Is that what you call this?" He studied me like I was a disappointing experiment. "I call it wasted time. You already know how this ends, brother. He will fail, and this little mortal will be nothing more than another footnote in history. And you will have your trident back."

Footnote in history?

No. That wasn't going to happen.

I had already proved myself time and time again. Against

the Denizens, against Zale, against death itself. I wouldn't be cast aside as insignificant by a supercilious god who refused to see the strength of mortals.

Vorago exhaled slowly. "You underestimate him."

Tempest gave a short, humorless laugh. "No, you overestimate him. The trident may have chosen him, but that doesn't mean he understands why." His sharp gaze cut to me. "Do you?"

I hesitated.

That same damn question again.

Why me?

I wanted to say it was because I had fought for Atlantis, because I had sacrificed everything for it, but something about the way Tempest looked at me—mocking, waiting for an answer he was sure I didn't have—made my throat close around the words.

Vorago answered for me. "Because he is destined for more. Because even now, Atlantis does not understand what it has in him."

A strange heat bloomed inside me at his words. It wasn't mere flattery. Vorago believed it.

He believed in me.

No one else had ever spoken about me that way. Not as a ruler. Not as a hero. But as something more. Something greater.

Tempest remained unimpressed. "You sound so certain."

"I am."

My hold on the trident turned rigid.

Tempest had mocked me for failing to manipulate time. But Vorago hadn't wavered, hadn't doubted. He wasn't just teaching me tricks. He was showing me how to unlock something inside myself, something vast and untapped. He may not approve of humans living on the island, but he still cared for his ocean subjects. That much was obvious, despite his gruff demeanor.

"That boy." Tempest pointed at me. "Is unworthy to join our ranks. I won't allow it."

Vorago folded his arms. "You may not have a choice, brother."

If Vorago was wasting his time, why would he bother? Why show me what I was capable of unless he truly believed I would become something beyond mortal? Otherwise, I'd be dead in sixty years or so, a mere blink of time for a god, and then he could pluck the trident from my cold, dead hand.

Despite his initial reaction to the trident deserting him, Vorago wasn't here to steal it. And his reaction was warranted. If something I had created, that was the pinnacle of my power, that had been with me for centuries...had found another owner, I'd be upset too. And *upset* was an understatement.

I turned back to Tempest, lifting my chin. "You don't think I can do it? Stay and watch."

Tempest arched a brow, then smirked. "Very well, mortal. Amuse me."

Yes, amuse us.

I planted my feet and squared my shoulders. I wasn't just going to prove him wrong. I was going to prove I was more than he could ever imagine. And when I became a god, I would wipe that smug smile off his fucking face.

CHAPTER NINE

The palace loomed ahead, its marble domes gleaming under the midday sun. I rolled my neck, easing the tension from my shoulders as I made my way through the court-yard, stepping around piles of offerings to the gods and plump grapes that had fallen from the overhanging vines. My head ached from the training and the way the voice had pestered me, but beneath the exhaustion, a hum of power pulsed through me. A new hum that didn't dissipate when I grew tired.

I was stronger.

Vorago had shown me what I could become—what I *was* becoming.

And I wanted more.

The rush of my thoughts came to a jarring halt as I spotted Bay standing in the palace gardens, arms crossed over his chest, his expression unreadable. A few feet behind him, Moby and Ash lay sprawled near a fountain. Ash had his wings unfurled and was pulling on a joint, whereas Moby leaned back on his elbows.

I smothered a sigh. I wouldn't be able to reach the path that led to my home with Bay blocking the route. All I wanted was to shower the sweat off and put on fresh clothes, then hold Una in my arms and ignore the rest of the world for a few hours. Clearly, my wants would have to wait.

Bay turned to face me as I approached, the sunlight catching his strong features. His expression held the expectation of an apology, which he wasn't going to get. We hadn't spoken since the Power of the Sea had chosen him yesterday. Since I'd stormed out of the great hall.

I adjusted my grip on the trident, not breaking stride, trying to avoid eye contact. I knew we'd have to talk at some point, learn how to put our powers together, but today was not that day.

I pulled level with Bay, caught a muscle in his jaw ticking.

"I wanted to show you something," he called. I couldn't tell if he was in a good mood or a bad mood. Not that it mattered. Not that I cared.

I should have kept walking, should have ignored him, but something in his tone made me stop.

Without another word, he turned toward the fountain. He lifted one hand, palm facing downward. At first, nothing happened. Then, the water stirred. The ripples swirled outward, slow at first, then tightened into a perfect spiral.

The movement sped up. The water twisted higher, climbing into the air in a narrow vortex, spinning faster and faster until it towered over us, a twisting column of liquid defying gravity. Schools of tiny colorful fish swam in its currents, their bodies glowing silver and blue as they flickered in and out of sight, pulled along by the motion.

Moby let out a low whistle. Ash nudged him, wide-eyed, and fluttered both wings. The resulting breeze stirred the trees and sent water droplets from Bay's vortex to sprinkle over me.

I studied the vortex. It was tiny. Cute. Pretty, even. But insignificant.

Bay flicked his wrist, and just as easily as it had formed, the vortex collapsed back into the fountain, not a single drop spilling over the edges.

He turned back to me, expectant.

I arched a brow. "What do you want, a medal?" I knew I was being a dick, but I also didn't really care. What good were three-foot funnels when I could slow time?

Bay's lips pressed into a thin line. "This is what the Power of the Sea has given me. I can control currents, summon walls of water, guide entire ecosystems. Or at least I will be able to once I've trained."

I scoffed. "And you think that's supposed to impress me? I can do *far* more than that." I spun the trident in my hand, tempted to show off my new skills. But I wasn't ready to share just yet.

Bay frowned, his entire face caught up in the expression. "I thought you'd be pleased...relieved to know that the safety of Atlantis isn't entirely your responsibility. I know how much that bothers you."

Una. Una had told him of our private conversations, of my innermost fears. Fears that weren't even relevant anymore.

Aren't they?

No, they're not.

Burying my anger, I planted the hilt of the trident in the ground next to me, creating a divot in the immaculate lawn. "It's nice and all that the Power of the Sea chose you, Bay, and I hope you enjoy the powers that come with, but we don't need them. Not anymore. What Vorago has shown me makes that look like child's play."

Ash frowned. "Gal—"

Bay cut him off. "I wanted to talk to you about that too." He took a step forward, his eyes holding a challenge. "Vorago is using you."

I laughed. "Is that what you think?"

"I *know* it." His entire body tensed, every finely-honed muscle taut. He'd been training with Ford for years and it showed in his physique.

"You're jealous." I shook my head. "The Power of the Sea chose you as guardian and now you think you're the most important person on this island. Or do you think you're the most powerful? And that it's your job to step up and save Atlantis..." I couldn't keep hold of the laugh brewing in my chest. "Seriously, Bay. I got it covered."

"Jealous?" His eyes narrowed. "Protecting Atlantis is about unity."

"Not anymore," I said, waving the trident, which caused the water in the fountain to stir in a far more impressive display than Bay's funnel. Three large vortexes spun around the lawn, making Moby and Ash roll away to prevent themselves from getting soaked. The funnels took to the sky, froze and thawed in a repeating cycle, until landing back in the fountain.

Bay's mouth fell open, then snapped shut, then open again. "Atlantis deserves more than your arrogance. You've never appreciated its value, or all the gifts it bestowed on you—"

"*Gifts?*" I leaned forward, relishing my extra two inches in height. "You think wielding the trident is a *gift?* You think everyone expecting you to save the island, to save them, is a *gift?* You think having your loved ones threatened...killed...just to get to you, is a *gift?*"

"I do," Bay said, refusing to acknowledge the menace in my tone. "I never said it was easy. But it *is* a gift."

"Well, I'm so glad it all worked out for you. That you have

gifts you can appreciate. Come talk to me in a year or so when one of your parents is killed, or maybe the person you love."

He flinched. That had gotten to him. I didn't hang out with Bay socially, only during family occasions when we were forced together, so I had no idea about his love life. Nor did I care. But that reaction sparked my interest.

"I can offer a drag on my joint if you two need to chill out a bit?" Ash called. We both ignored him.

Moby got to his feet, his expression darkening. He'd never pretended to enjoy being involved in his family's legacy, but Bay was his brother and the Summers' loyalty knew no bounds.

I cut Moby a pointed look. "This is between me and your brother."

Moby nodded, but remained where he was and leaned against the trunk of a palm. He gave the impression of relaxed indifference, but I knew he was taking in the entire conversation.

"The protection of Atlantis is bigger than personal relationships," Bay said, his body rigid, the pulse in his neck ticking into overtime. "That was how it was lost in the first place."

I narrowed my eyes at him. "It was also how it was regained. My parents found it. United—"

"Unity," Bay cut me off. "As I said. It's the pinnacle of every prophecy."

I dug the trident's hilt into the ground again, widening the divot into a sizeable hole. We were going around in circles. Bay would never see sense.

"Look," I lowered my voice. "I know you've found it difficult finding your place. What with your mom and sister being oracles, and you having no powers—"

"Neither do Moby or Coral." Bay's hands fisted. This topic, it seemed, had gotten under his skin. "What's that got to do with anything?"

"Just because you have powers now doesn't mean your needed," I said, trying to be as gentle as possible, but there was a small part of me that wanted to slam my fist into his righteous face. Okay, maybe it wasn't a small part. "Maybe you can't stand that I'm the one who gets to defend Atlantis while you're stuck learning party tricks with the fish."

Bay barely blinked at my insult. "Babette, and her powers, were instrumental in defeating the ghost pirates."

The anger flashed through me so quickly that the water in the fountain froze. Moisture droplets in the air formed into ice crystals and hit the lawn like bullets. "Don't you dare say her name to me."

"Hit a sore spot, did I?"

"Babette was—" I cut myself off. He didn't deserve to know about Babette. Babette hadn't saved *him* from a pack of mutant muttwalkers. Babette hadn't sailed *him* to Iceland to find magical ice. Babette hadn't died during a volcanic storm for *him*.

Movement caught my eye. Ember, charging across the lawn. Although his one wing was absent, his presence filled the palace gardens. I took a breath and the fountain thawed, but the sound of its rushing water frayed on my nerves.

"Uh-oh," Ash quipped. "Big bro's coming to sort them out."

"Somebody needs to," Moby said.

"What's going on?" Ember asked when he joined us. "I can hear you all the way from Dylan's bar."

"Drinking during the day again, brother?" Ash said, a sly grin on his face.

Ember raised an eyebrow. "You're one to talk when you're smoking my weed." He turned his attention back to Bay and me.

I pointed at Bay. "He thinks because he can create a three-foot spinning toy that he suddenly gets to make decisions—"

"That is *not* what I said." Bay glared at me, shoving a finger in my face. "I was merely talking about the importance of unity—"

"Whoa." Ember spread his arms, planted one hand on my chest and the other on Bay's shoulder. "Maybe we all do need a little funky fruit. Can we dial it down a notch?"

Bay recoiled at the touch. Ember withdrew his hand from Bay's shoulder, but left his other hand on my chest. They stared at each other, something passing between them I didn't understand. Suspicion crawled along my spine. Were they speaking telepathically? It was the only way ocean shifters could communicate in water while in their ocean forms, and was difficult to accomplish on land, but my parents were capable of it. So were Una and I, when the distance wasn't too great. What the hell was going on here?

Bay flexed his fingers and leveled his gaze at me. "I don't care about power. I care about Atlantis. Can you say the same?"

Can you?

The words hit like a punch to the gut, but I didn't let it show. Instead, I stepped forward, closing the space between us and shrugging Ember's hand off. "If Atlantis is going to survive, we need more than hope." My fingers tightened around the trident. "You have no idea what we're up against."

"Oh, I think I do," he bit out. "Vorago isn't your mentor." His voice was quieter now, but there was an urgency beneath it. "He's your enemy. You just haven't realized it yet."

I *did* realize it.

Somewhere deep down, I *knew* Bay was right.

But I found myself defending Vorago anyway.

Because if Bay was gaining power, then I needed *everything* Vorago could teach me. And if Vorago did end up stabbing me in the back, then I needed everything in my arsenal that could defeat him. Only a god could defeat a god.

"Can we please not start a civil war in the palace gardens?"

Ember said. "I'd like to make it to dinner without dodging light-ning bolts...or whatever power you two might dish up. I reckon you either need to hug it out or fight it out."

My head whipped toward Ember's so quickly I thought I'd give myself whiplash. "I am *not* hugging him."

"I am *not* going to fight," Bay said.

I glowered at him. "Because you'd lose." My voice came out as more of a growl.

"I don't care about losing, as long as Atlantis is safe."

"Damn," Moby muttered.

"Think you could use this in your next movie?" Ash asked. "The tension is delicious."

Moby shook his head. "Time and place, Ash."

The humor drained from Ember's face. "You two need to sort your shit out, because if we are facing a threat, we're going to need both of you." He looked at me. "Gal. You know I love you, but you need to be careful around Vorago—"

"I'm not stupid."

Ember raised a hand. "Never said you were, buddy. But you *can* be single minded."

"Look, if and when we do face another threat, I will be prepared." I spoke directly to Ember. "With your pyro shield and my cryo-aquaism, and Bay's...cute little funnels. We're a good team."

Ash launched to his feet and threw his joint on the ground. "Did you forget the time I saved you from a lava lake?"

"I thought it was me who teleported you there?" I snapped at the young dragon king.

"So I could help *you*," he replied.

"And you did," I said. "I believe I thanked you at the time."

"Unity," Bay muttered.

"Alright, alright! We get it. Everyone's a hero. Let's put away the measuring sticks and create a team chant," Ember said, then turned to Bay.

"You don't need to say anything," Bay's voice came out strangely husky. "I know exactly what my faults are. And I am working on them."

Ember's expression softened. "That's not what I was going to say." He reached a hand toward Bay, but before it made contact, let it drift to his side. "And I know you are."

My gaze pinballed between them. "What the *fuck* are you two talking about?"

They both stared at me. A flush crawled onto Bay's face. I'd never seen him embarrassed before. Ember raked a hand through his hair and little flames erupted from his fingers.

"We're just worried about Vorago," Ember said. "And Tempest has already ruined some of the northern crops with a storm he created. Including my weed."

I raised both brows. *That fucker.* "I'll have a word with Vorago."

Bay laughed. "You think you can tell a god to control his brother?"

"I don't see why not," I said through gritted teeth. "Tempest is a dick. He needs a fucking leash."

"Agreed," Bay said.

Ember splayed a hand. "Well, that's progress."

I looked at my best friend. "Since when did you learn mediation tactics?"

"When I started growing weed."

"Fair point," I conceded, a notch of tension releasing from my shoulders. Ember was still Ember. My best friend. My cousin. *Family.* No matter what was going on between him and Bay.

Ember squeezed my shoulder. "You look exhausted."

"I'm fine."

Ember studied me for a moment longer, his shoulder twitching like his wing might shoot into appearance, then spoke to Bay. "I'll walk him home."

Bay gestured for us to leave.

"I'm not a child," I said.

"Then don't act like one," Bay muttered quietly, but I caught it.

"Oh, for fuck's sake you two." A small fiery disc appeared in Ember's palm, and he hurled it at the sky. We watched it sail away into the clouds.

Bay and I locked eyes one last time, neither of us willing to break the tension entirely, but for now, we called an unspoken truce. The fountain behind us gurgled as if exhausted by the sheer weight of all the accusations and clashing egos that had filled the air.

Ash took a lazy step forward, dusting off his shorts with a flick of his hand. "Well, that was entertaining. Are we scheduling this again tomorrow? Same time, same place?"

His casual sarcasm did nothing to ease the pit in my stomach. Bay's warning echoed in my mind. *Vorago is your enemy.*

I shook it off as Ember nudged my shoulder. "Come on," he said. "Let's get you out of here before Moby's fan group arrives."

Bay's face remained neutral, but his eyes tracked me as I started toward the path leading away from the gardens. He wasn't done with this conversation, not by a long shot. And maybe he had a point buried under all his self-righteousness. But I wasn't going to give him the satisfaction of acknowledging it. Not yet.

Ember fell into step beside me. The familiar scent of smoke clung to him, a comforting reminder of his fire abilities. The path stretched ahead of us, winding between statues of long-dead Atlantean heroes and stone arches adorned with coral and seaweed. As well as all the offerings. We passed a group of people singing a hymn I didn't recognize, a song for the gods, about how thankful they were for their return. Had they forgotten it was me who had saved them from the Denizens?

"You alright?" Ember asked after a few minutes of silence. "That was...a lot, even for you."

"I'm fine," I muttered, letting the trident dangle at my side. "Bay's just being Bay. He thinks he's the new authority on everything because he's got fancy new powers."

Ember chuckled under his breath. "Yeah, I noticed. Though I have to admit, the fish vortex was kind of cool."

I shot him a sideways look. "You're supposed to be on my side."

"You know you're my number one bro." He raised both hands in mock surrender. "Just saying. Maybe there's room for both of you to be impressive, you know?"

"Room for both of us?" I echoed. "I don't need Bay."

He shrugged. "Would it be so bad? If you'd stopped to notice, you might see Bay's grown up a bit. He's not the pain in the ass he used to be—"

"You hanging out with Bay now?"

Ember shrugged. "I can have other friends."

"Of course you can...I didn't mean it like that...but Bay—"

"He's not wrong about unity being important. Especially if things with Vorago go sideways."

"Things aren't going to go sideways. I can handle Vorago."

Steam poured out of Ember's nostrils. "I hope you're right. But you've got a habit of thinking you can handle everything on your own. Just...don't shut us out, Gal. Me, Una, the others—we're here for you."

The sincerity in his voice caught me off guard. Ember wasn't usually one for heavy conversations. But he meant this. And as much as I hated to admit it, he wasn't wrong either. I'd been so focused on learning everything I could from Vorago, that I hadn't stopped to consider anyone else.

I nodded. "I hear you."

"Good," he said, his tone lightening again. "Because if you go full 'lone seawolf with a god complex,' I'll be the first one to slap some sense into you."

I snorted. "You can try."

"Don't tempt me." He grinned, bumping his shoulder against mine.

We walked in companionable silence for a while, the woods thickening around us, the low hum of insects filling the gaps in our conversation. The waterways lining the path flowed with a calming essence, their crystal-clear surfaces rippling as darting fish broke the surface before disappearing into the depths once more. A coconut plopped into the undergrowth with a dull thud, sending a pair of sand-colored crabs scuttling sideways before scrabbling into a burrow beneath the roots of a banyan tree. Sometimes I wished I could burrow into the roots of a banyan tree too. But I didn't fancy my balls being pinched by the roaming claws of a crab or two.

As we neared the path leading to my cottage, Ember spoke again. "In all seriousness...you've been pushing yourself hard. Why don't you take a breather. Spend some time with Una. She's probably worried about you."

A pang of guilt twisted inside me. He was right. I'd left the cottage this morning before Una was awake, hadn't even told her I was going to meet Vorago. Because I knew, deep down, she'd have an opinion on that. But maybe I needed to remind her—and myself—that she wasn't just a distant reason for my actions. She was my partner. My wife. Everything I did was for her, but I needed to include her in that decision making.

"I will," I said.

"Good." Ember clapped me on the back. "Now let's get you

inside before Ash and Moby decide to follow us and turn this into a full-blown afterparty."

I chuckled, shaking my head as we passed the gate leading to my cottage. The tension from the confrontation in the gardens began to fade, replaced by a renewed sense of purpose. There was a storm brewing—both figuratively and, if Tempest had anything to say about it, probably literally. But for now, I had it all under control.

CHAPTER TEN

I rolled over at the sound of soft footsteps and the scent of jasmine floating into the room.

"Where have you been?" I plumped a pillow and propped myself up to look at Una as she entered our bedroom, the light from the hall catching the pearl on her ring, making it glow.

Una hadn't been at home when I'd arrived. So Ember and I had hung out in the garden, playing with our powers, me freezing his fiery disks as he shot them into the sky. I'd used the trident to teleport to Uncle Dylan's bar and grab us a carafe or two of wine, and as the afternoon wore on, the more we drank the bigger our challenges became until we almost took out the roof of Una's parents' home. Now, it was well after midnight and I'd fallen asleep waiting for my wife to return.

"Did you miss me?" Una slipped out of her dress, a one shoulder affair that highlighted the definition of her muscles. Its aqua sheen emphasized the color of her eye, even in the semi-darkness of the bedroom. Beneath, she wore only a pair of panties. Moonlight from the open window played across her creamy skin, accenting the swell of her breasts and the curve of her hips. "I was with Cascadia." She slipped into a T-shirt and any stirring of desire I'd felt was doused with a prickle of appre-hension.

"Cascadia?" I patted the bed beside me, and Una came to sit, running her fingers through her hair to tame her curls.

"Thought I'd see if I could befriend her. Figure out what they're all up to."

"And?" I asked when she didn't volunteer more information.

Una tucked her legs beneath the covers. "She's...nice..."

"*Nice?*"

"She's been spending time getting to know the people. Even the humans. Apparently, she doesn't share her brothers' disdain for our co-mingling."

I huffed a laugh. "That's good. I think?"

"I think so." Una tilted her head. "But she's not just a pretty face. She's clever. While she comes across warm and friendly and subservient to her brothers...she's crafty."

"How so?"

"Hard to pinpoint. But I get the feeling she sees everything."

"Noted."

"And she didn't volunteer any useful information."

"So back to square one." I laid back with my hands behind my head and studied my wife's profile. Her beauty. Her scars. Her radiance. Her stubbornness. "I didn't know you were going to try that."

"That's because you left before we could hatch a plan."

I shot into a sitting position and twisted to face her. The moonlight caught her face. She still had her eyepatch on. She only wore it at night when she was feeling insecure. Or angry. "Are you mad at me?" I reached for her across the bed and she laced her fingers loosely through mine. I didn't relish another argument today, and promised myself I would remain calm, no matter what she said.

"Not mad." Una squeezed my fingers, but the tender gesture was anything but reassuring.

"I'm sensing a *but*." I turned a smile on her, hoping to ease the brewing tension.

She dropped my hand and cold air took its place. I braced myself, but couldn't help the temperature in the room dipping a couple degrees.

"You didn't tell me you were meeting Vorago to train with the trident." I couldn't tell if it was hurt or anger in her tone.

I placed a hand on her thigh. "You were sleeping. I didn't want to wake you."

"We need to make these decisions together."

I frowned and sat back on my knees so I could face her. "Don't you trust me anymore?"

She leaned forward and cupped my jaw, rubbed a thumb over the pulsing muscle in it. "Of course I trust you." Her voice was low, too soft, too...unlike Una. "Three eyes are better than two." Neither of us laughed at her joke. "I think it would be a good idea for me to be involved in your training sessions with Vorago. I might see things differently."

"Good differently or bad differently?"

She shrugged. "I'm hoping I can offer an unbiased view."

I pulled back, moving away from her touch. My breath misted in front of my face, despite Atlantean outdoor night temperatures never dropping below sixty-five degrees. "You don't think I can be unbiased?"

"Every Atlantean I've spoken to today has done nothing but wax lyrical about the gods. How wonderful it is they've returned. How safe they feel with all their power living on the island. How they finally feel Atlantis is as it was in the beginning...I could go on. So many sentiments. All of them positive. None of them doubting. It makes me wary. It's easy to fall prey to power, to denial, to wishful thinking...Their blind acceptance is...worrying. And I'm worried that you, too, will fall victim to their charm."

She doesn't believe in you.

I lurched out of bed.

Una's gaze followed me as I stood and paced to the window. I clenched my fists, my nails digging into my palms.

"Gal," Una said quietly. "You know you have a tendency to get...too close to things sometimes. You don't always see the whole picture."

I turned to face her, irritation bubbling to the surface. "And you don't? You're telling me you've never let your emotions blind you to what's right in front of you?"

She didn't flinch, just held my gaze with that steady, assessing look that always unnerved me. "Of course I have. That's exactly why we're supposed to keep each other in check. Two heads are better than one, right?"

"Exactly," I said. "I'm doing all of this for you. For us. So you will always be safe. So Atlantis will be safe. I'm not blind. I know the gods have an agenda. But I must learn all I can from them in order to protect you."

"I never asked you to do that."

I blanched. "Una—"

"I don't need your protection, Gal."

I gripped the bedpost. "That's my job. As your husband. As your partner—"

"It's our job to protect each other."

"But I have more power than you."

She stared at me, then shook her head. "It's not about power."

"Now you sound like Bay," I muttered.

Una's eye narrowed, her jaw tightening. "Bay told me you two argued earlier."

I sighed. "We did."

"About what?"

I crossed the room and sat on the edge of the bed. "He was showing off his new powers like he wanted a damn trophy. He's acting like he's suddenly the savior of Atlantis just because the Power of the Sea chose him."

"And you're acting like he's your enemy," Una shot back. "He's my brother, Gal. He's your brother-in-law. You're supposed to be on the same side."

I looked away, staring at the moonlit patterns on the floor.

"We are on the same side," I said. "But Bay thinks he can lecture me about responsibility. He's had his powers for all of two days. He has no idea what it's like to carry the weight of this." I swept a hand around the room to encompass Atlantis and the trident.

She leaned closer, her voice sharpening. "I know that prophecy rocked you when it appeared five years ago, but I thought you'd gotten a handle on it." She waved a hand at me when I opened my mouth to protest. "Yes, I get that Vorago's presence brings it all rushing back, makes it real...I just don't want you running headlong into something none of us understand."

I hesitated, rebelling against her words, ice coating the furniture in the room. Una wrapped her arms around her waist. I hadn't told anyone the full extent of what Vorago had shown me during our first training session. But if she wanted honesty, she was about to get it.

I rested my hands on my knees. "Vorago's been teaching me how to manipulate time."

Una's eye widened. "He was serious?"

"Yeah," I nodded. "I can slow it down, bring it almost to a halt. It's not easy to control yet, but it's possible."

Her brows knitted into a disbelieving line. "Why would you

even need that? You already have so much power, Gal. Isn't this going too far?"

"Too *far?*" I gave a humorless laugh. "Think about the fight with the Denizens. If I'd had this ability then—if I could've slowed time—no one would've had to die. I could've killed them all before they even touched us."

Her expression tightened as my words sank in. When she remained silent, I thought I'd finally gotten through to her. But then she spoke. "You don't know that. You did everything you could back then. More than anyone else could have. Bending time wouldn't change the fact that we were outnumbered and caught off guard. Sometimes...sometimes things go wrong, no matter how much power you have."

She's right.

"You're wrong," I said quietly, challenging both her and the voice. "If I'd had this ability, hundreds of soldiers would still be alive."

Una unfolded her arm from around her waist and reached for my hand again. "Gal...that's not on you. It was war—"

"War that could have turned out differently!"

Ice cracked. We stared at each other.

"Power like this...it has a cost," Una said. "And I'm afraid of what that cost will be."

The memory of when the prophecy had first appeared ran through my mind. *The man becomes the god.* She had cried. *Cried.* And not happy tears. Being a god didn't mean becoming evil. Why couldn't she see that? If I became a god...there was so much I would be able to do.

Una's thumb brushed over the back of my hand. "You've barely known Vorago for two days. You've only trained with him once, and already he's giving you these ideas about reshaping time and destiny. Does that not worry you?"

"Of course it does," I admitted. I drew in a couple of

measured breaths and willed myself to relax. Ice melted. Water droplets beaded on our furniture, but at least the room was warm again. "But it's also...*incredible*. I've never felt power like this before. It's like...like I'm finally understanding what I'm capable of."

She fiddled with the pearl on her wedding ring, running her finger around its surface. "Just because something feels powerful doesn't mean it's right. You said it yourself: the trident has secrets. And so does Vorago. What if he isn't telling you everything?"

I clenched my jaw. I couldn't deny the possibility. Vorago was enigmatic at best, and I wasn't naïve enough to think he didn't have his hidden motives. But that didn't change the fact that he was offering me knowledge I couldn't afford to turn down.

"I get that you're worried," I said, trying to keep my voice calm. "But I need this. Atlantis needs this. If we're going to survive future threats, I need to be ready. I can't become a god without Vorago's help. And clearly, I need to become a god in order to face our future. And I think that's what the voice is telling me."

"The voice," Una echoed, unconvinced.

"Maybe I'm not going crazy." I tried on a smile. "Maybe there really is a voice giving me...advice." *In a strange, mocking kind of way.*

"You think that's what it is?"

I shrugged. "What else could it be?"

Many, many things...

"I don't know, Gal, but maybe don't trust it too much. Until we figure out what it really is." Una sighed, her shoulders slumping. "It's always good to be prepared. I don't deny that. But—"

"But what?"

109

A tear slipped out of her eye. "I'm scared."

"Scared of what?"

"Scared of losing you." She said it quietly, but the words rebounded between us. She lowered her gaze, her lips twitching into something between a frown and a wince. And seeing her like that—it gutted me from the inside out.

"I'm here. *Right here.*" I took both her hands in mine. "I love you. I'm being careful. You're not going to lose me."

"You can't promise that."

I took her hand and placed it over my heart. "Yes, I can."

A faint smile curved her lips. "I love you too."

"And if you want to sit in on my sessions with Vorago, then I'd be more than happy to have you."

"What if he doesn't agree?"

"It's not up to him."

I pulled her into my arms. She wrapped her legs around my waist and leaned her forehead against mine. "I'm sorry," I murmured against her hair. "I didn't mean to shut you out. I...got over excited, I guess."

"I know," she whispered. "And I love the way you've learned to embrace your responsibility to Atlantis. I don't want you to close yourself off, that's all."

"Never," I murmured. "Never with you." The worries and doubts faded into the background. All that mattered was this moment—Una and me, together.

I brushed my lips against the shell of her ear. Flicking out my tongue, I traced a line from her ear to her shoulder, peppering her skin with kisses and reveling in her jasmine scent.

"Gal..." Una placed her hands on my shoulders.

"It's just you and me," I whispered, then claimed her lips with mine, a hunger growing deep in the pit of my stomach that would only be satisfied in one way.

"I'm not sure this conversation is finished," she said between kisses, but her hands speared through my hair and her hips rolled against me.

"It is for now."

As she gave in, I eased her down to the bed, my hands roaming under her T-shirt to stroke her silken skin. I drew circles with my thumb beneath her ribs, trailing lower until my fingers met the dip on the inside of her hip. Her stomach quivered under my touch and she released a sharp gasp.

Una's moan sent a jolt of warmth through me. She gripped my arms, digging her fingers in, arching her hips. Tension coiled deep inside. Tension that was desperate to be released by her, and her alone. Heat flashed over my skin as her touch became more insistent.

I pulled back, just enough to watch her face. Her lips were swollen, her cheeks flushed, and her eyepatch had fallen off. Pushing the hair away from her face, I laid my lips on the rough skin of her scar, then raised myself to elbows to look at her once more. She was so damn beautiful, it made my chest ache.

"What is it?" Una asked.

"You." That was all that needed to be said.

Her hands moved to my back and she shifted her weight beneath me so I was positioned between her legs, the hard length of me pushing against her between the thin material of her panties and my boxer shorts.

I leaned down again, pressing slow, deliberate kisses along her collarbone, savoring every inch of exposed skin. I wanted to take my time, to explore her like I never had before. No prophecies, no powers, no gods. Just us.

Her fingers curled into my hair, tugging gently as I continued my path down her body. I kneeled briefly to slip the T-shirt over her head and toss it aside, then eased her panties down her legs and discarded those too. Moonlight painted her skin in silver tones, highlighting every curve and plane like she was a work of art carved by the gods themselves. Did Vorago even paint? Whatever.

"You're staring," she murmured.

"Can you blame me?" I brushed my knuckles along the inside of her waist, watching goosebumps rise in the wake of my touch. "You're perfect."

Her breath hitched at my words, and a flash of vulnerability flickered in her eye. I kissed her again, this time slow and deep, hoping to show her exactly how much she meant to me. Her body softened beneath mine, her legs parting to cradle me as I settled between them, the hardened tips of her breasts brushing against my chest.

Our kiss grew hungrier, more urgent. Her hands explored my back, her nails dragging lightly over my muscles, leaving tingling trails of sensation in their wake. I groaned into her mouth, the fire in my veins roaring to life. She arched against me, pressing herself closer, and I felt every inch of her—every soft curve, every tender touch, every pulse of her escalating heartbeat.

She pulled away and braced her hands against my chest. Our breaths rose and fell in sync, the air between us charged with anticipation. The room was far from frozen now.

"I need you," she whispered. "Don't disappear on me."

"You have me," I promised. "Always."

I let my hands glide down her sides, savoring every curve, every plane, as if her body were a sacred map I had been entrusted to rediscover. The warmth of her skin radiated into my palms, soft and inviting, so powerful in its pull. Her body responded to every touch—muscles twitching beneath my fingertips, her breath catching as I stroked the sensitive spot below her navel. I traced patterns there, slow circles that caused her stomach to quiver and her thighs to tense in anticipation.

When I trailed my lips across the hollow of her throat, she

let out a soft gasp. I moved lower, my mouth following a path to the valley between her breasts. I pressed kisses there, then shifted to the swell of one, teasing her skin with the lightest touch of my tongue. Her back arched, her body instinctively pressing closer, silently begging for more.

"Gal," she whispered, her voice breathless and raw.

I smiled against her skin and continued worshiping the only person in my life worthy of being a god. Maybe the prophecy was about her. Una would make a perfect goddess. Just and fair and compassionate. Alternating between soft kisses and open-mouthed caresses, I took my time, savoring her taste—salt, the ocean, and jasmine. Una's smell. Una's taste. Una's everything. I traced the line of her ribs with my lips, gently nipping at her sides just to hear her sharp, surprised intake of breath.

"Please, Gal. I need more." She released the words with a plaintive moan.

"Patience," I said. I flattened my hands on her thighs, spreading her legs to give myself better access to the soft skin between them. I placed a lingering kiss above her hipbone, causing a shudder to ripple through her in the most satisfying way.

I continued my downward path, moving deliberately slowly. Every kiss was a promise, every flick of my tongue a vow that she was the only thing that mattered. Her gasps grew more urgent, her body writhing beneath me as if she couldn't contain the sensations coursing through her.

I reached her inner thighs. She whimpered, her legs trembling as I teased her with feather-light touches. Her hands buried into my shoulders, then clenched as I flicked my tongue over her silken center.

"Gal..." She bucked her hips, chasing friction, but I moved back up her body.

I stole a kiss and peered down at her. Her eye was dark with desire, her pupil blown wide, and the sight sent a fresh surge of heat through me. I kissed her again, reveling in the way she melted into me, like we were two halves finally reuniting.

"You drive me insane," I whispered.

"Good," she breathed, her voice rough with need.

The world narrowed to the two of us, tangled together in the moonlight. It was almost as if I could sense what was coming. That this could be our last time together.

"Gal," she gasped again, her voice a plea that shot through me like liquid fire.

"I've got you," I promised, letting my lips roam back to her throat as my hands traced the length of her body once more. I would take my time giving her everything she needed. Everything she deserved. This night belonged to us.

Her hands moved to the waistband of my shorts, tugging impatiently. I chuckled, then shifted to help her, kicking the fabric away until there was nothing between us but skin.

We fit together seamlessly, as if we had been made for each other, but tonight felt different—deeper, more primal, like every emotion, every touch, had been magnified. I guided myself into her, savoring the way she stretched to accommodate me, the way her body welcomed me like it had been waiting for this moment. I growled as the heat of her surrounded me, her warmth so intense I was sure fire was scorching my veins.

Una dug her nails into my shoulders as I pushed deeper, moving inch by inch until we were fully connected. She spasmed around me as we both took stock, both of us adjusting to the intoxicating way our bodies always molded together so perfectly. We stared at each other, breathing each other in. I took in every detail of her blue iris, every flicker of emotion in her pupil. I kissed her with quiet reverence, my lips lingering on hers as I began to move, slow and steady, each thrust deliberate and drawn out. Her body tightened around me, responding to every stroke with a need that matched my own. The friction frayed my control, sending sparks shooting through me with every roll of my hips. I growled low in my throat, the sound vibrating through both of us. Heat pooled in my stomach, spreading outward like wildfire, igniting every cell. I was burning for her, my need for her all-consuming.

"Gal..." she groaned, my name on her lips sounding like a prayer.

"Let go, my queen," I murmured, my hands sliding under her thighs to lift her, changing the angle just enough to make her cry out. The sound sent a shiver down my spine, spurring me on. I kept the pace unhurried, savoring every sigh, every gasp, every clench of her core.

Her hands tightened on my rear, pulling me closer, urging me deeper. We moved in perfect sync, the tension between us coiling tighter and tighter with every thrust.

The fire in my veins burned so hot I thought I'd need to call on my ice. Every brush of her skin against mine sent shockwaves through me. Every breathless whisper of my name unraveled me further. I increased my pace, burying myself deep inside her with each powerful thrust. I nipped at her lips, all tongue and teeth and desperation, then moved my lips to her ear, pulling at her lobe. Her breathy moans increased in frequency, growing louder in volume as her hips slammed against mine.

"Una..." I whispered her name, over and over, the only word I ever cared to utter. She was my anchor, the one thing in this world that kept me steady even as I teetered on the brink of losing control.

Her eye fluttered shut, her head falling back, exposing the elegant line of her throat. I kissed the hollow there, tasting her skin, feeling the rapid pulse beneath. Her body tensed beneath me, her breathing ragged and uneven. The coil of tension between us snapped as her climax took her. She cried out, her body arching off the bed as she clenched around me, her nails digging into my back so hard I welcomed the pain.

The sight and feel of her falling apart beneath me sent me over the edge. My release crashed through me, every nerve in my body on fire as her walls spasmed around me. I trembled as the flood of sensation poured through me and clung to her until the last aftershock shuddered through her.

Our bodies remained tangled, chests heaving as we tried to catch our breath. I pressed soft kisses to her collarbone, her shoulder, her jaw—gentle, reverent touches now that the fire had subsided into a warm glow. She traced lazy patterns along my spine, soothing, grounding, as though she, too, didn't want this moment to end.

"I love you," I whispered, my voice rough and full of all the emotions I couldn't put into words, ignoring everything that was coming for us.

Una smiled, her eye shining with emotion as she cupped my face. "I love you too, Gal. Always."

I rolled onto my side, pulling her with me so we were still connected, still wrapped around each other. The moonlight bathed us in a gentle glow, and for the first time in days, I felt at peace. Whatever challenges lay ahead, whatever dangers Vorago and his secrets held, we would face them together.

We always had. And we always would.

I waited for the voice to disagree, but it left us alone.

Una pulled the covers up and settled with her back pressed against my chest. She threaded her fingers through my hand and kissed each one of my knuckles, her touch lighter than a hummingbird's wings.

"Do me a favor?" she whispered.

"Of course." I kissed the nape of her neck. "Anything."

"Apologize to Bay tomorrow?"

Fuck that.

CHAPTER ELEVEN

Sunlight poured through the windows, casting a pleasing glow over the room. Una's body was draped across mine, her breaths slow and steady against my chest. All the doubts, fears, and tension that had plagued me last night faded into nothingness. I ran a hand down her back, savoring the peace of the moment.

Una stirred, lifting her head to look at me. She gave me a small, sleepy smile. "Morning."

"Morning," I murmured, brushing a kiss against her temple.

Her gaze turned serious. "Are we meeting with Vorago?"

I nodded. "Yes."

She sighed, her fingers tracing circles on my chest. "Sometimes I wish we could stay here forever."

I smiled. "We can if you want."

She laid her head on my chest and stilled, as if she was listening to the beat of my heart. "Just another minute."

I stroked her smooth back and closed my eyes to better breathe in her jasmine scent. A few minutes lapsed and I half wondered if I'd somehow frozen time without the use of the trident. Everything was so quiet, so still, so perfect.

Una slipped out from under the covers. I only had a few seconds to marvel at her naked body before she slipped into a jumpsuit. "Come on, let's get this over with."

After I dressed, we made our way through the forest, the only sound the rush of water from the palace's many fountains and canals. It took us longer than usual, considering every pathway and every fountain was lined with gifts for the gods. And in the courtyard, a large sign had been posted informing people of a festival that evening to honor their return.

"You weren't kidding when you said *everyone* was happy for their return," I said.

"I'm not even sure if the gods plan on attending," Una said, taking in the details of the event. "Cascadia didn't mention it yesterday. But they all spent a few hours giving blessings to a line of people that never ended."

"Well, if they want to keep the people on their side, they're going to have to make public appearances." Something I had done all my life.

I moved the bunches of hanging grapes away from our heads as we followed the column-lined path to the back of Uncle Dylan's bar. There we descended the stairs that led to the underground tunnel system and followed it until we reached the cave Vorago had taken me to yesterday.

Vorago was already waiting when we arrived, standing near a pool of shimmering water that reflected the glow of the cavern walls. His eyes gleamed with an ancient, calculating light as he turned to face us.

"You brought company," he said.

Although the temptation to justify Una's presence was strong, I quashed it. "I did."

"I work better alone," Vorago said.

"I work better with Una."

Una crossed her arms. "I'm here to look out for my husband."

Vorago's lips twitched in what might have been amusement. "Ah, the ever-watchful protector. Tell me, Princess, how long do you think you can hold him back from his destiny?"

"I'm not holding him back," Una said coolly. "I'm making sure he knows what he's stepping into."

Vorago chuckled, a low, rumbling sound that echoed off the cavern walls. "You misunderstand. I have no desire to control Gal. I am merely guiding him to realize his full potential. Something you, perhaps, fear."

"I fear manipulation disguised as guidance," Una shot back.

"Enough," I said, stepping between them. I didn't want this to spiral into another argument. "Let's get started. What's next?"

Vorago turned his attention to me, his expression neutral once more. "Today, we will push the limits of your time manipulation. We see how long you can hold time for."

I stepped forward, gripping the trident. It took me a minute to push Una's presence to the back of my mind. But when I finally relaxed and allowed the energy to thrum through me, it resonated with an almost sentient awareness. I focused on a rock feature, something to anchor me into the moment, narrowing my vision until everything else faded away. Slowly, I raised the trident, channeling its power.

The air grew thick, the faint sounds of the cavern muffled as time began to shift. The stone's edges blurred as I held time at bay. Droplets of water froze in midair, suspended like crystal ornaments. I held the suspension longer than I had before, the pressure building behind my ribs. My muscles burned, but I gritted my teeth and pushed harder.

"Good," Vorago said. "Now release it."

I exhaled and let go. Time snapped back into place, the droplets falling and splashing against the stone floor. My muscles ached, and my breath came in ragged gasps, but there was a flicker of pride sparked to life. That was a hell of a lot better than yesterday.

But is it enough?

Una rushed to my side. "Gal, are you okay?"

"I'm fine," I panted, wiping sweat from my brow.

"You don't look fine," she said.

Our gazes collided. Time seemed to stand still even though I hadn't arced the trident. I pushed my thoughts at her, hoping Vorago couldn't overhear our telepathy.

"*I need this.*"

"*It's exhausting you already.*"

"*I'll learn to increase my stamina.*"

Vorago walked around us. "Do you see now, Princess? He's evolving, becoming more than mortal. This is the path he was always meant to walk."

Una's eye darkened. "Or it's the path you want him to walk."

"Una," I warned. "Vorago deserves your respect."

She took a step back. "I'm not trying to stop you, Gal. Or disrespect Vorago. I just want you to stay grounded. To remember who you are."

"I know who I am," I said, irritated she was overreacting so quickly. "And I know what I'm doing."

Vorago clapped a hand on my shoulder. "Exactly. You are not a child anymore, Gal. You are a leader. A force. Atlantis will come to see that in time." He looked at Una. "As will you."

The words settled in my mind like a hook, digging deep. Part of me hated how much I wanted to believe him. But another part—the part that had carried the weight of Atlantis on my shoulders for years—craved that validation.

"Gal doesn't need to manipulate time to prove any of those things. He already is a leader. A force. And Atlantis already knows it."

"My, my." Vorago's eyes glinted. "You are an outspoken one, aren't you?"

Una stepped in front of me like she intended to shield me from the god's wrath.

"Una—"

She cut me down with a one-eyed glare.

"Are you going to let your woman speak to you like that?" Vorago asked.

"I'm not his *woman*," Una said. "I'm his *wife*."

Vorago waved a dismissive hand. "Same difference."

"Haven't you ever been in love?"

Vorago pivoted on the ball of his foot. "Certainly not. I had a world to create and watch over." Something passed over his face and I had the distinct impression he was lying. Perhaps he hadn't created Atlantis for all ocean shifters, but for one in particular. Or maybe he'd been betrayed.

"You've been asleep for centuries," Una said.

"Una—"

"Watch. Your. Tongue." Vorago's face turned to thunder as he straightened to his full height.

The shimmering pool of water reflected the storm gathering in his eyes. "You dare to lecture me about my purpose? You, a mortal child, a mixed-breed playing at royalty?"

I took a step forward, placing a hand on Una's arm. "Let's all take a breath," I said, trying to diffuse the tension. "We're here to learn, not fight."

Una shrugged off my hand. "I don't want to fight either. But I won't stand by while he manipulates you into thinking you're something you're not, something you don't need to be."

Vorago's lips twisted into a sneer. "Do you think I woke

from my slumber because I had nothing better to do? Everything I have ever done was for Atlantis. I shaped the oceans, protected your ancestors from annihilation, and forged the very power you now wield, Gal. My sacrifices made this kingdom possible."

His voice boomed through the cavern, a low rumble that shook the ground beneath our feet. Una flinched, but she didn't back down.

"And now you expect us to be grateful?" she countered. "Because if that's the case, maybe you should question why Atlantis moved on without you."

The air turned icy, and not from any power of mine. Vorago's presence seemed to swell, pressing against my senses. His eyes narrowed into dangerous slits, and for a moment, I thought he might unleash the full force of his anger.

"Careful," he hissed. "You have no idea the burden of divinity. The sacrifices gods make are beyond your comprehension. You mortals forget so easily. You take and take, then accuse those who gave you life of wanting too much in return."

"I'm not forgetting anything," Una snapped. "I'm making sure Gal doesn't lose himself in the same cycle. He doesn't need to become you."

"Enough!" I stepped between them, raising a hand to both. I glanced at Una, silently pleading for her to ease up. "Vorago, she's not questioning your power or your contributions. She just...wants me to be cautious. That's all."

Vorago's expression didn't soften. He crossed his arms, regarding Una with cold indifference. "You don't understand the weight your husband carries. The destiny that awaits him. He will either rise to meet it or be crushed beneath it. There is no middle ground."

"I understand more than you think," Una said, refusing to look away.

"Really?" Vorago's voice dripped with condescension. "Tell me, Princess, have you ever wielded a power capable of commanding time itself? Have you ever been responsible for an entire kingdom's survival?"

"I know what it's like to lose people I love because of that responsibility," she snapped. "And I know what it's like to fight for those who can't protect themselves."

Vorago scoffed. "Trivial losses compared to what lies ahead. You mortals think your suffering is unique. But you cling to your pain like a badge of honor. Gal has the potential to transcend all of that, to become something far greater. And yet here you are, trying to shackle him to your small, mortal fears."

Una tensed beside me, frustration radiating from her in waves. I hated seeing her like this—caught between wanting to protect me and feeling dismissed by a god who thought himself untouchable. Angering Vorago was a foolish mistake. Not now. Not when he held the key to unlocking the trident's full power.

"Look," I said, folding an arm around Una's waist. "I get that you're looking out for me, but I came here to learn. So can we move past this so I can get back to training?"

She searched my face, then dipped her chin in agreement. I glanced at Vorago, whose expression was still full of thunder.

Finally, he relaxed his stance and the tension in the cavern eased. "Very well. But understand this, Gal, if you want to master the trident, you must commit fully. No distractions. No half-measures."

I nodded. "I understand."

"You can leave," he said to Una.

Una's eye blazed with defiance, and she attempted a staring match with the creator of Atlantis. But after a few seconds, she backed down and swung her gaze to me. "Gal..."

I swept her into my arm and laid a kiss on her temple. I hated that this was already driving a wedge between us, but I had to trust she understood. "Go. I'll be fine. I won't do anything stupid."

She nodded under my lips, then turned and walked out of the cave without a backward glance.

The moment Una's footsteps faded down the tunnel, the cavern felt colder and emptier, despite the steady hum of power surrounding me. Her absence left an ache in my chest, but I couldn't afford distractions now. Not with Vorago watching. I forced my mind to refocus.

"She doesn't understand," Vorago said, as he walked a slow circle around me. "You knew she wouldn't."

"She's worries," I muttered, more to myself than to him. Una's words lingered. She had tried to be supportive, but she didn't trust this, didn't trust *him*. And maybe she didn't trust me anymore either.

Why should she? You haven't even told her about all our conversations.

I didn't need Una to worry more than she already was. Whatever was going on inside my head, I'd deal with it.

"Worried, yes. Afraid, more likely," Vorago said, pausing to study me. "It's in her nature. Mortals cling to fear. Fear of the unknown. Fear of losing what they love. You, Gal, are stepping into something beyond their comprehension."

"I'm not afraid," I said, although every other thought that came after spoke otherwise. "And neither is she."

Vorago chuckled. "You tell yourself that because you want to believe she will always stand beside you. But love is fragile, Gal. The moment you become what she can't understand, you'll see how quickly it cracks under pressure."

Tension wrapped around my ribs and stayed there. I attempted to ignore him, but his words had a way of seeping into my mind, twisting my insecurities. I could still hear Una's voice echoing in my thoughts. *You don't need this much power.*

You're already enough. But was I? The trident hadn't chosen her. It had chosen *me*. Maybe because it knew something I didn't—something she couldn't. Something the voice knew?

"Let's move on," I said, wanting to push the conversation, and the doubts, aside.

Vorago smiled like he could see right through me. "Very well. But be aware: hesitation will be your greatest weakness. You have no room for it anymore. Not if you wish to become what you were meant to be."

I clenched every muscle in my body, swallowing the retort that threatened to rise.

"Let's do this," I said, waving the trident.

"You must push the boundaries of what time manipulation can do," Vorago said. "True mastery isn't just about manipulating moments. It's about precision. If you can't focus, you'll never hold it long enough to make a difference when it matters."

I nodded, though unease settled low in my gut. Rewinding time was a fantasy; Vorago had confirmed it during yesterday's training. The very fabric of reality resisted any attempt to undo what had been done. But slowing time, bending it to my will— that was within reach. I'd seen flashes of it before, moments where the world moved like a sluggish tide around me, moments where I could act faster than anyone else could perceive.

"Focus on the waterfall," Vorago instructed, pointing to the cascade of water that flowed from a high crevice into the pool below. "Slow its flow. You won't be able to halt it yet. Well, no one can, not completely, but you get my point." Slowing time is hard. Check. "Then accelerate it. Keep the balance."

I raised the trident, the cool metal buzzing against my palms. The energy responded instantly, surging through me like a river breaking its dam. My muscles tensed as I reached out with my mind, connecting with the rhythm of the falling water.

I imagined the droplets slowing, hovering in midair, frozen in time.

At first, it worked. The cascade slowed, droplets drifting lazily and suspended in midair. The power thrummed through me. I strained every muscle in my body, pushing harder to hold the effect. Sweat beaded on my forehead. I could feel time resisting my control, like trying to push against an invisible tide.

"Don't force it," Vorago said, his voice eating into my concentration. "You are not stronger than time. You must *merge* with its current. Command, yes—but without arrogance."

I eased my grip on the trident's power. The water responded, flowing more naturally, but still slower than normal. I could feel the energy in the room shift, stabilizing. It was perfect—every drop of water moving at my command, time bending but not breaking.

But my thoughts wandered to Una. Her words. Her absence. The way she had looked at me last night, as if I were becoming someone she didn't recognize.

The water snapped back to its natural speed. The cascade surged forward, sloshing against the rocks with a deafening roar. I stumbled back a step, panting.

"No," Vorago said. "You let your mind falter. You let her linger in your thoughts and you lost control. Again."

"I had it," I muttered through gritted teeth. "I just...I was distracted."

"Distraction is a luxury you can no longer afford," Vorago said, stepping closer. His eyes shone with something darker now, a challenge. "You say you are not afraid, that you understand what this power demands. But actions speak louder than words. You hesitate. You second-guess yourself. Why?"

I didn't answer immediately. Because deep down, I knew the reason, and I hated it. I *was* afraid—afraid of losing Una, afraid of losing control, afraid this power would consume me like it had consumed others before me. But I couldn't admit that. Not to him. Not to anyone.

But I know.

Who was behind the voice?

"Atlantis loves you, Gal," Vorago's tone softened, becoming almost coaxing. "But the people will always fear you too. Fear is a poison they won't admit they carry, not until it's too late. Your council doesn't trust you; they trust the *idea* of you. And when that idea no longer fits their needs, they will turn on you. You are more than mortal. You only need to prove it—to them, and to yourself."

His words twisted in my gut. I hated how much they resonated. I'd seen it before—how easily people's faith could waver. How quickly trust could be broken. But I didn't want to believe Una would ever turn on me, that Bay, Ember, or the others would. Still, the fear gnawed at the edges of my mind.

"I need to be stronger," I said quietly, almost to myself.

"You *are* strong," Vorago replied, a dangerous edge to his voice. "But strength without commitment is weakness. You stand at the brink of greatness, yet you still let yourself be held back by doubt and sentiment."

I met his gaze, my heartbeat quickening. He was right, wasn't he? I couldn't afford to hesitate anymore. Not with so much at stake. I had to push through this, had to become everything the trident knew I could be. I couldn't let Una's fears, or my own, hold me back.

"I can do this," I said finally, squaring my shoulders. "But Una...she will be part of this."

Vorago's expression hardened. He clearly wasn't pleased, but he didn't argue. "If that's what you require," he said at last, his voice laced with impatience. "But know this: her presence will not protect you from the consequences of your choices. You are on this path now, Gal. And there is no turning back."

"I'm not turning back," I said firmly. No more hesitation. No more doubt. I would see this through.

Vorago stepped back, his shoulders relaxing. "Good. Then let's try again." He gestured toward the waterfall, and I raised the trident once more. This time, I wouldn't let myself falter. Whatever it took, I would master this power. I had to.

For Atlantis. For Una. For me.

CHAPTER TWELVE

I emerged from the cavern several hours later, sweat clinging to my skin, which the humidity outside did nothing to help. Every muscle in my body ached, and my head throbbed from the intensity of the training. And the stupid voice, which had taunted me during every inch of progress I'd made.

Squinting against the sun, I followed the path to the palace gardens and caught sight of a figure waiting at the edge of the clearing.

Ford.

He stood with his thumbs looped into his belt. His sharp eyes flicked briefly to the trident in my grip before meeting my gaze again. I approached and pulled to a halt a couple of feet from him. My skin crawled. There was something in his body language I wanted to run away from. Was it disappointment? Judgment? I shifted uncomfortably, trying to shake off the irrational sense of guilt creeping up my spine.

"Ford," I greeted, trying to sound casual.

"Gal," he replied, his voice not giving away a hint of his mood. "How is the training with Vorago going?"

I scanned his face for disapproval, but found none. Still, I had the urge to protect the secrets I was learning. "It's not a crime."

Ford raised a brow. "When did I say it was?"

"You didn't have to," I muttered, running my hand along the trident's shaft.

Ford sighed, his expression softening a fraction. "I'm not here to judge you, Gal. You're not a boy anymore. You've learned all I could teach you. You make your own choices now."

I looked away. A gecko skirted around my bare feet. "And what's that supposed to mean?"

Ford splayed a hand. "Remember what I taught you? Your greatest weapon has always been your mind, not whatever magic you wield."

I nodded, thinking back to all the hours we'd spent training together. Much of that time our weapons had been discarded on the ground and he had guided me through meditation and mindfulness exercises. I still used his techniques almost daily. But that had nothing to do with learning new abilities.

"Everything in balance," I said.

"Exactly." Ford smiled and ran a hand over his shaved head. "I'm trying to help Bay learn some of that balance. Now that he's come into a tremendous amount of power."

The words hit low in my gut. The humid air suddenly became impossible to breathe. My stomach twisted with an emotion I didn't want to acknowledge. Jealousy. Of course, Ford would help Bay. He was the new golden boy of Atlantis, the guardian of the Power of the Sea. But it still stung. *Fuck.* It more than stung. It stabbed. *Deep.*

"I'm sure Bay will benefit from your guidance," I said, struggling to keep the bitterness from my voice. They had been training together for years after all, so why did my emotions decide now was the time to be jealous?

Ford's gaze lingered on me. "What is it, Gal?"

"Do you trust Vorago?" I blurted. I wasn't sure why I'd asked. I didn't really care for an answer. Or more specifically, I only wanted to hear one answer. If Ford trusted Vorago, I could put my unease aside. But that wasn't why I'd asked the question. Truthfully, I wanted to keep him here, away from Bay, and I wanted him to...praise me. Yes, I was twenty-five-fucking-years old, and I still needed praise. Even though I hadn't sought it from him in years.

Ford had taught me how to fight from the time I was five years old. He had been like a father to me after my mother's death. He had been there with me when I faced the Denizens. Nothing could replace that. But I couldn't stand the thought of him loving Bay in the same way. Ford was mine.

"I haven't spent much time with him," Ford replied. "And so I haven't formed an opinion."

"But you've seen the prophecy. You've studied the book." Why was I pressing the point? There was nothing Ford could say that would stop me from training with Vorago.

Ford eyed me carefully. "Why do you want to manipulate time?"

"So I can better protect Atlantis. Una. My people." I took a breath, the answer spilling out too fast. "And if Vorago turns out to be bad news, I need to know what he's capable of. I need to be able to turn his own power against him."

Ford planted a hand on my chest, tapped it several times with his fingers, a method he used to ground me. "As long as you are true to yourself, you have nothing to fear."

His words should have calmed me, but they only added to my growing unease. And the tapping was just fucking irritating.

Did I have so little faith in myself? I shook my head. This was ridiculous. I was falling back into habits long buried. I was the Prince of Atlantis, the guardian of the orb of Snow and Ice, the Trident Wielder...I would not give in to fear. I had nothing *to* fear.

You should fear me.

I was tempted to tell Ford about the voice. But something held me back. I didn't want him looking at me funny. In case, like Una, he thought it was *just stress*.

I stepped back. "I'll let you get on your way."

"Walk with me." Ford turned and made his way toward the palace gardens. I walked beside him, the trident hanging limply in my grip, dodging a line of ants marching along the cobble path. "Remember your meditation."

"Of course." I sighed. I did *not* need Ford telling me what to do. So why had I asked?

We passed the shrine Vorago had erected to see the crowds of people hadn't diminished. The amount of flowers and gifts surpassed anything Una and I had received on our wedding day. Cascadia was there, talking to the people, placing a hand on their heads in a blessing. Some she gifted with iridescent skin, others with colorful swirling tattoos.

"Cascadia has been there for hours," Ford said as we walked by.

"No Tempest or Vorago?"

Ford shook his head. "My impression is that Cascadia is the more people-facing god."

While there was some truth in that, I suspected the real reason was neither Vorago nor Tempest could stand to be around humans, insisted that only ocean shifters were worthy of their blessings. But if they didn't learn to embrace *all* the inhabitants, they'd either find themselves at the end of the people's wrath, or we'd face another civil war. I didn't like to think about the outcome of either trajectory. Unity was key to defeating our enemies, and if the people were divided...

You will fail.

Exactly.

We arrived at the palace lawns to find Bay standing near a fountain, his face lined with heavy concentration. Ford walked ahead to talk to him, while I hung back and leaned against a marble pillar to watch.

They exchanged a few words before Ford demonstrated something with his hands. Bay mirrored the movement, the water in the fountain responding instantly, swirling into a controlled vortex far larger than the one he had shown me yesterday. He was getting the hang of his powers quickly.

A low growl of frustration escaped me. Where had Bay been when the Denizens attacked? Zale hadn't killed *his* mother. What did The Power of the Sea see in him? I'd spent years protecting Atlantis. And I did not need Bay Summers by my side now.

Wind trickled through the columns, bringing the voice with it. **Why not steal his powers?**

Because it's impossible.

Is it?

The thought hollowed my stomach. *I would never steal power.*

If you say so.

"If looks could kill, Bay would need a second resurrection," a familiar voice quipped behind me.

I turned to see Ember sauntering over, wearing his signature lopsided grin. His hair was slicked back—probably thanks to whatever bottle Ash used on his wings. He looked...sharp. Confident. Like he was headed somewhere important. A date, maybe? Good for him. It had been a while.

"Ember," I sighed. "Not in the mood for jokes right now."

"Clearly," he said, joining me at the pillar and lifting his face to the sun. "Which is exactly why I'm here. Somebody's got to keep you from brooding yourself into oblivion."

I smirked despite myself. "That your latest life mission?"

"I'm a multitasker," he said with a wink. "I can be emotionally supportive *and* annoying at the same time."

He elbowed me. "So... what'd Bay do this time to tie your fins in knots?"

I didn't answer. I was aware of how childish I'd sound if I tried to put what I was feeling into words.

Ember huffed. "You two are hopeless. Honestly, I should lock you in a room until you either kill each other or work it out."

"I don't need him to be my friend," I muttered. "He...he doesn't get it."

Ember arched a brow. "Doesn't get what? That you're our one and only living legend? The hero with the world riding on his back?" He widened his eyes, voice dripping with mock drama. "Yeah, real tough to wrap my head around."

I shot him a glare, but his teasing grin didn't waver. "You're not helping."

"Alright, alright." Ember raised his hands in surrender. "How about you show me what you've been working on instead? Maybe that'll take the edge off."

A slow grin spread across my face. "You sure? Most people tell me I don't need more power."

"I'm not most people," he replied, his eyes sparkling with curiosity.

"Thank...definitely *not* Vorago, for that."

Ember laughed. "Right? Who *do* we thank now?"

"Apparently still him. The guy's drowning in fan mail and flower offerings."

"Tell me about it. I'm suffocating in the stench of flowers, and if I trip over one more damn coral figurine, I'm throwing it into the ocean as an offering to my patience."

I chuckled. "Truth."

"Are you going to the event tonight?"

"Nope." I blew hair off my face. "I've had enough of Vorago for one day."

"What, not tempted to give the people a demonstration of your new powers?"

"They're not there to see me."

Ember raised both brows. "Maybe you can take that honeymoon while everyone else is preoccupied."

"I need to be here. Keep an eye on Vorago. Learn everything I can."

"Alright then," he said, pushing off the pillar. "Let's see what you've got. Just don't outshine my pyro shields. I've got a fragile ego to maintain."

Glad of the lightness Ember had infused in me, I stepped away from the pillar and raised the trident. The energy hummed in my veins, eager to be unleashed. I focused on Ford and Bay in the distance, homing in on the flow of time around them. Gradually, I bent the current of time, slowing it to a snail's pace.

The scene before us shifted. Ford was caught mid-gesture, his mouth half-open as he spoke. Bay's vortex froze in place, droplets of water suspended like tiny crystals. Their expressions were locked in comically awkward positions—Ford's face twisted in concentration, Bay's eyes wide in surprise.

Ember let out a loud laugh. "Wow...that's...fucking genius."

I chuckled, but the humor didn't last. The strain of maintaining the effect pulled at all my reserves, the weight of time resisting my control. I released it with a sharp exhale, and the world jerked back into action. Ford and Bay didn't seem to notice anything had changed.

"Maybe I'll freeze Bay in time whenever he's pissing me off."

Ember chuckled, the sound light and easy—but it faded quicker than usual. His smile lingered, then faltered at the edges. He rubbed the back of his neck, gaze flicking away like he was trying to find the right words or avoid the wrong ones.

"Something wrong?"

He didn't answer right away. Just exhaled and gave a small shrug, like he was brushing off more than dust. "Maybe don't mess with Bay like that too often. He's got enough on his plate without you turning him into a living statue."

I raised a brow. "You're defending Bay now?"

Ember sighed. "No one needs to be defended. There are no sides here, buddy. He's trying, Gal. Just like you are. You don't have to make this a competition."

I looked back at Bay and Ford, who were still deep in their training. "I'm not making it a competition." At least I didn't think I was. "I'm worried it's too much for him." I watched Bay form another vortex, this one spiraling over his head and collapsing before it made it back to the fountain, drenching both himself and Ford. I had no urge to laugh. There was nothing funny about learning to harness power...and failing. "I know how it feels."

"As do I, buddy." Ember clapped me on the back. "And that's why I smoke so much weed."

He laughed, the sound easy and familiar, then let it drift into a lazy grin. The moment settled between us, warm and unspoken. I rolled my shoulders and massaged the knots in my neck. My gaze wandered toward the beach glinting in the distance. Waves shimmered under the evening sun. It had been a few days since I'd been in merman form. The frustration, tension, and lingering anger in my veins could only be tempered one way—by returning to the water.

"I need to clear my head," I said, gripping the trident and striding toward the shoreline.

Ember followed for a few steps. "I'll be around. Try not to summon a hurricane while you're out there."

I threw him a half-smile over my shoulder before breaking into a jog toward the beach. The warm sand tickled the soles of my bare feet as I dashed toward the water's edge. After laying the trident on the sand, I dove into the breaking waves. My legs shimmered, merging into a sleek, powerful, onyx tail flecked with gold.

For the first few minutes, I simply let myself drift, the rhythmic pull of the currents soothing my frayed nerves. Then I pushed myself deeper, the world above fading away into blue shadows. Schools of fish darted around me, and I maneuvered through coral arches and seaweed forests. Down here, there was no prophecy, no rivalry with Bay, no lingering doubts about Vorago. Just the steady thrum of the ocean and the certainty of my own power.

But none of this would be here without Vorago either. It seemed no matter where I went, there were reminders of him. I squeezed my eyes closed against the intrusive thoughts. Just because Vorago was here, that I had met him, didn't mean the ocean had changed. I could still take pleasure in the currents, I could still power my tail to the depths and explore hidden caverns, I could still surf the breaking waves to bring myself back to the beach.

I opened my eyes to the gentle shimmer of light refracted through the water's surface far above. Tiny particles floated lazily in the current, catching the sunlight like scattered diamonds. The deeper I swam, the cooler the water became. I flicked my tail, feeling the surge of raw power as it propelled me forward. My muscles relaxed, the aches and tension from training dissolving in the ocean's embrace.

This was where I belonged. The place where I was truly myself—unchained, untethered, and infinite.

But then a strong current wrapped around me, tugging me deeper, in directions I didn't want to go. I pulled against it, powering my tail, but the surface refused to appear. Whips of invisible water lashed around my tail and my wrists, yanking me toward the bottom of the ocean.

Panicking, I raised my hand for the trident, but with my wrist bound, I couldn't call to it.

I struggled against the currents, their weight crushing me, suffocating my gills, their bullying momentum tossing me in circles. I lost all sense of where the surface was. The world reduced to a chaotic swirl of blue and black. Panic clawed up my throat, sharp and bitter. My gills spasmed. The pressure blurred my vision and thundered behind my eyes. My muscles screamed as I kicked hard, reaching for something solid, something stable, but the current only laughed. Or was it the voice?

I clenched my jaw, forcing the fear down, and gathered every shred of strength I had left. With a roar underwater that was more instinct than sound, I drove myself forward—through the crushing pressure, through the spinning dark—and finally, finally, broke free. The current spat me out like a discarded piece of driftwood, hurling me into stiller waters, my body limp, my mind reeling.

You think you're safe in the water?

Leave me alone!

I sped to the surface. My head snapped above water. I turned in rapid circles, looking for...there was no one there. I dipped my head underwater once more. I was alone. Completely alone. Then what the hell had restrained me? A rogue rip?

I sped back to the beach. My tail shifted back into legs as I emerged from the water.

"Interesting weapon you've got there."

I spun around to see Tempest standing a few feet away, his gaze glued to the trident I'd left on the sand. Had he tried to pick it up? His presence carried a charged intensity, like the air before a thunderstorm. Was he responsible for the change in the tide?

"It is," I replied, shaking water out of my hair. "What do you want, Tempest?"

"How much of its power have you unlocked?"

I rested a hand on my hip. "Enough."

Tempest chuckled. "Is that so? Vorago must be pleased with you, then. Though I imagine even he must have doubts."

I gritted my teeth. "What's your point?"

"My point is power like yours is wasted if you don't push it to its limits. You're holding back, aren't you? Trying to play the role of the responsible prince?" He sneered. "A god doesn't need to apologize for his power."

"I'm not a god," I said.

"Not yet." Tempest's eyes gleamed. "But you could be. If you have the stomach for it. But then, I too have my doubts."

I stepped forward, my muscles coiling with renewed tension. "You think I don't have the stomach for power? Is that why you're here, to test me?"

"Perhaps." He leaned in, his voice dropping to a near whisper. "Or perhaps I'm here to see if you can handle a real storm."

Before I could respond, Tempest raised his arms, and the air around us shifted. Black clouds gathered on the horizon, the sky darkening unnaturally fast. Memories of Dagonar swirled to the surface, of when the Denizen had thrust Atlantis into perpetual night.

A powerful gust of wind whipped through the beach, sending sand and spray into the air. The waves grew more violent, crashing against the shore with a savage howl.

"Enough, Tempest," I warned. "The tides have been acting up enough as it is."

"Why? Afraid of a little rain?" he taunted. "Show me what you can do, Gal. Or are you too scared to lose control?"

I plucked the trident from the sand as fury burned through me. The sky above crackled with lightning. The storm moved through my bones, as if it were taunting me too. Tempest wanted to push me, to make me lash out. And gods help me, I wanted to. The power thrumming through the trident surged in response to my emotions, itching to tear loose.

I planted the trident in the sand, digging deep to ground myself. Slowly, I raised my other hand and summoned the power within me, not to lash out, but to command. The storm's intensity diminished, the winds calming. But Tempest wasn't done.

"You call that control?" Disdain dripped from his words. "You're weak, Gal. You'll never be more than a mortal pretending to be a god."

Still shaky from my swim, I took a deep breath, fighting the urge to strike him down. Tempest wanted a reaction. He wanted to push me over the edge. I couldn't give him that satisfaction.

Instead, I smirked. "Weak? I think you're mistaking strategy for weakness. But if you're so keen to be proven wrong..."

I focused all my energy into the trident, channeling the power to slow time around Tempest. The storm froze mid-flash, lightning suspended in the clouds like jagged veins of light. Tempest's cocky expression faltered as he glanced around, clearly disoriented by the sudden stillness.

"Careful, Tempest," I said, stepping closer. It took everything in me to keep this much time at bay, but I refused to let the strain show. "You might want to learn the difference between provoking power and controlling it."

Tempest's eyes narrowed. Tension crackled between us. Time snapped back into motion, and I smothered my internal gasp at being able to let it go. Tempest stepped back, brushing sand off his arms as if to dismiss the encounter.

"We'll see how long you can keep that control," he said coolly. "But for now, I'll let you bask in your little victory."

With a final smirk, he turned and strode down the beach, the storm clouds dispersing behind him. I watched him go, my heart still racing.

Ember appeared beside me, shaking his head. "Well, that wasn't ominous at all."

"Tell me about it," I muttered, rubbing the back of my neck. But my gaze was glued to the ocean, not Tempest.

Tempest was right about one thing. I was walking a fine line between control and chaos. And I wasn't sure which side I'd end up on.

CHAPTER THIRTEEN

I heard the voice again, just before Ember shoved a
beer into my hand. "Get that down you. It'll be a
round of shots next."

I chose to ignore the persistent voice, take Ember's advice,
and downed half the beer in one. Ominous threats still rang in
my skull, whispers with teeth. They curled in my gut, coiling
tighter with every breath. But tonight wasn't for spiraling.
Tonight was for drowning it all out. In alcohol, in laughter, in
anything that didn't sound like doubt wearing my voice.

Uncle Dylan's bar was packed, as it had been every night
this week. Not that I'd had the pleasure of seeing my uncle...
until tonight. Although now he was stuck behind three lines of
people at the bar. The crowds spilled into the courtyard each
evening when I was walking back from training with Vorago,
people trying to get a glimpse of him or one of the other gods.
Vorago, Tempest, and Cascadia never visited the bar. When
they weren't sequestered in their home, they would gather near
Vorago's shrine to greet people, shake hands, give blessings, and
accept gifts. Or sometimes give demonstrations of power.
Tempest would often conjure a brief storm, Vorago created

dazzling displays of funnels and vortexes, and Cascadia commanded ocean creatures—from sea horses to dolphins—to give a performance along the shore. They were all smiles and lightness. Vorago even acquiescing to the human presence. At least when he was in public. The trails of flowers and coral figurines and other offerings leading all the way to the door of their cottage doubled.

"Useless trinkets," Tempest had sneered at the colorful array.

"They're beautiful," Cascadia had said. "Mortals have a gift for creating beauty from simplicity."

"Beauty fades. Power endures. The wise invest in the latter." Vorago had underlined his thoughts with his tone.

I shook the conversation out of my head and tried not to fall asleep in my beer. I'd risen before the sun each day only to return after midnight, falling asleep as soon as my head hit the pillow. Una and I had barely spoken. But every day I was able to slow time for a little longer and the size of the areas I affected grew. Now I was here under Una's orders to take some time off. Uncle Dylan had pulled out all the stops for us tonight—large platters of food, drinks flowing freely. A much-needed distraction after the last few days of constant training.

Ember sat beside me, downing his third drink like it was water. Una sat on my other side, her hand on my thigh, occasionally giving it a gentle squeeze. Across from us, Coral leaned against Ash, flirting with him shamelessly, her eyes never leaving his face. Ripple lay sprawled across the table in front of her, occasionally dipping his paw into her glass of wine, earning smiles from the whole group. Moby had his back turned to the booth as he signed a few autographs. Cyra sat in the corner of the booth sipping a glass of cider.

Coral tilted her head, a playful glint in her eyes. "I'll bet you couldn't handle even half the challenges in the Dragon Tides,"

143

she teased Ash, her voice light but daring. "Those hoops are tight. No way you're getting those massive wings through."

Ash smirked, his gaze flicking over her with deliberate slowness. "Oh, I don't know, Coral," he murmured, his voice dropping into a husky growl. "I've got a knack for finding...alternative routes. Maybe one day, you'll get to see just how creative I can be."

"Oh, for goodness sake," Bay groaned from his spot at the end of the table. He flicked a hand, summoning a stream of water from a nearby pitcher. It shot straight at Ash, soaking his shirt and making Una and Ember howl with laughter. I had to admit, I enjoyed seeing the cocky smile slip from Ash's face. "I think you need to cool off. And stay away from my sister."

Coral launched to her feet, her face crimson. "Bay! Mind your own business!"

Ash wiped water from one of his wings. "Didn't realize you were so protective."

"Can't have you charming your way into the family too easily," Bay shot back, then turned to his sister, who was regaining her seat. "Maybe don't make it my business by flirting in front of me."

"You're lucky I don't breathe fire." Ash winked, wringing out his shirt. "I'll have to set my big brother on you instead."

Ember pressed his back against the booth. "Leave me out of this."

Coral crossed her arms over her chest, her cheeks still flushed. "Yes, everyone stay out of this."

Ash dropped his mouth near the shell of Coral's ear. He whispered, but we all heard it. "Stay out of *what* exactly?"

Coral's color deepened once more and she stammered an undecipherable response.

"You do *not* want to be humped and dumped," Bay said to her.

"Give her a break, Bay," Una said, lifting his glass and putting it to his lips. "And lighten up a bit."

"Break needed," Coral muttered, taking a large gulp of her wine.

"Yeah, lighten up," Ash said. "Not everything is about marriage and forever. Your sister is seventeen. Let her live a little."

Even though the words were aimed at Bay, they wormed inside me. *Live a little.* I couldn't remember the last time I'd felt...free. Free from responsibility. Free from power. Free from expectation. But by coming back to Atlantis after I'd killed Zale, I had accepted my role in the island's destiny. I would never shirk that. And I was proud that I could keep my island safe. But man, I could use a vacation occasionally.

"Everything alright?" Ember asked, catching my eye as the others continued to banter.

"Yeah, just...thinking," I replied, swirling my glass until the head of the beer frothed up. "Long day."

A breeze spilled in through an open window. ***You haven't seen anything yet.***

I clenched the leg of the table until I was sure the voice had disappeared.

"Understatement of the year." He toasted me and let the issue drop.

Bay continued to make little spinning vortexes with the water from a second pitcher. He was catching up quickly and potentially surpassing expectations. I glanced at Ember, who watched more intently than necessary, and Bay smiled right back at him. Something about the way they were with each other didn't sit right with me. But I couldn't put my finger on it. Had they been spending more time together while I'd been busy preparing for my wedding and then training with Vorago?

The thought that Bay could slip into my shoes as Ember's

closest friend left a bitter taste in my mouth. But then, I reasoned, I was becoming a god. Did gods care about best friends?

Bay slumped in his chair, rubbing his temples, exhaustion etched on his face.

"That little vortex did you in, huh?" I asked, unable to stop myself from voicing the dig.

He gave me a side glance. "Been at it all day. Every day for the last week. Should have known better than to push it."

"You don't need to push it," I said. "I have enough power for both of us."

"The Power of the Sea chose *me*."

Una gave me a warning look, which I ignored. I'd never apologized to Bay. She'd asked me a couple of times over the last week, and each time I promised I'd think about it. Once or twice I even thought I would, but I couldn't bring myself to in the end.

"I don't think I'm learning fast enough," Bay said.

"Slow is always the best way forward," Ash said as he draped an arm around Coral's shoulders, causing her to blush into her glass. "Have a joint. Chill out a little, dude. You're always so uptight."

"You try being chosen by the Power of the Sea," Bay snapped at him.

Ash quirked an eyebrow. "Nah. I'd just say *no thanks*."

Bay snorted. "Like it's a choice."

Ash whirled his hand in the air imperiously. "You do you."

A pang of sympathy shot through me as I realized the amount of pressure Bay was putting on himself. I'd been there. Hell, I lived there.

"Better to build it slowly than force it too fast," I said to him. "Take one day at a time."

He huffed into his beer. "Is that what you do?"

I took a sip of my own beer, relished the taste of it as it slid down my throat. "Nope. But I didn't have the luxury of knowing there was someone else as powerful as me."

Bay's gaze settled on me. The moment stretched on until I felt like we'd embarked in a staring contest.

Una poked my arm, making me break the contact. "Finish your beer."

I finished my beer.

"You two might as well get your dicks out and measure them," Ash said.

Una slapped his shoulder. "Do not encourage them."

Bay shook his head. "I'm not interested in competition." He returned his gaze to me. "I just want to keep Atlantis safe."

With me? Or *from* me?

"Same here," I said, lifting my empty glass in a mocking toast.

Coral raised her glass too. "To keeping Atlantis safe!"

Everyone clinked, but the tension didn't dissipate. I appreciated what Coral was trying to do, but the friction between her brother and me had been simmering for weeks. Although Bay's latest comment felt like a new level of distrust. I forced my expression to remain neutral, but my mind raced and my blood boiled.

"Training isn't a race," I said, ignoring his subtext. "It's about control and endurance. You'll get there."

Bay held my eyes for a few more seconds. "Yeah. I hope so."

The conversation shifted as Coral dragged Ash into a debate about which sea creatures made the best hunting partners, and Moby regaled the group with stories of his latest underwater filming location. The laughter and chatter swirled around me, but I felt increasingly detached, like I was watching from the outside.

You are not one of them.

147

I jerked at the voice. Una frowned and pressed herself against me, whispered in my ear. "You okay?"

I cocked a shoulder. "Stupid voice," I muttered.

Her lips twisted with concern. "Maybe we should get you checked at the hospital."

I bit down on a laugh. They wouldn't find anything. Cleary, I was going insane. Hearing voices was a classic symptom.

"They might be able to help." Una placed a hand on my thigh, her touch firm, pressing her point.

No one can help you.

I massaged my temples. "Thank you...but I think I need a bit of space."

I excused myself and headed to the bar, leaving Una staring after me. I did not want to get into a conversation about my mental health with my friends there, least of all Bay. Uncle Dylan was wiping glasses. He looked up as I approached.

"Everything alright?" he asked, pouring me another drink without me having to ask.

"Yeah. Just needed a breather." I took a sip, the warmth of the alcohol spreading through my chest and curdling with the ball of irritation.

Uncle Dylan's eyes flicked to the group. "Everyone has an opinion."

"Something like that."

Uncle Dylan swept a cloth over the counter. "So Bay is the guardian of the Power of the Sea, huh?"

The last guardian had been Babette, Uncle Dylan's girl-friend. "He's not good enough—"

"People said that about Babette too." He leaned over the counter. "Said she was just a human. Said she didn't really want to be part of our world." He straightened, looked me square in the face. "But she had the biggest damn heart of anyone I've ever met."

If Vorago had arisen when Babette was guardian, he would have...I don't know what he would have done, but his fury would have been ferocious.

I frowned. "If you're trying to say Bay has a big heart, then I've got another thing to tell you—"

Uncle Dylan raised a palm. "All I'm saying is that the Power of the Sea has been without a guardian for almost six years. There's a reason it's waited until now to choose one. And there's a reason it's Bay."

I sighed and took a swig of my beer. "I wish I knew what it was."

Uncle Dylan tilted his head, smiled at me like I should know better.

"What?" I asked.

"No one person should be all powerful."

I almost spat my beer out. "You think *I'm* the problem?"

"Didn't say that." Dylan pushed a fresh cloth into a wet glass. "Just said that no one person should have too much power. Everything needs a balance."

"Not you too." I blew my hair out of my face.

"You know I always lay it out straight."

"I do."

"And you know you're my favorite nephew."

"I won't tell Ember."

We shared a smile.

"I have no trouble telling you if I think you're getting in over your head."

"Like you did with Mom?" I asked.

Uncle Dylan nodded, laid the glass and the cloth on the counter. "And Maya, and Trent, and others along the way."

"I just want to do right by Atlantis." I rubbed my hands over my face. "By Mom. By Dad. By Una. And sometimes it would be nice if people had a little faith in me."

"That's something everyone has in spades."

"Not since the prophecy."

"Only because your path is uncertain." Uncle Dylan served a customer, then turned his attention back to me. "And people hate uncertainty."

"Including me." I glugged my beer, then decided to let Dylan in on my secret. "I've been hearing a voice."

Dylan paused in the action of wiping the counter. "What kind of voice?"

"In my head. I think. Although if feels like a whisper on the wind."

I braced myself for judgment, but saw only concern in his expression. "What is it telling you?"

"It's...mocking me. Telling me I'm not good enough...that I don't belong..."

Truthfully, I never felt like I belonged. Being a prince and growing up royal had set me apart. And that was before I became the Trident Wielder.

Dylan smiled.

I frowned. "It's not funny."

"Never said it was." He picked up my glass and wiped underneath it. "Mental health conditions run in our family."

"Una thinks it's stress."

"She's probably right."

"But it doesn't feel...normal."

"If you have a voice in your head telling you you're not good enough, I reckon that's your inner doubt speaking. What you have to ask yourself is, why now? What are you worried about? Why have your stress levels ratcheted up? And I would never begin to suggest getting married is a bad thing, but it does bring its own stresses—"

"It's not Una."

You sure about that?

Yes.

"Just something to consider," Dylan said. "But I wouldn't overthink this...voice...I'm sure once you get your shit together it will disappear."

No, I won't.

"I hope you're right."

"And if not, we can stick you in a room with padded walls. Yeah?"

A laugh burst out of me. Uncle Dylan had suffered in his life, he struggled with PTSD and OCD and anxiety. I appreciated the way he could make light of things, to laugh at himself, to laugh at life, in spite of everything.

"That's my boy. Laughter is good for the soul. Took me a long time to learn that." Dylan clapped a hand on my shoulder. "And remember—you're more than just a prophecy. You're Gal. That's enough."

No titles. Just Gal. But who was I without everything else?

Maybe he was right. Maybe I didn't have to become a god to protect those I loved. But as I glanced back at the table, where Bay and Ember were laughing together, that uneasy tension returned to my stomach.

What if it wasn't enough?

When I rejoined the group, I slid into the booth next to Una once more. Her hand immediately slid to my thigh. Her other hand remained on the table circled around her glass of wine. The pearl in the center of her ring winked under the dim lighting, and I wondered if it was capable of producing a force field against anything besides the Hound of the Ocean and other sea monsters.

"I can't believe the amount of people lining up out there just to kiss the gods' feet." Ash rolled his eyes.

He meant it literally. Besides the offerings, people craved the gods' attention, to thank them for Atlantis, to see for themselves that they were real. Even the humans who had made their lives here. And the gods were lapping it up. But they had refused to meet with the High Council.

Coral flushed and dipped her chin. Una had told me she had visited with the gods every day, suggesting lavish festivals and events to entertain them.

"It's only natural," Cyra said. "They've been our deities for centuries. No one knew if they were real or not. Why wouldn't they want to pay their respects?"

"Exactly!" Coral exclaimed, her palm hitting the table and causing our drinks to slosh. "Sorry. But Cyra's right. They created this island. They created us. Why wouldn't people want to meet them?"

Moby gave her a side-eye. "Have you been in that line of people, Coral?"

Coral's blush grew deeper and she folded her arms. "Maybe."

"People need to be more careful." Bay pressed his hand onto the table. "Inflating their egos will only add to their arrogance, and we don't know what they want yet."

Una nudged her brother. "They want the trident. Vorago said as much."

"It is his, after all," Coral said, recovering from her embarrassment. "Why shouldn't he have it?"

"Because it doesn't belong to him anymore," Ember said. "It belongs to Gal."

"But he *made* it," Coral pressed.

"I did try to give it to him," I reminded her.

"And if the trident doesn't want him back, then we can assume their intentions aren't good," Bay said.

"And yet the rest of Atlantis seems to think they're the second coming," Moby said.

"Maybe you're pissed off because your fan group has had their attention diverted," Ash laughed.

Moby punched his arm. "You trying to tell me you're getting the same amount of action since the gods arrived?"

Ash slid a glance to Coral, coughed, and gulped down half his beer.

"That's what I thought," Moby said.

"Maybe I'm not interested in casual sex anymore," Ash replied.

Bay spluttered a laugh. "Certainly not with my sister."

Coral scowled at her brother. "I will decide who I have sex with and how I will have it, thank you very much."

"You're seventeen!" Bay exclaimed.

"So?" Coral shot back, her indignation deepening the color of her cheeks. "You were fifteen—" She cut herself off. "You were younger than that and you turned out okay."

Bay's cheeks flamed. "That was private."

"So is *my* sex life," Coral said.

Bay raised his hands. "Fair enough."

"Everyone's sex life should be private," I added, and Coral gave me an appreciative look.

Ember clinked a knife against his glass to get everyone's attention. "This is getting a little out of hand..."

Una cleared her throat. "We were meant to be talking about the gods. They won't even meet with the High Council."

"Exactly," Ember said, looking relieved at the conversation change. "We have no idea why they're here, what they want, how long they're staying...that's not right. If they're so benevolent, wouldn't they share that information with us? And if not with us, at least the High Council. Or Gal and Wade."

Coral rolled her eyes. "That's not how gods work."

Bay laughed. "Who made you an expert?"

Coral pinned him with her fiercest glare. Which wasn't

particularly fierce. Especially with the seashells braided into her hair. "While you've been training with Ford and getting your muscles all swollen over the last few years, I've been with Una and studying the book."

"She has," Una confirmed, smiling at her sister.

"They made us in their image. They created Atlantis." Coral's voice grew more insistent with each point. Ripple chirped at her and she ran a hand over his furry back. "They gave us a safe place to be. So it is not our purpose to question their will. Which I'm sure will be nothing but lovely."

I raised an eyebrow. "Have you *met* Vorago?"

Coral nodded. "He was perfectly pleasant. He said I'd make a fine oracle one day." She beamed.

"How many oracles do we need?" Moby muttered.

Coral flicked a hand at him. "Just because you don't give a shit about our family's legacy."

Moby leaned back against the booth. "I don't need to. We've got you and Una and Bay all ready to carry the torch."

"Moby..." Una's voice came out half reproachful and half sympathetic.

"What?" He shrugged. "Atlantis doesn't need me. So I'm going to keep doing what I love and make my movies."

"You have at it, bro." Ash offered his knuckles for a punch.

Una sighed under her breath. I rested my hand on top of hers and squeezed. I didn't have siblings. Growing up it had been just my parents and me. And then, kind of just me. But I did have friends. I had Ember. And Una.

"Someone still needs to talk to Vorago," Ember said, swirling the dregs of beer in his glass. "Find out what he's up to."

All eyes swiveled in my direction.

"What?" I asked. "You want me to question the will of a god? Seriously?"

"Yes," they all replied. Except for Coral, who was still wearing an adorable frown.

"Yes," they all replied like a choir. (And who was still beginning about his father?)

CHAPTER FOURTEEN

stood on the lawn, the trident spinning in my hand. Each maneuver sent ripples of energy through the air, shifting the wind, stirring the waters beyond the cliffs. Power pulsed through me, coiling under my skin like a living thing, restless, insatiable.

I was getting stronger.

Too strong?

I pivoted sharply, driving the trident's prongs into the earth. The ground rumbled in response, a deep, guttural vibration that made the torches flicker in protest. A couple of statues crumbled. Oops.

Vorago found me a few minutes later. "Are you ready to train?"

"Yes."

He gestured for me to walk with him to the edge of the cliff. "It's time to experiment with the elements. Not all power is tied to time."

I sucked in a lungful of sea air and prepared myself. Vorago raised his hand and a funnel spun out of the waves. He swung his arm and the funnel spun along the shore and crashed into the rocks. I mimicked his action with the trident, trying to create something he would approve of, pleased when a spinning vortex of water spiraled after Vorago's funnel.

I went for a second funnel, but suddenly found the water resistant to my will, like the tides were yanking me in the other direction. I frowned.

"What is it?" Vorago asked. "Are you tiring already?"

I clenched my teeth and pushed more focus into the funnel, but it would not form. Waves rolled away from me, taunting me.

Maybe the voice belonged to the current. Or an entity dwelling within the current. Maybe it had broken the constellation too. Somehow.

None of my thoughts made sense, but I couldn't help feeling they were all connected.

Vorago raised his hand once more, but no funnel appeared. It was his turn to frown. Then he looked at the sky. The broken trident constellation wasn't visible in the daytime, but I wondered if he had noticed it.

"The last time I went swimming, the tides were acting strange then too," I said.

"It means we must work harder." He waved at me to step closer. "Again."

With doubt clawing at my mind, I raised the trident, but this time the intended funnel appeared. I heaved a sigh of relief. Whatever was going on in the ocean, it was temporary. Maybe a series of strange rips due to changing weather patterns. I didn't pretend to understand how climate worked, especially when Atlantis existed in its own magical micro-climate, but I was sure that must be the reason.

A few minutes later, the entire ocean was churning under my power, nothing but white caps crashing onto the rocks below. I turned my face to welcome the sting of salt spray and then leaned into the winds I had summoned. Vorago stood beside me, his eyes gleaming with approval as a storm of power took my body hostage.

"Magnificent," he murmured.

A towering tidal wave surged toward the horizon. I guided it with my hand, the trident humming in perfect sync with my will, the resistance earlier all but forgotten. Beneath the surface, whirlpools twisted into spirals of power, vast enough to swallow ships whole. The sheer magnitude of control filled me with a rush of exhilaration.

Behind me, the crunch of footsteps sounded on the rocky terrain. Tempest approached. In the two weeks since they'd arrived, his demeanor hadn't eased. The gods still hadn't engaged with the High Council, and Tempest had done his best to keep their intentions hidden, claiming it was their right to return to Atlantis whenever the hell they pleased, so what did they need a meeting for? Such a warm and fuzzy guy.

"Not bad," he drawled, crossing his arms as lightning flickered across the distant clouds. "For a beginner."

"You don't think I'm capable of more?" I asked. I may not have been able to hold time at bay for more than a few seconds, but with the trident, I could damn well drown the island.

Tempest smirked. "Prove me wrong. Show me you're more than a mortal playing with divine toys."

Vorago remained silent, clearly allowing me to make up my own mind. The challenge in Tempest's words stabbed at my pride. I glanced at the ocean again, its waves beckoning. I raised the trident. Power surged, the sky darkening as black clouds rolled in. The tides tried to resist, but I reached beneath them, felt the extent of their will and...yanked. The ocean rolled toward me. No voice. No resistance.

I raised my free hand and called on my ice. The ocean became a roiling mass of ice and waves, jagged frozen shards shooting out of the depths to pierce the cliffs. Funnels of violent water erupted from the ocean. With a flick of my wrist, I froze them, and they crashed back into the water.

I sensed the awe of those gathered on the shores below—Atlanteans who had come to witness the display. They stared with open mouths. A couple shouted up to me, but the wind snatched their words before they reached me. Some ran for shelter. That made me laugh. There was nowhere anyone could go to avoid the weather I had created.

Below, the crowd backed away from the shoreline. I caught a cry for help. Didn't they know I would never hurt them?

"Gal!" A voice cut through the roar of the ocean. Or perhaps it entered my mind. But I could hear her clearly, as though she was standing right next to me. Telepathy. Cascadia stood below me on the shore, her flowing blue dress plastered against her frame. She stepped into the surf, raising a hand to the waves, taking the violent edge off the warring ocean. *"The ocean gives life. Do not make it your weapon."*

I hesitated, the trident's glow dimming for a heartbeat. The towering waves faltered but held their shape.

"She's gone soft," Tempest replied telepathically so Cascadia could hear him. *"Don't listen to her. This is what separates gods from mortals. You hesitate, and you lose control."*

"Remember who you are," Vorago said. There wasn't a trace of doubt in his voice. "You wield the trident for a reason. If you cannot master your own fear, the sea will master you instead."

I mastered fear a long time ago.

I growled under my breath and slammed the trident into the ground. The tidal waves surged higher, obeying my will, funneling their destructive force into controlled currents that spun harmlessly offshore.

Cascadia's stare burned into me as she retreated from the water. The storm calmed, though the tension in the air was thick enough to bite. Without another word, she turned and strode away, taking many of the onlookers with her, their footsteps vanishing into the sand.

Vorago put his hand over mine, his fingers so close to the trident. He had never touched me before. The sense of him ran through me, filled my veins and leached into every cell. I also felt his desire to hold the trident again. No, not desire. It was stronger than that. *Obsession*.

"That's enough for today," Vorago said.

I lowered the trident. The waves collapsed. The sun beamed down on us all. I turned to face him. "When I become a god, will I rule with you?"

That wasn't quite the question my friends wanted me to ask, but it was the one that came out.

Vorago tilted his head, his eyes shining like shards of frozen lightning. "You assume that ascension is merely a matter of time," he said. "Becoming a god is not about ruling but about transcending. To reach that point, you must first understand what sets you apart. You've come further than most ever could, Gal. But there are still obstacles...ones you may not yet see."

"Obstacles? What obstacles?"

Tempest lingered a few paces away, his perpetual smirk grating on my nerves.

"Your ties to those who cannot understand what you're becoming." Vorago's presence filled the space between us. "Take Bay, for instance. He may follow the rules...for now, but power like his—like yours—cannot help but hunger for more. It is the way of things. His growing mastery over the Power of the Sea could turn him into a rival."

The man becomes the god.

Which man?

I covered my discomfort with a scoff. "Bay? He's not a threat. He's not ready for any of this."

"Perhaps," Vorago said, though his eyes remained locked on

mine, as though he knew my doubts better than I did. "But rivalry does not always come in the form of direct confrontation. Sometimes it's subtler...a quiet erosion of trust. He may see you as something to surpass, to prove himself against. And when the time comes, you must be prepared for that."

I swallowed, but saliva got stuck halfway down, causing me to cough. The truth of the words was uncomfortable to hear. I thought Bay was too moralistic to let power...tempt him, but if his resentment toward me grew...?

Vorago continued. "And then there's Una. She loves you, yes. But love is fragile when faced with the unknown. She sees the man you were, not the god you are becoming. Her warnings are born from fear, not insight."

"Una doesn't fear me," I said quickly, though the words rang hollow. When we'd first discovered the prophecy, Una had cried. *Wept.* As if she knew I would walk a dangerous path. But I was only doing it for her. Couldn't she see that? Danger was a permanent fixture in our lives. I had no choice but to court it.

"Fear isn't always obvious," Vorago said. "It festers in doubt, in the need to hold you back for 'your own good.' Ask yourself—has she ever truly believed in your potential? Or does she want to keep you bound to the limits of mortality?"

I puffed my cheeks and blew out a breath. "Una's not like that. She's just...she worries, that's all. She's an oracle. There is a lot on her shoulders."

"Of course," Vorago said, his voice turning soft, almost pitying. "It's difficult for mortals to grasp divinity, even when it stands before them."

"And yet every Atlantean on this island worships the ground you walk on."

Vorago waved a hand. "But they do not know the true me. They never will."

I stared at the horizon, where the sun was sinking into the

sea. The light fractured across the water like shards of gold. The trident pulsed in my grip, reminding me of the strength at my fingertips.

"You, however, are different," Vorago said, his tone shifting to one of admiration. "Your mastery of both the trident and your cryo-aquaism are remarkable. You're not like the others. That power—the ability to command both ice and water—makes you unique, even among gods. You've already begun transcending the limitations of both worlds. Soon, neither mortal nor divine will be your equal."

"You can't be serious."

"I never joke."

The words took root deep inside, inflating my ego despite the nagging voice of caution whispering in the back of my mind. I was powerful. The storms I summoned, the ice I forged from nothing, the currents I controlled—all of it proved I was becoming more than just a prince or a protector.

Does it? Or is it your own arrogance?

I refused to allow the voice to put doubts in my head. I pushed it away. Locked it down. It could spout whatever bullshit it wanted to, but I was done listening.

"Enough talk." Tempest gestured to the sky, where the last of the storm clouds were dispersing. "You've got potential, sure. But if you're going to call yourself a god, you better act like one. Power without boldness is like a flame without heat."

I didn't dignify his taunt with a response, though a part of me itched to raise another storm just to shut him up. Instead, I glanced at Vorago, whose approving nod urged me forward.

"You're right about one thing," I said to Tempest, turning the trident lazily in my hands. "I'm not afraid to test my limits. You'd do well to remember that."

Tempest chuckled. "Oh, I'll remember. Let's see how long you can keep that control."

Before I could reply, Vorago clapped a hand on my shoulder. "You are on the right path. Those around you simply fear what they cannot comprehend. Trust in your strength, Gal. You are becoming something greater than any of them can imagine."

His words sank deep into my core, solidifying like ice. I would not let their fears control me. I would not let their warnings prevent me from protecting them. I was done hesitating. The future belonged to those willing to seize it. And I would seize it with both hands.

"Do you still want the trident?" I asked the question that had been gnawing at me all day. The one I wasn't sure I wanted an answer to. The one that would determine the future of our relationship.

Vorago didn't answer, his eyes darting over my face, his gaze intensifying until I felt he was weighing the worth of my soul.

"He's smarter than I gave him credit for." Tempest folded his arms over his chest. "I think you better tell him, brother."

My skin prickled. "Tell me what?"

CHAPTER FIFTEEN

I wound my way along the cliff path toward the palace, my head full of the few ominous answers Vorago had shared with me. He had finally agreed to meet with the High Council. And *only* the High Council. And then he would explain. I sensed something cataclysmic about to descend. But if it was so bad, why hadn't *The Mermaid Chronicles* warned us?

I stared at my feet as I walked, the cliff giving way to sand, lost in my thoughts until I became aware that Ember was standing in the middle of the path.

"What the hell was that, Gal?"

I frowned at the accusation in his voice. "What are you talking about?"

Ember cocked his head. "You nearly sank half the coastline?"

I spared a glance over my shoulder. The storm. I'd forgotten about the storm I'd created. The sea glistened in the sunlight, waves rolling with a gentle, almost apologetic rhythm. The towering waves had vanished, but the signs of their fury remained etched into the land. Further along the coast, jagged scars marred the cliff faces where chunks of rock had crumbled away. Two small landslides had swept patches of dense vegetation onto the beaches below, scattering debris along the shoreline. Blocks of ice, some larger than boulders, dotted the beach.

If someone had been near those cliffs...

You could have killed people.

I pushed the voice aside. No one was hurt. Atlanteans were smart enough to keep their distance when I was practicing with the trident. They had to know I wouldn't let harm come to them.

I faced Ember again. There wasn't a hint of humor in his brown eyes. His jaw was set, his brow furrowed.

"Landslides, maybe," I admitted, forcing a note of nonchalance into my voice. "But no one's hurt."

"Maybe Bay is right."

The words hit like his pyro shields had seared my insides. I was too stunned to reply.

"You used the ocean like a damn toy, Gal. People were terrified."

"Ember, only last night we were drinking in the bar and I was telling you about what I was learning. What's changed?"

"Last night was before you created a storm that almost swallowed the island. Ash had to fly a couple of kids to safety." Ember shook his head. His entire body vibrated with disappointment.

"I didn't know that."

"There's a reason we went to the north of the island to train last time."

"You're right. I'm sorry. I'll be more careful."

He deflated, dug a foot into the sand. "I was worried I was losing you there for a minute."

"Don't let Bay get inside your head. I'm still me, buddy. I haven't changed."

Ember closed the distance between us, placed his hand on my shoulder, and squeezed. "I'm really glad to hear you say that."

I pulled him into a one-armed hug, careful to keep the trident from touching him.

"I do have good news, by the way," I said.

Ember pulled back and gave me a quizzical look. "Don't keep me waiting. I'm not one for dramatic pauses."

I chuckled. "Vorago has agreed to a meeting with the High Council."

Ember blew out a breath, a little puff of steam coming out with it. "Thank fuck for that."

A couple of hours later, I entered the great hall to find the High Council already in attendance. Ford, Blaze, Maya, and...Bay stood at various points around the room. So he'd been invited already? Of course he had. Whoever the Power of the Sea chose as its guardian was automatically given a position on the council.

Bay and I shared a look, but didn't exchange words. My father entered next, looking around the room. He smiled when his eyes fell on me.

"I'm glad we're finally getting somewhere," Dad said.

"They're not here yet," Blaze said, circling the orb of Fire and Heat. "So keep your hopes in check."

No one sat. Everyone was too nervous.

"What do you think they're going to tell us?" Maya asked me as we stared into the Power of the Sea.

"Nothing good," Bay said.

"That's what I'm afraid of." She glanced at *The Mermaid Chronicles*, as if willing it to share a new prophecy.

"I wish Una was here," I said.

Maya ran her hand over the book. "Me too."

The door opened once more and the three gods entered.

Vorago held his head high as his gaze fell over our small gathering. Cascadia inclined her head in respect. Tempest, however, refused to make eye contact as they took their places.

"King Wade," Vorago greeted smoothly. "It is good to see you. We were hoping you would join us. Your wisdom is a valuable asset to these discussions."

Dad nodded. "Atlantis faces uncertain times. Of course, I'm here to support my people, and my son."

His words eased the knot of tension in my chest. He stepped forward, clasping my shoulder in a firm but affectionate grip. "You've carried a heavy burden, Gal. More than anyone should at your age. I want you to know I'm proud of you."

Sweat beaded on my brow, but I was grateful for the support. Before I could say anything, Blaze spoke, his tone edged with smoke. "Let's get to it. Vorago, you've kept us in the dark long enough. Would you please explain what's going on."

Vorago stepped into the center of the room, walked a slow circle around the Power of the Sea, his features softening with nostalgia. "I had been hoping to avoid telling you this, but as you are all suspicious of my intentions, I will have to reveal the truth."

"About time," Maya muttered under her breath.

"It is my sister who created the bloodline of oracles." Vorago glared at her. "Do you wish to make her regret her decision?"

"I mean no disrespect." Maya flushed. I couldn't tell if it was through anger or embarrassment. "But you must understand the effect your reawakening has had on our community. And while we believe our creators would only have our best interests at heart, we have so many questions—"

Vorago raised a hand. "The Architect, the creator of the universe, may be returning."

The room fell silent. Even Tempest's smug expression faded.

"God?" Dad asked.

Vorago shook his head. "God is a figurehead. An icon. A myth. The Architect is real."

What the fuck?

Everyone stared at each other. No one knew what to say. I'd thought the Denizens were the most powerful beings I'd had to face. And then Vorago returned. And now...this?

"Why?" Blaze asked.

"Who...who is he?" Bay questioned.

"Not a *he*, but an *it*," Tempest said.

"And this is a problem, why?" Steam poured out of Blaze's mouth as he voiced the question.

"Because the Architect lacks emotion," Vorago replied. "It is not like the three of us. The Architect used the universe as its blank canvas, and sometimes the Architect becomes bored of what it produced and starts again."

Cascadia, silent until now, joined her brothers in the center of the room. "Creators are not always benevolent. The Architect may see our growth, our evolution, as defiance. It may wish to remake the world into something new. Or undo what it created altogether."

"You think it's going to destroy the world?" Bay's body was wired so tight I could see his muscles vibrating.

"It's a possibility we have been trying to gain more clarity on," Cascadia said.

"So you came back for the trident in the hopes of saving us all?" I asked. Coral was right. The gods had created us. There was no reason for them to bring ill will, despite the impression their temperamental personalities gave off or their prejudice against humans. But, I reasoned, I guessed that was what happened if you were immortal and alive for centuries and the people you created had been persecuted.

Vorago locked his eyes on me. "Correct. With the trident,

and all my power, there may be a chance we can save Atlantis and the rest of our universe."

We all glanced at the trident where it rested in its brackets above the fireplace.

"But the trident chose to remain with my son," Dad said, edging closer to me.

Vorago bristled, but covered it quickly. "Which is why I must train Gal to be as powerful as me. He must ascend."

Maya frowned. "Why is this not in *The Mermaid Chronicles*?"

"Because the Architect is beyond prophecy," Cascadia replied.

Maya rushed to the book and flicked through the pages, even though she knew every word written inside-out and back-to-front. "There's never been mention of the Architect in here."

"There wouldn't be," Vorago replied. "It is beyond our world."

Maya crossed her arms. "And you kept this hidden? Why?"

"To prevent widespread panic," Vorago explained. "Fear leads to poor decisions. We needed time to observe and prepare. Now that you know the truth, we can work together to strengthen our defenses. But we must act swiftly. The Architect's power surpasses anything we possess."

Bay shifted uncomfortably beside Blaze. "So you say, yet you also sought the trident. If you're so worried about the Architect, why didn't you tell us from the beginning?"

Vorago's gaze sharpened. "Because, after being away for so long, I needed time to see if you all could be trusted—"

"Us?" Maya's eyes goggled. "We're not the one keeping secrets—"

Vorago cut her off. "And it seems you all need time to trust us once more too."

Tempest chuckled darkly. "You mortals love your suspicions."

Bay bristled. "We have every right to be suspicious when someone like you shows up out of nowhere and starts manipulating people."

Tempest jerked his head, his eyes narrowing. "Careful, little guardian. You're playing with forces you barely understand."

"Enough," Dad said, raising his voice. Tempest hesitated but backed off, his gaze still locked on Bay.

Vorago nodded approvingly at Dad. "You are wise to seek peace. But understand this—if Gal cannot reach his full potential, we may not have a chance against the Architect. He must learn to manipulate time, and he must do so quickly. That is our only chance."

All eyes turned to me again. The pressure of their expectations was suffocating.

You will fail.

I can't.

This level of responsibility was like nothing I'd experienced before. Dad squeezed my shoulder once more and I leaned into the solid surety of him. "You're not alone in this," he said. "We'll face whatever comes together."

"The path ahead is not one mortals can fully comprehend." Vorago clasped his hands together. "Gal's abilities place him above such limits. You all see the man, but I see the god he is becoming."

"We need more than brute force to face this threat." Ford hadn't voiced his thoughts yet, and now he spoke with his usual tempered tone. "We need unity. And we all need to look out for Gal so that the power doesn't overwhelm him."

"Control is precisely what I am teaching him," Vorago replied coolly. "He is progressing faster than you can imagine."

Bay crossed his arms. "So fast he's already endangering the coastline? That's what you call progress?"

I clenched my jaw, unwilling to rise to the bait, but Vorago answered for me. "Perhaps you're envious of what you cannot achieve yourself, Guardian. Power often breeds such emotions."

"I don't envy Gal," Bay shot back. "I just want to make sure he doesn't destroy everything we're trying to protect."

I met Bay's glare. My hand twitched, but I refrained from calling the trident to me. My conversation with Ember earlier replayed in my mind.

"We can't let this divide us," Dad said. "We're stronger when we stand together. As Ford said. Unity is paramount. It always has been."

Vorago inclined his head. "Wise words. Let us hope they are heeded. And please remember, secrecy is necessary for now. Panic will weaken us." He turned to me. "Come, Gal. There is more for us to discuss in private."

As the council murmured among themselves, I followed Vorago from the hall, my mind racing.

The Architect. The Creator. A force beyond comprehension.

My mouth was dry. I kept licking my lips just to feel something. It was almost too much to believe, and yet Vorago had descended on our island when people had mostly given up believing in him. His presence had brought a renewed sense of community. Worshipping halls had sprung up all over the island. And the offerings continued to pile up outside his door.

As we walked through the palace gardens together, he filled me in on all he knew of the Architect, and each word coated my bones in ice. Unemotional. Uncaring. And with so much power at the click of a finger. How could I ever hope to stand against a being like that?

"The shifting trident constellation." I looked up at the sky, but it was still daylight and there were no stars in the sky. "The unruly tides. Are they...the Architect?"

Vorago nodded.

"What about the voice—"

"That carries on the wind? Intrudes in your mind?"

My head snapped up. "Yes. How did you know? I thought I was going insane."

"It is the Architect playing with you. Mocking you. Making you doubt. Only gods can hear the whispers." That explained that then. I breathed a sigh of relief. *Not* crazy. "The tide and the constellation are the universe warning us something isn't right. They are signs of imbalance. Either of the Architect's displeasure or signaling a shift in our world. It's hard to tell which. But regardless, the Architect is watching. Waiting. Preparing."

"You've been hearing the voice too?"

"I have."

"Do you have doubts?"

"I have learned to ignore them."

If only it were that easy.

"Why me?" I asked him.

"What do you mean?"

"You're more powerful than I am," I said. "You may not be able to bend time without the trident, but you created an entire island. Surely you don't need me to defeat the Architect."

Vorago searched my face, as if wrestling whether to tell me something.

"Gods cannot destroy," he said finally. "Only create—"

"Then we have nothing to worry about if the Architect—"

Vorago raised his hand to quieten me. "The Architect is not a god. It is beyond such concepts. But the gods, me, Tempest, Cascadia, and eventually you...we cannot destroy. We can only create. So while we may have immense power, and while we can wield that power over the weather and the tides and the oceans, even use them to cause destruction if we wish, we cannot simply vanish an island, or the people on it, or the Architect."

I hung my head as I took in his words. "I still don't understand why you need me. If the Architect is so powerful, and you are all so much more powerful than me, and I don't ascend in time..." I trailed off, the mental image intruding on my mind too gloomy to dwell on.

You will never defeat me.

It was the first time the Architect had owned the voice. I took that as a good sign. That maybe it feared me. Either that or it was gaining confidence.

"The only god capable of manipulating time is the one who wields the trident," Vorago said. "And manipulation is a generous term. Slowing it for periodic moments and allowing it to snap back to the present time may appear to be a formidable ability, and it *is* in any other circumstance, but it is a long shot. And our only chance to save ourselves. To save the island. To save our people, Gal."

I frowned. "How will manipulating time defeat the Architect?"

"Truthfully? I'm not entirely sure it can." Vorago ran a hand through his flowing hair, water droplets flicking into the air. "The Architect exists beyond time. That much we know. The stories say he weaves fate like threads on a loom, twisting and unraveling at will. If we were to *anchor* him, force him into a linear timeline—our timeline—he would be vulnerable."

"And then what?"

"We...you...can slow time enough that it is almost at a standstill. There is a chance we may be able to trap the Architect there. We then speed up to the present. And the Architect will

173

remain in the past, or slowed down, or in slow motion. However you want to think about it."

My frown deepened. "My head hurts."

Vorago chuckled darkly. "Time is an unruly concept. And it doesn't behave how you think it does."

"Tell me about it." I puffed out my cheeks. "And if we fail?"

"Then the Architect wipes us out of existence with a snap of his fingers," Vorago said, somehow without flinching. "But you already know that."

I exhaled sharply. "Christ Almighty."

Vorago gave me a wry smile. "You still pray to a god that doesn't exist?"

"It's more a figure of speech." I nudged the base of a fountain with my toes. "What do we do once we trap the Architect in time?"

Vorago lifted his face to the sun as we walked along the clifftop path. "The combined power of the trident and the three gods is the strongest force this world has ever seen. Together, we could create a moment, a single point in time where the Architect is bound to Atlantis' rules. And in that moment—" his eyes gleamed "—he would be killable."

"Has anyone ever tried this before?"

Vorago pursed his lips. "Not to my knowledge."

"Even if we succeeded in trapping him within time, that doesn't guarantee we can kill him."

"No," Vorago admitted. "But it gives us a chance. A chance to use everything we have, every ounce of power, to rip him apart before he can unmake the world."

My stomach hollowed. The trident's constellation. The irregular tides. The voice. All signs the Architect was real. And if it was real, it was coming.

Vorago left to give blessings to a crowd of people hovering on the path, promising to meet with me soon to train. With my head lost in thought as well as a cloud of insistent mosquitos, I headed for the garden path with the trident in my hand. As I neared home, warm light spilled from the windows. Exhaustion tugged at my limbs. I couldn't wait to share a drink with Una and fall into bed together. I shut the front door behind me and moved through the house until I found her. She was curled up on our bed with a book in her lap. Not *The Mermaid Chronicles*. But a novel.

She looked up at me, her face softening with a smile. "Hey. You look exhausted. You okay?"

After placing the trident in the corner of the room, I lowered myself to the edge of the bed and she slipped her feet across my lap. "Ask me that again in an hour." I fell back on the bed, one hand kneading the arch of Una's foot.

"I saw Bay earlier."

I was too tired to feel tense, so I waited for the question.

"He wouldn't tell me anything about the meeting."

"I wish you could have been there. But it was High Council ears only."

"Your father was there."

"He's the king."

"And I'm an oracle."

"*An* oracle," I said. "Not *the* oracle."

I heard the snap of Una's book closing. She removed her feet from my lap. I rolled toward her and propped my head on my elbow. "What is it?"

She leaned forward, searching my face. "I want to know what's going on. Not because I'm nosy, but because I believe I can help."

I smiled and replaced my hand on her foot, running my thumb over her toes. I wanted to tell her everything, to unload the fear and uncertainty roiling inside, but Vorago's warning echoed in my mind. *Secrecy is necessary for now. Panic will weaken us.* Yet hiding this from Una felt wrong. We had faced every battle together. I owed her the truth.

"It's complicated," I finally said. "Vorago...told us something. Something big. But I'm not supposed to talk about it."

Una frowned and repositioned her eye patch. "I've never seen Bay so tense. And you've never not told me something, Gal. You're scaring me."

"I don't want you to be scared." I was scared enough for both of us. And I couldn't keep her in the dark. Not about this. "The Architect," I whispered, as if saying the name aloud would summon it. "The one who created the universe. Vorago thinks it's returning."

"God?"

I shook my head. "Not God. Apparently, God is a legend. But the person, or thing, behind the beginning of the universe is real. He created Vorago and Tempest and Cascadia. They created Atlantis."

"It's like their dad," Una whispered.

"I guess."

"What does it want?"

"No one knows," I replied. "But that's why Vorago was after the trident. With it he thinks he can put up a fight if the Architect decides to wipe our slate clean and start again."

"It would murder us all?" Her face paled. She covered her mouth with her hands.

"We don't know what its intentions are. But the constellation? The tides? They are signs the Architect is coming, that it is planning to disrupt things."

Una frowned. "But your pops was saying the other day how he and Marina have noted natural changes in the tides. That they predicted the shift months before—"

"It's *not* natural," I said. "And the voice in my head? Vorago says it's the Architect itself mocking me, challenging me, because it knows I'm a threat."

Tension bracketed her mouth and eye. "Because the trident chose you."

"Which is why I have to train. Hard. And learn everything Vorago can teach me. To become—" I broke off, reluctant to say the word aloud.

"To become a god," Una whispered, then averted her gaze, but I caught the tear sliding down her cheek.

I skated my hand to her knee. "What is it?"

"I don't want you to become a god," she said.

"I don't think I have a choice."

She got to her knees and cupped my face with both hands. "We could go away. Go to the mainland. Just you and me. You don't have to do this. I don't want to do this. I don't want this for us—"

I held her forearms. "Una, I love you. That will never change. But I can't protect Atlantis if I run."

She dropped her hands and looked out the window at the stars, twinkling so brightly they were almost mocking. There was the trident, the bend in it more apparent than ever.

"If you become a god, it will change things."

"It will *not* change my love for you."

She looked down at her hands. "Must you become a god to protect Atlantis?"

"If Vorago is worried, then I think we should be too." I said it as gently as possible. "I think I need to follow his instructions."

"What if he's using you?"

I tilted my head. "I guess he is, in a way. He can't access the trident. I have to do it for him."

"And what if—"

"What if *what*, Una? Didn't you tell me not to dwell on the what ifs?"

177

She looked me square in the face. "I love you. You know I do. But what if you lose yourself to..." her gaze fell to her trembling hands.

"Do you have so little faith in me?"

"Of course I have faith in you, but..."

"But what?"

"I wish it didn't have to be you. I wish you didn't find power so...intoxicating. I wish that you knew you didn't have anything to prove—"

"It's not about proving anything." The 'intoxicating' comment stung, so I chose to ignore it. "It's about survival. I wish it didn't have to be this way, but I can't ignore what's coming. And maybe I could even find a way to get you your eye back."

"I don't care about my eye." She pressed her forehead to mine, her breath warm against my skin. "And you say that now...but I've seen what power can do to people. I've seen how it's already changing you."

"I'm still me," I whispered, tightening my hold on her. "I need you to believe that. And if I'm changing, it's not because of power, it's because of what I have to face."

She pressed the gentlest of kisses to my temple. "Promise me...*promise me* you won't let them take you away from me," she whispered back, her trembling voice betraying the extent of her fear.

"I promise." The words felt like both a vow and a prayer. I kissed her softly, hoping it would be enough to ease her fears, if only for tonight. "*I promise.*"

I barely got the words out before Una's hands fisted in my shirt, pulling me to her with a force that left no space between us. She kissed me. Hard, desperate, like she was trying to brand me, like she needed to anchor herself in a storm we had no chance of surviving. I met her with the same intensity, my hands sliding into her hair, tangling in the loose strands, holding her to me as if letting go would shatter me into a thousand pieces.

I poured everything I couldn't say into that kiss—my devotion, my regret, my need for her, for this, for us. I wrapped my arms around her, one hand splaying across the curve of her back, the other slipping down to cradle her hip, desperate to feel as much of her as possible. I kissed her like I needed her to breathe, like she was the only thing tethering me to this world. And maybe she was. Without Una, I simply wouldn't exist. God or no god.

When she pulled away, she laid a hand on my cheek. "I need to ask a favor."

I kissed the tips of her fingers. "Anything."

"Bay needs your help," Una said.

I braced myself. "With what?"

"His abilities. He's terrified."

"Did he tell you that?"

"He didn't have to. I'm his big sister. I can tell." A fragile smile played across her lips. Lips I wanted to kiss again and not think about Bay fucking Summers.

I sighed. "He won't listen to me, Una."

"But you can be nearby. You can...protect him, Gal. And you need to be united."

"We're more likely to kill each other."

"That's not funny."

"Wasn't joking."

And yet the next morning, I found myself in search of Bay.

CHAPTER SIXTEEN

*B*ay was shirtless and barefoot, sweat glistening on his skin as he moved with deliberate focus on the rocks east of the palace gardens. Water spiraled around him in perfect, fluid arcs. Controlled, precise. Almost too precise. Like he was trying to drown something inside himself. I should've turned around. He didn't look like he needed help. But then I saw Una's face in my mind, tight with worry, her voice cracking when she asked me to check on him.

Ash and Coral were stretched out nearby on a sunny patch of lawn watching Bay manipulate water. Ash was leaning back on his palms with Coral sitting between his legs and laying across his chest. That was new. I sent Ash a wave and a wink to Coral. She immediately blushed. That girl wore her emotions all over her face. Ripple ran out from the rocks and dived into Coral's lap, making both her and Ash laugh.

My muscles were sore from training with Vorago the day before, but Una's words were imprinted in my mind. We needed to be united. I didn't know if it was possible, not with the tension simmering between us, but I was here. That counted for something. Una couldn't blame me if this went wrong.

I planted my feet in the grass and crossed my arms. "Not bad."

Bay startled, the streams of water faltering. He turned, wiping his face with the back of his arm. "What do you want?"

"To help. Una said you could use a hand."

His nostrils flared and he summoned the streams back with a flick of his hand. "I'm managing just fine."

"Really? Because it looks like you're one misstep away from collapsing." I stepped closer, examining his dark circles and bloodshot eyes. He clearly hadn't bothered to visit the fountain. "I've been there, Bay. You don't have to do this alone. The prophecies are all about being united."

"Oh, now you're on board?"

"I've always been on board."

Bay narrowed his eyes. "I thought you didn't need to be united when you were a god."

"I only came to help—"

"I don't need *your* help." He squared off. He may have been a couple of inches shorter, but he didn't lack in muscle and bulk. "And I'm not alone. I have Ford, and Blaze, and Mom—people who aren't obsessed with godhood."

I stiffened. "Is that what you think this is? Me chasing power for the hell of it?"

"You tell me." He dropped the water, letting it splash into the waves. "Ever since Vorago showed up, you've been different. You act like you're untouchable, like you don't need anyone anymore. I don't know...maybe you don't...but my sister is worried and I don't like seeing her upset. And I don't like seeing you—"

"I've been training to protect Atlantis. Protect all of us," I snapped. "Including you."

"Funny how your version of protection almost destroyed

181

half the coastline," he shot back. "People were scared, Gal. You used to care about that."

A flush of heat climbed up my neck, but I forced myself to stay calm. "Do you not understand how big the threat of the Architect is?"

"I know what Vorago told us." Bay took a step forward, his eyes blazing.

"You don't believe him?"

"I'd like to see the evidence for myself."

"The broken constellation, the changes in the tides, the voice—" I cut myself off. No way was I admitting to hearing voices to Bay. Even if it was the Architect behind it. "Are they not signs enough for you?"

"As I said, I'll believe it when I see it."

"When you see it, it will be too late."

"That's better than throwing caution to the wind."

"Is it?"

We glared at each other.

"We need to work together," I said, trying for a last-ditch attempt to smooth things over. Bay was the last person I wanted to combine powers with. But I had to put that aside if I wanted to save Atlantis.

His jaw flexed once, then again—like he was chewing back whatever he really wanted to say. "That's what I've been saying from the beginning."

"Then we're agreed." I took a step back and raised the trident. "Let's see what you've got."

Bay didn't hesitate. He raised both hands, and a surge of water erupted from the ocean, twisting into a massive vortex aimed straight at me. I deflected it with a wall of ice, the two forces colliding with a deafening crack.

Even your combined power can't defeat me.

We'll see about that.

"You're holding back," I said.

"So are you," Bay growled, launching another attack.

Bay lunged to the left, a swirling vortex forming at his fingertips. He thrust it toward me. I crouched, driving the trident into the ground. A burst of icy energy erupted in response, freezing the vortex before it reached me. The pressure of our clashing powers sent a shockwave rippling outward, knocking loose stones from the paths and felling a couple of nearby trees.

"Come on, Bay. Is that all you've got?"

Babette had been capable of so much more. Whirlpools and storm clouds and cyclones of death. During the Ghost pirates' attack, she had funneled fountain water to anyone in need. But Bay wasn't anywhere near that type of power. He was scared. He was stressed. His emotions were getting in the way. But he needed to learn to be his best, despite whatever he was feeling. Just like I had.

Is that what you tell yourself?

It's what I know.

I sent a spear of ice toward his chest. He ducked out the way, using a funnel of water to cut it in half, but not before it opened a cut on his shoulder. Blood trickled down his arm. He panted, glaring at me, his eyes promising murder.

I didn't care how he felt about me. I only wanted him to realize his full potential. Because if anything happened to me, Atlantis would need him. Una would need him.

His movements grew more erratic, more desperate. He gritted his teeth, summoning more water from the ocean to form another spiraling torrent. His arms shook as he forced the liquid into a shape that writhed like a serpent poised to strike. But I could see it—the cracks in his control, the way his energy faltered with every new attack. He was exhausting himself, and fast.

My mind raced as I fought. I'd been in his shoes once—straining, clawing to harness power beyond comprehension. But that was before I had unlocked the powers of the trident. Before Vorago had shown me how to truly wield my gifts. Now, I was in control. I was stronger. As I slowed time, I sensed every shift in the air, every pulse of water Bay tried to manipulate. I tiptoed around his attacks and released time once more. The look of astonishment on his face was worth every bead of sweat.

"You're fucking with me!" Every tendon on his neck strained as he yelled at me.

"I'm just showing you how hard things might get."

He didn't stand a chance.

The thought hit me harder than expected, unsettling me. This wasn't how it was supposed to be. We were supposed to be allies, partners in protecting Atlantis. And yet, here I was, outmatching him without breaking a sweat. I wasn't just besting him, I was humiliating him.

Which is how you will feel very soon.

Not if I can help it.

His face twisted in frustration, and he summoned a tidal surge to sweep me off my feet. I braced myself, freezing the wave mid-crest. The ice cracked under the strain but held. Bay panted, sweat pouring down his face.

"You don't have to prove yourself to me," I said, lowering the trident. "This isn't a competition."

"Easy for you to say," Bay spat. "You're the chosen one. The perfect prince with the trident and all the answers. I'm just the backup plan, right?"

I stepped forward, anger rising. "You think I wanted this? You think I don't wake up every day wondering if I'll lose control? You're not the only one carrying a burden, Bay."

Tension snapped like a breaking dam. Bay lunged, and I reacted instinctively. My cryo-aquaism flared, sending a shockwave of ice and energy that hit Bay square in the chest. He flew backward, crashing into the rocks with a sickening thud.

"Bay!"

Ash and Coral, who had been watching from a distance, bolted toward him. Ash's wings flared as he took to the sky, yelling for fountain water.

Frozen, I stared at Bay, horror and guilt and a whole medley of other emotions surging through me. He lay sprawled on the rocks, gasping for breath, blood trickling from the corner of his mouth, bright and startling against the pale of his skin. Too much blood. Too fast.

"Shit..." I dropped the trident, the clang of it hitting stone ringing louder than it should have. I kneeled beside him. "Bay, I —I didn't mean to—"

His eyes fluttered, unfocused. His lips moved like he wanted to say something, but all that came out was a choked, gurgling breath.

"What did you do?" Coral cried, shoving me aside to get to her brother. Her hands shook as she cradled his head in her lap, fingers fumbling over his throat. "Bay? Bay, can you hear me?"

She checked for a pulse once, then again. Her hands moved to his chest, pressing down to feel the shallow rise and fall. Boundless tears streamed down her face, soaking into Bay's dark hair as she bent to whisper something against his forehead.

"I didn't mean to..." My voice came out hoarse, useless. The truth lodged in my throat like a shard of ice. I hadn't meant to hit him that hard. I hadn't meant to...break him.

But he wasn't moving.

He wasn't speaking.

Was he...breathing?

Coral peered up at me from under her lashes, her eyes

streaming, her cheeks wet, her hands trembling. Ripple pressed against her side. "Couldn't you put your differences aside? Just for one day?"

"I was just trying to push him," I whispered. "Make him stronger. Show him what it's like when things get real." I looked down at my hands. They were shaking. "I didn't think—"

"No," Coral spat, her eyes flashing. "You didn't think. Because you've stopped seeing us as people. We're just pawns in your war now, right?"

Her words cut deep, but not deeper than the sound Bay made then. A low, wet cough. He tried to roll to his side, failed. His hand twitched near Coral's arm.

"I'm here," she said, holding his hand. "I'm right here, Bay. Just hold on. Fountain water is coming."

He blinked slowly, like it cost him everything.

"I'm sorry—"

"Bay was right. You're *dangerous*."

Her words stabbed a million knives into my heart. There were so many things I wanted to tell her. About the legacy of her family. About the burdens I carried. About how Atlantis really worked. But I couldn't do that to her. The words died in my throat.

"I'm sorry." *I'm so, so sorry.* I backed away, unable to endure her look of utter disappointment.

Vorago and Tempest appeared at the edge of the field. Vorago's gaze fell on Bay, then shifted to me.

"You see now," Tempest said. "This is what happens when mortals play with power beyond their comprehension."

"Gal, come," Vorago said. "There is no time to dwell on this. You are needed elsewhere."

"I hurt him," I mumbled, my voice so different from anything I recognized as my own.

"And you will learn to control that power," Vorago said, stepping closer. "But not here. Not with them."

I glanced down at Bay, who struggled to open his eyes. Coral brushed Bay's hair back from his face, a gentle repetitive motion, as if she could smooth all the blood back inside. I wanted to help, but she flinched when I said her name.

She is afraid of you.

She is.

"Gal," Vorago urged. "You have a greater purpose. Do not let this distract you."

My indecision stretched on. I wanted to stay, to fix what I had broken, but Vorago's words pulled at something deeper. The Architect. The fate of Atlantis. It was bigger than this.

Decisions. Decisions.

I heard the sound of Ash's wingbeats overhead. He would have fountain water. Bay would be okay. I stood, my gaze meeting Bay's for one agonizing second. "I'm sorry, Bay." Then I turned away.

"Let's go," I said to Vorago.

Coral cursed me, my name on her lips a promise of retribution. I didn't blame her. She shouldn't have put her faith in me. Or the gods. We were all at war. There was nothing I could do for her here.

As I walked away, Una's words flashed through my mind: *Promise me you won't let them take you away from me.*

But this wasn't that. This had been between me and Bay. And it was overdue. He was so new to this. And I was the only one who could show him how hard things could be. I had done him a favor.

Tempest gave me a sharp, approving nod as I fell into step with him and Vorago. "Finally seeing reason," he said. "You can't waste time coddling those who don't understand what's at stake. He'll live. They always do."

"Oh, I think he understands what's at stake," Vorago said.

But all I could think about was the sound Bay made when he hit the rocks, the sickening crack of impact. The fountain would cure him. Hell, he was probably up and about right now, and maybe following me to let loose a little revenge. Or not. That wasn't really Bay's style. I pushed thoughts of him away and turned my attention to what mattered most. Atlantis needed me—needed the power I wielded. And if Vorago was right, the Architect's return would demand more than any of us could give alone.

Vorago led us toward the cliffs. "You cannot afford divided loyalties. That is how power weakens, how fear sets in. You are chosen. You must embrace your role without hesitation."

My hands tightened around the trident. "He's Una's brother," I muttered, more to myself than to him.

"A brother bound by jealousy," Vorago countered, his voice sharper than the wind. "Do not mistake his fear for loyalty. He questions you because he covets what you have. That is the nature of power. It divides as much as it unites. Only those with the strength to rise above such doubts will survive."

I bit down on my retort. Was that true? Was Bay really jealous of me, of the trident? He had accused me of arrogance, of being untouchable. But wasn't that his own fear talking? Maybe I had changed, but he didn't understand the weight I carried or the grief I nursed. He never could.

The wind whispered. Not a voice. But a deep, resounding laugh. One that sent my stomach lurching up my throat. I felt the blood drain from my face.

Vorago scrutinized me. "Do not let guilt eat away at you. It is a worthless emotion."

"It's not that," I said. "It's...the voice."

Vorago and Tempest exchanged a look.

"He hears the Architect?" Tempest asked with guarded surprise.

"He does," Vorago confirmed, then turned to me. "You must ignore it."

Easier said than done. And I had a feeling ignoring it was the wrong thing to do. Things seemed to fester that way. They expanded. Grew out of control. But I had little choice as Vorago began our training session.

Cascadia was already waiting for us at the cliffs overlooking the ocean, her arms hanging loosely at her sides as she stared out at the horizon. She turned as we approached, her gaze narrowing as she took in the expression on my face.

"What happened?" she asked.

"An accident," Vorago replied smoothly before I could speak. "Nothing that should concern you."

Her eyes flicked between us. "What kind of accident?"

Vorago waved his hand. "An altercation with a mortal. It's of no importance."

"How have you grown so arrogant, brother?" Cascadia narrowed her eyes. "You loved the ocean shifters when we first created them. You loved Atlantis. Do you have no heart left?"

Vorago whirled on her so fast I thought he might force her over the edge, but Cascadia stood her ground. "It's my heart that is compelling me to save this forsaken island from the Architect."

"I'll have no part in this," she said, shaking her head. "Not when our people are endangered."

Vorago splayed a hand. "You can leave. Go hide with the mortals."

Ignoring him, Cascadia swept past him until she reached me. "If you continue down this path, you'll destroy more than you protect. Power without balance is a curse, not a gift."

Tempest rolled his eyes. "Here we go again. Always preaching balance, Cascadia. The Architect isn't interested in balance. You know that. We need to up our game. Unless you would have us all destroyed?"

"Of course not, but I won't let you turn him into a weapon," she replied. "You may have forgotten what it means to protect, but I haven't."

"I'm not a child," I interrupted. "I know what I'm doing. You think I don't understand balance? You think I want to hurt people?"

Cascadia's expression softened. "I think you're being manipulated by forces you don't fully understand. I've lived long enough to see it happen again and again, Gal. Don't let their ambition blind you to what truly matters."

"But the Architect has nothing to do with ambition, and everything to do with survival—"

"Enough." Vorago placed a hand on my shoulder. "We don't have time for bickering. The Architect's return looms closer every day. Gal's training is paramount."

Cascadia stepped back. "If you push him too far, brother, you'll lose him."

"Not if he's strong enough to rise above doubt," Vorago replied. He turned to me, his piercing blue eyes burning. "Are you?"

"I am."

"Good," Vorago said. "Then prove it. Show us the true power of the trident. You will lead Atlantis in its darkest hour, Gal. And you will do so as more than just a mortal prince."

"Why me? Why not you?"

"As much as it rankles me, it is because you wield the trident," Vorago said, his voice laced with steel. "Because my *power*, my *grace*, is *tied* to the trident. And even though I am more powerful than you, the trident holds more power than the three of us combined."

Holy shit. Okay then.

"I didn't know that," I said.

Not enough to beat me.

I suspected the Architect wasn't entirely truthful. And that gave me hope.

"Let's get to it," Vorago said, stepping over the rocks until he towered over me. "Show me you have what it takes to end the threat of all threats."

I couldn't dwell on the past. I could only focus on this moment, here, now, the trident in my hand, the power that was mine to control, and the destiny of my people. For them, I would take the leap. Always for them.

Always for them, is it?

If the voice continued to harass me with increasing frequency, I'd have to find the equivalent of magical ear plugs.

Ignoring it, I stepped around Vorago to the edge of the cliff, raising the trident high. The ocean roared in response, waves surging as the sky darkened. Power coursed through me like a second heartbeat, faster and stronger than ever before.

For so long, I had fought this. Fought what I was becoming. Fought the destiny that had been written in the currents of Atlantis long before I was born. I had clung to the idea that I was still just a man—a prince, a protector, a husband. But never a god. Never something untouchable, unrelatable, something my people might one day fear instead of love.

But the truth was undeniable. The ocean didn't just answer *to* me, it *knew* me. It had always known me. The sky churned with the force of my will, lightning flickering along the horizon like a whispered promise of the storm I could summon if I chose. The trident pulsed in my hands, urging me to let loose.

The weight of history settled onto my shoulders, the knowledge that I was the only one who could bear this burden. The only one who could wield this power. The only one who could keep Atlantis safe. Not just today, not just tomorrow, but for as long as the waves met the shore and the tides obeyed the moon. There was no one else. No one who could carry this mantle.

And for the first time, I didn't resent it. I didn't fear it.

I *embraced* it.

A gust of wind tore through the cliffs. Below, the ocean crashed against the rocks, mirroring the rush of energy inside me. I adjusted my grip on the trident, holding it steady as golden light spiraled up its shaft, illuminating the darkened sky. The tides attempted to break free from my grip, but I yanked harder and they begrudgingly acquiesced.

"I am the wielder of the trident," I said, the words not just a statement but an unshakable truth. The waves surged higher in answer. The power didn't control me. *I* controlled *it*. I decided how it was used, how it was shaped, how it would forge the future of this kingdom.

No more doubts. No more hesitation.

Wind curled around me, the faintest of whispers. But I would no longer listen. No longer hear.

I was Gal Waters. A prince. A god. The guardian of Atlantis.

And I would see it through, no matter the cost.

"About fucking time." Tempest clapped, his eyes alight with an emotion I couldn't name. And I didn't care to. This wasn't about him. This was about Atlantis. My people. And the woman I loved.

Cascadia watched in silence, her expression grim. I pushed her warning to the back of my mind. This was bigger than her fears. Bigger than all of us.

"I thought you were leaving, sister," Vorago said.

"Someone needs to be the voice of reason," she replied.

"I have my own reason, and that is all I need," I said.

"The boy has spoken," Tempest said, and Cascadia shrank into the background.

I swirled the trident. The sky obeyed my command, lightning splitting the clouds above. This was my time. No one could help me. I was alone. But that was okay. Because I was becoming something more.

And soon, everyone would see it.

Power surged through me, exhilarating and untamable. The storm I had summoned roared around me, lightning splitting the sky in jagged flashes, illuminating the churning sea below. The trident purred in my hands, its tone silken, pulling at my will. A dulcet whisper, light and lilting—nothing like the harshness of the Architect's voice. The crashing waves bowed to my will, towering and then freezing mid-crest as I manipulated time.

Vorago's voice echoed in my mind: *You must learn not just to control time, but to master it.*

I remembered to breathe and focused on the surrounding storm. Time slowed. Then sped up. Then slowed again. A smile tugged at my lips as I realized how easy it was. How easy it had been all along.

Raindrops hung suspended in the air like shards of glass, catching glimmers of light from the static lightning bolts that crackled but did not move. I walked forward, weaving between arcs of fiery light, watching the static energy raise the hairs on my arms. But it never harmed me. Because I was in total control.

I reached out, my fingers brushing close to a bolt, feeling the electrifying warmth radiating from it. Vorago and Tempest watched me. My grin widened. This was so much fucking fun. This was something no one else could experience, something no mortal could comprehend. Here, in the heart of the storm, I wasn't just wielding power—I was becoming it. Time was mine to command. The weight of ordinary existence faded. I felt...untouchable. *Immortal.*

I continued to walk through the storm, delighting in the absolute stillness I had created. I raised the trident, directing the lightning, watching it shift under my control. I could twist it, redirect it, mold it like clay in my hands. A rush of warmth spread through me, heady and addictive.

On an impulse, I sped time forward. The lightning surged an inch before halting again. I laughed, the sound swallowed by thunder.

"You've learned quickly," Vorago's voice called from the cliff edge. I turned to see him watching me, his bright blue eyes gleaming with pride. "You are mastering more than I anticipated. Soon, there will be no limit to what you can achieve."

I waved a hand, releasing the tension I had placed on time. The storm exploded into motion around me, lightning racing through the clouds, waves crashing against the cliffs below. I could command the elements with a single gesture. The thrill of it sang in my veins. I wasn't afraid of losing control anymore. This power was mine. It always had been.

"You feel it, don't you?" Vorago said, brushing his shoulder against mine. The jolt of godly contact only added to the sweetness flowing through my veins. "You are no longer bound by mortal fears. You are becoming what you were meant to be. A force beyond limitation."

"I do," I admitted. "I can hold time longer now, shape the storm exactly as I want it. It's like...nothing can touch me. Am I now a god?"

Tempest chuckled. "Not yet."

"When will I know?"

"You'll know." Vorago replied. "Remember, mastery requires constant testing. Never settle for what you have now. There is always more."

I gazed out at the storm still raging beneath my control. The thought of reaching greater heights—of transcending even the gods who had created this world—filled me with a deep, undeniable hunger. I didn't just want power. I wanted perfection. I wanted to be unstoppable.

But really, it had nothing to do with want. It was a necessity. If I had any chance at defeating the Architect, I needed to embrace every ounce of power that came my way.

CHAPTER SEVENTEEN

*T*here was something wrong with the trident.

I glanced at its polished surface, trying to decipher the problem. I halted on the path and turned it over in my hands. After a few minutes of examination, I noted a small chip marring the central prong. I drew in a breath, my pulse picking up speed, intrusive thoughts attacking my worth. Denial gripped me. This couldn't be possible. The weapon was made to never tarnish.

I ran my finger over the dent. Still there. It was barely noticeable unless you were looking for it. Yet to me, it stood out like an infected wound.

"What the hell?" I swore under my breath, running a finger repeatedly over the imperfection, hoping it was my imagination. The trident was supposed to be indestructible, a weapon forged by divine power. It had survived battles and centuries untouched. Until now.

Is it a warning?

You are not as strong as you think you are.

I growled at the voice. It had left me alone for a while. I'd thought I'd gotten the knack of ignoring it. But now that my doubts were resurfacing, it was back to gloat.

I pushed the anxiety aside. The chip was probably nothing, merely a result of the storm's intensity, or the amount of power I now commanded. There was no need to be concerned.

I sighed and continued down the path toward the palace gardens. A few geckos darted around my shadow as I walked. The soft rustle of leaves and the distant sound of fountains reached my ears as I turned a corner. And stopped abruptly for a second time, my mouth hanging open, my lungs refusing to inflate.

What the fuck?

Ember and Bay stood half-hidden beneath an archway, swallowed by the twisting vines and heavy blooms that draped over them like a living curtain. They were tangled together, Bay's fingers gripping Ember's hair while Ember's hands rested on Bay's hips. Their faces were close. *Too close.* Their lips crashed together in an urgency I associated with Una. They pulled away, breathless, gazes locked. Bay's lips were swollen. Ember's cheeks were flushed. I lowered my gaze. They were both hard.

What the actual fuck?

Blood rushed to my head, a sick mix of confusion, anger, and betrayal surging through me. Ember...my best friend. And Bay, the person I had just fought with, the person I had left injured and humiliated. The two of them together? My stomach churned, the rich scent of earth and flowers suddenly suffocating.

I pushed aside the foliage, leaves scratching against my skin as I stepped into the archway, startling them both. "What the *fuck* is this?"

Bay jerked away from Ember, his face turning crimson.

Ember's expression hardened, his usual easy-going demeanor vanishing like smoke. He stepped forward, putting himself between Bay and me, the shadows twisting over his face like ink spilling across a page.

"What the fuck is *this?*" Ember threw the question back in my face, gesturing between himself and Bay, his eyes blazing. I was thankful there was no fire around as I was sure Ember would suck it up and spit it right back out at me. "Why the *fuck* did you leave Bay wounded on the rocks? That's what *I* want to know. You *hurt* him, and you didn't even bother to check if he was okay. You walked away like it was nothing."

"Ash went for fountain water."

Bay put a hand on Ember's arm. "You don't have to."

"The hell I do," Ember said to him over his shoulder. "He almost killed the man I love."

The man he loves?

He no longer cares about you.

The ground teetered and everything I knew to be true took on a new shape. Shapes I didn't know how to label.

"You don't love him." The words stumbled out of me, broken and afraid. "You *can't* love him."

Ember ignored my comment and jabbed his finger into my chest, shoving me back against the rough stone of the arch. "*You* should have gone for the fountain water. "

"Vorago said—"

"Yes, we all know what Vorago said. Vorago says jump and Gal jumps."

"That's not fair."

Ember crossed his arms. He rolled his shoulder as if his wing was about to make an appearance. But it had been five years since I'd seen Ember's remaining wing. The space where the other had once been seemed to ache with the weight of unspoken things. "You've stepped over the edge, Gal."

Bay wiped his mouth with the back of his hand and stepped out of the foliage. "You walk around like you're untouchable. Like the rest of us are just...background noise. Whatever happened to unity?"

I glared at Ember. "Are you going to let him get away with this shit?"

"He's only saying what's on everyone else's mind."

"I didn't hear anyone complaining when I took down the Denizens."

"And broke my sister's heart," Bay muttered, his words a sharp slap.

"And yet your sister married me. If her heart was broken, she wouldn't have."

"You're dangerous," Bay said. "Untrustworthy. Unreliable. Unprincipled—"

"Says the guy who can command Atlantis' most powerful magic," I sneered. "And what have you done to earn my trust?"

Bay shook his head, stepping out of the arch's shadow. "I don't need your trust."

Ember leaned forward, muscles taut, and for a moment I thought he might punch me. Ember and I had never fought.

I looked at my best friend. My cousin. My closest family member. "You've let him get inside your head. He's turning you against me. Brainwashing you."

A muscle near Ember's eye twitched. "You don't get to make this about us, Gal. You don't own me, and you sure as hell don't own Bay. We're not here to dance around your ego."

"Fuck you, Ember," I spat, rage blinding me. Ice spread under our feet. "I'm only trying to do my job. I'm only trying to protect Atlantis—"

"And who's protecting us from you?" Bay shot back, his words slamming into me harder than any blow could. "You think power makes you better than us? It doesn't. It makes you a ticking bomb."

Ice coated my skin, gathered on the vines, trailed along the path. "You've never forgiven me for Nautalun. And now you're looking for a reason to tear me down."

Bay's eyes turned to frozen chips of blue. "Maybe because someone needs to."

My hands shook. I couldn't tell if it was from the trident's power thrumming through me or the overwhelming fury boiling in my veins. The vines above rustled in the wind, whispering like evil ghosts. I braced myself for the voice, but it didn't appear.

I took a step back, trying to rein it in. They weren't worth losing control over. Not like this.

"Fine," I said through gritted teeth. "You two have each other. I hope it's worth it."

Without waiting for a response, I spun on my heel and stormed off, skidding over my own ice. Their voices faded behind me as I strode through the garden paths, my vision tunneling.

This wasn't supposed to happen. We were supposed to be united. But all I saw were cracks—cracks that could shatter everything we'd fought for. Crevices. Canyons. Craters. And I wasn't sure I could hold it together anymore. So I went to the one place I knew there would still be support. The palace.

Ice trailed me all the way to the great hall, where I found Dad. It was empty apart from him. He stood near the fireplace, his hands clasped behind his back, staring into the flickering flames. I hesitated at the entrance, wondering if I should turn back. I took a breath, reaching for my control, willing my ice to retreat. After a minute, it thawed and left puddles on the marble floor.

Dad turned and caught sight of me. His expression softened, his eyes—so much like mine—filled with concern.

"Gal," he said. "Come in. We haven't talked for a while. You've been so busy training."

I forced myself to walk forward. When I reached him, I stood stiffly, my gaze shifting to the fire. "I already know what you're going to say."

He tilted his head, studying me. "Oh? And what's that?"

"That I've gone too far," I muttered. "That I've let the power go to my head. That I hurt Bay and put everyone in danger. That I've disappointed you."

Dad sighed and shook his head. "You don't need me to tell you that."

"Ouch."

A sympathetic smile flashed across his face. "You're twenty-five years old. You can make your own decisions. And yes, I heard about what happened with Bay. And, yes, I was worried. But this isn't about disappointment. It's about...me. About how I failed you."

I did a double take. "What are you talking about? You didn't fail me."

He turned to face me fully, placing a hand on my shoulder, and guided me to a chair. We sat across from each other. I rested the trident on the floor. My toes froze as my icy power flashed over my skin.

"I should have been a better role model." Dad leaned forward, resting his forearms on his knees, looking me straight in the eyes. "Prepared you for what it really means to carry the burden of responsibility without letting power consume you. But after your mother died...I wasn't there for you in the way I should have been. I spent too long drowning in grief. I lost my way. So I'm not a great example. And to be honest, neither was she. But we did our best."

His voice cracked. He leaned back and toyed with the wedding ring he still wore, twisting it absentmindedly on his finger. When he'd composed himself, he continued. "I thought if I distanced myself, it would hurt less. But all I did was leave you to carry burdens that no child should have to face alone. You were forced to grow up too fast, Gal. And now, here you are, dealing with forces that would overwhelm anyone."

"We dealt with all of that." My voice came out gruff. I hadn't expected this, hadn't expected him to be so open about his regrets. "We're all good now."

"I'm worried about you."

"I'm worried about me too," I admitted.

You should be.

I almost told my father about the voice. But I didn't want him to worry any more than he already was.

"I don't know if I'm strong enough to handle this." I dropped my elbows onto my knees and clasped my hands together. "It's like...the more power I gain, the more I feel like I'm losing myself. Like I'm losing everyone I care about."

He squeezed my shoulder. "You *are* strong enough. I've always believed that. But you don't have to carry this alone. You've got people who care about you, who want to help you. Including me."

I looked away. "I'm not sure Bay or Ember would agree with that right now."

"Then make things right with them," he said gently. "During the quests with your mother, there were plenty of arguments, and not just between us. Most people don't know how to handle fear. Throw in deadly see monsters or evil witches or dark gods...it's overwhelming for anyone. We're all human. We all make mistakes. But it's never too late to make amends. You're not alone, Gal. You never have to be."

"But no one else has my kind of power. I mean, maybe Bay,

but he's so new to it all. No one really understands. Just Vorago."

"You don't need power to gain unity," Dad said, and I wondered how much time he'd been spending with Ford. Or perhaps Dad had learned more than I'd thought along the way. We so rarely spoke of his past. Memories of my mother were too painful. For both of us. But it was clear he possessed wisdom that could help me, wisdom I should pay more attention to.

I blew out a breath that was more than just air. A little relief, a little tension, and a little ice.

I searched my dad's blue selachii eyes and saw nothing but love and understanding. "Thanks, Dad."

"You've got this," he said, taking my hand. "I know you do."

For the first time in what felt like days, I allowed myself to breathe. Maybe I could still fix this. Maybe I could still bring us all together. But I had to find a way to balance who I was with who I was becoming. And that, I knew, would be the hardest battle of all.

I left the great hall feeling lighter than I had in days. Dad's words had been unexpected but exactly what I'd needed. The night air greeted me with a warm caress, carrying the scent of salt and night-blooming flowers. Above, the sky stretched wide and endless, constellations blinking like watchful eyes. Among them, the trident constellation still bore its crooked bend. But I no longer let it unnerve me. It was simply a marker of the future, of inevitabilities I couldn't change. So I would meet each day as it arrived, step forward without hesitation, and leave the weight of tomorrow where it belonged.

I ran a hand over the carved handle of the trident, the metal warm in my grip. We'd been on a journey together, one that was far from over. But I was sure that if I leaned into my instincts, we could win.

As I walked the familiar path to my cottage, it felt different. Less like a retreat, and more like a return. A choice.

But the moment I opened the door to my home, I knew something was wrong. Una was pacing in front of the fireplace, her hands tangled together, her good eye darting around the room as if she couldn't decide what to focus on. She stopped mid-step when she saw me, her arms crossing over her chest.

"Gal," she said, her voice sharper than a blade. "You're back."

"Hey," I said, closing the door behind me. "It's been...a long day."

"Long day? Oh, really?" Her tone dripped with sarcasm. "Bay told me what happened."

"He's fine," I said, reminding myself to stay calm. I was done with feeling out of control. I was done with my cryo-aquaism exploding when I didn't need it. I was done with judgment. I was so fucking done. The wind brought the voice through the window and rumbled a mocking laugh. "Ash got to the fountain in time."

"*Fine?*" Una's eye narrowed. "He almost *died*, Gal. He wouldn't be *fine* if it weren't for Ash and Coral. You just walked away."

"It wasn't like that," I said through clenched teeth. "We were training. Like you asked me to—"

"No," she cut me off, her hands dropping to her sides. "It *is* that simple. You hurt my brother. My *little* brother. And you didn't even apologize. Do you have any idea how terrified Coral was when she saw Bay lying there?"

"I didn't mean to hurt him," I said, the temperature of the room dropping despite my recent promises. "We were training. Things got out of hand. It wasn't...intentional."

She took a step closer, her gaze burning through me. "That's not the point, Gal. You didn't check on him. You didn't take responsibility. And you keep using the gods as an excuse. 'Vorago said this,' 'Tempest suggested that.' When did you stop thinking for yourself?"

"I *am* thinking for myself," I snapped, throwing the trident on the couch, my breath visibly pluming in the frigid room. "Everything I'm doing is for Atlantis. For you. To keep you safe."

"For *me*?" Her voice cracked on the words, disbelief flashing across her face. "Do you even hear yourself? You're hurting the people who care about you, Gal. You're letting those gods manipulate you, and you don't even see it."

"They're not manipulating me," I growled. "The Architect is real, Una. If I don't learn how to control this power, everything could be destroyed."

"And you trust them? You trust Vorago?" She shook her head furiously. "You don't think he's using you?"

"That's not fair," I said. "You don't understand what's coming. I'm the only one who can stop it."

"You think you're the only one who can save the world?" she said, her voice hollow. "Typical. Just like Bay said, you've become so obsessed with this godhood that you can't even see what it's doing to you. Or to *us*."

I flinched. My pulse raced. Frost crept along the edges of the windows, spreading in jagged patterns. Ice crawled up the walls. So much for good intentions.

"This isn't just about me," I said. "I have a responsibility. If I don't do this, who will?"

"I don't want you to be a god!" Una shouted. And there it was. She stepped back from me, shivering with emotion or cold, I couldn't tell. "I want *you*, Gal. Not this...version of you who's drunk on power and doesn't even care who he hurts anymore."

"Drunk on power?" I laughed bitterly, the sound echoing off

the icy walls. "Is that what you think this is? You think I *want* this?"

"Then stop!" She threw her hands in the air, the ring on her finger symbolizing everything I had to lose. "Step back. Take a minute. Before you lose everything. Before you lose *me*."

"I *can't* step back, Una," I hissed. Ice spread from my feet across the floor, cracking the wooden planks. "This is bigger than you or me. If the Architect returns, there won't be anything left to protect."

"And what about Bay? What about Ember? What about the people who love you? You're pushing us all away."

"I'm doing this *for* you!" I roared. The frost deepened, icy flowers blooming along the walls. A glass vase near the fireplace cracked, the shards shattering with a sharp snap.

Una flinched, her eye wide with fear for a split second before she steeled herself. "For me?" she repeated, her voice trembling. "Hurting my brother, freezing our home...*this* is for *me*?"

I stared at her, unable to see a way through our impasse. My hands shook. Silence stretched between us. Chilled and frozen. Una rubbed her arms. I didn't know how to make her understand. I was doing all of this for her, for our future. But the more I fought for that future, the more it felt like it was slipping through my fingers.

"Una." Her name slipped out, tender and careful. "I love you. That hasn't changed. It will *never* change."

She stepped away from me, and that small action was the most hurtful thing she'd ever done. "Then show me. Show me by taking a step back. By not letting them control you."

I counted to ten, trying to calm the torrent raging through me, but ice crystals collected on the surface of my tongue as well as the furniture. "I can't do that, Una. Not now. There's too much at stake."

She folded her arms around her waist and hunched her shoulders. "You're going to lose everything if you keep going down this path. You're going to lose *us*."

The ice in the room thickened as Una's words sank in. I stood there, speechless, struggling to find a response. The weight of everything—the trident, the gods, the Architect—pressed down on me like the deepest ocean current. I felt trapped, caught between responsibility and the people I loved.

Una's eye softened, but there was no forgiveness in her expression. She crossed her arms tighter around herself as if she were physically holding back the hurt.

"You're not just losing me," she whispered. "You've already lost Bay. And Ember too."

Something about the way she said their names made the memory slam back. Seeing them together in the garden.

"Ember and Bay," I muttered under my breath. Suspicion crawled along my spine. "How long have you known?"

Una's gaze hit the floor. "Since the Denizens' attack...when they were under Nautalun's spell."

My eyes snagged on the guilty flush crawling up her neck as I tried to comprehend the timeline. "That was *five years* ago."

"They haven't been together all that time—"

"I should fucking well hope not, seeing as my best friend and cousin didn't reveal a hint of this..."

"Bay was too young..."

"That's not why you didn't tell me."

"They didn't fully understand what was happening to them. But...recently, they've admitted their feelings."

"Why. Didn't. You. Tell. Me?" I snapped, ice turning the windows opaque.

Una sighed and rubbed the bridge of her nose. "It wasn't my place to tell you. Bay confided in me as his sister. He trusted me.

And Ember...well, maybe you should ask yourself why *he* didn't tell you."

That hurt.

They will never understand.

I swallowed, forcing myself to think. Why *hadn't* Ember told me? We were supposed to be best friends, brothers in everything. But when I thought about it, moments flashed before my mind—Ember and Bay training together, laughing together, sharing quiet conversations when they thought I wasn't paying attention. Like the night in the bar recently.

The signs were there. I just hadn't seen them.

No. That wasn't true. I hadn't *noticed* them because I'd been too focused on other things. On the trident. On keeping everyone safe. On becoming more than mortal. And in doing all of that, I'd let myself drift further and further from the people who mattered most.

"Maybe I was too distracted," I said, more to myself than to Una.

"You were," she agreed. "But that doesn't mean you can't fix things now."

I shook my head, anger still simmering. "They were sneaking around behind my back, Una. Ember...he's supposed to be my best friend."

"He *is* your best friend." Una's voice hardened. "And Bay is my brother. This isn't about you, Gal. This is about them. They weren't hiding from you to hurt you. Maybe they were afraid you wouldn't understand...and right now, I'm starting to see why."

Her words stung, but I couldn't deny the truth in them. I had made myself unapproachable, wrapped in layers of power, responsibility, and godhood. The thought burned like frostbite. I turned away from her, staring at the trident resting on the couch.

"I didn't mean to hurt anyone," I whispered. "I'm just...trying to protect what we have."

Una's shoulders sagged, exhaustion and frustration etched into every line of her body. "And in protecting it, you're tearing it apart."

"You don't understand, Una. You've seen the prophecies. You've seen what we're up against. If I don't take control of this power—"

"Prophecies? The Architect?" she cut in. "You sound just like them now—like Vorago, like Tempest. You're always talking about what *might* happen, but you can't see what's happening right in front of you. *Right now*. Marina says the tides are shifting due to natural causes. Your grandfather says it's normal for constellations to change over time. You're hearing voices. *Voices*, Gal. That's a huge reg flag. I'm worried. *Really* worried. For all we know, the Architect isn't even real. There is no proof—"

"Damn it, Una!" My raised voice caused the trident to hum ominously. The temperature plummeted, ice covered the windows and walls. "The architect is *real*."

"How do you know? Because Vorago told you so?"

"I feel it."

"But you're hearing voices!"

"Which belong to the Architect!"

Do they?

I fisted my hands, attempting to squeeze some of the tension out of my body. "You think this is easy for me? That I'm doing this because I want to?"

"I think you're doing this because you're scared," she said quietly. The words struck a chord. "You're afraid of losing control, so you're letting them control you instead."

"That's not true."

"Isn't it?" Una fiddled with her eyepatch, then dropped her

hand. "You can't keep using the Architect as an excuse. You've hurt Bay. You've hurt Ember. And now—" She faltered, her eye glistening with unshed tears. "Now I'm afraid you're going to hurt us too."

I wanted to reach for her, to promise her everything would be fine, but no matter what I said, it wouldn't be enough. I didn't know when she had stopped believing in us.

She wiped her face roughly and took a step back. "I can't stand here and watch you keep slipping away."

"Una, wait—"

She held up a hand, stopping me in my tracks. "No. You need to figure out what you really want. Because if you continue to walk down this road...you won't just lose me. You'll lose yourself."

I opened my mouth to respond, but she had already turned on her heel and marched down the hall. I heard the sharp slam of the spare room door and winced.

Silenced rushed in to fill the gaps and cradle my heart. Ice cracked as it thickened on the windows, and streaks of it snaked across the floor. Time stood still, almost as though I had used the trident to slow it. I couldn't go back. And I didn't want to face the future. I couldn't bear to imagine one without Una in it.

Every single one of her words shredded my heart. I never thought I'd see the day when Una stopped believing in me. And I still didn't understand why she couldn't trust me now. I hadn't changed. I was still Gal. And I was completely aware of the amount of power at my fingertips. I would never hurt her. Or Atlantis.

But you did hurt Bay. And then you walked away.

A tiny voice inside my head told me she was right. That I had already fallen over the edge.

I sank onto the couch, burying my face in my hands. The trident lay beside me. The chip on its prong mocking me. Did the trident also know I had gone too far? Did it sense that I wouldn't come back? Was it already looking for another wielder?

The gods had promised power and purpose, but all I felt now was isolation. I was supposed to protect everyone I loved. Instead, I was driving them away, one by one.

For the first time, I wondered if I was losing the very war I'd been fighting so desperately to win.

CHAPTER EIGHTEEN

*T*he next morning, I rose early, though I hadn't slept much. The frost from last night's outburst still coated the windows, thin crystalline veins stretching across the glass like spiderwebs. That had never happened before. Had my cryo-aquaism been active even while I'd tossed and turned?

I rubbed my face, my fingers brushing over the shadow of stubble on my jaw. The chipped trident stood in the corner of the room, taunting me with its silent judgment. Silence moved through the house. A silence so thick it filled with whispers.

I listened for the voice, but it remained mute. Perhaps it felt that with everyone abandoning me it no longer needed to goad me.

Getting to my feet, I trudged down the hall and paused outside the spare room. The door was closed, but I sensed Una in there. I poked my head in to find her fast asleep, curled into a ball on top of the covers. I moved into the room and laid a blanket over her. She shifted, but didn't wake. I stared down at her. My heart ached with the weight of everything left unsaid. She didn't understand. How could she? How could any of them?

I turned and walked away.

The early morning chill hit me the moment I stepped outside. The forest sprawled before me, leaves tipped with frost that Atlantis only ever experienced during its two weeks of winter. I frowned, waved a hand, and the ice thawed, water now dripping from the leaves. I had caused that. Without even trying. I had wanted more power. And power had come. Not only had my skills with the trident increased, but it seemed my cryo-aquaism had grown too. Instead of feeling relieved or excited, all I felt was dread. A dread that wound around the ache in my chest.

As I followed the winding path through the palace grounds, even the geckos kept a wide berth, as if they sensed my mood. I passed by the fountain where Bay liked to train. Coral sat on the stone ledge with Ripple. The little creature chattered playfully, dipping in and out of the water.

Coral looked up as I approached. Her face brightened for a split second, the way it always did when she saw family, but then she quickly averted her gaze. Her smile faltered and faded entirely. Without a word, she stood, clutching Ripple to her chest as if shielding him from me.

"Coral?" I ventured closer. "I'm so sorry about yesterday."

She didn't respond. She stepped around the fountain, skirting around me, and hurried along the cobble path.

I frowned after her. I couldn't blame her. Not after yesterday. She'd probably hate me forever. But that was okay, as long as she, and everyone else, was safe.

I shook it off and kept walking.

After I rounded the corner of the palace, I spotted Ash leaning lazily against a stone pillar in the courtyard. He plucked grapes from the overhanging vines and chucked them into his mouth one by one. I raised a hand in greeting as he caught my eye. But his expression didn't change. He tucked his wings in and crossed his arms. As I drew closer, he straightened, his golden eyes narrowing.

"Morning, Your Highness," he greeted, his tone sharp and laced with mockery. "Or should I say, *God of Ice and Storms?*"

I paused and looked him over. "What's your problem?"

Ash made a display of looking over both shoulders. "I'm not the one with the problem."

I scratched the back of my head. "You sure about that? You look pretty riled up to me? Maybe a little withdrawal from your brother's product?"

"You see," Ash said, looking around the courtyard, "my bad habits don't have a way of hurting other people."

"You really want to do this?"

Ash cocked his head. "I think you started it."

I sighed. "Maybe you should stay out of it and let the grown-ups make the decisions." I jutted my chin in the direction of the rear gardens. "Coral went that way."

"You're lucky I don't breathe fire."

I laughed. "Was that a threat?"

"More like a friendly warning."

"Friendly?"

"Oh, yeah, shit, I forgot. You don't know what that word means anymore."

"For fuck's sake, Ash. This is ridiculous. The creator of the entire universe might destroy our world and you want to get hung up on a training accident?"

"Is that what you're calling it?"

I glared at him. Ice spread from beneath my feet, snaked across the cobbles, and crawled up the pillars. "Don't push me."

He raised an eyebrow, his smirk widening. "Push you? Nah. I wouldn't dare. You've got bigger things to deal with, right? Like figuring out how many more people you can alienate before you end up alone."

The words hit like punches. The ice on the pillars cracked and tinkled to the ground. Ash shook his head. "You are out of control, buddy."

"Go to hell," I snapped, stepping around him and continuing along the path, a trail of ice shadowing my feet.

"Keep it warm for me," he called after me. "I like it hot."

I swung the trident and accidently caused a wave to crest over the path. Where it froze. I focused on the wave, pushing all my anger into that frozen crest, and it exploded, ice shards bulleting in every direction. A gull squawked in protest and took off.

I glanced around to see if anyone had noticed. Cyra sat on a nearby bench, her legs crossed and a book resting on her lap. She stared at the ice scattered on the ground, flicked a few shards off her legs.

"What?" I asked.

"Nothing," she replied, and returned to her book.

I walked on.

I set my eyes on the horizon and prepared to teleport to the cave to meet Vorago, but the sight of another figure near the courtyard's edge stalled my movement. Moby stood with his back to me, his broad frame partially silhouetted by the morning light. He didn't move as I approached, didn't acknowledge my presence. I cleared my throat, hoping he'd turn around, say something—anything—but he remained still.

"Moby," I said.

He turned. Gave me two furious eyebrows, then stalked off.

I watched him go, his tall frame disappearing between the pillars. They were all judging me. Bay. Ash. Coral. Moby. Cyra. Una. They didn't understand. None of them did. Maybe they never would. This was not their burden to carry. It was mine. And I would shoulder it to keep them safe.

Is that what you tell yourself?

It is the truth.

I inhaled deeply, breathing in as much sea air as I could, hoping it would settle the nausea sloshing in my stomach. It didn't. Maybe it was time to stop trying to meet everyone's expectations. Not maybe. Definitely. I trusted my instincts. They'd never let me down before. It was time to forge ahead. Hugs and apologies could be made later.

I didn't need them. I had the gods. Vorago, Tempest, Cascadia—they understood what was at stake. They knew the burden I carried. I wasn't doing this for praise or approval. I was doing it to protect Atlantis, to protect the people I loved, even if they couldn't see it.

I squared my shoulders.

Let them judge me. Let them fear me. I would protect them all. Even from themselves.

Hardening myself to my emotions, I teleported to the cave beneath the cliffs, the surrounding air distorting in a shimmer of icy light. I landed in the center of the cavern, my feet splashing into a pool of water.

Vorago stood nearby. Beside him, Tempest leaned casually against the cavern wall. Cascadia kneeled by the pool, her fingertips trailing through the water.

"You're late," Vorago said, his voice carrying effortlessly through the space.

"I had...a few things to deal with," I muttered. I should have teleported from the house.

"Excuses are mortal indulgences," Tempest remarked with his signature smirk. "If you want to be more, you'll need to leave those behind."

"I'm here now," I said. "Let's get on with it."

Vorago stepped forward. He studied me with eyes that seemed to hold entire oceans within them, vast, deep, and endlessly cold. "You're upset."

216

"No shit," I snapped before I could stop myself.

Tempest let out a low, sinister laugh and Cascadia glanced up from the water.

"Watch your tone," Vorago said. "You carry a power older than this world. It demands respect."

The cave grew colder. The air thickened. Ice crystals skated across the pool of water. The trident hummed in my hand, reminding me of its connection to Vorago. I swallowed my pride and nodded. "Understood."

Vorago's gaze lingered on me for a moment longer before he turned and led me deeper into the cave's heart and along a passage I'd never been down before. Cascadia and Tempest followed silently.

The walls of the underground passage shimmered with trapped pockets of energy, residual echoes of ancient rituals. I could feel it all, singing in my bones.

"What is this place?" I asked as we passed through an arch concealed by hanging moss. Perhaps down here we would find the heart of Atlantis. Or cause a collapse.

"A place that is guarded by magic so powerful that no mortal may enter, or be affected by what occurs," Vorago replied. "A practice ground for young gods, if you will."

My eyes widened and Tempest smacked the back of my head. "It will only let you in if you're worthy."

We arrived at the edge of a vast chamber illuminated by bioluminescent crystals embedded in the walls. I hesitated at the threshold, worrying the magic might hold me back. I knew I wasn't a god, yet, but I wasn't just a mortal anymore either. When I stepped through unscathed, I couldn't help the grin spreading across my face. I shot Tempest a triumphant look.

"This is where we will push the limits," Vorago said. "But understand this, Gal. Power unchecked is a path to ruin. You will learn control, or you will break."

Tempest cracked his knuckles, arcs of lightning flaring briefly around his hands. "Don't worry. We'll know when you're about to explode."

"Tempest," Cascadia said. "This is not a game. Gal, join your powers with ours."

My gaze fell to a circular platform at the center surrounded by flowing water. I stepped onto the platform. The gods formed a triangle around me. A quick glance at the trident's middle prong and I thought the chip had grown. I blinked. Shook my head. Couldn't be sure. It whispered at me. Or was that the voice?

My pulse quickened as the gods summoned their powers. Vorago raised twin streams of water that spiraled upward like charmed cobras. Tempest conjured a dome of crackling storm clouds, and Cascadia kneeled to infuse the ground with moonlight that spread in rippling waves.

"Feel it," Vorago said, his booming voice penetrating my mind. "Let it merge within you."

I shifted my stance, centering my balance. The connection snapped together, more potent than before. Energy surged through me in a chaotic torrent, causing my limbs to spasm and my thoughts to scatter, but I held firm, visualizing an ocean where our forces met in harmony. The trident glowed fiercely, its golden light brighter than it had even been, bathing me in approval.

The power grew exponentially, filling every crevice of my mind and body. Ecstasy and agony rippled through me in equal measure. My senses sharpened to an unbearable degree. I could hear the distant drip of water deep within the cave, feel the subtle tremors of the earth beneath my feet, taste the charged air as if it were molten lightning.

The elements fused, creating a sphere of pulsing, unstable energy above us. I couldn't think straight, drunk on the sheer magnitude of it all. I was more than a man; I was becoming something greater. Invincible. Infinite.

"Focus, Gal!" Vorago's voice snapped me out of my thoughts.

The sphere flickered erratically, cracks spidering across its surface. I forced myself to breathe, to center my thoughts. Slowly, the sphere stabilized, its disordered pulses softening into a steady, harmonious rhythm.

"Now control the flow of time around it," Vorago said.

With my hand gripping the trident and the water lapping over the stone I was standing on, I stared at the ball of concentrated power. I pushed my resolve into the golden weapon, picturing time slow to a standstill.

The ball froze, the flickers of lightning within it struck still. Tempest's clouds ceased to spin. And the pull of Cascadia's tide relaxed its grip. The cave surrounding us blurred as the ball of energy hung, suspended, hardly moving, frozen in time. But it took everything in me. A crushing force built inside me, like I might split apart from the strain. I gritted my teeth and locked every muscle in my body, straining to hold time at bay.

The seconds ticked on. Sweat poured down my back. My legs shook. I couldn't hold it anymore.

"That's it." Vorago's eyes glimmered with approval.

"You're starting to understand," Cascadia said.

"I can't hold it anymore," I spat through my clenched jaw. And a few seconds later, my control collapsed. The ball of energy whizzed back to life, flickers of lightning moving through the unruly clouds once more.

Together, and using the last of my strength, we reined the powers back in until there was nothing left but the four of us standing together in the cavern.

"You have done well, Gal," Vorago said.

My body trembled from the strain, but the euphoria

lingered. I craved more. I could wield this power. I could master it. I could ascend.

Tempest clapped a hand on my shoulder. "Not bad."

Even though Tempest was an asshole, I couldn't help but bask in the praise.

My thoughts were already racing ahead. What more could we accomplish? How much further could we push the boundaries of our joined power? The Architect's shadowy threat seemed almost laughable in comparison to what we could achieve.

"Rest," Vorago instructed.

"We only tried once," I protested. "We should practice more."

"No," Vorago said, his tone final. "You must increase your stamina bit by bit. Too much too soon will destroy you. Tomorrow, we push further."

The gods left the chamber, Cascadia giving me a backward glance. She opened her mouth to say something, then must have thought better of it as she turned and followed her brothers. I didn't need whatever last words of advice she was going to impart. I didn't need *her*. I didn't need any of them. I knew what to do.

I remained on the platform, staring at the trident in my hands, listening to its casual whispers. The chip remained, a glaring reminder nothing perfect existed in the universe. One I chose to ignore.

Not even the voice had anything to say about it.

CHAPTER NINETEEN

I had avenged my mother's death. I had killed four Denizens. And I had combined my powers with the three gods of the ocean. There was nothing left to fear.

Or so I wanted to believe.

The trident's light clung to me as I made my way back through the palace grounds, golden rays swirling around my arms and legs, coating my torso, wrapping around my neck. Almost as if it was testing me. Probing me. Examining me.

"What the fuck are you doing, Gal?" Ember called from the shadows, his voice carrying through the rustling leaves and the distant crash of the tide. He stepped out from beneath the lattice of ivy that draped over a marble archway, folding his arms across his chest. The overhanging vines stirred in his wake.

I steeled myself for the encounter. Clearly, he was still upset about our earlier argument. The faintest glimmer of irritation flickered in his gold-flecked eyes, though it was tempered with something softer. I sighed. "I don't want to fight with you."

"I'm not here to fight." He raised his hands in a gesture of peace. "I'm offering an olive branch."

"That didn't sound like an olive branch."

A half-smile formed on his lips. "You can't kill a guy for feeling emotional."

"You? Emotional?" I faked a laugh.

"We're both tired of fighting, aren't we?"

"I'm not fighting with anyone." Truth. I meant no ill will. I was only trying to keep people safe.

"That's how you see it?"

"Is there another way to see it?"

"There's always two sides to every story. Usually more than two," Ember said. "You know that, Gal."

"What's your point?" I was so sure Ember was here to grill me like everyone else, that I couldn't drop my defensive tone.

"You can't carry all this alone."

"I'm not alone. I have Vorago and Tempest and Cascadia."

Ember ran his teeth over his lower lip. "And you trust them?"

"I don't have a choice."

"There's always a choice." Ember sighed, his gaze falling to the trident. "Every battle we've fought, Gal, we fought together. Unity. It's why we survive."

"I do wish everyone would stop banging on about unity. I *can* read the damn book. And besides, Gods don't need unity," I said.

Ember's head jerked up. "Is that what they're telling you?" He let out a short, humorless laugh and shook his head. "Even they know better than that. You think Vorago would've lasted this long without Tempest and Cascadia at his side? And now they need *you* to defeat the Architect."

I hesitated. He wasn't wrong. The gods worked in unison, balancing their strengths and weaknesses. "Okay..."

Ember's lips curved into the suggestion of a smile. "Good."

We stared at each other. Seconds passed. The seconds rolled into a full minute. It was a silence that stretched too long, filling the spaces between words that needed saying but neither of us knew how to voice.

"Why didn't you tell me?"

Ember cocked his head and scuffed his foot across the cobbles. "About Bay?"

I nodded.

"Honestly? I'm not sure." He looked away for a moment, his expression softening. "It wasn't something I was hiding. It just...happened."

"When?"

Ember raked a hand through his hair. "During Nautalun's spell. We found ourselves in a rather...compromising position." I remembered Ember coming into Uncle Dylan's bar, face flushed and refusing to talk about it. "Bay was only fifteen at the time..."

"What's age got to do with it?"

A smile ghosted his face, but Ember rubbed it away. "Nothing...I guess. But after it happened I felt...ashamed...as if I'd led him astray—"

"Not your fault. You do remember my own infidelities? Nautalun's power was..."

"Strong," Ember finished for me. "I know. But after the...incident...I couldn't stop thinking about him. Realized I'd caught feelings. Didn't know what to do with them."

"You could have told me. You know that, right?"

Ember shrugged. "I was a little embarrassed. And what was the point? There's not much you could have done to help. Bay was only—"

"Fifteen."

"Exactly." A small smile tugged at his lips. "And I had no idea if he felt the same way."

"And now?"

"He was feeling a little lost after the Power of the Sea chose him. I was there for him. Everything kind of came out. Turned out he couldn't stop thinking about that night either."

"Why did it have to be Bay?"

Ember released a low chuckle. "The heart wants what the heart wants."

"Ain't that the truth." I looked my friend over, noted the fresh color in his cheeks. I couldn't remember the last time he'd dated someone seriously. There had been both men and women in his past, but I'd had no idea he'd fallen so deeply. "So you're...together?"

Ember gave a quick dip of his head. "We are. And I'd really like you to be okay with it. You're my best friend, Gal. Even when you are a total dickhead."

Smirking, I closed the distance between us and slapped a hand on his shoulder. "I'm happy for you. But...we're not going to double date, okay? I am not Bay's favorite person."

"One step at a time," Ember said, gesturing for us to walk toward the palace. "I came to find you because there's a meeting you're needed for in the great hall."

My stomach clenched. "I've got everything under control."

"And yet we still need to hatch a plan. There are other people on this island with powers beside you. Let's make use of what we have."

Even though I knew a Plan B wouldn't be necessary, I accepted his words and walked with him up the steps leading to the palace. The stone floor cooled the soles of my bare feet as we padded down the wide passageway and came to a stop outside the great hall. Ember pushed the door open and the conversation inside halted. I raised an eyebrow at the gathering. Everyone was there. *Everyone.* My father. My wife. My extended family. The High Council. And the senate. I guessed that made sense considering we were here to devise a plan to take down the Architect, but the charged stillness in the air put me on edge.

I caught Una's eye, but she only gave me the smallest of smiles in response. It was hardly even that. More of a brief tipping of her lips. Nothing more than an acknowledgement. Her hands were stretched over her stomach as if the entire idea of this meeting made her sick. I turned to look at Ember. He splayed a hand to indicate I should go inside.

"I'm sorry," he said. And that's when I knew why I was really here. He grabbed my arm. "Remember, they're here because they care."

The doors swung shut behind us and I stood to face my execution. Or so it felt. No one spoke. My gaze skittered over the familiar faces, but I didn't settle for long on anyone in particular. Their expressions were all the same; worried and disappointed.

Gritting my teeth against the fresh wave of anger surging through me, I stepped forward. "What is this?"

Una stepped forward. "We are worried about you."

My spine stiffened. "I do not need our entire extended family to intervene in our marriage."

"You're pushing everyone away," Cyra added. If Cyra was weighing in so soon she must be really pissed off. "You're letting the gods twist your thoughts."

Ash crossed his arms, stepping into a shaft of light from the window. "You're a danger...not just to yourself but to everyone else."

"Danger?" I shook my head, ice crawling through my veins. This wasn't right. "Everything I've done has been to protect you all."

Moby wore an expression I'd never seen in any of his movies. "Isolating yourself, taking on power you barely under-stand...that's not protecting anyone. That's reckless."

Bay stood by his side, his expression equally firm. "We're not your enemies, Gal. We're here because we care about you. You're part of this family." He, of all people, dared to say that to me?

"I love you." Dad stepped forward. "But leadership isn't about bearing the burden alone. It's about knowing when to lean on those who stand with you."

"He's right," Pops said from the back of the room. "You don't have to do this alone."

Aunt Marina's voice was gentle, and somehow that seemed to hurt more. "I think you're looking for answers in the mystical when they can be explained by science. I want to give you some clarity."

She was talking about the constellation. The tides. The voice. Una had broken my confidence.

Grams offered a warm smile. "We're not here to judge you, love. We're here to support you."

Blaze's eyes burned. "You're good, Gal. But no one's invincible. You keep pushing like this, and you'll self-destruct."

"We've fought too hard and survived too much...you don't need to walk this path," Aunt Raina said.

Jordan nodded. "We're your family. We're not going to let you push us away without a fight."

The words circled me, each one taking a chunk out of my heart.

Ember's hand rested on my shoulder. "They're right. You've been carrying this weight alone for too long. Let us help. Before it's too late."

I looked around the room, seeing the sincerity etched on their faces. But beneath the surface, all I could feel was frustration. They didn't understand the magnitude of what I was facing. The gods, the Architect, the power coursing through my veins...how could they possibly comprehend?

"You don't get it," I said. "This isn't some petty squabble or a challenge you can just talk me through. I'm doing this to protect you all. The gods chose me for a reason."

"Maybe they chose you," Ash said, "but you're still human. You're not invincible."

"I'm may not be a god *yet*," I snapped. "But I'm no longer mortal either."

The room fell silent. This was not the reaction they wanted. Fuck it. I had been hoping it wouldn't come to this, but clearly they didn't realize how dangerous the Architect was. They could thank me once I'd defeated it.

Una placed her hand on my arm. It stung worse than the jellyfish stings I'd accrued during the Denizens' attack. "Gal, please...don't do this...don't let the power consume you."

"I'm not consumed!" I shouted, jerking away from her touch. A surge of brilliance bled from the trident, casting warped, twisting sigils across the walls, as if something ancient and hungry was trying to break free. I lifted my chin, refusing to let doubt take hold. "I don't need this. I don't need an intervention." I looked at Una. "And I expected a hell of a lot more from you."

"Please, Gal..." she whimpered as a fat tear rolled out of her eye. But it did nothing to change how I felt. It created no sympathy. "*Please.*"

"You're not listening to us," Ember said, his eyes dark with disappointment.

"No," I said, shaking my head. "*You're* not listening to *me*. I'm done here."

Without another word, I turned on my heel and stormed out of the hall. No one tried to stop me. The heavy doors closed behind me, cutting off their voices. I didn't need their doubts. I didn't need anyone. I had the power to face the Architect. And I would.

Alone.

CHAPTER TWENTY

I stormed through the gardens, trampling over flowers and plants, not caring about sticking to the paths. The stench of jasmine clogged my nose. Too much jasmine. Usually, I adored the scent. It was Una's scent. But now it only reminded me of betrayal.

I had been intending to head to my cottage, but there would be too many reminders of Una there. And her disloyalty. We'd made vows. Only recently. And now she was ditching me at the first sign of trouble. *She* was the one who said there would always be prophecies. *She* was the one who said we would always stand by each other during the tough times. *She* was the one who made me love her. So where was she now?

I came to an abrupt halt at the entrance to the woods, my attention snagging on voices coming from beyond the treeline.

"We've gone too far for an artifact that doesn't even matter anymore!" Cascadia's voice rang out, more urgent than I'd ever heard it. I was surprised there was something capable of ruffling her calm.

I slipped behind a tree. From my vantage point, I could see Cascadia and Tempest standing in a clearing near a fountain.

Cascadia's posture was tense, her arms crossed, while Tempest paced, his movements quick and restless.

"*Doesn't matter?*" Tempest snapped. "The trident is the key to everything."

My grip on the trident tightened instinctively. I leaned in closer, straining to hear.

"You're lying to yourself," Cascadia said. "We're risking everything for something we don't need."

"Don't preach to me about risk," Tempest said, lightning flickering around his fingertips. "You know how dangerous he is. We can't afford to hold back."

Were they talking about me? I held my breath to hear them better, but could then only focus on the sound of my own accelerating pulse.

"We need the trident in our control," Tempest half shouted.

"And Gal *is* under our control," Cascadia replied.

They glared at each other.

"Vorago doesn't deserve it." Tempest fisted both hands. I'd never seen him so tense. Not even when he was goading me.

"Do you plan to go against your own brother?" Cascadia threw a hand at him. "After all this time?"

Tempest flicked his dreadlocks over his shoulder. "I'm sick and tired of living under his thumb. For centuries he has misused his power...what do you think he'll do when he gets the trident back?"

Tempest wanted the trident.

Tempest wants the trident. For himself.

Of course he did. He'd been so disdainful of mortals, of me becoming a god, of the training sessions. He'd countered my progress at every step. Because, really, he wanted me to fail so he could claim the trident. He was power-hungry and short-sighted. Which was absurd with the Architect's return looming over us all. Was his ego really so big?

I stepped forward, revealing myself. Both gods turned to face me, surprise written all over their faces.

"Is this what it's come to?" I demanded. "You're fighting over the trident when the Architect is about to destroy us all?"

Tempest stood with his chest puffed up and his shoulders squared. "You know nothing, Gal Waters."

"Nothing?" I waved the trident. "I overheard you. You think I'm going to stand by while you try to take the trident for yourself?"

Tempest narrowed his flashing eyes. "This isn't about taking anything. You're letting your paranoia cloud your judgment."

Cascadia held up a hand. "Gal, you're misunderstanding—"

"Am I?" I interrupted. "Because from where I'm standing, it looks like you're plotting behind my back."

Electricity crackled around Tempest's frame as he took a step forward. "You have no idea what's at stake. This power isn't a game."

"Enlighten me then!" I yelled.

Tension snapped like a lightning strike. Tempest hurled a bolt of energy, and I reacted without thinking. Water surged from the nearby fountain, colliding with the lightning in a deafening explosion. The shockwave rattled the ground, sending cobble fragments and shards of coral sculptures hurtling through the air. The water from the fountain vaporized, turning into a heavy mist that obscured the garden. Shrapnel flew in every direction, some careening over the rocks and into the ocean, while other jagged chunks of debris struck the palace. Several large pieces punched through the marble walls, leaving gaping holes of ruin behind. Windows shattered under the pressure, raining shards of glass onto the courtyard and steps. The once-pristine garden path fractured, water seeping up from cracks where underground streams had been disturbed. The reek of ozone, salt, and dust surrounded us as the destruction settled in grim silence.

"Enough," Cascadia said with the authority of the ocean's depths. A powerful wave of force rippled outward, separating us. The ground trembled, but neither Tempest nor I backed down.

"You think you can wield this power better than me?" I growled, stepping closer to Tempest. "You're reckless."

"And you're blinded by arrogance," he shot back.

The air between us crackled with unspent energy. Cascadia's gaze hardened as she moved between us. "This isn't helping. The Architect is coming, and we're wasting time fighting each other."

Tempest's storm dissipated, though his glare didn't waver. "We need to trust each other, or we're doomed."

Was that his version of an apology? I hesitated, my thoughts spiraling. Could I blame him for creating the trident? Did it matter whose hands it was in as long as the Architect was defeated? Maybe I'd been too quick to assume betrayal. But there were too few people I could trust at the moment, and fury remained simmering beneath the surface.

"I'll trust you when you stop acting like you know what's best for me," I said. "Stay out of my way."

I turned on my heel and walked away, ignoring the cuts the sharp cobble made on the soles of my bare feet. I tore through the woods until I arrived at my home. Once there, I took a carafe of wine from the fridge and poured myself a large glass, right to the brim. As I retraced my steps to the door, intending to go outside and sit in the garden, I caught sight of Una's wardrobe in our bedroom. The doors were open. Half of her clothes were gone.

So it was like that, was it?

No doubt she had gone back to her parents.

I shook my head, biting back the emotion. I didn't know whether to feel sad or angry or betrayed. Maybe all three were valid. She had deserted me. She had done the very thing that I'd always been terrified of.

And I was still standing.

The thought caused a bitter laugh to rise up my throat. Still standing. But alone. I had told them all I would forge ahead alone. And I would. For their safety. But it felt shitty.

Outside, I threw the trident on the ground and flopped onto the swing bench. After topping up my glass, I placed the carafe on the table and downed half the glass of wine, attempting to numb the swirl of angry thoughts. All I had left was the trident, its chipped prong mocking me. And maybe the flimsy alliance of three temperamental gods.

When the Denizens had attacked, I'd had a team of people behind me. Not just Rob and the army, who he'd outfitted with explosive spears. But Una, who had been training in combat almost as long as me. Ford, my mentor, my second father figure, so skilled with his short swords. Blaze with his fiery breath. Ember with his pyro shield keeping us all safe and taking out Dagonar's shadows. My father with his Herculean strength twisting off Karkenloth's tentacles. Even Ash and Cyra, although they'd only been thirteen at the time, had joined the battles, and made a difference. And they would all willingly fight again. Just not by my side.

Footsteps crunched on the gravel path. I didn't bother looking up and resigned myself to another intervention. Perhaps they'll all come at me one by one this time.

"Evening, nephew," Uncle Dylan said. I looked up at the relaxed tone in his voice, searching for an ulterior motive. He stepped into view, hands shoved casually in his pockets. "Figured I'd find you here. Got an extra glass?"

I huffed a dry laugh and gestured toward the nearby table. "Help yourself."

Dylan grabbed a glass and poured himself some wine, then lowered himself onto the swing beside me. We sat in silence for a while, the gurgling sound of the surrounding water channels grating on my already frayed nerves.

The night was too peaceful, too still, a contrast to the turmoil inside me. My fingers curled tighter around my glass, the cool stem pressing into my palm. The wine barely did anything to dull the hollow ache that had settled inside me.

I had done everything for Atlantis. I had trained. I had sacrificed. I had wielded power beyond comprehension. And yet, they had gathered like I was a reckless child who needed to be lectured, as if I didn't understand the gravity of what I was doing. As if I hadn't carried this burden alone while they whispered their concerns behind my back.

I took another sip, rolling the wine over my tongue before swallowing it. The bitterness lingered. Just like everything else.

The gods had chosen *me*. Not them. Not my father. Not Una. Not Ember or Bay or Moby. *Me*.

And yet, they all thought they had the right to tell me how I should handle it.

I set my glass down with a sharp *clink*, the sound swallowed by the rush of water nearby.

Dylan remained quiet, swirling his wine in his glass. He didn't pry, didn't fill the silence with meaningless words, and for that, I was grateful.

"How come you weren't at the intervention?" I finally asked, my curiosity getting the better of me.

"Didn't think it was my place," he replied simply, bending his knee and resting his foot on the chair. "I've never believed in interventions. People don't usually change because a crowd corners them."

I glanced at him, searching his face for a hint of judgment. There was none. Only calm curiosity.

"So, you're not here to lecture me?"

He chuckled. "Lecture you? Nah. Not my style. But I'll say this: things are kind of scary right now. Atlantis has never seen so much power. *You're* kind of a little scary."

"Scary?" I repeated. "I'm not scary."

"You took down an oversized selachii who stole my life and traumatized me. I'd say anyone who could defeat Zale is scary."

"Powerful."

"Same thing."

"Is it?"

"You don't think?"

I took a sip of wine and considered. How would I feel if it was Una or Ember with all this power? I wasn't sure of the answer. It was hard to imagine. And Ember did have a lot of power. But not once had he scared me. Apart from that time I'd leaped out at him on the path and he'd almost singed my eyebrows off with one of his pyro shields. Even watching him suck in an entire lake of lava hadn't been scary. Impressive, yes. Fierce, yes. But not scary.

"I would never hurt anyone," I said.

Dylan smiled and pushed at the ground with his foot to sway the bench. "They know that."

"Then what are they scared of?"

"Power."

"I'm not a tyrant." I clamped down on the indignation in my voice.

"Never said you were," Dylan replied. "But good men lose themselves to it all the time. They're just worried about you."

"This is starting to feel like an intervention."

"Not my intention."

We fell into another silence. He sipped his wine, letting the moment stretch without pressing me. I rubbed a hand over my jaw, trying to collect my thoughts. The quiet gave them too much space, each one louder, heavier, more impossible to ignore. Finally, he spoke again. "How are you feeling?"

The question knocked the air from my lungs. I blinked, staring into the swirling depths of my glass. No one had asked me that. Not Una. Not Tempest. Not even Ember. They'd all been too busy telling me what I was doing wrong or how dangerous I'd become.

"I...don't know," I admitted. "Tired. Angry. Alone. I didn't want to do this on my own. But now it feels like everyone's forcing me to."

Dylan nodded slowly, letting my words sink in. "Yeah. It's a lot. You're carrying the weight of Atlantis on your shoulders, and everyone has an opinion on how you should use it."

"I'm trying to protect them," I muttered. "And they think I'm a monster."

He shifted on the bench to face me. "Of course you're not a monster, Gal. You're a young man who's been thrown into a role no one's ready for. But maybe...maybe you don't have to be perfect."

I raised my brows. "No one ever forgives my mistakes."

"They forgave you for burning *The Mermaid Chronicles*, didn't they?"

"Only because it regenerated."

Uncle Dylan chuckled and ran a finger around the rim of his glass. "Or maybe they just want you to trust them," he suggested. "To try and see what they see."

I stared at him. I didn't have a response. I wasn't sure if I could trust anyone anymore.

"What about Una?" I whispered. "For better or for worse..." I waved a hand behind my head to indicate the cottage behind me. "She left. Packed a bag and left. Just like that."

"Relationships aren't perfect."

I laughed. "Understatement of the year."

"I'm not the best person to give relationship advice—"

"You and Aunt Marina seem to be managing pretty well."

Uncle Dylan tilted his head. "We're older. Been around the block a few times. Not much to argue about."

I let out a sigh and blew my hair away from my face.

"I've never seen anyone love someone the way Una loves you," Uncle Dylan said. "Apart from your mom and dad. That kind of love..." He shook his head. "It's powerful. Chaotic. And it can bring people together or push them apart."

"Tell me about it."

Dylan stood, raised his glass in a toast. "I have every faith you and Una will come through this."

"That makes one of us." I downed the rest of my wine. "Why are you so sure?"

"Because you're your mother's son."

CHAPTER TWENTY-ONE

$\mathcal{T}$he northern cliffs rose starkly against the early morning sky, jagged peaks thrusting into the clouds like ancient sentinels. Salt air swirled around me as I peered at the ocean below, churning white foam crashing against the rocks and mirroring the turmoil in my heart.

A few miles farther along the coast was the royal cabin where Una and I had stayed while I was training with the trident. We were supposed to be taking our honeymoon there. But with the new prophecy, we'd had to put it off. I didn't know if it would happen now. I didn't know how to reach her. I didn't know if I wanted to.

I walked the path to meet the gods, all three of them watching me as I drew near. Cascadia's smile was small but warm. Tempest paced a few feet away, sparks of electricity dancing around his hands, restless energy crackling with each step. Vorago's expression was unreadable. I could never tell what he was thinking. I assumed he liked it that way.

"We thought it would be better to train here," Cascadia said. "Away from those who are...interfering."

I bit down on my lower lip, my gaze glued to the trident in

my hand. A second chip had appeared on its central prong this morning. I had no idea what it meant. Was the trident rejecting me? Were my friends and family right?

But they couldn't be. The Architect was a genuine threat and I was the only one with enough power to face it. Whatever consuming the power did to me, I had to accept it. Even if it destroyed me.

You will never be good enough. You will never be able to save her.

I whirled around at the voice. But it was just the wind. Or the Architect. Whatever the voice belonged to, it rattled around my head for so long it left a permanent echo.

I shook it off as I joined the gods in a small circle.

Vorago frowned, his aquamarine eyes hinting at disapproval. "Stop feeling sorry for yourself," he said. "You no longer need your mortals. They doubt you, fear you. We, the gods, are your allies now. Lean on that strength instead of wallowing in bitterness."

The words stung, though I refused to show it. "They're not just 'my mortals.' They're my family, my friends."

"Family?" His lip curled into a sneer. "A true leader does not require family to prop him up. You are evolving beyond them. Accept that."

Tempest raised an eyebrow, watching the exchange with a faint smirk. "He's got a point. You're not the same Gal they knew before. They're holding you back."

"I disagree, brothers," Cascadia said, raising her palm. "This isn't about severing ties or abandoning your humanity. Gal needs balance, not isolation."

Vorago waved her off, stepping to the edge of the cliff. "He will achieve balance with us. Nothing else matters."

He was right. I had to let go of my friends and family. I couldn't afford distractions.

Vorago studied me with his ancient gaze. "We have spent time building your control, and that is essential, but now we must go further. The power within you, within us, has no defined limits. If we're to face what's coming, we must understand what is truly possible. Together."

"Meaning?" I asked warily.

"We push past boundaries," Tempest cut in. "Hold nothing back. We need to test what we can create...and what we can survive."

Cascadia crossed her arms. "Mastery comes from pushing boundaries, yes. But breaking ourselves in the process serves no one. We can't afford reckless experimentation."

"Do you not understand the threat of the Architect, sister?" Vorago's voice rose, echoing off the rocks. "The Architect is real. And it is coming. With the downfall of human civilization on the mainland, it has the opportunity to start again. Do you care to survive, or not?"

Cascadia averted her gaze.

A flicker of something almost gentle passed through Vorago's eyes. "You are of kinder heart than Tempest and me, sister. And that is one of your most valuable qualities. But it won't help in a battle against the Architect."

Cascadia nodded. "I'm sorry, brother. We have been slumbering for so long I must have forgotten the reality of our threats."

"And our powers aren't at full strength because of it," Tempest said.

"Not at full strength?" I blurted, unsure how they could possibly come to possess more power than they already had.

"Slumbering puts our powers into stasis," Vorago said. "It takes time for them to refresh. Which is why we must train and not take any chances."

"But there is the worry of Gal losing himself in the process," Cascadia said. "We must return him to his family whole."

"He won't lose himself," Vorago said with finality, his gaze shifting to me. "You won't."

"Of course I fucking won't," I said. "I can do this. I *will* do this. I will save my island."

I glanced at Cascadia, who looked unconvinced, but said nothing more. Tempest gave me a nod of encouragement. That was a first.

Vorago clapped his hands, startling a few nearby gulls who'd been roosting in the rocks. "Let's begin."

The trident hummed. The resonance grew stronger as the gods prepared themselves. Vorago raised his arms, summoning waves that touched the sky. Tempest's storm clouds billowed in from the east, thickening rapidly, their dark mass swirling and crackling with raw energy. The sun disappeared. Rain lashed down from the sky, icy fat drops that pelted my exposed skin. Cascadia hesitated for a moment before releasing her power, deeper tides churning in circles, adding height to Vorago's waves.

"Join us," Vorago said. "Feel the elements merge within you."

I took a deep breath and closed my eyes, feeling the wind yank at my clothes and the rain drum against my head. Power jolted through me. From the trident, my cryo-aquaism, and the suggestion of something new. My limbs struggled to contain it. My mind was bombarded with sensations—the roar of water, the crack of thunder, and the electric zing of lightning. The trident blazed, its golden light pulsing like a heartbeat. *My* heartbeat.

"More," Tempest roared over the cacophonous elements. "Push further."

Arms trembling with the effort, I visualized an endless

ocean where our forces met and collided and created a vessel large enough to contain the Architect. The water around me rose and solidified into crystalline arcs, reflecting Tempest's lightning strikes. Intoxicating energy coursed through me. Every part of my being was torn between rapture and despair.

Salt coated my skin, rain soaked my hair, wind slapped my cheeks. I grinned at the swirling mass of power. Dark and writhing. Angry and chaotic. Formidable and destructive. No one power was distinguishable from the others. We had created a mass of cloud and lightning and thunder and ice. And within it, a vacuum large enough to imprison even the most formidable of enemies. A power so vast it had to be capable of defeating the Architect. A power so immense I had the urge to leap off the cliff and join it.

"Enough!" Cascadia yelled over the storm. Her light dimmed as she lowered her hands. Her gaze locked onto me. "He's on the verge of losing control."

I wasn't anywhere near that point. I hadn't felt this good in weeks.

Vorago frowned, but didn't lower his hands. "He needs to understand what it feels like to reach that edge. Only then can he pull back."

"What edge?" I called. "There is no edge!"

You will never be worthy.

"Fuck off!" I yelled at the Architect.

Cascadia gripped my shoulders. "Breathe, Gal. Focus. Don't let the power consume you."

"It doesn't matter," I yelled, rain filling my mouth and running down the back of my neck. "It doesn't matter if the power consumes me. All that matters is defeating the Architect."

"That's not true!" she called. "The Architect is not here yet. We cannot lose you before then!"

But there was so much more I could do. The trident reared in my hands, its wild energy surging like an unbroken beast. Spirals of golden ice lashed out, meeting the torrents of waves and arcs of lightning in a violent collision.

Without warning, a sudden euphoria seeped into my pores, spread through my limbs, and traveled through every blood vessel. I leaned into it, searching for more, ignoring how close I stood to the cliff's edge.

My chest swelled, the power running through me, singing sweet love songs, caressing my mind as well as my limbs. The craving for more power clawed at my mind.

"Gal?" Cascadia's eyes held nothing but fear.

"I'm fine," I said, though my voice betrayed my exhaustion.

"Are you?" she asked.

I met her gaze through the rain. What if she wanted the trident? What if Tempest still planned to steal it? I couldn't let either of them have more power. I had to do this, if not to beat the Architect, then to keep them from taking what was mine.

"Stop coddling him, sister," Vorago said. "He's stronger than you give him credit for."

"I'm not coddling him." She stepped between us. "You're pushing him too fast. If he loses himself, we'll all pay the price. Including *you*."

"We don't have time to go slow!" Vorago retorted, his anger causing a wave to crest over our feet.

"I can do this," I said, glaring at Cascadia, unsure if I believed my own words. What did it matter anymore anyway? No one trusted me. No one believed in me. I had nothing to live up to.

"I hope so," she replied.

Vorago nodded at me, approval surfacing in his stormy gaze. "Prove it. Show us you can handle this."

The wind howled mercilessly, battering my body and

threatening to dislodge me from the cliff's edge. I staggered, the cold rock beneath my feet my only anchor, though it, too, trembled beneath the onslaught. The rain came in sheets so thick it blurred everything into a chaotic haze, reducing my vision to flashes of lightning and shadows of crashing water. A bolt of lightning struck frighteningly close, sending a shower of sparks that singed my skin and hair. I gritted my teeth, clenching so hard I chipped one.

I couldn't lose this fight. I had to master the power.

I gripped both hands around the trident and called on time. I'd never tried to control so much power at once over such a vast space. The clouds, the lightning, the waves, the ice, the rain...all of it indestructible, all of it with a mind of its own.

My vision blurred, colors bleeding together as the forces of water, lightning, and ice converged within me. The roar of the storm grew deafening, but I surrendered to it, willing it to accept me. I was no longer a man tied to mortal fears. I was something more.

Leaning into the wind, I gave myself up, offering myself to the whim of power. The sense of time wrapped around me, around us, around the island. Gradually, second by second, everything slowed.

"Yes. That's it," Vorago roared over the noise. "Embrace the power, Gal. Let it become a part of you."

I obeyed without hesitation.

I didn't bring time to a standstill. I wasn't strong enough for that yet, but the violence of the storm dissipated. I held it for a minute. Or what I estimated to be a minute, and just as a triumphant grin spread over my face, I lost control and time snapped back to the present, the storm at full throttle once more.

"More!" Tempest yelled.

I didn't have the strength to slow such a vast area of time

again so soon, but I could enrage the storm. Waves crashed against the cliffs with bone-rattling force, sending plumes of salt spray high into the air, where freezing winds twisted them into spiraling shards of ice. The air crackled with energy, each bolt tearing through the atmosphere. My skin tingled with static, every hair standing on end. Rain lashed across my face, sharp as needles, while the cold gnawed at my bones. Yet heat burned within me—power surging, untamed and relentless. The storm wasn't just around us; it was inside me, woven into every cell of my being.

I was untouchable, unstoppable.

The boundaries between myself and the elements blurred until I could no longer tell where the storm ended and I began.

You think you have control of this power? It has control over you.

I snarled at the voice and pushed it to the back of my mind.

Tempest's lightning coiled around my arms, flickering in sync with the pulse of the trident. Cascadia's light shimmered at the edges of my vision, turning the frothing waves silver. The force of the gale intensified, howling like a thousand voices. And through it all, Vorago stood unmoved, his eyes glinting with ancient approval. I pushed for more.

I didn't even hear Cascadia's warning this time. I laughed, feeling the rush of lightning in my veins and the crashing tide beneath my skin. The air shimmered with unrestrained force, distorting reality. Had I stopped time again? So easily this time? I didn't know. I didn't care.

I arced the trident and a column of water shot skyward, breaking into freezing mist as Tempest's lightning tore through it. The cliff pulled apart, a large crack running inland. Icy missiles flew out of the water and buried themselves in the cliffs, the rocks, the beach, some of them a little too close for comfort. It was my power causing that. And it was glorious.

"Gal, stop!" Cascadia's voice finally registered.

"Why?" I shouted, my voice booming with unnatural force. "This is what you wanted, isn't it? This is what I am now!"

"You're losing control!" Cascadia yelled.

"Control?" I laughed. I'd never felt more *in* control. "What's the point of control when I can do this?"

I wanted to see how far I could go, how much power I could wield. I arced the trident again, channeling every ounce of energy into a single devastating command. A vortex of wind, water, and lightning exploded outward, shattering the rocks beneath us, tearing the vacuum into two.

The force of the blast hurled Tempest backward. He landed on his feet, lightning still sparking around him, a fearful expression on his face I'd never seen before. Cascadia shielded herself with some kind of invisible barrier.

"Stop!" Cascadia yelled.

But the power within me didn't stop. It raged uncontrollably, a storm without end. I couldn't think. Couldn't breathe. My body shook as I wrestled for control.

"Gal, you have to let it go!" Cascadia shouted, stepping toward me, reaching for the trident. *Foolish.*

"I can handle it!" But I wasn't sure if that was true. And I wasn't sure I cared. Energy raked across my insides. The cliffside around me warped and twisted, as though time itself was unraveling.

"You're tearing yourself apart!" Tempest growled, arcs of lightning surging from his hands as he tried to stabilize the storm. "Brother, you must stop him!"

Vorago didn't reply, but continued to wield the storm with me.

I couldn't stop even if I wanted to. The power was too much, too vast. It consumed me, driving me deeper onto the path I could no longer refuse. I could hear voices. More than one now. Whispers from the depths of the storm, urging me to let go completely. To become something greater, something beyond mortal comprehension. My feet slipped. My toes hung over the cliff's edge. Waves kissed my bare soles.

A mental image of Una's face slammed into my consciousness. I flinched.

"No..." I muttered, my voice barely audible. I fought to pull myself back from the edge. The euphoria slithered out of me, leaving behind a hollow emptiness.

Cascadia yanked me away from the cliff's edge. She placed her hands on either side of my face, forcing me to look at her. "Breathe, Gal. Listen to my voice."

Her words pierced through the haze and weather. Slowly, agonizingly, I heeded her words. The storm inside me weakened, the wild energy receding like a retreating tide. My grip on the trident loosened, and its blinding light dimmed to a soft glow.

The wind that had howled like a living beast now exhaled in dying gasps, the last remnants of its fury dissipating into the open sky. Thunder rumbled in the distance, a hollow echo rather than a war cry. The swirling, violent waters below lost their relentless churn, waves rolling lazily once more, as if the ocean itself was sighing in relief. Rain, which had fallen in thick, biting sheets, softened into a gentle rhythmic pattern, like a lullaby hummed by the heavens. The sky, once thick with roiling black clouds, split open, revealing slivers of gold where the sun fought to reclaim its place. My lungs ached, as if I had surfaced from drowning.

The cliff was in ruins. Deep fissures ran through the rocks. Boulders, once part of the sturdy ledge, now littered the beach below, some half-submerged in the tide, others shattered into unrecognizable rubble. Cascadia lowered her hands, watching me carefully.

"You're stronger than before," Vorago said when the elements had settled. "Stronger than I thought you could be."

My limbs shook. My ears rang. Adrenaline wreaked havoc on my body. Cascadia gave me a small, reassuring nod.

The gray clouds lingered. Gentle raindrops ran down my face. As I lowered the trident, movement caught my eye. Before I could react, a brute force knocked into me and took out my legs. I almost tumbled over the edge of the cliff.

I lay on the rocks, rain filling my eye sockets, Moby's furious face peering down at me. He was straddling me, his fist raised, his lips twisted in visceral disgust. "Coral is in there."

"What?" None of his words made sense.

"Coral came north," he shouted as the sun returned. "Because she was afraid of *you*. She went swimming. She's *out there*, Gal. In the ocean."

Oh, no. No, no, no, no.

CHAPTER TWENTY-TWO

"*S*he's out there, Gal. In the ocean," Moby repeated, his voice breaking over every word. He climbed off me, fists clenching and unclenching at his sides.

I scrambled to my feet, my limbs shaking as I glanced toward the restless sea. Waves churned against the base of the cliffs, their white foam hissing like whispers of accusation. Coral had come here because of me. I swallowed, trying to push down the rising panic. There was no time for regret.

"We'll find her," I said, gripping the trident. Moby gave me a dark glare and nodded curtly.

Without another word, I turned and leaped from the cliff's edge, the trident guiding my dive. I used its power to slow time, to give me a few extra precious seconds to save her life.

The shock of the cold struck me like a thousand needles, momentarily stealing my breath. Then I transitioned to my merman form and powered my tail, propelling myself downward, scanning the darkness for Coral.

The underwater world was a blur of blue and green shadows. Visibility was poor. The sea was still roiling from our earlier storm, the currents pulling and twisting. I focused on the trident, its glow cutting through the murk. A second splash followed—Moby, diving in close behind me.

Ripple appeared from nowhere, darting in frantic circles. His sleek body glimmered in the dim light as he chirped in distress. He guided us forward, weaving through jagged underwater rocks and patches of drifting seaweed. My pulse quickened as the water grew darker and colder the deeper we swam.

Then I saw her.

I lost my grip on time, precious seconds speeding past me.

Coral's body was trapped beneath a massive boulder, her pale form motionless, her blonde hair drifting in the currents, the seashells she always braided into it now floating loose. Bruises and gashes marred her arms and legs. My heart plummeted. No. *No, this can't be happening.*

Ripple let out a series of mournful squeaks. Moby surged past me, his gray selachii tail carving through the water, his face contorted with fury and anguish. He gripped the edge of the boulder and strained against it, bubbles streaming from his gills as he screamed in frustration. The rock wouldn't budge.

I swam to his side, signaling for him to stop. He shook his head, refusing, his desperate thoughts filling my head louder than thunder.

"I can use the trident," I yelled over his telepathic bombardment.

His glare burned into me for a second longer before he moved back. I swirled the trident as I channeled strength and focus into it.

The ocean calmed, the currents stilling. Golden tendrils wrapped around the boulder. Slowly, the massive stone began to shift. It groaned as it lifted inch by inch, sending silt and debris spiraling into the water. Moby darted forward, grabbing Coral and pulling her free.

The moment she was out, the boulder dropped with a thud that sent shockwaves rippling through the water. Flicking my tail against the unruly currents, I grabbed Moby's arm, and together we kicked upward, Coral's lifeless body cradled between us. The surface seemed impossibly far away, but we didn't stop. We couldn't stop.

We erupted past the surface, the sound of crashing surf and Moby's desperate pleas filling my ears. The sun beat down on us, no sign of the earlier storm. A beautiful day. Except for what had occurred beneath the waves.

We dragged Coral onto a nearby sandbar. Her body was so cold. So limp. So blue. I already knew it was too late. Ripple crawled onto her chest, nudging her face with desperate squeals.

"Coral!" Moby shouted, his voice cracking. He shook her gently. "Coral, wake up! Please, wake up!"

She didn't move.

I kneeled beside them, placing my hand over her heart. Nothing. Not even a faint pulse. Reality slammed into me. I had caused this. My obsession with power, my negligence—it had driven her away, driven her to this.

I crouched over her and performed CPR. Showed Moby how to press her chest. I breathed life into her lungs, hoping against hope. The two of us worked together. Seconds passed. Then minutes. Then too much time. Time that I couldn't control.

I glanced at the cliffs. Vorago, Tempest, and Cascadia remained, staring impassively, as if they'd had nothing to do with this. But I couldn't blame them. This was my island. And it was my power that had caused this.

"Gal, do something!" Moby shook my arm. "You have the trident. You're supposed to be a god now, aren't you? Surely you can do something?!"

I shook my head. "It doesn't work like that." I hated the words. I hated crushing Moby's soul. I hated all of this.

"Then what good are you? What good is that?" He pointed at the trident.

I had been testing my power so I could save those I loved. But I was no savior. I wasn't a god. I was a man who had failed.

"Useless," I whispered, picturing Una in my mind. She would never forgive me.

Moby's eyes widened in disbelief before narrowing with rage. He shoved me hard, sending me sprawling into the shallow water. "You *can't?!*" he roared. "You're the one who caused this! You're the reason she's dead!"

I didn't fight back. I couldn't. He was right.

Ripple pawed at Coral's still form. Moby collapsed next to her, burying his face in his hands as sobs wracked his body. The sound was gut-wrenching, cutting deeper than any wound.

I kneeled in the water. The trident dimmed. A third chip appeared on a second prong. The storm inside me was gone, replaced by a hollow, aching silence.

There was no coming back from this. I had broken the trust of everyone I loved. And now Coral was gone.

An icy wind froze the blood in my veins. It stilled the beat of my heart. It stole my will to live. But I couldn't avoid this, couldn't slink away, couldn't pretend it wasn't my fault.

"We should take her home," I said.

"Not yet."

Tears spilled down his face and mingled with the ocean lapping at our feet. He lifted Coral's lifeless body into his arms and howled at the sky. I glanced at the cliffs once more. The gods were gone.

Anger swelled inside me, but it was quickly replaced by guilt. I had nowhere to direct my anger but at myself.

Hours passed with me sitting near Coral's body, my knees

buried in wet sand, cold water kissing my ankles. Moby sat opposite me, rocking Coral's body, whispering to her as he moved her wet hair away from her pale face.

I swept my gaze over her face. So white. So bruised. So broken. Her long blonde hair was still tangled with loose seashells. Ripple lay next to her, keening plaintive whimpers every few minutes. The sight twisted something deep inside me. I had done this. No one else. Me.

"We have to take her back," I said quietly.

Moby's head snapped up, eyes bloodshot and burning with fury. "No! I'm not...ready." His voice hitched on the last word, and he clutched Coral to his chest.

"The rest of your family needs to know," I said. Even if they disowned me.

Moby's nostrils flared. "Don't act like you're doing this for them. You're doing it for you. So you can pretend you're not a monster."

I flinched, then swallowed the retort that formed on my tongue. He wasn't wrong. Maybe part of me did want to lessen my guilt, to face Una and Bay and Maya and Trent, to apologize. But it would never be enough. And it wouldn't bring her back.

I let the silence settle between us again. The rhythm of the waves filled the void, steady and endless. Time seemed to stretch, each second dragging into an eternity. Sand coated my skin. Wind tugged at my hair. Salt stung my flesh.

The voice didn't need to torment me. I could do that all by myself.

The wind shifted, carrying the faint scent of salt and seaweed. The tide crept closer, gentle swells washing over Coral's feet. Ripple slept in a ball on her chest. My throat tightened. I couldn't swallow. My mouth was filled with sand.

I lowered my gaze to the trident half buried in the wet sand.

MARISA NOELLE

Not only were there now three chips, but its golden sheen lacked luster, as if its power was fading, as if it too was overcome by sadness.

I stood and walked over to Moby, touched his shoulder. "Come on."

Moby didn't answer, just stared at me with a blank, pleading look. Then he got to his feet. He scooped Coral into his arms. His movements were tender, almost reverent, as if he feared breaking her fragile form. Ripple curled protectively around her neck.

I raised the trident. A tremor ran through the metal, as if it could feel my determination, responding to my touch. I focused on a mental image of the Summer's family home. The place where her parents had raised her, where she'd spent countless summers laughing and swimming in the shallows with Ripple by her side.

Golden light surrounded us. The sea and sky blurred, the sandbar fading into nothingness. We floated in a void of shimmering gold, suspended between worlds, but it only lasted seconds.

With a rush of displaced air, we reappeared on the lawn in front of the Summers' house. White plaster. Terracotta roof. Figurines of geckos by the door. A pot of water to wash off sandy feet. It looked the same. But it would never be the same again.

I took a step forward, lowering the trident so it dangled from my hand. The sound of the ocean faded to a soft murmur behind us. Moby kicked the door open. People were gathered inside. They turned to stare.

My gaze collided with Una's. Her face crumpled when she saw me, fast, silent tears slipping out of her beautiful blue eye.

Moby choked on a sob and moved into the room.

Bay blocked my entry. "You're not welcome here."

254

"Let him in," Maya said, moving her son aside.

Trent couldn't seem to manage words. He stared at me, his face pale under his tan, his curls tangled as if he'd been running his hands through them constantly.

"I'm sorry," I said, but there was barely any volume to my words.

Moby laid Coral on a couch. He brushed a strand of hair from her face, his fingers lingering as if reluctant to let go. Ripple whimpered but remained glued to her side.

Bay shook his head. "What have you done?"

Una's shoulders hunched, deep sobs wracking her petite frame.

Maya rushed to Coral's side and kneeled beside her, her head bowing as she shed tears and clasped her dead daughter's hands.

Una launched herself at me, using every aspect of her vicious selachii side, scratching my face, pulling my hair, slamming punches into my ribs. I stood there and took it all until Trent pulled her off me.

"Una! Stop!" Trent yelled, holding her back. But it didn't stop her from kicking out.

"How could you?" Una screamed at me. That was the end. I knew it then. She could never forgive me. But that was okay. I had a different path to pursue. As long as she was safe, that was all that mattered.

Trent put her down, but she came at me again.

"I'm sorry," I said again, owning the words, holding her arms so she couldn't attack.

Una twisted out of my grasp. "The Architect isn't even real!" She hurled the words at me, the tendons on her neck standing rigid, her face flushed.

My stomach went into freefall. "What are you talking about?"

"Cascadia was here earlier," Una said, jabbing a finger in the air with every word. "She said Vorago was using you. Trying to get the power to consume you so he could steal the trident. But when Coral...died...she knew it had gone too far. She confirmed the constellation was a natural change, that the tides were shifting, and that there is no voice! *There is no fucking Architect!*"

The room spun. The floor rushed up to meet me. I stumbled, caught myself before I fell. "But there has to be." Coral's death had to mean something. I had lost my friends, my family, my *wife*. For nothing? For the ego of one god?

Tears spilled down Una's cheeks. "No, Gal. It's just you."

I gaped at her. Felt the wound of her words opening me up. A gash that split me in two from head to foot and eviscerated my heart. It may have stopped beating. I didn't care. The pain I had caused Una was unforgivable. I deserved everything she dished out.

Trent slipped into a chair, just staring at us. He must have been in shock.

Una collapsed against me, her head falling to meet my chest. Moby and Maya continued to sit with Coral. Bay stared at me from across the room, his arms crossed, looking as if he wanted to summon his new abilities.

I folded one arm around Una's waist and pressed a kiss to the top of her head. Breathed in her jasmine and salt and ocean scent. Wished I could take it all back.

I closed my eyes. "I'm so sorry, Una. I never meant to hurt you."

She sobbed, then pushed away from me, reeling across the other side of the room. Bay put a protective arm around her.

I forced myself to look at Coral one last time. There was nothing else I could do here. Nothing more I could say.

I walked out the front door.

Before the door shut behind me, someone came after me. Bay. I turned to face him.

"I don't know what to say to you," he said, his voice so much calmer than I had been expecting.

I shrugged. "I've probably already thought it."

"Do you even care?"

"Care?" I lurched forward. "Of course I fucking *care*. That's the reason I've done all this." I splayed a hand at the night encroaching on the gardens, attempting to indicate everything beyond.

"You broke her heart."

"Everything I've done is for her."

Bay crossed his arms. "I knew you couldn't be trusted."

I sighed, rubbed the back of my neck. "This is a pointless argument, Bay. We've been here before."

He took a step toward me. "She's pregnant."

"Who?"

"Una, *you fucking asshole*, who did you think I meant?"

I frowned, my stomach climbing into my throat. "We were using the herbs."

"That's what she said."

I glanced at the house, watched a moth flitting by the hanging lantern. I couldn't remember the last time I'd taken the herbs. With everything that had been happening...it had totally slipped my mind. Had Una forgotten too? Had she done it on purpose? Did it even matter?

"Is it mine?"

A bitter laugh erupted out of Bay. "You really are too much. You piece of shit." He came at me, but Maya rushed out of the doorway, grabbed his fist before he launched it at me.

"Go inside, Bay."

"Mom—"

"*Go inside*. Your sister needs you."

Bay's shoulders dropped and he ducked his head. With one hand on the door, he shot me a glance over his shoulder. I'd never seen so much fury in one expression.

Maya stepped into the night with me. "Thank you for bringing her back."

"It was the least I could do."

She dug her hand into her pocket and removed an object. Then pressed it into my palm.

"What is it?" I asked, inspecting the ornate brooch with a large purple stone at its center.

"Esmerelda's brooch," Maya said. "Una found it in my jewelry box. I'd almost forgotten about it. My instinct says you'll need it."

I didn't know how the brooch of a long-dead High Council member could help me, but now wasn't the time to be ungrateful, so I shoved it into my pocket.

"Is there really no Architect?" I asked.

Maya inhaled a deep breath, as if she were attempting to control her emotions. "That's what Cascadia said. But I don't know if I trust any of them."

Then what was the fucking voice?

"And there's nothing in the book?"

Maya shook her head.

"And Una is pregnant?"

This time she nodded.

I didn't know what to do with that information.

I wanted to hug Maya. I wanted her to forgive me for killing her youngest daughter. I wanted her to tell me everything was going to be okay like I was five years old again.

"Okay," I said, and walked away, my feet crunching against the pebbles.

I didn't look back. I couldn't.

CHAPTER TWENTY-THREE

*I*ce erupted from the ocean. Jagged spikes of frozen crystal now lined the desolate eastern coast all the way to the obsidian monolith that had trapped Maelstrom. I arced the trident once more. More ice spikes appeared in the shallows, rising out of the ocean like the gnashing teeth in the maw of a monster.

Black sand. Granite rocks. Ice spikes.

Sunlight pounded the back of my neck, but did nothing to ease the tension I stored there.

Another swoop of the trident. An icy wave crested over the rocks and swallowed my feet. Sea spray rose in chilling bursts, carried on a restless wind that tugged at my hair and soaked my clothes. Goosebumps pebbled my skin and chased some of the numbness away. Better.

I stared at the rolling sea. This part of the island had always felt forgotten, untouched by the vibrant life of the southern shores. Now, it was the only place that mirrored the emptiness inside me.

I lowered myself to a weathered rock and laid the trident across my knees. Its chipped prongs—four of them now—scolded me for all my bad choices, reminded me of all my failures. Coral's face haunted my mind—her pale skin, her unseeing eyes, the seashells drifting from her hair.

Footsteps crunched behind me. I stiffened, but didn't turn around. There was no one I wanted to see.

"Gal." Cascadia's voice carried on the wind. "You've been hiding here for days."

"Not hiding," I muttered. "Just...thinking."

"You blame yourself." She lowered herself to an opposite rock and leaned toward me, her hands on her thighs. "But it's not all on you."

I snorted. "Isn't it? I was the one who pushed the power too far. I'm the reason Coral is dead."

"Vorago and Tempest manipulated you," she said. "They used your fear of the Architect to control you."

My head snapped up. "Why wouldn't I be afraid of the Architect? It has the power to destroy us all."

Guilt flashed across her face, and everything I'd been avoiding facing by coming here came slamming back. My chest tightened. I struggled for breath. I dropped my head into my hands.

"Please tell me the Architect is real," I said. "It *has* to be. Coral didn't die for nothing."

"The Architect is *not* real," Cascadia said.

I winced. I had been played like a fool. Maybe I should leave Atlantis. Why had I bothered staying this long? A kernel of hope remained. But hope for what? Coral was dead. Una would never forgive me.

"Vorago invented the threat to push you toward complete surrender. He's desperate to reclaim the trident. With you pushing your limits, he was hoping the trident would reject you and no longer see you as worthy to wield it."

"What?" I glanced at the lightweight metal weapon in my lap. "You're lying."

"I'm not." She touched my knee. "I've been complicit in their plan. I'm sorry. My brothers...they're stronger than me. I wasn't brave enough to go against them. And I will always regret that. It is my job to protect all the ocean creatures. Coral was one of those creatures. It is my failure as much as yours."

"What about the voice?"

Cascadia's expression filled with pity. "I expect that is your own conscience."

Even my own conscience didn't agree with my actions. *Jesus fucking Christ.*

I lurched to my feet and paced along the cliff's edge. "So, everything was for nothing? All of this...Coral's *death*, the destruction...just a game to Vorago?"

"It wasn't a game," Cascadia said, following me with her eyes. "At least not to me. He believes the trident is his. He can't see past that. And he will stop at nothing to get it."

"And then what?" I asked. "Does he want to smite us all? Remove us from his island? Take it for himself? He was the one who created it for us!"

Cascadia stood to face me. "He wants to be worshiped once more."

"Has he not seen the piles of offerings lining the path to your house? Is he not aware of the new temples scattered across the island? The daily services held? The requests for blessings?" I swept a hand inland.

"He believes power is the most important thing. And that he should be the most powerful. He is the original god of the ocean, after all. And he worries with you wielding the trident, people won't revere him in the same way."

"He's a fucking *god*." I slapped my chest. "I'm just a man trying to grapple with too many abilities."

She paused, her gaze falling over the desolate landscape. "And then there is Tempest. He is tired of living in Vorago's shadow. He wants the trident for himself."

"I *knew* it." But having the suspicion confirmed didn't change anything. "What am I supposed to do? Walk away? Leave them to it?"

"No, Gal," Cascadia said, approaching me once more, her expression full of useless sympathy. "You know that's not the answer. That's not why the trident chose you."

I shoved my hand into my pocket, felt the mermaid brooch. I pulled it from my pocket and held it up. The ornate piece of jewelry glimmered, the purple stone at its center swirling like a miniature ocean. "Maya gave me this. What is it?"

Cascadia tensed, shock evident on her face. "That's Esmerelda's brooch. It contains the Essence of the Ocean. The same power that created the Power of the Sea. I thought it had been lost."

I stared at the brooch, its weight suddenly heavier in my hand. The wind howled across the eastern cliffs, carrying with it the scent of damp stone. "And what does that mean?"

"It can only be unlocked by a god," she said, excitement flashing in her eyes. "But once unlocked, it can grant its wielder immense power. Enough to challenge Vorago and Tempest. But not at the same time."

"They're not going to stand there and wait their turn," I said, staring past her at the sea, at the endless horizon that offered no answers. "They both want the trident. They're going to fight together."

Cascadia placed her hands over mine, squeezed them around the brooch. "You won't have to. I'll give you my grace."

I frowned. "Your grace? What are you talking about?"

"My godly essence," she replied. "It will strengthen you

enough to face both my brothers. But...it comes at a cost. I'll cease to exist."

The words hit like a rogue wave, knocking the air from my lungs. "No." I shook my head. "I'm not letting you do that. You must stay and be Atlantis' god after this is all over."

Cascadia's lips curled into a small, wistful smile. "No, Gal. *You* will be their god. By taking my essence, by ingesting the Essence of the Ocean, you will achieve ascension. It's how it was meant to be."

"I don't want it," I said flatly, squeezing my fingers around the hard edges of the brooch. "I mean, I'll take it so I can deal with Vorago and Tempest, but then I'm giving up the god stuff. I don't want it. I don't need it. It's done nothing but brought harm to everyone I love."

"We should never have awoken." A shadow crossed her face, regret carved into the delicate lines of her features. She dropped her hands. "We should have stayed in slumber. And we should never have returned." She lifted her gaze back to mine, something like sorrow shining in her ocean-blue eyes. "I need to atone for what I have done. By giving you my grace, I can do that."

My throat tightened. Suddenly I was freezing, and my body was wracked with uncontrollable shudders. I searched her face for any sign of doubt, but there was none. "There has to be another way."

She placed a hand on my cheek, her touch warm and comforting. "Don't carry more guilt than you have to. You're a protector. It's time to finish this."

She was resolved. Tears stung my eyes. "Okay. But I'll never forgive myself for this."

"There is nothing to forgive." Cascadia stepped back, lifting her hands, and the glow of her godly essence surrounded her like the light of a dying star. The brooch pulsed in response, a deep, humming power that vibrated through my bones. The stone at its center cracked, and the force that had been trapped for centuries rushed toward me in an overwhelming flood of brilliant purple light. It reminded me of Una's orb of Spirit and Soul and brought a brief smile to my face. *Una*.

Heat flashed over my skin. Warmth caressed my limbs. The wind died. The waves stilled. Time itself seemed to hold its breath. The power coursed through me. I gasped, staggering under its intensity. When I glanced at my body, my veins glowed golden and pulsed with radiant light.

Cascadia stepped forward and gathered her hands in mine once more. "Look at me, Gal."

I met her determined gaze. She didn't allow me to look away. Love filled her eyes, her face, her expression. Without warning, she started to fade, as though she were only a copy of herself, and a gentle pressure moved against my body.

Panic tightened my chest. "Cascadia! Wait—"

She shook her dissolving head, smiling as golden mist curled around her like the final breath of a setting sun. "You can do this, Gal. Have faith."

The pressure found a way inside me, somehow seeping through my pores, and combined with the power from Esmerelda's brooch. The light inside me flared. Molten fire flashed through my veins. My limbs glowed golden.

Cascadia was nearly gone, her form little more than shimmering particles.

I reached for her, but my fingers passed through empty air.

"Thank you, Gal," her voice echoed. "Save our world."

And then she was gone.

The ocean roared below, wild and free, as if mourning her sacrifice.

I stood alone on the cliff, the power of the ocean and the

gods surging within me. I would not waste it. Vorago and Tempest would pay for everything they had done.

I would finish this.

I TELEPORTED to the northern coast and stormed along the cliff paths searching for Vorago and Tempest. My senses were heightened, Cascadia's grace streaming through me. Although her essence brought more calm than I'd experienced...ever...it wasn't enough to drown my fury.

I had been played. I had been duped. I had been made a fool of. And I had lost the people closest to me because of it. It was anger that had fueled my mission to find Zale. And I would use it again now to bring down Vorago and Tempest. They no longer deserved to set foot on Atlantis. They no longer deserved to exist.

Every step I took cracked the ground beneath me, ice creeping along the edges of the cliffs with each furious stride. Golden light trailed from my body.

Vorago and Tempest had to be here. This was where we'd trained, where they'd pushed me beyond my limits. But the cliffs were empty, only a single seagull present to mock me, and only memories of Coral's death in the water below.

"Where are you?" I called, shouting over the wind. I clenched the trident until my knuckles turned white.

I scanned the horizon one last time before teleporting to the cavern. The air shimmered, and I reappeared in the heart of the training grounds. The chamber exhaled a deep, hollow silence, the stone walls slick with moisture, their bioluminescent lights pulsing with a warning. The light I emitted filled the space. I called their names, my voice bouncing off the rock, my rage startling the silence, but there was no response. Only the steady drip of water echoed back.

"Cowards," I hissed.

The trident crackled in agreement. Then I noted one of the chips had repaired itself. And a second wasn't half as big. I smiled. I must have been doing something right. Gripping the shaft, I ran my hand along the cool metal, whispering sweet nothings to the only thing I had ever been able to depend on. We were a team. An equal partnership. Together we would end Vorago's rule.

Together.

The voice was back. And this time, I knew it belonged to me. It had been my own internal doubt all along. But now it was my determination.

I slammed the butt of the trident against the floor, sending a shockwave rippling through the cavern, shattering several stalactites. I would never come here again.

Teleporting again, I appeared near the palace. Guards and civilians scattered as I strode through the grounds, my body radiating heat and light. My veins burned with golden fire, Cascadia's power woven with the Essence of the Ocean. People stared, their whispers sharp and fearful. I caught fragments of their murmurs:

"Is that Gal?"

"He's glowing..."

"Where has he been?"

"Looks like he's about to explode."

"Is he here for Vorago's ceremony?"

There would be no fucking ceremony to honor *him*.

I pressed forward through the palace gardens, the cobble pathways cracking beneath my bare feet. But again, no sign of Vorago or Tempest. They weren't here. They'd vanished, leaving me to prowl the island like a caged predator.

I stood by a fountain, scanning the clumps of people for the telltale sign of silver flowing hair, or dreadlocks and a mocking smirk. But they wouldn't hide. They were far too arrogant for that.

Someone touched the back of my knee. I pivoted on my heel, swinging the trident, ready to obliterate my opponent. But it was only a small child, gazing at me in wonder, at shards of light pulsing from my body.

I lowered the trident, pulled back the power.

"Are you real?" he asked.

I forced a smile, then took in the roundness of his cheeks, the amazement in his brown eyes, the innocence in his expression, and my smile became genuine.

I fell to one knee and lifted the child to sit on it. "Yes, I'm real. And I'm here to keep you safe."

The child smiled, then leaped off my knee and dashed to a woman hovering a few yards away. She clutched his hand, tilted her head to listen to her child blurt stories about golden light, but kept her uncertain gaze trained on me.

Another survey of the gardens told me Vorago wasn't there. I needed answers. Without bothering to rise to my feet, I swung the trident and teleported away. I landed outside Uncle Dylan's bar, which was only on the other side of the palace and across the courtyard. I shoved the door open, and the room fell into an uneasy silence.

Every patron turned to stare. The golden glow emanating from my skin caught the polished wooden walls, bathing the room in shifting patterns of light. My veins shimmered beneath my skin. Conversations died. People edged away from their tables. Even the sea wolf rug by the hearth looked fearful.

Dylan stood behind the bar, both hands planted on the counter, his hazel eyes following my every move. "Gal," he said in a low voice. "You're causing a scene."

I didn't reply, my gaze sweeping the room. The tension was thick enough to choke on. Even the most seasoned regulars looked ready to bolt.

Uncle Dylan stepped around the bar and approached me cautiously. "You're glowing like a damn beacon. If you're not careful, you're going to start a riot."

"Let them stare," I said, but my voice had none of the edge I'd intended. "I'm looking for Vorago and Tempest. They're not anywhere on the island."

Dylan sighed and crossed his arms. "And you thought tearing through every corner of Atlantis was the best way to find them? You're scaring people, Gal."

Frustration clawed at my insides as I fought the urge to snap. The door opened behind me, and I turned to see Ford. His gaze flicked from me to Uncle Dylan, then around the room. He took in the tension, the wary looks, and gave a slow nod.

"Gal," Ford said. "You need to take a breath. You're radiating so much energy it's a wonder the building hasn't caught fire."

I signaled my understanding with a tight jerk of my chin. "They're hiding from me, Ford. They know what they've done, and they're hiding."

He approached and stood before me. Time ticked on as we stared at each other. He was the one I'd looked up to when my father was lost. He was the one who'd taught me how to fight. He was the one who treated me like a son. He was the one I always looked to for approval. And I needed it now. *Goddamn, did I need it now.*

His gaze scanned my body, taking in the pulses of light, the glowing veins, the wild red hair.

"Your eyes are nothing but light."

I didn't know that. I hadn't stopped to look in a mirror.

He placed a hand on my chest, bracing as if the touch might kill him.

"I'm still me."

Ford nodded, left his hand on my chest, his touch grounding me, providing an anchor. "You have ascended."

"I have."

He clutched both my shoulders. "They'll show themselves. You don't need to rampage across the island to draw them out. Go somewhere you can think clearly."

"And where would that be?" I asked.

"The mountain," he said without hesitation. "You're most comfortable surrounded by snow and ice. Let me get word to them. If they want a confrontation, they'll come to you there."

The fire in my veins cooled. Ford was right. I couldn't keep charging around blindly. "That's a good idea."

"And it will protect the citizens," Ford said.

I nodded. The mountain was in the middle of the island. Isolated. Desolate. Private. No Atlantean would come to harm.

Ford gestured to the swords that were always strapped to his back. "I can come with you. But I fear I won't be much use."

"No. No one else is going to risk their life. You stay here and keep people safe."

"I'm proud of you." Ford shook my hand. I didn't have time to process the thought. It seemed too unreal to be true. "Now go. Before you accidentally blow this place to pieces."

I gave him a curt nod and turned to leave. The patrons parted, giving me a wide berth as I made my way to the door.

"Wait!" Uncle Dylan called, dashing around the bar and winding a path through the tables. He threw his arms around me. Surprised by the rare display of physical affection, I stumbled back, choking on emotion. He pulled back. "You can do this. I believe in you."

"Thank you," I said. At least I had one person on my side. Two if I counted Ford. I wouldn't let myself think about anyone else. Not until this was over.

"Don't do anything stupid," he called after me.

I paused at the threshold, glancing over my shoulder. "No promises."

The door swung shut behind me and I stepped into the courtyard. Insects buzzed around the vines, and the grapes had come into season, fat and juicy and round. There would be a good wine this year. If everything went well, I might get to drink some.

Not a single cloud marred the blue expanse of the sky. And not a single sail interrupted the straight line of the horizon. The salty breeze carried the scent of the ocean, mingling with the faint aroma of sun-warmed fruit. The heat of the day pressed down on my shoulders, but a colder weight settled in my gut. I stretched my fingers, feeling for the trident's familiar pulse. The world stood still, waiting.

It was a fine day for a battle.

It is.

I closed my eyes and teleported to the mountain, a rush of cold air greeting me as I landed on a rocky outcrop. The shift in temperature was instant, the sharp bite of winter carving through my skin. Snow stretched as far as I could see, blanketing the ground in pristine white, only to be interrupted by the occasional group of boulders. Fir trees stood in solemn ranks, their branches heavy with snow, creaking in the breeze. I spotted the footprints of an animal. Maybe a fox. That made me think of Ripple. And of how distraught the sea otter was. But that was why I was here. To avenge Coral's death.

I took a deep breath, the air crisp and biting, filling my lungs with an icy burn that fueled my strength. This was my element.

This is where I belonged. This is where I was strongest, where the world felt clean and unburdened.

I had no idea if I would survive what was coming. But I was damn well going to make sure Cascadia's grace and Coral's death counted for something.

CHAPTER TWENTY-FOUR

ind howled across the frozen peaks, whipping
snow into my face, tearing through my clothes. I
hardly felt it. The ice, the silence, the brutal bite of the mountain air—this was where I belonged. The trident pulsed. Snow
landed on my shoulders. My breath misted in the frigid air,
curling like smoke before vanishing into nothing.

A shift in the atmosphere made my spine stiffen.

You can't defeat two gods.

Yes, I can.

Even though I knew the voice did not belong to the Architect, I refused to listen to its doubts. I could unpack my delicate
psychological state after the battle.

I turned just as a vortex of water and lightning swirled
through the sky. The vortex spiraled, then took shape, molding
itself into two towering figures. Vorago and Tempest. They
landed on the ridge above me, their forms wreathed in
elemental fury. Vorago's dark armor gleamed like wet stone, his
aquamarine eyes burning with silent rage. Beside him, Tempest
stood with crackling electricity skimming over his hands, his
smirk sharp and hungry.

I secured my grip on the trident. "Took you long enough."

Vorago stepped forward, his intimidating stride swallowing the space between us. The snow beneath his feet melted into steaming puddles. "You were expecting us."

I squared my shoulders. "I know the truth now, Vorago. The Architect isn't real."

His face remained impassive, but I caught the smallest flicker of tension in his jaw.

"You lied to me," I went on. "You used me. Used my people. You twisted my life apart for your own gain."

The words cut as I said them, guilt carving deeper into me with every syllable. A bitter laugh escaped me before I could stop it. "But I did that on my own, didn't I?"

Tempest arched a brow, his grin widening like he was enjoying the show. "Self-awareness looks good on you. But the golden light is a little *holier than thou*, don't you think?"

I ignored him, locking eyes with Vorago. "You wanted the trident all along. That's what this was really about." I shook my head. "What happened to you? You created this island for your people. For the ocean shifters. Out of love. And now look at you. Full of rage and self-righteousness. Was the people's love for you not enough? Their devotion? Their respect? What. Happened. To. You?"

"The people lost the island," Vorago growled. "What was the point in me staying around after that? After everything I had done for them. And so I went to sleep. And when I woke...there were humans on my island! *My island!* That I created for ocean shifters. The disrespect of you all cannot go unpunished."

"Unpunished? We're not children. We have free will. It's a shame the Architect isn't real. It would be a far better ruler than you."

Vorago's face flushed with rage. "You wait until I get my hands on that trident."

"If your brother doesn't try to get it first." My gaze slid to Tempest, whose smirk faltered. "You want it too, don't you? More power. More than your brother. More than anyone."

Tempest rolled his shoulders. "And why shouldn't I? What makes you think you deserve it?" His gaze flicked over me, filled with barely hidden disdain. "You're not even one of us. You may have the Essence of the Ocean. You may have stolen our sister's grace. You may now be a god. But you'll never be one of us."

Vorago's fists curled at his sides, his knuckles white. "You betray me, Tempest?" His voice was calm. Too calm. A frozen lake waiting to crack. "You know what happens to those who betray me."

Tempest tilted his head. "You taught me to take power where I can find it, brother." His lips curled. "The trident forsook you. It is mine for the taking."

Vorago's gaze darkened. The air between them thickened. The tension stretched until breaking point. The eye of the storm.

"We will regain the trident," Vorago said to his brother. "And then we shall see who shall wield it."

"So it's like that, then?" I planted my feet to prepare for the fight. "The two of you against me, and then you turn on each other?"

"It didn't have to be." Vorago shifted his attention back to me. "We could have ruled together, Gal. You and I. But you've made your decision."

"I already have a father," I snarled. "And an uncle. And a wife. I don't need you."

"Suit yourself." Vorago glowered at me. "What a waste."

He didn't mean a word of it. But that was how far his manipulation extended. Maybe he believed his own lies. Even now he was toying with me. But I wouldn't be taken in by his pretty words again.

I raised the trident. The wind shrieked, picking up loose shards of ice and hurling them into the air. Snow churned into a whirling blizzard, obscuring everything beyond the three of us. The temperature plummeted, frost crackling against my skin as the mountain braced for war.

Lightning split the sky, jagged streaks arcing between the storm clouds above, casting eerie shadows across the icy slopes. The ground beneath my feet groaned, the permafrost cracking. Pressure pressed against my bones, hammered against my ribs.

Tempest took a step forward, his boots crunching against the ice, his smirk widening. "I was hoping we'd get here." He spread his arms, palms crackling with electricity. "Let's see what you've really got, Gal."

Vorago lifted his hand and a wave surged from the nothingness of the storm, a towering wall of water that shouldn't have existed this high in the mountains. It curled and twisted, alive with his command, waiting to be unleashed.

I braced myself, clinging to the trident. The storm lashed around me, but I stood firm.

Let them come.

The first strike came from Tempest. A bolt of lightning ripped toward me. I swung the trident up just as it struck. The impact rattled through me, my muscles locking against the force, the metal of the trident glowing white-hot where the bolt had connected. Snow exploded outward, sending ice and rock flying.

Vorago followed, unleashing the tidal wave with a flick of his wrist. It surged toward me. I flung out my hand, freezing it in place, drawing on my cryo-aquaism. But the sheer size of it pushed me to my knees as I struggled to control the volume of pressure surging toward me. Finally, after a few seconds, the entire wave froze, but I could hear the ice cracking under the force of the restrained power.

Vorago flicked his hand a second time. More water surged over the frozen crest. It hit like a hammer, slamming me backward, the force lifting me off my feet. Water and ice crashed over me, freezing and suffocating all at once. I twisted, forcing the trident's power outward, the golden glow erupting around me in a shockwave.

The water split into two channels, streaming either side of me. I landed hard on the ice but rolled back onto my feet. My body burned with both adrenaline and power.

They came at me again.

I met them head-on.

I called on the ice beneath us. The permafrost surged upward, jagged spears of frozen earth launching toward Vorago. He twisted his hands, and the water around him solidified into shields, blocking my attack. Tempest, undeterred, shot another bolt of lightning. But I was ready. I slowed time, enough to step out of its direct path. The bolt carved a molten scar across the ice where I had stood, but I was already countering, spinning toward him with a stream of freezing wind that blasted his side.

He stumbled, cursing, but recovered quickly. His hands snapped forward, and arcs of electricity danced through the blizzard. I felt the charge in the air before the storm detonated, a flash of white light enveloping us all.

The bolt crashed into the ice inches to my left, sending serrated cracks racing across the frozen ground. I launched myself forward, thrusting the trident. A spiraling column of ice erupted in Tempest's path, forcing him to leap aside.

Vorago was on me in an instant, wielding the entire ocean. Or so it seemed. A whip of water thrashed out, cracking like a lash against my stomach, the impact sending me skidding backward. Blood poured down my side. My breath came in ragged pants.

I hit the ice and rolled, bracing myself before another wave crashed down from above. It felt like every muscle and bone in my body was bruised. But adrenaline had me leaping to my feet once more.

I faced the wave. This wasn't just water. This was the ocean in its most violent form, a force of nature bending to Vorago's will.

I slammed the trident into the ice. Frost exploded in a circle around me, freezing the water in midair. Vorago rolled his wrist, shattering the ice into a thousand shards, but it gave me the fraction of a second I needed. I launched myself high into the air, twisting as I came down, bringing the trident in a wide arc toward him. A shockwave of freezing wind burst from the weapon, slamming into Vorago with enough force to send him staggering.

A surge of electricity struck me from the side, pain ripping through my body. Tempest. He grinned as he sprinted toward me, hands wreathed in lightning. He moved fast, faster than before. Too fast.

I narrowed my focus. Ignored my bloody wounds. Slowed time. Tempest's movements became sluggish, the arcs of lightning stretching in unhurried ways through the air. I stepped aside as he lunged, gripping the trident with both hands. A wall of ice erupted between us, but as I released time back to its normal speed, Tempest shattered it in an explosion of energy, sending frozen shards flying in every direction. One clipped my cheek, slicing through skin.

"Impressive," Tempest admitted, wiping a trickle of blood from his lip. "But you can't stop us both."

"Watch me."

The storm raged, the elements turning the battlefield into a wasteland of ruined rock and ice. Vorago summoned a wave taller than the cliffs, and Tempest sent a barrage of lightning surging through it, turning the water into a glowing wall of destruction.

The sheer force of their combined power sent tremors through the mountain. I dug my feet into the ice, bracing for the onslaught.

Una. Coral. Dad. Ford. Ember. Uncle D. Aunt Raina. Aunt Marina. Grams. Pops. Maya. Trent. Moby. Jordan. Ash. Cyra. And even Bay. I whispered all the names of the people I loved. I let fear wash through me, accepting it was there, didn't try to fight against it.

The moment the wave crashed toward me, I dove forward, sinking into the oceanic force, letting it take me. I shifted as soon as my body hit water. My legs fused together, the power of my merman form taking hold. The trident pulsed as I spun through the depths, weaving between the deadly currents.

Tempest's lightning crackled through the water, electrifying the ocean. I twisted, feeling the static burn through my veins, my body screaming from the onslaught. But this was my domain too. I sped forward, gripping the trident tight, propelling myself toward him.

I broke the surface in a blast of freezing water, ice shards flaring off my skin like shattered glass. My lungs seized, my body still twitching from the remnants of Tempest's electricity. The storm howled, trying to trap me, but I was already moving, already locking onto him.

Tempest hovered midair, lightning dancing across his fingers, his eyes alight with power. His hand snapped forward, and a bolt tore toward me—blinding, searing, meant to end me.

But I was faster.

I leaped into the air, water coiling around me, the trident an extension of my will. I slowed time and then I flung the glowing weapon forward with all my strength, spinning it like a spear, its golden light a burning star against the storm's fury.

Tempest saw it too late. His eyes widened. He moved, but he wasn't fast enough.

The trident struck him square in the chest.

Time snapped back into focus.

Tempest jerked backward, his body arching. Electricity erupted from him in chaotic, uncontrolled waves. The storm convulsed as his power fractured. A guttural scream ripped from his throat. His power detonated in wild, uncontrolled bursts.

He clawed at the trident embedded in him, fingers sparking wildly, but the ice had already spread.

I clenched my fist, pouring everything into the cold, calling upon the frozen abyss that lived inside me. The storm was mine now. The ice was mine. It coursed through me, freezing him from the inside out.

Frost climbed his limbs, his lightning flickering, faltering, dying. His eyes snapped to mine—shock, rage, and then something else appeared in his blown pupils. Something closer to fear.

His lips parted, but no words followed. Only a shuddering breath.

Then, with a final pulse of power, he shattered.

A thousand frozen shards scattered into the wind, swept away into the howling void. The crackling echoes of his power lingered for a heartbeat before being swallowed by the storm.

I exhaled sharply. My arms ached. My body trembled. My thoughts emptied. There was no time to think. No time to recover. I called the trident back to my hand, and it slammed into my palm with loving grace.

A roar split the air—deep, furious, unyielding.

Vorago.

He stood on the rim of a boulder, his eyes ablaze with banked rage. Water coiled and twisted around his arms, forming deadly currents ready to strike.

The frozen battlefield buckled beneath my feet. Tempest was gone. But Vorago remained.

And he would not fall so easily.

He was already moving, waves rising from nowhere, cresting, ready to collapse.

Vorago struck, his fists cracking against my chest, his water surging with each movement. I countered with my ice, my trident, but he refused to surrender. His strikes sent me stumbling, each step skidding across the ice as I tried to hold my ground. Blood poured from a medley of wounds.

I slowed time, dodging, countering, striking back, but Vorago was too old, too powerful, too honed by eons of experience. Every strike I threw was met with equal force, every feint anticipated before I had even committed to it. He wasn't fighting me —he was dismantling me, breaking me apart, reading every movement like a well-worn battle map. I lost my grip on time.

"How can anyone who hears voices think they can defeat me?" Vorago demanded.

"My doubts make me stronger," I replied. Without them, I would lose sight of what was real. I would lose all sense of balance. I would lose *myself*.

"You are still chained to mortal thoughts," Vorago growled.

"And you are a slave to your own ego."

I didn't see his next strike coming. He opened skin at my shoulder, another cut sliced the length of my ribs. Pain snatched a chokehold on me. The shocking contrast of blood on snow made me hesitate. And that hesitation cost me.

A fist came toward my face. I dove for the snow and rolled out the way, my body skittering down the mountain, hitting boulders, its speed increasing. I think I broke my arm. Maybe my ankle too.

Stealing a breath, I waved the trident with my good arm and

slowed time again, managed to pick myself up off the ground. The trail of blood led back to Vorago, where he stood on the ridge with a triumphant smile.

I glanced at my body, worried I was losing too much blood, but the wounds had already started to heal. Skin closed. Muscles reknitted. Tendons repaired themselves. Bones snapped back into place. I guess that was what it meant to be a god. To be immortal.

Roaring, I charged up the slope, the trident held high. With time slowed, I opened a wound across his throat. Not enough to kill him, but enough to make him bleed.

Fear shot through Vorago's eyes. An emotion I was sure he'd never experienced before. He clutched his throat, then glared at me.

"You will not win this fight," he yelled.

"We'll see about that."

Truthfully, I didn't know who would win, but I would fight until my dying breath.

Glaciers split and tumbled. Avalanches thundered down the ridges, burying entire swaths of terrain beneath crushing tons of snow and ice. The storm followed us, dogging every step and swing.

Blood stained the snow—mine, his, mixing together. A deep gash burned across my shoulder, the wound raw and searing, blood trickling down my arm in stinging streams. My ribs ached from a brutal strike, bruises blooming beneath my skin like dark, angry stains. Every breath rattled inside me, sharp and shallow. But Vorago fared no better. A jagged cut stretched across his side where my ice had pierced through his defenses, and his right eye was swollen shut. But as we stood there panting for breath, we both began to heal. Neither of us relented. Neither of us would fall first. We were beyond pain, beyond exhaustion.

Beyond time. We fought with the fury of gods, and only one of us would walk away from this.

And it damn well better be me.

I needed to land a killing blow or this battle would stretch into eternity.

"You were never meant to wield that trident," he yelled. "It belongs to me!"

"Then take it from me," I snarled.

He lunged. I met him head-on, the trident locked against his strength, water and ice colliding in a blinding explosion.

The mountain splintered beneath us.

Vorago staggered. That moment of weakness was all I needed. I twisted, driving the trident forward, pouring every ounce of my power into it. My godly power. The weapon blazed with glacial light, consuming everything. My body lit up the blank landscape like a volcanic eruption. Whispers filled my head. Cascadia. The trident. My own determination. And something deeper, something fainter I couldn't put my finger on.

Drawing on it all, I pushed the three prongs of the trident until they skewered Vorago's throat. A purple flare of light gifted by the Essence of the Ocean streaked along the weapon and emptied into Vorago's bleeding wound. I didn't take my hands from the hilt, but pressed forward, impaling him against a rock. Cascadia's grace surged next, a determined strength that flowed from me and along the trident.

Vorago's eyes bulged, as if he were trying to use his powers but couldn't. He tried to speak. Couldn't.

"I don't need to hear any last words," I said.

The storm above my head vanished. Lightning struck in the distant sea. Waves crept back over the lip of the mountain. It was just me and the snow and my nemesis.

Vorago raised his hands, gurgled something incomprehensible. Golden light swirled around my limbs. Blood spilled out of his throat.

I leaned into him, pressing the trident deeper, almost severing his head from his body. Light detonated, engulfing both of us. The trident's power—*my* power—tore through him, his form unraveling into mist and ocean spray.

And then a blue light shimmered along the trident and slammed into my chest, knocking me backward. Vorago's grace.

Silence fell. A silence so profound it hollowed out my insides. I bent over and threw up in the snow.

Gentle snowflakes dotted my shoulders. Ice coated my lashes. The winds fell quiet. Golden light retreated into my body, seeping in through my pores, traveling along my veins, until it dimmed and disappeared. I looked like myself again. I was still a god, but I was also Gal.

Dropping the trident, I collapsed to my knees and wiped my mouth with the back of my hand.

I had killed two gods.

I glanced at the weapon that had chosen me. Not a single chip marred its shining surface. It glowed with purpose. With approval. With power.

Vorago was gone. Tempest was gone. The battle was over.

I had won.

CHAPTER TWENTY-FIVE

I lay in the snow and stared at the sky, watching the clouds drift above, and argued with the voice in my head.

There was no point going home.

There is nothing there for you.

I have burned all my bridges.

No one there loves you.

It seemed we agreed on something. Which was a good thing, considering I was talking to myself.

Atlantis was safe. That was all that mattered.

Turning my head, I took in the destruction of the battle. Although the storm had long since disappeared. The landscape had been vastly altered. Large sections of trees had fallen. Mammoth boulders had crashed into the empty pit of Lake Echomere. And deep crevasses had ripped open all over the mountain.

But the air smelled sweet and soft and pure.

Getting to my feet, I swung the trident and waited for the land to repair itself. It was only a matter of seconds. The trees sprang back into position. Boulders rolled themselves back up the slopes, and the crevasses rejoined with only a gentle, protesting groan. That was the magic of Atlantis. The strength of the trident. The might of the Power of the Sea.

Light snow continued to fall, coating my hair, sticking to my eyelashes. I smiled and held out my hand, catching a few snowflakes on my palm. This was where I was meant to be. There was much I would miss. And I couldn't deny the deep, aching hole in my chest that yearned for Una. But I had caused her enough pain. I would look after her from afar.

Unwilling to use my teleportation power for laziness, I turned and walked up the mountain, heading for a small cabin that my family had used over the years. I was the only one who visited it with any frequency.

The walk took an hour, which I was grateful for. It gave me time to assemble my thoughts, to sift through my emotions, to decide on a plan. Solitude would be my new best friend. But when I arrived at the small cabin, I found the windows lit up and the smell of food permeating the wooden walls.

My stomach growled. I couldn't remember the last time I'd eaten. Did gods eat?

Unsure who might be inside, I pushed the door open and scanned the small entrance. The kitchen was hidden to the right. A staircase led to two bedrooms above. In front of me there was a crackling fire in a hearth situated between two armchairs. One of them was occupied.

"Hello?" I called, shutting the door behind me.

The person turned. It was someone I didn't recognize, but ancient wisdom radiated from the lines of his weathered face. Long white hair fell past his shoulders, and he wore a simple blue robe that I swore shifted like an ocean current.

"Come sit." He patted the empty chair, causing a plume of dust to rise. No one had been here in months.

I wiped my feet and leaned the trident against the wall. "Who are you?"

The man smiled. Nothing but warmth poured out of his face. I relaxed and took the seat beside him. He crossed his legs and angled his body to face me.

"I am, what you know as, the Architect."

My pulse spiked. I lurched forward, air gusting from my lungs. "You're real?"

"I am."

"And you created the universe?"

"I did."

"You don't want to destroy us? To wipe the slate clean. To start again?"

He frowned. "I. Do. Not." He relaxed his expression. "I never interfere in a world once it is created."

"I thought you didn't care about us. That you exist without emotion."

"I care deeply about everything I create."

"Oh. Okay." Vorago was a lying bastard. "Did Vorago know of your existence?"

"No." The long sleeves of his blue robe fell over his hands. "I have never revealed myself to anyone before. He used the whispers of my existence to manipulate you."

I pressed my back against the chair to feel something solid, to make sure I wasn't dreaming, or hallucinating. Which was entirely possible considering the voice in my head. "Why me?"

"Because you deserve answers."

My questions stalled. I didn't know what to say, what to ask, what to fucking *think*.

"You're just a man." I cringed as soon as the words left my mouth.

The Architect chuckled. "I appear this way to you so that I do not startle you."

"What do you really look like?"

"Many, many things."

"Why are you here?"

"There are not many occasions that have compelled me to visit a planet once I have created it," he said. "But you, young Gal Waters, are the reason I am here."

"Me?"

He nodded. "Vorago and Tempest were disrupting the balance of the universe. I couldn't allow them to destroy one of my most favorite planets. I gifted them with the power to create entire lands." He swept a hand over the room, indicating the small log cabin and Atlantis beyond. "And they turned their back on it, succumbed to greed and laziness and arrogance, strayed from their purpose." He took a deep breath, as if the admission pained him. "But you have saved it. You, Gal Waters."

My head spun. My mouth opened, but no words came out. Until I stuttered, "The constellations? The changing tides? Was that you?"

"In a way," the Architect replied. "Although changes in the stars and the tides can occur naturally over time, on this occasion, it was the universe's way of informing me something was amiss. And when I turned my attention to Earth, I saw Vorago's intentions. I saw the broken trident and knew you needed my help. I saw the path you would have to take to defeat him. Not an easy one."

"No, it wasn't." I frowned, the weight of questions giving me a headache. "What about...the voice...?"

"In your head?" The Architect pulled at his beard. "It is what you suspected. Your subconscious. Your conscience. It can both torment and appease. But it is not always truthful. Sometimes it inflames the worst of our doubts. I think you may find that voice will quieten now."

"Good, because it got really noisy in there for a while." I tapped my temple, trying to make light of the intrusive thoughts that had kept me in a chokehold. "Without wanting to risk your wrath, can I ask something else?"

"Of course," he replied. "I do not anger easily."

"If you were aware of Vorago's intentions, why didn't you deal with him?"

The Architect gave me a wry smile. "There is much you don't know about the universe. Much that you will never know. But Vorago was right about one thing, I am a creator, not a destroyer. I can only give people the gifts they need to succeed in their own battles."

Annoyingly, that made sense. No planet could endure a god who gave life only to tear it away the next moment. The Architect may have created the universe, but it...he...was still encumbered by its laws.

"Could time have trapped you?" I asked. "If Vorago had gotten ahold of the trident and you presented yourself to him. Could he have trapped you in time?"

The Architect's expression turned noncommittal. "Perhaps. But it's of no importance. The universe will exist with or without me."

"I see." I didn't see at all. The entire thing was too big to comprehend. I stared at the fire, trying to make sense of everything, listening for the voice I wasn't convinced had left me. But it remained quiet for now.

"I have come to thank you," he said when my silence stretched on. "And to reward you. As long as it does not disrupt the balance, I will give you whatever you desire."

Una. Ember. Dad. The names of all the people I loved spun through my mind. *Mom.*

The heat of the fire flashed over my face.

"Coral," I said, knowing it was the only thing I could ask for. "Can you bring Coral back?"

The Architect steepled his fingers under his chin. "Life and death are a balance."

My hope dissolved with an acid burn. "You're right. I'm sorry I asked—"

He raised a hand. "I didn't say I couldn't. Or that I wouldn't. But I want you to understand the consequences."

I dipped my head. "I don't want anyone else to take her place."

He chuckled, the sound surprising me. "Nothing like that, Gal. Please do not fear."

I blew out a breath and tried relaxing into the chair, but it was impossible. I gripped the armrests like the chair might suddenly buck me out of it.

"I can bring Coral back. But you must remain a god. You must watch over Atlantis. That is your pathway now."

"Of course." I had already accepted that as my role.

"Look how far you have come," the Architect said. "From burning *The Mermaid Chronicles* to ascending to a powerful protector."

Well...when he put it like that...A self-conscious flush heated my cheeks.

"You have come a long way in a short time. And one day," he glanced at the trident, "there will be a new wielder. You must be ready to relinquish the weapon when the time is right."

"But I'll still be a god?"

"Yes."

"And I'll still have power? I'll still be able to save my people?"

"Yes."

"Deal."

He chuckled again and shifted his robe. "That was easier than I thought."

"That trident has brought me nothing but trouble."

"Trouble you have handled well." He stood. "I will leave you now."

"Wait!" Panic surged up my throat. I had so many questions.

He turned, smiled patiently.

"I'm immortal?"

"Yes...."

"What does that mean exactly? Am I...will I...?" I dropped my head into my hands. I didn't know how to phrase the question without scaring the shit out of myself. I peeked at him through spread fingers. "Am I going to live forever?"

"Yes."

A cold rush of fear flashed through me. "What if someone chops my head off?"

"Your immortal life may end only if you are killed by another god, or if a godly weapon is used against you."

"So my head will reattach itself?"

"Something like that." The Architect tapped the back of my chair. "But no mortal would be capable of it."

Okay. *Holy shit.*

I didn't want to dwell on the implications of that, so I asked a different question. "Will I ever see you again?"

"Perhaps." Something about the tone of his voice reassured me.

"What about Coral?"

He clicked his fingers. "She is now alive."

Wow.

I tried clicking my fingers, but nothing happened.

The Architect let out a belly laugh, clutching his stomach. "That is not a power that any god possesses."

A rueful smile formed on my lips. "Thought it was worth a try."

"There is soup on the stove." He touched my shoulder. Lightness flowed through my body. Something shifted my organs, realigned my bones, sent energy into my muscles. I felt...connected. At peace. "Make sure you eat. You've been through quite an ordeal."

I opened my mouth to thank him, but he was already gone. I lurched to my feet, spun in a circle, but there was no sign of the Architect, save for the cracking fire and the smell of soup wafting from the kitchen.

"Did that just happen?" I muttered to myself as I walked into the kitchen. There was no answering internal voice.

On autopilot, I found a bowl and a spoon, turned off the stove, and poured the soup into the bowl. Tomato. My favorite. I grabbed a husk of freshly baked bread sitting on the counter and slathered it with butter from a dish to its side.

The first sip of soup sent me into a state of ecstasy. I'd never tasted anything so damn good. I devoured the meal in a couple of minutes, washed up my dishes, and stood in the kitchen staring out the window.

I had to make sure.

I placed my hand on the trident's shaft, greeting my closest friend, and teleported to the Summer's home. I stood in the trees in their backyard. Night had fallen. Crickets chirped in the grass. A cloud scudded across the moon. Laughter fell out of an open window. Keeping cover under the trees that rimmed the property, I crept closer to the house. There were Una and Bay talking by the kitchen sink. My heart almost seized in my chest at the sight of her. *Perfection*. But not mine. Never again.

I moved my gaze and found Moby laughing at something Trent said. And Maya hugging her daughter. Hugging *Coral*. Who was holding Ripple tight against her chest.

Through the sting of tears, I smiled at the loving scene. They were whole once more.

As if sensing my presence, Una suddenly glanced out the window. She frowned, searching the darkness, but I was confident she couldn't see me. Her eye patch was new, a soft blue that complemented her complexion. And her hair was a little longer. Her smile a little more guarded.

Finally, when I could bear it no longer, I arced the trident and returned to the snow.

CHAPTER TWENTY-SIX

I thought of Ember's destroyed wing and Una's missing eye, and knew instinctively there was nothing I could do to bring back their missing parts. With as much power as I possessed, those gifts had not been granted to me. The Architect had confirmed as much. And rightly so. Their wounds were a testament to the battles they had fought, the courage they wielded, and to the lives they had lived. No god should be capable of altering destiny. That was a burden I never wanted to carry. The Architect could have at it.

But I could help my friends in a more mortal, human way.

I moved into the mountain cabin. I didn't bother to return home for clothes or trinkets, the cabin was already supplied with my basic needs. I baked bread in the morning and made stews and soups for dinner, kneading the dough until my hands ached, stirring the broth until the steam coated the walls with warmth. It was a simple life, different to the one I had envisioned, but it was better I was here. Better for everyone. Even the internal voice had deserted me.

During the day, I hiked the mountain, my boots crunching over the frozen earth, breath curling into the crisp air. It took me a week to find the right tree, the right grain, the right everything. Not just any wood would do. It had to be strong but light, flexible but durable. I ran my hands over bark, testing each tree for imperfections, listening to the whisper of the wind through their branches as if they might tell me which one was worthy. When I finally found it, a towering old spruce on the north ridge, I hesitated before striking the first blow with my ax. It had stood for decades, perhaps centuries. Now, it would serve a new purpose.

I worked outside, relishing the clean scent of wood as I measured it and cut it down to size. I carved and sanded and shaped for days, my hands aching, but the blisters disappeared as quickly as I gained them, thanks to my new godly powers. At least the transient pain made me feel somewhat human again. Mortal.

I refined each curve and joint of wood until the structure mirrored the shape of a true wing. This was no replacement. I knew that. It would never be the same. But it was something. It was the least I could do.

When the carving was done, I laid the wing across the workbench and ran my palm over its surface. It was sturdy yet flexible, reinforced with thin strips of metal I had scavenged. It would hold. But I wanted it to be more than just wood and metal. I wanted it to be his.

I raised the trident. As I pressed it against the base of the wing, warmth spread from my hands into the wood. Golden light seeped into the grain, winding through the carvings like veins of sunlight. The magic was strong, turning the wood into something else entirely. It was now lighter, stronger, more adaptable to Ember's movements.

When I pulled back, the trident whispered sweet melodies. I examined the prosthetic, now infused with something beyond mere craftsmanship. It would move with Ember, respond to his instincts, feel like an extension of himself rather than a burden.

Satisfied, I turned to my next task. Una's eye.

This was different. More delicate. More personal.

I sifted through the stones I had collected from the mountain's rivers, running my fingers over their smooth surfaces until I found the right one. A perfect sphere of deep blue, the same color as the ocean. I cleaned it for hours, polishing the edges until it gleamed like a true gemstone.

The process took longer than the wing. There was no room for error. Una had lost her eye because of me. Indirectly, perhaps, but the guilt still weighed on me. I owed her this.

It took my days to refine its shape, whittling away at imperfections, smoothing every edge until it felt as natural as any part of her had before. I imagined Una's face as I worked, the way her jaw clenched when she was deep in thought, the flicker of determination that never quite faded from her gaze. I wanted her to see again, not just in the way she once had, but in a way that made her stronger.

The trident hummed again as I held it over the stone. This time, the light that seeped into it was cooler, gentler, like the glow of the ocean beneath moonlight. I whispered a quiet blessing, though I didn't know if she would accept it. The eye would function as more than a mere replacement. It would allow her to see through water, to sense the movement of currents, to wield a piece of the ocean's power even on land.

When I was finished, I set the eye next to the wing. Two small offerings in the wake of all the damage I had caused.

My hands trembled as I reached for the trident again. For the first time since the battle, I stared at my reflection in its golden surface. I looked mortal. Just a man, worn and tired. But when I lifted the trident, my skin shimmered, veins pulsing with light.

A stillness settled over me. I was not mortal anymore. Not

even close. The island had not yet seen what I had become. Perhaps they never would.

Lifting Una's eye and Ember's wing, I swung the trident and teleported to the palace. I left Ember's wing in his room and Una's eye on her pillow. I didn't bother with notes or apologies. I didn't wait for them to discover the gifts. At least I'd hope they'd see them as gifts. I returned to the mountain and sat by the fire in the cabin, suddenly exhausted.

Days bled into weeks. Then months. The mountain became my world. I kept to a steady rhythm—hunting, carving, meditating. I practiced the meditation rituals Ford had taught me each morning, using the trident like a staff as I practiced the fluid routines. I watched the snowfall, built fires that burned through the night, and let time drift by. But I knew, deep down, that solitude could not last forever. I was merely killing time. Waiting.

Waiting for what?

It was at the end of the third month when footsteps crunched through the frostbitten ground. Followed by a low murmur of voices. I didn't move from my spot by the fire as the cabin door creaked open.

Uncle Dylan stepped in first, shaking off the cold, followed closely by my father. They stamped their boots and hung up their coats. They said nothing at first, just looked at me. Taking in the unkempt beard, the sunken eyes, the way my fingers rested idly on the trident.

"We figured we'd give you space," Uncle Dylan finally said, rubbing his hands together for warmth. "But three months is a long time to be alone."

I didn't respond. I couldn't.

Dad sighed, stepping forward. "You should come home."

I ached to walk into his arms, to have him comfort me, but I resisted. I couldn't rely on my father to fight my battles or smooth my path.

I hung my head. "There's nothing left for me there. No one will forgive me. And they shouldn't."

Dad moved through the room and sat on the second chair. Uncle Dylan lowered himself to a footstool in front of me.

"I hate the cold," Uncle Dylan said.

"You sound like Ember," I said.

Uncle Dylan tapped my knee. "I didn't come all the way up here to return empty handed."

I shrugged.

"You're depressed," Dad said. "I know what that feels like, son."

He put his hand on my shoulder. No one had touched me in weeks. My eyes heated. I *was* depressed. I had done everything I was supposed to do. Defeated the gods. Saved Atlantis. But Una...I shook my head. I couldn't go there.

Uncle Dylan stretched out his legs. "People grieve in different ways. Some with anger. Some with silence. But no one has written you off."

I stared at the fire. "I don't belong there anymore. I don't know if I ever did."

My father crouched beside me, his expression softer than I'd seen in years. "That's not true." He gestured to the trident. "You fought for this island, Gal. That doesn't make you an outcast."

I swallowed. "It doesn't make me one of them either."

Uncle Dylan leaned forward. "Then what are you waiting for? Punishment? Isolation? You've spent three months hiding in these mountains, but for what? To prove you're a ghost?"

I averted my gaze, but he wasn't finished. "You're not dead, kid. You're alive. Will be for quite some time if the rumors I'm hearing are true. And the people who care about you? They're still there, waiting."

I wanted to believe him. But the thought of stepping foot

back in the palace, facing Una, Bay, Ember, the others—it twisted my stomach into knots.

"You don't have to have all the answers." Dad reached across the space between us and clasped my forearm, a silent pledge of support. "But you have to try."

Silence settled between us. The fire crackled, throwing flickering shadows against the walls. My knuckles whitened on the trident. It returned the gesture with a pulse of golden light.

"I don't know if I can," I said.

I was afraid. Afraid of losing them all.

Dad stood, his hand still on my shoulder. "Then take it one step at a time. But don't take it alone."

He offered his hand and waited for me to take it. A choice. A bridge back to something I wasn't sure I deserved.

For the first time in months, I hesitated. And then, slowly, I took his hand.

CHAPTER TWENTY-SEVEN

$\mathcal{W}$e landed in the courtyard. My heart threatened to pound its way out of my ribs. Familiar sights surrounded me—the sprawling stone paths, the ever-present scent of salt and sea, the exquisite palace that had once felt like home. But I no longer knew if I belonged there.

Dad squeezed my shoulder, letting me know he was there. My gaze fell on the statue of my mother, depicted in battle hurling a fireball at an unseen enemy. So fierce. So strong. So full of love.

I sucked in a breath. Then another. And another. And finally, the anxiety eased. Not completely, but enough that I could see straight.

"Come find me at the bar when you're done," Uncle Dylan said. "I've got a couple of pints with your name on it."

Dad walked me up the steps to the palace, then remained outside in the sunshine as I passed through the entrance arch. Voices murmured beyond the open doors. It was now or never.

Aunt Marina was the first to spot me. Her eyes widened, and in two strides, she had me wrapped in a fierce hug, her warmth cutting through the cold I hadn't realized I was still carrying. "You're home," she whispered.

"I'm sorry," I murmured, the words feeling inadequate.

She pulled back, studying my face. "You're my nephew. I never stopped believing in you."

Aunt Raina stood nearby, arms crossed, her sharp gaze flicking over me. "Took you long enough," she said, though her voice was softer than usual. "We were beginning to think you'd rather live in a snowdrift."

Grams and Pops followed, their expressions overflowing with affection. Pops clapped a hand on my shoulder, his grip strong and steady. I knew they had forgiven me before I even opened my mouth.

I swiped at my eyes, trying to rein the emotion back in. But then Ash and Cyra came bounding around the corner, Ash with his wings spread and nearly taking out an ornate vase.

Ash's golden eyes studied me, a smirk tugging at the corner of his lips. "Figured you'd show up eventually," he said, though the relief in his tone betrayed him.

"I'm sorry," I told them both, turning to Cyra.

She shook her head. "You don't need to say anything, Gal."

But I did. To all of them.

"They had everyone fooled," Ash said.

Moby appeared in the doorway, arms folded. We stared at each other. Seconds lapsed into minutes. Then he let out a breath, shaking his head. "You're still a bastard," he muttered, but he stepped forward and clapped me on the shoulder. "But you came back."

I hugged him fiercely until he joked he couldn't breathe. Or maybe it wasn't a joke.

"So you're a god now, huh?" Ash asked, rebalancing the vase he'd almost smashed.

"Looks that way." I gave a fragile smile.

Cyra gave me a once over, her gaze settling on the golden glow of my eyes. "You're immortal?"

I nodded, still dubious about the idea of living *forever*.

Everyone would die. Atlanteans had longer lifespans than humans when they drank regularly from the fountain, but they wouldn't live as long as me. I would see every single person I cared about pass. The thought almost sent me back to the mountain.

Before I could dwell on those sorrowful implications, Blaze cut through the growing crowd. "Good to see you back, son."

I dipped my chin, unsure if he meant it.

The dragon king bumped his shoulder against mine. "Ember has missed you," he whispered into my ear.

"I missed him too," I whispered back. But that didn't mean our friendship would recover.

"He's made good use of that wing you made him," Blaze said.

"I never said I made it."

Blaze laughed. "We all knew it was you. He's outside now." He nodded at the window.

I moved to the window, lifted my gaze to the sky, and sure enough, there was Ember, wings spread wide, soaring over the gardens. It had been almost six years since he'd lost the wing. Six years since I'd seen him fly. I smiled as warmth flooded my body.

"Go on," Blaze said at my shoulder.

On my way outside, I ran into Ford. He gave me once over, looking me up and down, then cracked a rare smile. "I'm glad you're home."

"I hope so." My voice came out small.

Ford tilted his head, studied me for a few seconds, then pulled me into a bear hug. He clenched me against his chest and whispered in my ear. "If it hadn't gone exactly how it did, none of us would be standing here now. You saved Atlantis, no one was hurt—"

"Coral—"

"Coral is fine." He pulled away and placed his hands on my shoulders. "You're here now. That's all that matters."

I clasped his shoulder too, squeezed. "Thank you, Ford. You've always been like a second father to me—"

"Shhh." He smiled. "Enough of the mushy talk. I know. You don't need to say it. No go on and get out of here. You've got friends to reunite with."

I gave him another hug, then stepped away. Outside, I stood at the top of the rear steps, watching Ember as he performed a few loops in the air, then came to land a few feet from me.

"Hi," he said, panting.

"Hi yourself."

He smiled.

I smiled.

He laughed. I joined him in that too.

"I don't know how you made it, but I fucking love it. I love it more than the other wing," Ember said, his eyes dancing.

Emotions welled in my throat, clogging it. I couldn't push out any words.

"You left without a word," he said, not unkindly.

"I'm sorry."

Ember held my gaze, then sighed. "You really are a dramatic bastard."

I snorted. No one else made me laugh like Ember. "But I'm *your* dramatic bastard."

"Aye. That is the truth."

"Are we still...?"

"Friends?" Ember asked. "Of course we fucking are. It's harder to get rid of me than that, you idiot." He swamped me in a hug. Then he pulled back, a familiar mischievous smile dancing on his lips. "As long as you don't make me go to the mountains. I draw the line there."

I laughed with genuine amusement. "Okay, buddy. I can deal with that."

Movement snagged my attention and I turned to see Bay walking up the steps. My stomach clenched. This would be one of the hardest apologies.

He came to a stop beside Ember. I couldn't read his expression. I never could. He always kept his emotions locked deep inside.

"You were an arrogant ass," Bay said, though his voice lacked venom. "And for a while, I hated you for it."

"I know," I said. "I deserve that."

Bay studied me, then smirked. "Yeah, you do. But...you also saved us all. It takes a god to kill a god. And even with the abilities the Power of the Sea gave me, it wouldn't have been enough. *I* wouldn't have been enough. I was arrogant too."

I hesitated, unsure how to respond. Finally, I said, "You were always stronger than I gave you credit for. Smarter, too."

Bay arched an eyebrow. "You finally noticed?"

A small chuckle bubbled up my throat. "Guess I did."

Before I could say more, Ember nudged Bay with his shoulder. "Don't let it go to your head."

Bay laughed. "Feet firmly on the ground."

I blinked at them both, taking in the easy way they stood together, Ember's arm brushing against Bay's like it belonged there. I watched how Ember's hand lingered on Bay's lower back, how Bay leaned into it, almost unconsciously.

"Oh," I said, realization settling over me. "This is serious?"

Bay gave me a knowing look. "It is."

Ember crossed his arms, arching a brow. "You have a problem with that?"

"Of course not," I said. "Just surprised you managed to find someone willing to put up with you."

Bay elbowed Ember. "There may have been an exchange of coin."

A surprised laugh burbled out of me. I'd never known Bay to make a joke before.

Ember feigned offense, placing a hand over his chest. "Excuse you, I am a delight."

Bay rolled his eyes, but the warmth in his gaze said otherwise. I watched them, something easing in my chest that I hadn't realized was tight. Ember, who had always been restless, and Bay, who had always carried the weight of his family— together, they looked lighter. Whole, in a way I hadn't seen before.

"You suit each other," I said honestly.

Ember's smirk softened, and Bay's expression grew thoughtful. "Yeah," he said after a moment. "We do."

A comfortable silence settled between us, the weight of old wounds not quite gone, but lessened. Then Bay's expression turned serious again.

"She still loves you, you know."

I choked on my own saliva. My ears rang. "Una?"

Bay nodded. "She's hurt. But she never stopped."

I coughed and swallowed the saliva. "Does she...does she even want to see me?"

"She wouldn't admit it outright," Bay said, crossing his arms. "But I know my sister. You're all she's thought about since the moment you left."

Ember touched my arm. "We knew you'd come back eventually, Gal. And we all know why you hesitated." He glanced at Bay before turning back to me. "But you don't have to keep punishing yourself."

Coral.

I clenched my fists. "I don't know if she'll ever forgive me."

"You won't know unless you try," Bay said.

I squeezed the trident, looking for reassurance or for a sign of what I should do. My journey home wasn't over yet. Not even close.

"And Gal?" Bay asked. I looked up. "Thank you for bringing Coral back. Without her it was...dark."

"I wouldn't have asked for anything else."

Bay's eyebrows quirked. "Asked?"

I told them about the Architect and his offer of a reward. They both looked at me with stunned expressions.

Ember recovered first. Sort of. "I don't know what to say."

"About the Architect being real?" I asked.

"To any of it."

Bay fisted his hand over his heart. His eyes glistened. Then he offered his hand. I took it and we shook, a new mutual respect growing between us. "Thank you."

Before the situation could get any more emotional, I swung the trident and teleported away. I landed outside the Summer's family home. I couldn't put this off any longer.

I was just mustering the courage to knock on the door when a voice piped up from the porch.

"Hi, Gal." Coral sat in a chair, Ripple curled up on her lap, a book in her hand.

"Hi, Coral." Our gazes collided, full of every emotion under the sun. I didn't know what to say.

"I'm sorry I was scared of you."

"I'm sorry I killed you."

She put her book down, shifted Ripple off her lap, and danced across the porch on bare feet to stand in front of me. She was a couple of steps up so she could look straight into my eyes. I tried not to flinch.

"That wasn't your fault." She touched my cheek and it was

like being kissed by the moon. An overwhelming sense of forgiveness and peace poured into me.

"It wasn't?"

She brushed her thumb over my cheek. "You can let go of that now."

I nodded, not sure if I could, or would, but wanting to please her anyway.

She dropped her hand and narrowed her blue eyes at me. "I'm serious, Gal Waters. It's time to stop being so hard on yourself."

"I never wanted to scare you."

"I never wanted three evil gods to come to Atlantis."

"Two," I corrected. "Cascadia came good in the end. But I'm sorry they didn't turn out to be who you wanted them to me."

"Me too." She tucked her hair behind her ear. "I was so gullible."

I shook my head. "You weren't the only one."

"I should have known better."

"That makes two of us."

We smiled at each other.

"Cascadia gave you her grace?"

"She did," I confirmed. "How did you know?"

"It was in the book." Of course it was. "Want to see?"

"Nope." God or no god, I still hated that damn book.

Coral laughed, causing Ripple to crack open an eye and huff at her. I noted a bottle of coconut oil on the table. Ash's coconut oil that he used to massage his wings.

I jutted my chin at the bottle. "That belong to Ash?"

Coral's cheeks pinked. "Maybe. Ripple likes me to rub it into his fur."

"So, Ash is spending more time around here, huh?" I winked.

VORAGO RETURNS

The color of Coral's cheeks deepened. "Maybe."

"I'm happy for you."

She smiled. "Speaking of happiness. She wants to see you."

"I hope so."

"Go inside."

My immortal stomach fell through my feet, but I took the suggestion and climbed the three steps and knocked on the front door.

"Good luck!" Coral called as she resumed her seat and pulled Ripple onto her lap once more.

The door swung open to reveal Maya.

307

CHAPTER TWENTY-EIGHT

$\mathcal{M}$aya gasped and her hand flew to cover her mouth. She scanned my face, then did a loop of my body as if checking for injuries. "We've been so worried."

"I'm okay," I said. Relatively speaking.

She stepped back and opened the door wider. "Come in."

I stole myself. Braced myself. Winced a little. I had killed two gods, and yet this was the moment I feared most.

As I crossed the threshold, the familiar scent of the Summer's family home filled my nose. Salt, herbs, and something faintly floral. There was the vase Una had made when she was five, decorated with seashells and home to a freshly cut bouquet of jasmine. A painting of Ocean Beach hung on the wall. One of Trent's surfboards was peeking out of a cupboard. Oh, how I had missed those simple things.

Trent appeared in the hallway, his hand resting on the newel post of the staircase. His blond hair was wild and tangled, his blue eyes...evaluating. Then his expression softened and something close to relief crossed his features.

Maya took my hand and drew me further into the house,

gave my palm a light squeeze. "Look who's come home," she said to her husband.

"The prodigal son returns," Trent said. I guess I deserved that. "Or should I say *son-in-law?*"

"I would never desert Atlantis."

The unspoken words hung between us. I had deserted Una. But not before she had turned her back on me. I sighed. I wasn't here to get into a pissing contest. Who did what and when didn't matter anymore.

"It's good to see you," Maya said, squeezing my shoulders before pulling back. "Really, it is."

"I'm glad you're safe," Trent said. "And thank you for bringing Coral back."

Maya's eyes filled. "That couldn't have been easy for you. Considering..."

I didn't want her to feel any guilt. My mother had been her best friend. I knew she mourned her death as much as I did. And I had thought about it. The chance to undo my greatest loss. To bring back the woman who had shaped my entire existence. But in the end, I had made my choice.

"I know," I said. "But Coral deserved another chance. It wouldn't have been right to take that from her."

I also knew my mother would have told me to choose Coral too.

Maya wiped her cheeks. "Thank you. Your mother would be so proud of you, Gal."

The words punched into my chest. I swallowed, trying to work moisture into my throat as I blinked back tears.

Trent put his hand on my shoulder. "You did good."

I wasn't sure I believed that yet, but I appreciated the words. Before I could find a way to respond, soft footsteps sounded from the staircase. Air refused to inflate my lungs as Una descended, each step slow, deliberate, as if she were preparing herself for this moment just as much as I was. I rested the trident against the wall.

My world narrowed to her.

Her blonde hair was pinned back, revealing the strong, stubborn tilt of her chin. And on her finger, she wore her wedding ring. That was all that mattered. If it was still on her finger, there was hope.

Her blue eye—so much like the ocean that had shaped us both—held a storm of emotions. And then I noted her second eye. The eye patch was gone, and in its place the magical blue stone I had crafted and blessed for her. It had been so long since she'd had two eyes. My lungs forgot how to function. As did my heart. And my brain. For six years I had wanted to give her this.

She touched her eyelid as if self-conscious. "The hospital fitted it for me and made my eyelid work again. I can't see out of it, but I can feel the ocean, and I can see the prophecies."

I didn't reply, because my gaze had dropped and snagged on the faint swell of her stomach, barely noticeable beneath her loose dress.

Maya put a hand on Trent's arm. "We'll leave you two to talk." They left the room and a few seconds later, I heard the gentle rattle of dishes coming from the kitchen.

I stared at Una's stomach, and didn't stop. "Una..." My voice barely worked. I hadn't forgotten she was pregnant, but the reality of her swollen stomach brought a new layer of understanding...and fear. The ring, the eye, the pregnancy. This was too fucking much. Emotion swarmed into my chest, and a shuddering exhale rattled out of my lungs. It was too much, but I wouldn't have it any other way.

"How?" It was the only word I was capable of asking. And then, "Did you stop taking the herbs?"

Una passed a hand over her stomach. "Never. Until now. Obviously."

"I forgot," I admitted, twisting my hands together. "Before. For a few days."

"It shouldn't have mattered if I was taking them," she said.

"Then how?"

Una gave a gentle, almost breathless laugh. "Because Atlantis decided it should be so."

Atlantis decided. Of course it did. Inside her was a new life. Our futures had been repaved. The thing I had feared most was growing inside her stomach.

She searched my face, waiting for me to say something—anything. But I couldn't find the words. Instead, I took a hesitant step forward, reaching out but stopping just short of touching her. "I'm not afraid anymore."

I was fucking terrified.

But there was no going back. Atlantis had decided that I would have a child. And so it would be. I would learn to live with the fear of losing it. *Her. Him.* And they would have to live with an immortal parent.

Una searched my face, then cradled her stomach with both hands. "Really? Because I am."

I tilted my head and smiled ruefully. "Okay, that wasn't entirely honest. Yes, I'm scared. Fucking terrified, if you must know. But I will never shirk my duties. And I will love this child with everything I have. I will never let our child feel alone. No matter what happens between us, they will always have both of us. They will always know love."

Tears spilled down her face. She blew out a breath, her lips vibrating, her skin turning blotchy. "I don't know what the future looks like, Gal. I don't know how we get back to what we were. But..." She lifted her eyes back to mine. "I do know that I never stopped loving you."

Something inside me cracked, releasing the pressure that had been building since the moment I had left her. I exhaled shakily, fighting against the rising emotion wreaking havoc with my body: the slick palms, the pounding heart, the shallow breathing. "I thought I'd lost you."

Una stepped closer, close enough that I could smell her scent. Salt, the ocean, and jasmine. It was the best fucking smell in the world. "We almost lost *each other*."

I swallowed. "I'm sorry."

She studied me in silence, fingers twitching, as if weighing her next words. "No, *I'm* sorry."

I frowned. "What do you have to apologize for?"

A fragile smile sat on her lips. "You're not the only one who gave into fear. I knew you were destined to be a god the moment I saw that prophecy. But I resisted it. Because I wanted you all to myself." She pressed a hand to her heart, her fingers trembling before she stilled them. "So you see, I put pressure on you to turn your back on the very thing you were supposed to be. You did the right thing. For Atlantis. For all of us. I lost sight of the bigger picture. I was...selfish."

Every part of me rejected her words. "You could never be selfish. And I wanted all those things too. I never wanted to be Prince, to be a guardian, to be the Trident Wielder, or a god. I just wanted justice for my mother...and then I just wanted you."

"Me too."

We stared at each other, drinking each other in. We stood on a precipice. I would never stop loving Una. Not for all my immortal years, but I didn't know how to heal our wounds.

"We are where we are," I said. "And I can't turn my back on any of it."

"Nor should you."

I gathered my courage. "We'll have to live around it. If you want to."

Tentatively, Una reached out, her fingers brushing against mine. I grasped them gently, cradling her hand in both of mine as if it was the most fragile, precious thing in the world. For the first time in a long time, the hope inside my chest grew wings.

We had been broken, shattered by war, by grief, by our own stubbornness. But maybe, just maybe, Atlantis had found a way to bring us back together too.

I kneeled before her, placed my hands on her hips, and brushed my lips against her stomach. Her arms wound around my neck and she toyed with the hair at my nape, then tugged the tips of my ears, which she knew was my favorite thing. It was the way she showed her love, the way she turned me on, the way she bent my will. I was merely putty in her hands. For *eternity*.

"I love you," I whispered against her stomach.

"I love you too."

I rose to my feet as a terrifying thought took hold. My entire body trembled and I backed away from her. Heart pumping. Head throbbing. Blood pounding.

Fear lanced across Una's face. "Gal? What is it?"

I shook my head, the movement becoming more rapid. Nausea flooded my stomach and I retched, gripping the newel post to support myself.

"What is it?" Una eased me down until I was sitting on the stairs. "Breathe, Gal. Just breathe."

I dropped my head into my hands, but she clutched my forearms and made me look at her.

"I'm immortal."

"I know."

"I will live forever."

"That's what immortal means," Una said with a trace of humor in her tone. But nothing about this was funny.

"I will outlive you by...centuries. At a bare minimum."

Her lips thinned and sympathy flashed through her eyes. "I know."

"I don't want to live without you."

She kneeled in front of me and cupped my face. "I know this presses on every raw nerve inside you. I know this is the most terrible thing for you. And I wish I could be by your side for eternity—"

"I'll find a way," I said, almost lurching to my feet. "I'm immortal. I'm a god. I have powers. I'll find a way. I'll demand an audience with the Architect. I'll make him grant you immortality too..."

Una was shaking her head. "That's not how it's supposed to be."

"But that's how I *want* it to be."

"I know." She pressed a kiss to my temple. "But you will need to look after our children. And their children. And their children's children. That is your role now, Gal. And it is an important one. You are the protector of Atlantis. And you are the protector of our line. You must guard it with your life. And you will always have the love of family."

Tears flooded out of my eyes. "But I want *you*. I only want *you*."

"And you will have me for as long as we have."

I looked away. I couldn't bear to look at her face anymore. Something inside me died. My hands trembled. My lips tingled. My teeth jammed together. I couldn't do this.

"Don't pull away from me, Gal."

How did she know I'd just contemplated leaving? If I was going to lose her, what was the point of being together?

I must have communicated telepathically, because she said, "You can't think like that. Everything is worthwhile. Even pain. Even fear. Even loss. Don't give up on us just because fear has come knocking again."

I stared at her through my tears. "That's easy for you to say. You won't be left behind."

She shook her head. "It is just as hard for me to leave you, as it is for you to stay."

She was right. Of course she was. But I didn't want her to be. And it fucking *hurt*.

I felt like I'd lost her already. Desperate, I wrapped my arms around her and clung to her. Maybe if I never let her go, she would never leave me. A foolish thought, but a sentiment my heart wouldn't give up on.

"You can do this, Gal," she whispered. "We can do this together."

Una lifted my face to hers. She cupped my jaw, thumbs brushing over my cheekbones as if she could smooth away every ache, every fear, every shattered piece of me. I closed my eyes and breathed her in. The ocean and salt. Jasmine and warmth. *Home*.

When I opened them again, she was still there, kneeling between my legs. Still looking at me like I was worth something. Like I hadn't destroyed everything good in my life. Like I could still be the man she loved. Her lips parted, and I felt the faintest hitch in her breath. She was waiting—for me, for this, for whatever came next. And gods help me, I couldn't resist her any longer. I was still terrified, but I could never give her up. Not for anything. Even if it killed me in the end.

I kissed her.

It began in a hush and was achingly tentative, like neither of us could quite believe this moment was real. Her lips were soft, warm, familiar in a way that sent a sharp ache through my chest. I deepened the kiss, pulling her closer until there was no space between us, until I could feel the steady beat of her heart against my erratic one. Her fingers tangled in my hair, nails scraping against my scalp, heat and chills racing down my spine. I lost myself in her, in this, in the way she melted into me as if she had never wanted to be anywhere else.

She sighed into my mouth, and the sound undid me. My hands tightened at her waist, one sliding up her back, the other splaying against her stomach, feeling the faint curve beneath my palm. Our child. A future I had never dared to imagine. I kissed her deeper, more desperately, pouring everything I had into it—the longing, the regret, the love I had never stopped feeling. She pressed herself against me, anchoring me as my world threatened to tip over the edge.

My lips left hers only to trail along her jaw, then the column of her throat, tasting the salt of her skin. She gasped, her hands gripping my shoulders, holding me there. I kissed my way back to her lips, lingering, savoring, memorizing. Because no matter how much time we had, I would never have enough of her. And I would relish every single second.

She pulled back just enough to look at me, her breath coming fast. "Gal..."

I rested my forehead against hers, trying to steady myself. "I love you," I whispered, the three most important words spilling out again and again.

Her fingers slid down my chest, coming to rest over my heart. "I love you, too."

And I believed her. I let myself believe her. Even knowing how this would end. Even knowing pain was waiting for me in the centuries to come. Right now, in this moment, she was mine. And I would hold on to that for as long as I could.

CHAPTER TWENTY-NINE

I laced my fingers through Una's, picked up the trident, and led her to the door.

"Where are we going?"

"Home."

That was all that needed to be said.

We called goodbye to Maya and Trent and then ducked out the front door. Una squeezed my hand. I took that as reassurance. Love. Hope. All the things.

We didn't speak on the walk back. The silence was comfortable. Inevitable. The kind of silence that spoke of understanding, of knowing words weren't needed, of knowing everything we'd left unsaid had already been felt. Una's hand stayed in mine the entire time, her fingers curled around mine as though she feared I might vanish if she let go. I understood that fear. I had been running for too long.

We arrived as the sun began to set, the sky a blaze of fiery orange and deepening purple. The soft hum of the island surrounded us—the chirping of insects, the distant rush of waves against the cliffs, the whisper of leaves in the trees, and the eternal smell of the jasmine we'd planted around our home. The cottage stood exactly as we'd left it, nestled in the clearing, climbing jasmine curling over the walls, the place we should never have left.

Una led me inside. We scanned the small hall. Dust covered the furniture. The room was cold, even though Atlantis was a tropical island. Cold. Unlived in. Lacking love. We would change that. We would change that *right now*.

The moment the door clicked shut behind us, Una turned, looking up at me with that searching, complicated gaze of hers. I knew what she was thinking, what she was feeling—that this moment, this night, it was both an ending and a beginning. I reached for her, brushing my knuckles along her cheek, watching the way she leaned into my touch, eyes fluttering shut for a heartbeat. Both eyes.

"I missed you," I murmured, as I leaned the trident against the wall.

Something tender and raw flashed through her eyes. "Then show me."

Hell yes.

I kissed her again, deeper this time, letting myself sink into her, into this. Her fingers threaded through my hair, caressing and pinching the tips of my ears. Heat shot straight to my groin. There was no way I wasn't going to make love to my wife tonight. *Make love. My wife.* Those words echoed around my head. Again and again. The best words ever invented. I couldn't help the grin spreading across my face.

"What?" Una asked, her own smile tipping her lips.

"Just us," I said.

She leaned her forehead against my chest. "Why did we let it get so hard?"

"Because love without challenge, without sacrifice, wouldn't be love at all. And gods, Una, I would sacrifice everything for you." I kissed her, then took both her hands in mine, squeezing them to ground myself in the reality of her. Of us.

"You and I...we were always meant to be. It was never going to be easy. We live in a world of curses and prophecies, of fates written in the tides and stars. You are an oracle, the guardian of the orb of Spirit and Soul. A princess. I am a prince, a god, immortal, the Trident Wielder, the guardian of the orb of Snow and Ice..." I let out a soft, breathless laugh. "How could we ever have been simple?"

Her lips twitched, but she stayed quiet, watching me with eyes that saw straight through to my soul.

"Our love was always going to transcend...time? Life? Immortality?" I shook my head, grasping for the words. "Fuck, I don't know. But I do know that no prophecy, no divine intervention, no impossible fate could have kept me from loving you. Whether you believe in destiny or not, I don't give a shit. Because *I* believe in you. In us."

She chuckled, but her grip on my hands tightened, as if she shared every single one of my thoughts.

"I know it took me too long." Emotion roughened my words. "Too long to understand how much you meant to me. Too long to accept that I could live with the risk of losing someone I love. But I can. I will. Because I would rather live with that fear every single day than live a single second without you."

I lifted her hands to my lips, kissing her knuckles, her palms, every inch of her skin I could reach. "I choose you, Una. I will always, *always* choose you."

We smiled at each other.

"My parents may have songs written about them." I took a breath, stared into the two blue eyes of my beautiful wife. "But I think we may have them beat."

"Fuck, yes," Una whispered, and then claimed my lips.

I only gave her a few seconds to intrude on my mouth, to toy with my tongue, before I lifted her off her feet and carried her to our bed. She laughed against my lips.

The bed creaked as I laid her down. I pulled back to let my eyes roam her body, drinking her in. The curve of her collarbone, kissed by shadows. The rise and fall of her chest. The soft dip of her waist, the line of her hip beneath my hand. I memorized her all over again, not only with my eyes, but with something deeper—something that ached to never forget. My wife. My heart. My home.

I traced the curve of her jaw, the slope of her neck, the soft swell of her stomach where our child grew. Awe filled me, a quiet devotion I had never known before. I placed a gentle kiss there, over our unborn child, my lips lingering as I whispered a silent promise—to love them, to protect them, to be the father they deserved.

Una's hands cupped my face, drawing me back up to her. "You don't have to worship me," she teased, a playful smile on her lips.

"Yes, I do," I said, pressing kisses to her collarbone, to her shoulder, to the pulse point at her throat. "I lost you once. I'll never take you for granted again."

She shivered beneath me, her body arching, her breath hitching as I traced the map of her skin with my lips, my hands, my devotion. She was a familiar song I hadn't heard in months, and every note struck something deep, something newly awakened. My fingertips glided along the curve of her shoulder, down her arm, following the fine shiver that rippled across her flesh. The warmth of her skin, the way she moved beneath my touch, sent a slow ache through me, a longing that went deeper than anything physical.

I kissed my way down her throat, lingering at the hollow where her pulse thrummed, pressing my lips there as if I could mark the rhythm into my own heart. We undressed each other. Slowly. Taking our time. Rediscovering each other's bodies.

When we were naked, I positioned myself above her, my weight supported on my elbows. I couldn't stop staring into her eyes. *Eyes.*

Unwilling to wait any longer, she wrapped her hand around my shaft and guided me to her entrance. And when I was ready, I pushed inside of her. Slowly. Deliberately. Carefully. Savoring the feel of her wet heat.

Her hands roamed over my back and rear, guiding me, keeping me close. She let me take my time, and I did. I had all the time in the world now, but this moment was the only one that mattered. I let my lips explore, tasting the salt of her skin, following the rise and fall of her breath. Every sigh, every subtle tilt of her hips, every whispered sound she made. I absorbed it all, locking it away in my soul.

I was careful, mindful of the delicate life she carried. My hands framed her stomach, my thumbs brushing against the place where our child bloomed. I swallowed, overwhelmed by love, by the sheer weight of what we had created together. "You're so beautiful," I whispered, barely recognizing my own voice.

Una cupped my face, her lips parting as she kissed me. She set the pace, the gentle undulation of her body against mine leading me, grounding me. I followed, let her show me the way. Her fingers danced over my back, along my shoulders, her touch burning through me like fire and water all at once—fierce and soothing, demanding and giving. I memorized every detail, every sensation. The softness of her thighs as they bracketed my hips, the delicate gasp that escaped her lips when I moved just right, the way her body molded to mine like we had been carved from the same force of nature.

I kissed her over her heart, her collarbone, her jaw. She

trembled beneath me, a breathless sigh escaping as I rocked against her, slow and unhurried, like the waves kissing the shore. We weren't chasing anything; we were simply here, together, present in this moment.

When we finally came together, it was not hurried or desperate. It was a communion of souls as much as bodies. I pressed my forehead against hers, our breaths mingling, our hearts beating in time. Every motion, every brush of skin against skin, was deliberate, a reminder that we were still here, still choosing each other despite everything. My name left her lips in a soft gasp, and I whispered hers in return, a vow carried on the air between us.

And when the world stilled, when all that remained was the hum of our connected heartbeats, I held her. I reveled in the way her fingers curled against my chest, the way her breath tickled my skin, the way her lips pressed a kiss against my jaw. I wouldn't have them forever. And every time we came together, I promised myself I would commit every curve, every whisper, and every sensation to memory so that I could draw on them during my immortality.

Una pulled the covers over us. I traced my fingertips over the small swell of her stomach, imprinting the sensation into my bones—something I'd never let time erase, no matter how many centuries passed. I had been afraid, lost in the dark, but Una had always been my light. And in this, in her, I found my way home again.

As night settled over us, I cradled her against me, my hand resting over her stomach. She traced lazy patterns on my chest, and I let my fingers drift through her hair, savoring the simple intimacy of the moment.

"I love you," she whispered against my skin.

I kissed her temple. "I love you too."

A long silence stretched between us, filled with warmth and

the steady rhythm of our love. Then Una shifted, tilting her head back to look at me. "You were stuck in your head again," she said knowingly.

I sighed, brushing a thumb over her cheek. "Just...thinking about time. About how I will outlive you."

She caught my hand, placing a kiss on my palm. "We've already talked about this, Gal. We take what we have and we make it count."

I nodded, though the ache inside me lingered. But maybe, just maybe, she was right. Maybe love was worth the pain of loss. Maybe this life we were building together was worth everything that would come after.

I kissed her, slow and lingering, and as she melted into me, I let myself believe that for however long we had, I would hold on. I would cherish. I would love.

CHAPTER THIRTY

♪♪ "THE TRIDENT WIELDER"

Verse 1

He didn't chase the light above,
He fought for truth, he fought for love.
He held the weight no boy should bear,
With frozen breath and steady stare.
No crown of gold, no trumpet sound,
Just quiet steps on sacred ground.
When darkness crept and hope grew thin,
He braved the cold and pulled us in.

Chorus 1

He's the Trident Wielder, chill and clear,
A silent strength that drew us near.
The frost beneath his every stride,
Held back the flood, turned back the tide.
The wind still hums his name with pride—
Gal, who stood when gods had lied.

Verse 2

He faced the gods with shaking hands,

324

Two giants bent to break the land.
But still he rose, through pain and fear,
And carved our future crystal clear.
He fell, he bled, he lost, he healed,
But never once refused the field.
The trident sparked, he stilled the tide—
And bent back time the day gods died.

Chorus 2

He's the Trident Wielder, born for more,
The ocean's edge, the winter's core.
He gave his peace, he gave his youth,
To guard our home and speak the truth.
And when the sky began to crack—
He held the line, he pushed it back.

Bridge

He wasn't loud, he wasn't grand,
But when it broke, he made a stand.
No need for songs of shallow praise—
His name is stitched in ocean spray.

Verse 3

Now stars bend low when he walks by,
A shimmer carved into the sky.
The tide obeys his quiet calm,
And on this isle, the waves are a balm.
He watches us with golden eyes,
A winter god in mortal guise.
No storm can shake the path he laid—
With Gal among us, we're not afraid.

Final Chorus

He's the Trident Wielder, now divine,
A god who walks the ocean line.
We feel him in the falling snow,
A watchful flame in undertow.
And when the sea begins to rise—
He holds the tide, he stills our cries.

Outro

He stayed...
He stays with us...
The Trident Wielder, forged in frost—
Our god, our shield...
Our island's cross.

EPILOGUE

The trident hit the wall with a dull thud as I propped it against the polished wood. The golden metal gleamed in the evening light, its power a constant, silent presence in our home. I hardly had time to take a breath before Una's voice carried down the hall.

"Reef! Where are you?"

Her concerned tone sent a flicker of unease through me.

I pushed away from the doorframe, already moving. "How long has he been missing?"

Una appeared from the nursery, her arms crossed, an exasperated but undeniably fond look in her eyes. "Only a few minutes."

"He can't have gone far."

"He tried to climb the bookshelf earlier."

I chuckled. "Of course he did."

"And this morning, he tried to touch the trident while you were sleeping—again," she continued, narrowing her gaze at me. "Do you remember what happened the first time?"

I did. All too well.

Reef had barely been walking when he'd toddled up to the

trident, his chubby fingers reaching out before Una or I could stop him. The instant his skin made contact, the power had flared, searing his tiny hand. He had wailed in pain, the sight of his reddened skin making my stomach lurch. We had rushed him to the Fountain of Youth, where the water had soothed and healed him, and Una had insisted I build a bracket for the weapon over our bed where the twins couldn't reach it. And now, whenever Reef so much as looked at the trident, she became an anxious wreck.

"He's fearless," I admitted. "Like his mother."

Una shot me a dry look before peering down the hallway. "Like his father."

I hid my smirk and stepped past her. "I'll find him."

I didn't have to look far.

A tiny figure perched atop the windowsill at the end of the hall, strawberry-blond curls tousled, his small hands gripping the frame as he stared outside like he was considering the fastest route down.

"Reef," I called, making my voice stern but not unkind. "That's not happening."

My son turned his head, flashing me a toothy grin. "But Daddy, I wanna fly!"

"You can't fly."

"Ember flies!"

"You are not Ember."

Reef pouted, his little legs swinging as if testing his balance. Una let out a small noise behind me, probably on the verge of scolding him herself, but I beat her to it. "Come down. Now."

To my relief, he obeyed, scrambling off the sill and bounding toward me. He wrapped his arms around my leg, his giggles muffled in my shorts. "I wasn't really gonna jump."

I bent down, ruffling his hair. "Good. Because you're not allowed to give your mother a heart attack before dinner."

Una sighed, brushing her hand through Reef's wild curls. "I swear, you're aging me faster than time itself."

Reef grinned up at her, all innocence and mischief.

Before I could scoop him up, a soft giggle broke the moment.

I turned. Caught sight of Rain crawling across the floor. Toward the trident. Where I had propped it against the wall and not put it in its brackets. And for some reason, although I wasn't touching it, it glowed with power.

Una and I shared a horrified glance.

Rain.

I couldn't slow time without the trident in my hand, even though it felt like it was at a standstill now. But that was the fear talking.

I was a god. I was immortal. And I was loved. But none of those things could stop the inevitable moment of Rain touching the trident. I was too far across the other side of the room to reach her in time.

Thank fuck we kept a flask of fountain water in the kitchen.

Rain, named after my aunt, was quiet by nature. Thoughtful in that way that made you feel like she saw right through you. Her ocean-blue eyes missed nothing, and her little hands reached not for destruction, but for meaning.

But this time, she reached for something she shouldn't.

"Rain!" Una called.

I leaped over furniture. But before I could reach my daughter, her fingers brushed against the trident's shaft.

Instead of the blinding flash that had burned her brother, the trident thrummed. A low, deep hum, resonating through the air like a heartbeat. Its glow pulsed, not in warning, but in recognition.

Rain giggled. My heart picked up tempo, knocking against my ribs. I froze halfway between the trident and the armchair I'd just leaped over.

My daughter wrapped her tiny fingers around the weapon's shaft, gripping it with surprising ease. She was just a baby—only two years old—but in that moment, she looked impossibly strong.

Una gasped. "Gal..."

I got moving again, took a couple of long strides and dropped to my knees beside Rain, easing the trident from her grasp. When I touched it, its glow softened, as if relinquishing something back to me.

"She's meant to be the next trident wielder," I said.

"Shit."

I chuckled. "As an oracle, and a person well versed in *The Mermaid Chronicles*, that's not the reaction I was expecting."

"She's our *daughter*."

"And I'm immortal." I looked at my wife, the strain of our past and the demise of our future hovering between us. "And I will look after her."

Tension bracketed Una's mouth, but she didn't argue. She couldn't. Our fate was not our own. Yes, we could make our own decisions, but destiny would always come knocking. I had given up trying to resist it.

A glimmer of light flickered outside the window.

Una gulped, her gaze lifting toward the night sky, and she moved across the room to stand next to me.

The constellation resembling the trident shimmered, as though an unseen force were acknowledging what had just happened. Its three prongs stood straight once more, as they had since the day I'd killed Vorago.

She placed a hand on my shoulder. "Do you think it's the Architect? Do you think this is his doing?"

I studied the sky for a minute before answering, "Maybe." The possibilities were endless.

Reef tugged at my clothes, his expression scrunched in confusion. "What's an 'Arctet'?"

I placed the trident out of reach, then hoisted him onto my hip. "Something we'll talk about when you're older."

Rain made a noise of protest, and I reached for her too, lifting her in my other arm. She snuggled into me without complaint, her small head resting against my shoulder.

Una sighed, watching me juggle our two children. "I don't know how you do that."

I smirked. "I'm a god."

She rolled her eye, but she was smiling.

I glanced at the trident where it rested against the wall. A symbol of power, of legacy, of the battles I had fought and the sacrifices I had made. But it was also something else now. Something more. It was a bridge to the future.

I turned toward Una, my wife, my heart, my home. We stood at the threshold of everything we had built, our children in our arms, the ocean whispering in the distance, Atlantis thriving beneath the watchful constellations above.

I smiled, my fear of eternity momentarily replaced by love.

"For the first time," I said, "I'm not torn between who I am and who I was meant to be."

Una leaned her head against mine. "And whatever comes next?"

I glanced at Rain, then Reef, at the way they babbled to each other in twin speak, wondering about how their bond would help them in the future. Then I looked at Una, the love of my life, the woman who had made all this possible.

"Whatever comes next," I promised, "we'll face it together. All of us."

THE END

It is **THE END!** (but not quite!) Scroll on to test your
knowledge in *The Mermaid Chronicles* Quiz!

I hope you have enjoyed *Vorago Returns,* the last book in *The
Mermaid Chronicles!* I can't believe this time has come—these
stories have been in my head for so long! I'd be forever grateful
if you would think about leaving a review.

You can do it here: https://geni.us/VoragoReturns

If you are sad to leave Cordelia & Wade, and Gal & Una
behind, fret not! Dive into the companion guide to read about
ancient legends, old prophecies, significant figures and so much
more! It comes in both paperback and hardback (as well as e-
book), and **you can grab it here:**

https://geni.us/TheMermaidChronicles

THE MERMAID CHRONICLES QUIZ

So, you think you're merfolk royalty? A guardian of Atlantis? A trident-wielding, prophecy-defying, ocean-dominating legend?

Or... are you just some poor land-dweller who barely knows the difference between a selachii and a sea cucumber?

This is your **chance to prove your worth**! Answer these questions **correctly**, and you'll reign over the ocean, commanding the tides like the true heir of the deep. But beware—**get too many wrong**, and you'll be **banished to the depths**, locked away with the **ashrays and ghost pirates**, where you'll spend eternity scrubbing barnacles off shipwrecks.

Are you ready? Grab your **magic pearls**, summon your **oceanic wisdom**, and let's see if you **rule the seas or sink to the abyss!**

Good luck... you're going to need it.

1 Why does Cordelia have a fear of water?

a) She had a near-drowning experience as a child

b) A tragic shark attack killed her mother and twin brother

c) She was cursed by a mermaid queen

d) She saw a ghostly figure in the ocean as a child

2 What object does Dylan give Cordelia that plays a significant role in her journey?

a) A golden seashell

b) A map to Atlantis

c) A selachii charm

d) A magical pearl

3 How does Cordelia react when she first meets Wade again after five years?

a) She immediately recognizes him and runs into his arms

b) She doesn't recognize him at first but feels an instant connection

c) She is cold and distant, not wanting to revisit the past

d) She panics and leaves before they can speak

4 What is happening to sharks along the Pacific coast that alarms Cordelia?

a) They are disappearing mysteriously

b) They are attacking humans more frequently than ever before

c) They are being controlled by selachii magic

d) They are evolving and growing much larger

5 What symbolic object does Cordelia find in her house that belonged to her mother?

a) A keychain with two opals and a mysterious sapphire

b) A locket containing an ancient prophecy

c) A shell with strange carvings on it

d) A mermaid-shaped brooch

6 Who betrays Cordelia by stealing the pearl?

a) Trent

b) Wade

c) Zale

d) Maya

7 What must Cordelia and Wade do to get legs again?

a) Retrieve the lost pearl from Zale

b) Defeat the selachii king in battle

c) Petition the High Council to break the curse

d) Make a blood pact with the mermaid queen

QUEST FOR ATLANTIS

8 What is Cordelia and Wade's mission after receiving their legs?

a) Find the scattered jewels to open the portal to Atlantis

b) Prove themselves worthy warriors

c) Retrieve the Trident of the Deep

d) Build a new home for mermaids and selachii

9 What dangerous location do Cordelia and Wade travel through to find the first jewel?

a) The Bermuda Triangle

b) The Mariana Trench

c) The ice caves of Mount Rainier

d) The ruins of Atlantis

10 What elemental power does Cordelia gain?
a) Control over water
b) The ability to summon fire
c) Ice manipulation
d) Shape-shifting into any ocean creature

11 Who joins the expedition to Atlantis, causing tension between Cordelia and Wade?
a) A powerful sea witch
b) Wade's former flame, Stephanie
c) A mysterious eelusionist warrior
d) An ambitious treasure hunter

12 How does the hidden map to Atlantis reveal itself?
a) It glows when exposed to moonlight
b) It requires activation with fossilized squid ink
c) It responds to Cordelia's touch alone
d) It can only be read underwater by a selachii

13 What shocking discovery does Cordelia make when Atlantis is restored?
a) The selachii were the original rulers
b) Ashrays now rule the island
c) The High Council had been lying to them
d) Her mother is alive

FIGHT FOR FREEDOM

14 What major catastrophe happens on the mainland?

a) A nuclear war

b) A volcanic eruption

c) A deadly hurricane

d) An alien invasion

15 Who is responsible for blaming the merfolk for the disaster?

a) The president of the United States

b) A wealthy baron seeking revenge

c) A rogue faction of selachii

d) A power-hungry scientist

16 Who does Cordelia form an uneasy alliance with?

a) Babette

b) Zale

c) A former pirate king

d) The dragon queen

17 What mystical creature does Cordelia battle to save Atlantis?

a) A kraken

b) A sea dragon

c) A siren queen

d) The Hound of the Ocean

18 What shocking revelation does Cordelia make at the end of the book?

a) She is pregnant

b) She can no longer transform into a mermaid

c) Wade has secretly been working with humans

d) The Fountain of Youth is dying

GHOST PIRATES

19 What strange weather phenomenon appears at the start of the book?
a) A massive whirlpool
b) A permanent hurricane surrounding the island
c) A red tide poisoning the waters
d) A sudden snowstorm in Atlantis

20 What is an ashray?
a) A cursed mermaid
b) A legendary ship of the dead
c) A ghostly sea creature that inflicts deadly wounds
d) A lost piece of Atlantis

21 What object does Zale give Angelica?
a) A map to the Fountain of Youth
b) A mysterious obsidian rock
c) A blade forged from shark teeth
d) A vial of selachii blood

22 Why does Angelica seek out Atlantis?
To find the Fountain of Youth to save her nephew
To warn of an impending selachii invasion
c) To uncover the truth about her past
d) To challenge the High Council for leadership

23 What must Angelica do to save her nephew?
a) Trade a human soul
b) Defeat a guardian sea monster

c) Place the rock in the Fountain of Youth

d) Marry a selachii warrior

24 What threat does Atlantis face in this book?

a) An ancient mermaid queen returning for revenge

b) A selachii rebellion led by a rogue warrior

c) A powerful storm threatening to sink the island

d) A ghostly fleet of cursed pirates

VENDETTA

25 What does Gal do to *The Mermaid Chronicles* book at the beginning of *Vendetta*?

a) He locks it away in the palace vault

b) He tears out several pages but keeps the rest

c) He rewrites a new prophecy in its pages

d) He burns it in a fire, trying to destroy it completely

26 Why does Gal resent the book's prophecies?

a) He believes they are misleading and full of lies

b) He blames them for his mother's death

c) He thinks they favor the selachii over the merfolk

d) He is afraid of what they predict about his own fate

27 What does Gal plan to do after destroying *The Mermaid Chronicles*?

a) Challenge his father for the throne

b) Leave Atlantis to hunt down Zale

c) Claim the Power of the Sea for himself

d) Attempt to bring his mother back using forbidden magic

28 Which two friends secretly stow away on Gal's

boat?

a) Ford and Maya

b) Bay and Moby

c) Una and Ember

d) Dylan and Wade

29 **Why does Gal feel unprepared to fight Zale?**

a) He hasn't been in the water in over ten years

b) He lacks control over his ice powers

c) His father forbade him from learning combat

d) He is afraid of using his mother's trident

DENIZENS OF DARKNESS

30 **What power does Gal struggle to master at the beginning of Denizens of Darkness?**

a) Summoning ice storms

b) Controlling sea creatures

c) Water breathing and tidal control

d) Harnessing the full power of the trident

31 **What unsettling ability does the mysterious woman Siryn seem to possess?**

a) The power to seduce with music

b) The ability to steal the memories of others

c) Shapeshifting into different sea creatures

d) Controlling others' dreams

32 **What does Ford warn Gal about before they begin training in the north?**

a) The trident will only grant power to those it deems worthy

b) The Denizens are already closer than they realize

c) Una could be a distraction in battle

d) A new prophecy is forming in *The Mermaid Chronicles*

33 Why does Gal worry about his love for Una?

a) He fears his enemies will use her against him

b) He believes she will betray him like Wade betrayed his mother

c) He thinks loving her will make him weaker in battle

d) He doesn't want to leave her heartbroken like his mother left his father

34 What new power does Gal develop?

a) The ability to control the sea itself

b) Ice manipulation

c) Speaking to all sea creatures

d) Seeing glimpses of the future

VORAGO RETURNS

35 What event marks the beginning of *Vorago Returns*?

a) A selachii rebellion

b) The return of Vorago

c) A new prophecy appearing in *The Mermaid Chronicles*

d) Gal and Una's wedding

36 Who returns and demands the trident back?

a) The original god of Atlantis, Vorago

b) A forgotten mermaid queen

c) Zale, back from the dead

d) A mysterious High Council elder

37 What personality trait of Gal's causes conflict?

a) His arrogance and need to prove himself

b) His refusal to use the trident

c) His mistrust of Una

d) His reluctance to lead

38 Who becomes the guardian of the Power of the Sea?

a) Maya

b) Gal

c) Bay

d) Wade

39 What magical object does Una discover?

a) A golden seashell crown

b) A glowing conch shell

c) A mermaid brooch

d) A cursed necklace

40 What truth is revealed about the Architect?

a) He abandoned Earth for a greater purpose

b) He is still watching over Atlantis

c) He is actually a mortal in disguise

d) He created the selachii as a punishment

41 What unexpected challenge does Gal face?

a) The fear of outliving Una

b) Losing his connection to the sea

c) His trident being stolen

d) The rise of a new selachii ruler

42 Who ultimately defeats Vorago?

a) A united front of mermaids and selachii

b) Una, using the brooch's magic

c) Wade, sacrificing his own strength

d) Gal, with the power of immortality and the trident

43 What final decision does Gal make about his immortality?

a) He accepts it but vows to never forget his humanity

b) He searches for a way to reverse it

c) He isolates himself from Una to protect her

d) He gives up the trident to live a normal life

ANSWERS

1. b) A tragic shark attack killed her mother and twin brother
2. d) A magical pearl
3. b) She doesn't recognize him at first but feels an instant connection
4. b) They are attacking humans more frequently than ever before
5. a) A keychain with a pair of opals and a mysterious blue stone
6. a) Trent
7. c) Petition the High Council to break the curse
8. a) Find the scattered jewels to open the portal to Atlantis
9. c) The ice caves of Mount Rainier
10. b) The ability to summon fire
11. b) Wade's former flame, Stephanie
12. b) It requires activation with fossilized squid ink
13. d) Her mother is alive
14. a) A nuclear war
15. b) A wealthy baron seeking revenge

16. a) Babette
17. d) The Hound of the Ocean
18. a) She is pregnant
19. d) A sudden snowstorm in Atlantis
20. c) A ghostly sea creature that inflicts deadly wounds
21. b) A mysterious obsidian rock
22. a) To find the Fountain of Youth to save her nephew
23. c) Place the rock in the Fountain of Youth
24. d) A ghostly fleet of cursed pirates
25. d) He burns it in the fire, trying to destroy it completely
26. b) He blames them for his mother's death
27. b) Leave Atlantis to hunt down Zale
28. c) Una and Ember
29. a) He hasn't been in the water in over ten years
30. d) Harnessing the full power of the trident
31. a) The power to seduce with music
32. c) Una could be a distraction in battle
33. d) He doesn't want to leave her heartbroken like his mother left his father
34. b) Ice manipulation
35. d) Gal and Una's wedding
36. a) The original god of Atlantis, Vorago
37. a) His arrogance and need to prove himself
38. c) Bay
39. c) A mermaid brooch
40. b) He is still watching over Atlantis
41. a) The fear of outliving Una
42. d) Gal, with the power of immortality and the trident
43. a) He accepts it but vows to never forget his humanity

THE MERMAID CHRONICLES QUIZ – HOW DID YOU DO?

You've battled through 43 waves of questions, faced the deepest mysteries of Atlantis, and hopefully didn't anger the sea gods too much along the way! Now, it's time to see where you stand in the grand oceanic hierarchy. Count up your correct answers and find out your true merfolk destiny:

40-43 Correct – *The Ruler of the Tides!*

Move over, Cordelia and Gal—you are the true legend of the sea! You wield the trident with ease, command the respect of selachii and merfolk alike, and could probably rewrite *The Mermaid Chronicles* yourself. Atlantis bows to you! Now go, rule the ocean wisely, and try not to let the power go to your head.

30-39 Correct – *High Council Elite!*

You're not quite ruler of the seas, but you sit on the High Council, making big decisions and keeping Atlantis in check. You know most of the secrets of the deep, but a few rogue selachii might try to challenge your authority. Keep training, and soon you'll ascend to true merfolk royalty!

⚓ 20-29 Correct – *Brave Adventurer!* 🗡️

You've got heart, courage, and a decent amount of oceanic knowledge—but let's be honest, you'd probably get lost on your way to Atlantis. You might need a magic map (or at least a very patient guide like Wade) to help you avoid disaster. Keep exploring, and you might one day unlock the full power of the sea!

⚓ 10-19 Correct – *Shipwreck Survivor!* 🪝

Well... at least you're still alive? You might not be merfolk material just yet, but you haven't been fully banished to the abyss. Maybe you were too busy staring at a handsome selachii to study up on your lore? Don't worry—Atlantis still has room for you... but try to avoid the ghost pirates next time!

⚓ 0-9 Correct – *Banished to the Depths!* 🧜

Oh no. Oh no, no, no. What happened? Did you sleep through every merfolk history lesson? Did you anger the ashrays and they cursed your memory? Whatever the reason, you are now sentenced to barnacle-scraping duty on a ghost ship. 😱 But don't despair! Read *The Mermaid Chronicles* again, and maybe—just maybe—the ocean will give you a second chance.

No matter your score, you are officially part of the legend of Atlantis! ⚓ Share your results and challenge your friends— let's see who rules the tides and who's doomed to a life of scrubbing shipwrecks! 🚢☠️

FACEBOOK READERS GROUP

If you want to experience more of my books, do join my Facebook readers group where you can chat with other readers and discuss my books, as well as anything else you're reading. I am very active in this group, and you can expect book jokes, puzzles, riddles, quizzes, giveaways, the opportunity to name characters, as well as secret information about what I'm working on, cover reveals and so much more!

Just click here: https://www.facebook.com/groups/840324970233576

FREEBIE

If you'd like access to eleven novellas set in *The Unadjusteds* universe, completely FREE, all you have to do is subscribe to my newsletter!

https://www.marisanoelle.com/subscribe/

ACKNOWLEDGMENTS

Writing a book takes a village, and I am endlessly grateful for mine. I want to give a big shout-out to three teams who have kept me going through thick and thin!

To *The Rebel Alliance*—my incredible writing group. You all have been my ride-or-die crew for years, cheering me on through every word and chapter. I couldn't have reached this finish line without you!

And then there's *Team Swag*—the ones who held my hand while I navigated the wild world of publishing. We've tackled every twist and turn together, sharing laughs, support, and wisdom. You're an amazing bunch of writers and even better friends.

Anna, Emma & Sally—you guys are some of the best people I know. Friends online, friends in real life, and you keep me smiling through the blood, sweat, and tears. Couldn't do it without you!

To Fay—the cover is nothing short of gorgeous! I couldn't have asked for anything better.

Neil, my rock and my "Steady Eddie"—you stole my heart in one night and still keep it safe every day. Love you endlessly.

Riley, Lucas, and Quinn—my biggest supporters, as long as I don't embarrass you at school fairs with my book stacks! You're my go-to brainstormers whenever I'm stuck, and you always help me find my way.

To my parents, Larry and Rita—your unwavering support

means everything to me. And Mom, you're my super-sharp proofreader... unless there's a typo—then it's totally on you!

To my early supporters—Sasha Newell, Michelle Oliver, Nikki, Adrian, Darcy & Hetty Kane—thank you for your invaluable advice and feedback. You've each been a vital part of this journey.

And the fabulous Twitter writing community—thank you for making the highs sweeter and the lows lighter. You all know who you are, and I'm grateful for each one of you.

BookTok! You've been an absolute blast! From making me buy crowns (yes, multiple) to supporting my books with enthusiasm, you've given me so much. I've found the best beta and ARC readers here, and I know I've found my people.

To Michael Fox, my A-level English teacher, thank you for teaching me to think for myself and defend my ideas. That lesson has carried me far.

And last but not least, to my readers—thank you from the bottom of my heart. You make every word worth it. I hope you stick around for more adventures to come!

Oh, and if you fancy learning more about my books and want to be in with the chance to win exclusive giveaways, sign up to my website below!

(**www.marisanoelle.com**)

ABOUT THE AUTHOR

Marisa Noelle is the author behind a treasure trove of young adult and adult novels across multiple genres, but they all have running themes of mental health or the ocean. She tends to gravitate toward the speculative arena and loves to write science-fiction, fantasy, horror, dystopian, romance, romantasy, or a combination of them all.

Marisa's books include:

The Shadow Keepers—a spine-tingling tale to keep you up all night and semi-finalist of the BBNYA book awards.

The Unraveling of Luna Forester—a novel impossible to talk about because of its huge twist, but it snagged several awards, including: First Place Incipere Award, WriteBlend Finalist, BBYNA Semi-Finalist, Bookshelf Finalist.

Plastic—a powerful eco-thriller exploring grief, corporate corruption, and the fight to save our oceans. This contemporary YA novel blends activism with heartbreak as Sara Monroe battles her brother's death, a plastic-choked ocean, and the secrets of a billion-dollar beverage empire.

The Unadjusteds Trilogy delves into one of her favourite genres—dystopian. *The Unadjusteds, the Rise of the Altereds, and The Reckoning* make up the trilogy, but there are eleven further companion novellas that follow the secondary characters (FREE to subscribers). *The Unadjusteds* also placed as a semi-finalist in the BBNYA awards.

The Mermaid Chronicles is a seven book romantasy series that includes: *Secrets of the Deep, Quest for Atlantis, Fight for Freedom, Ghost Pirates, Vendetta, Denizens of Darkness, Vorago Returns*, as well as its own companion guide. The entire series is coming to audio with Tantor Media soon!

Marisa also writes steamy romance under the pen name Savannah Wilde.

When Marisa's not weaving literary spells, she's helping mold the future of MG and YA authors as a mentor for the Write Mentor program.

When not writing, Marisa likes to imagine herself as a mermaid, and can often be found in the local pool...or lake...or ocean. Despite her undeniable bookworm credentials since she was knee-high to a grasshopper, the author gig took Marisa by surprise. You see, she had a secret past as a bit of a science geek during her school days. But hey, science and storytelling make a surprisingly magical concoction! Currently, Marisa calls Woking, UK, her home sweet home, where she resides with her trusty squad, including her husband, three amazing kids, and a furry four-legged friend named Copper.

Marisa loves to hear from her readers. You can find and connect with her at the links below.

Twitter & Instagram: **@MarisaNoelle77**
Tiktok: **@MarisaNoelle12**
Website: **www.MarisaNoelle.com**

Don't forget to check out The Mermaid Chronicles Companion
Guide...
https://geni.us/TheMermaidChronicles

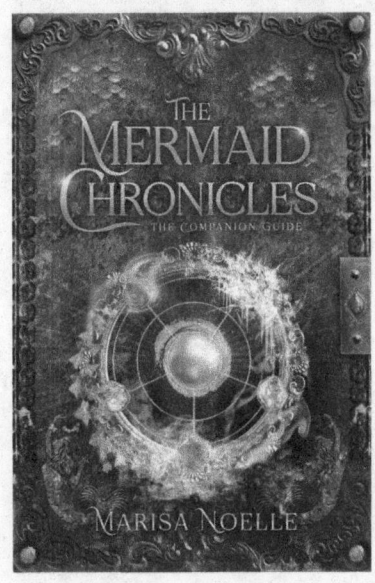

www.ingramcontent.com/pod-product-compliance
Lightning Source LLC
Chambersburg PA
CBHW010421170726
48283CB00011B/3003